MW01223529

ADVENTURE CAT

A CRAZY CAT LADY MYSTERY

BY MOLLIE HUNT

Adventure Cat, the 8th Crazy Cat Lady mystery
by Mollie Hunt

All rights reserved. This book or any portion thereof may not be reproduced or used in any manner whatsoever without the express written consent of the author except for the use of brief quotations in a book review.

ISBN: 9798544984320
Independently published

Copyright 2021 © Mollie Hunt

Editing and Design by Rosalyn Newhouse

Published in the United States of America

This book is a work of fiction. Names, characters, places, and incidents either are products of the author's imagination or are used fictitiously. Any resemblance to actual events or locales or persons, living or dead, is purely coincidental.

Cover Art: "Here Comes Trouble"
© 2008 Leslie Cobb www.lesliecobb.com
"I fostered Genevieve for Sunshine Rescue Group starting in 2007 because she had four different upper respiratory infections at the same time and the rescue had too many cats to give her the one-on-one attention her condition required. By the time she recovered, I couldn't let her go so I finalized her adoption. She was one of my most affectionate cats, and it broke my heart when she died of cancer in 2020." —Leslie Cobb

E1

Other Books by Mollie Hunt

Crazy Cat Lady Mysteries
Cats' Eyes (2013)
Copy Cats (2015)
Cat's Paw (2016)
Cat Call (2017)
Cat Café (2018)
Cosmic Cat (2019)
Cat Conundrum (2020)
Adventure Cat (2021)

Tenth Life Cozy Mysteries
Ghost Cat of Ocean Cove (2021)

Other Mysteries
Placid River Runs Deep (2016)

Sci-Fantasy
Cat Summer (Cat Seasons Tetralogy 2019 Fire Star Press)
Cat Winter (Cat Seasons Tetralogy 2020)

Short Stories
Cat's Cradle
The Dream Spinner

Poetry
Cat Poems: For the Love of Cats (2018)

Praise for Mollie Hunt, Cat Writer:

"I know Mollie as a true, dyed-in-the-wool cat person, as a cat guardian and a foster parent and, most importantly, as a human being. One thing I can spot a mile away is true passion... and Mollie Hunt has it. People like Mollie are rare in this world because they infuse their own curiosity... with true empathy... the recipe for not only a quality person, but, in the end, a great artist as well." —Jackson Galaxy, Cat Behavior Consultant

Praise for the Crazy Cat Lady cozy mystery series:

"I knew this novel was about cats but its theme is cats! Cats are as much the main characters as the main character is! —Sharon from Goodreads

"...Each book drew me right into the story and kept me intrigued and guessing all the way. They're as cozy as can be for cat enthusiasts, but there are also some real scares..." —Catwoods Porch Party

"...an outstanding amateur sleuth mystery that will delight cat lovers and mystery lovers alike. **Cats' Eyes** *has so many exciting twists and turns; it keeps the reader fascinated until the final thrilling scene. I liked the addition of 'cat facts'" at the heading of each chapter. I learned a few fascinating tidbits that I didn't know."* —Readers Favorite 5-Star Review

Praise for Cosmic Cat, Crazy Cat Lady mysteries #6, winner of the Cat Writers Association Muse Medallion Award for best mystery book, 2020:

"Mollie Hunt brings to life another dazzling mystery that finds Lynley on her most unusual case yet... Cosmic Cat is another brilliant installment in Lynley's adventures with a mystery that brings her into the world of Comic-Con, cosplayers, and planet vigilantes where she meets new cats and new characters."
—Liz Konkel, Readers' Favorite 5-star review

Praise for Cat Conundrum, Crazy Cat Lady mysteries #7:

"This story is the kind of cozy I love to read. The clues are all there... but I was totally surprised by the big reveal. If you enjoy this series, then you will love this latest installment. If you have never read the series, then jump right in. It holds up well as a standalone with everything you need to know about Lynley, her friends, and her cat obsession all included."
—I Read What You Write reviewer

"Cat Conundrum is my idea of the perfect cozy mystery book. It's totally clean, has quirky characters among its cast, has cats, and a mystery that takes most of the book to figure out. I highly recommend this cozy to all of you cozy mystery lovers! I can't wait to read more!"
—Christy's Cozy Corners

Dedication

This book is dedicated to all those who tirelessly fought through the trials and tribulations of 2020, those who continued the fight into 2021, and those precious souls who will be faced with things to come.

To the first responders, the EMTs, paramedics, firefighters, and police officers. To the people on the front lines, doctors, nurses, medical assistants, and those who cleaned up after them. To the people who went to work, risking their mental and physical health so we could have food and toilet paper. To the selfless who stayed home, wore masks, social distanced, and got vaccinated, not because someone told them to but because it was the right thing to do. To the artists, musicians, actors, and celebrities who took to Zoom to entertain us as we hunkered in our isolation. To the folks who found ways to help, to show compassion, and to reach out like never before. As life moves toward a nearer normal, let's not forget what it means to be kind.

Adventure Cat

Five years ago,
a fifty-something cat shelter volunteer
found a gym bag in a warehouse.
Inside the bag were
a kitten,
a cat toy,
and ten thousand dollars.

Prologue

The Lady tapped a blood-red fingernail on the lacquered table. The Man in Black cowered before her, looking much like a naughty child.

"You lost the Mafdet?" It was a curse.

"There were unforeseen circumstances, ma'am."

"There are always unforeseen circumstances, Kurt. That's why I pay you the big bucks."

"Yes, ma'am."

The woman rose and began to pace. Her Chinese robe swept the ground as she walked in spite of her four-inch spike heels. She paused and faced the window, a black void of night. Tossing back a long lock of pewter hair, she returned her attention to Kurt.

"We will retrieve the Goddess—the kitten is microchipped. But the artifact, Kurt. The artifact. How are we to recover it now?"

"It's hidden in the ball, the cat toy. Maybe whoever took the Goddess will keep it with her, figure it's hers."

The woman said nothing, and Kurt lowered his head, knowing what a long shot that would be. The Mafdet, ancient and beyond price, cleverly encased in a fifty-cent bauble, could be anywhere by now.

"Find the Goddess. Find the artifact."

"And the money?"

Ice-green eyes shot a gorgon stare. "The money will come out of your cut."

"Yes, ma'am," Kurt sighed.

As the fingernail began to drum the table once more,

Kurt turned and exited the room. He breathed with relief as he always did upon leaving the Lady's deadly presence, but his relief was short-lived as he considered the impossible task before him.

Chapter 1

Five Years Later

"Harry!" I called after the brawny tuxedo cat who was eagerly tearing up the side of the hill.

Rats! I thought to myself. *I can't believe this is happening!* With one Houdini move, old Dirty Harry had slipped out of his purple harness and was off at a gallop. It was the first time he'd done anything like that. He usually enjoyed his adventure walks and had never tried to run away — until now.

Something had caught the old boy's attention. A squirrel? Another cat? A will-o-the-wisp? Who knew? I didn't care so long as I could catch up to him before he disappeared into the wilds of Mt. Tabor Park.

My name is Lynley Cannon, and back in my youth, I could have sprung up that incline like a tiger. Now that I'm sixty-something, the dash left me winded before I'd made the first plateau. Was it too much to ask for Harry to pause on that grassy plain? Apparently it was, because there he went, skimming through the tree shadows, ever upward.

"Harrrreeee…" I cried again.

Harry paused and peered back at me.

"Harry," I said softly as I continued my climb, careful not to spook him now that he was within reach.

I was almost there.

I held out my hand, a friendly greeting.

"Harry kitty dear…"

1

With a *purrumph*, he gave me a sweet love blink, then took off down a side path that skirted the hilltop. At least it was level going and not difficult to track.

Sighing, I adjusted my glasses and followed through the cathedral corridor of ancient Douglas firs and ruddy maples. The approach of summer had brought the leaves to their full measure, shimmering, tender and green in the cool of the day. Flowering currant bloomed in fiery profusion; the native Oregon grape that flourished on the forest floor was putting forth blossoms of brightest yellow. A few leftover daffodils persevered, their gray-green spikes shooting from the loamy soil, but I took no notice. I just wanted to catch my cat.

The adventure cat program, a fast-growing faction of felines who accompany their humans on outdoor excursions, had sounded like so much fun when Blake put out the word. Blakely Brooks, fellow volunteer at Friends of Felines cat shelter, started the group as a way to get indoor cats outside for exercise and enrichment. The club's first meeting had thoroughly covered the safety issues of harnessing your cat. Number one was to make sure your equipment fit snugly so said cat couldn't wiggle out of it. The fact that Harry was now free and running amok was no one's fault but my own.

Dirty Harry was a mere ten feet ahead of me but keeping speed—the moment I moved to catch up, he trotted that much faster. He was teasing me; to him this was a game. At least he didn't seem to be chasing the whatever-it-was anymore. I hoped he would tire—after all, the guy was coming up on his sixteenth birthday. That would make him older than me in cat years. So how was he able to run like the wind when I could barely hobble?

I stopped to catch my breath. He looked at me with

what I'd swear was a challenge, then took off again, cutting from the nice, level pathway to scamper up the hill once more. Resigned, I followed. What else could I do?

In leaps and bounds, he pushed over the rise and disappeared. I panicked when I lost sight of him. Spurred by adrenaline, I made it up in ten long strides. When I got there, he was nowhere to be seen.

Desperately I scanned the quiet street that marked the border between the parkland and the adjoining neighborhood. Across the lane, a stepping-stone trail led up a gentle slope to a wrought-iron gate set in the center of a brick wall covered with rose vines. The gate was open, and in its hollow stood a figure. The sun was at their back so all I could see was a silhouette, but it seemed as if they were holding something about the size of a cat.

The person broke from the backlight, and I saw the bundle was Harry.

"Is this yours?" she asked.

At least I assumed it was a woman. The voice sounded female, but the look and dress gave no clue—boots, shapeless dark brown pants, a Carhartt jacket, and a wide-brimmed straw hat putting the face in complete shadow. A short woman or a very small man, this person was nowhere near so tall as the wall, which I gauged to be six feet at the most.

She took a few steps nearer, exposing an intriguing feminine face.

"I see you've found my Harry," I said, closing the distance between myself and my cat.

She passed me the big boy, and I slipped on his harness, this time making sure to fully tighten the straps.

"I assumed he was here to visit Hermione," said the woman. "She's very gregarious and sometimes attracts the neighbors."

Stepping aside, she revealed one of the most beautiful felines I'd ever seen. And one of the most unique. The predominantly white fur was marbled with marks of the deepest gray. The closest I could come to a label for that mesmerizing pattern of stripes and spots was paisley. She was like no other cat I'd come across.

No, I take that back.

There had been another.

* * *

I studied this exceptional cat with her bright red collar complimenting the fur of opposing shades. Needlessly I remarked, "She's absolutely gorgeous."

"Yes, she is, isn't she?" the woman grinned.

I did a bit of mental math. "Where did she come from, if you don't mind my asking?"

"No, I don't mind, but I would like to sit down. Won't you join me? We can have a cup of tea on the veranda, and I'll tell you all about my sweet Hermione."

I hesitated. Something in the woman's open manner served to disturb and compel me at the same time. If it had been a man offering an invitation into the secluded garden, I would have surely declined, yet this small woman was another matter.

She must have sensed my vacillation. "I promise I'm quite harmless," she said with a demure smile. "Please. I get very few callers nowadays."

Her insistence on innocence only increased my wariness, and the admission that no one visited her even though she lived smack dab in the middle of Portland made me more nervous than ever. I looked around: the parkland with its huge, old trees on one side; the

4

rose-twined brick wall of her property, like something out of a fairytale, on the other. If a nefarious deed were to be done, this absolute solitude would be the place to do it.

I chided myself for my mistrust. So much going on in the world these days—violence, theft, murder—but I was letting my imagination run away with me. What were the chances this reclusive cat person would turn out to be a psychopath?

Then my attention returned to Hermione. I had a feeling about her, a feeling that sent excitement shooting through me like electricity through fur. Could it be? Was it true...? My cat-like curiosity eclipsed my anxiety, and the decision was made.

"Yes, thank you. But I'm with a group. Let me text my friends and tell them what I'm doing so they don't worry." *And so they'll have my last known location when I go missing,* I added to myself.

"Of course." The woman turned and retreated up the path, Hermione by her side. "Straight ahead, whenever you're ready," she called back. "Please close the gate behind you."

I watched her tiny form recede from sight through a crimson bower of vine roses and wondered again what I was getting myself into. Such an odd-looking creature, almost elfin if not for the bulky, manly dress.

Harry wanted to follow the woman and her paisley cat and was tugging on his leash. Afraid he would escape his harness again in spite of the strap adjustment, I let him lead me along while I tapped out my text.

Patty, met a friend who lives at the crest of the hill. Stopping for tea. See you later.

I wasn't sure why I had referred to the woman as a "friend" since we'd barely met. Maybe for convenience sake, or maybe because I didn't really want to admit what I was about to do. I paused halfway through the gate, wondering if I should just turn around and leave while I still had the chance. But something drew me, and it wasn't just Dirty Harry pulling like a tugboat on his purple leash.

Chapter 2

The Adventure Cats movement is said to have started in 2013 when an Iraq War veteran from Oregon posted on Instagram that hiking with his cat helped him manage his post-traumatic stress disorder.

The rose bower spanning the gateway trellis was in dire need of pruning, and the wayward vines jabbed thorns into my hair and sweater as I passed. It was almost as if they didn't want to grant me entrance. But that was ridiculous, another freak imagining from some long-forgotten fairy story. Carefully I unhinged the clinging claws and stepped through, only to pause again, this time in wonder.

The red rose vines with their deep burgundy foliage were merely a preview of what was to come in the garden proper. All the plants, bushes, shrubberies, creepers, climbers, and even the large old trees boasted foliage of red. A red maple wound its gnarled branches into a leafy bower above a little orchard of dwarf flowering plums. Profusions of coral bells, purple stonecrop, and other crimson-leafed flora grew up around the trunks. I picked out a few vegetables among the collection: a row of tiny red beet leaves, just sprung from the ground; a few ruby spikes of Swiss chard, gnarled and shaggy from wintering over. It was like looking out on an alien landscape, a cultivated version of the red planet, Mars.

Dutifully I shut the gate, watching the latch click into

place. As I turned, I wondered if I had indeed seen the crimson tableau or only dreamt it. But there it was, layer upon layer of cherry, burgundy, red, pink, magenta. The path was made with red volcanic gravel, possibly from Mt. Tabor itself, the little inner-city cinder cone that at one time had been quarried for its pretty, porous stone.

Harry had paused to sniff a leaf but was now ready to move on, propelling me toward a small, one-story bungalow built of the same old brick as the wall that surrounded the garden. A covered porch of traditional style ran across the front, and in the doorway stood the woman, just as she had in the gate, Hermione sitting tall by her side.

As I approached, she turned and disappeared into the shadows. Harry padded up the step without hesitation, and I tagged along behind, blinking my eyes in the dimness.

The woman was now seated in an antique oak and velvet armchair writing in a large book. Tea things were set out on the wicker table—a red clay pot and two china cups.

"I thought you weren't expecting company," I commented, eyeing the pair of cups.

"One never knows." She closed the journal, put it aside, then began to pour the tea, hot and steaming. "Come. Sit. Enjoy."

Maybe it was the sudden cool of the enclosed veranda or the half-light that filtered in through slatted blinds. Maybe it was the scent of the tea—fragrant and slightly exotic. The air hummed with the drone of bees but was otherwise strangely quiet. We were in the center of the city—where was the urban clatter? The traffic, the sirens, the trucks? It was almost as if within these walls was an oasis. Or a magical world.

I shook my head to cast off my fantasies and took a seat at the table. The wicker chair, which by its design I reckoned to be nearly as old as I was, sighed with my weight. Harry, still on his leash, hopped onto my lap, eliciting another sough from the old rattan.

"I'm Carry," said the woman, extending a small, calloused hand for me to shake. "With a 'C'. C-A-R-R-Y," she spelled out, noting my look of confusion. "Not the other kind, the one with the 'K'."

"Alright," I replied, a bit at a loss. "I'm Lynley and this is Dirty Harry," I said of the big tuxedo boy. "I have to tell you, Carry, I grew up in this neighborhood, but I've never noticed this house before. Have you lived here long?"

She pulled off her hat, revealing short, blunt-cut hair of no particular color and sparkling turquoise eyes. "Quite a while," she replied ambiguously.

I expected her to say more, but instead she leaned back in her chair holding her teacup in both hands like an offering. Slowly, almost reverently, she brought it to her lips and sipped.

The silence between us was becoming awkward, at least to my mind—Carry seemed perfectly content to sit and ponder. Then I suddenly recalled why I was there. How could I have forgotten the beautiful and singular cat who now lounged on the table by the tea set, giving me her lively blue stare?

"You were going to tell me about Hermione," I announced. "Where did you find such an extraordinary cat?"

Carry smiled, lovingly running a hand down the marbled back. "She came from a local shelter. Can you believe it?"

"Which shelter?" I asked cautiously.

She thought for a moment. "Something *Felines*, if I remember rightly. Companions? Colleagues?"

"Friends?" I offered. "Could it have been Friends of Felines?"

Carry nodded vigorously. "Yes, yes! That's it. An acquaintance put me in touch. She knew I was looking for someone remarkable. And they don't come any more remarkable than Hermione here." She studied the cat, her gaze tracing the sleek lines and unique coloration. "She was a special case. I don't recall the details, but she was never officially put up for adoption. It took weeks before I was even allowed to see her. But I persisted."

Hermione jumped onto the empty chair between us, continuing all the while to give me the eye. I couldn't tell if she was mocking me, questioning me, or just wondering if I had a treat in my pocket—which as a matter of fact I did. Harry glared, then turned and resettled on my lap with his back to her. She sniffed the air in his general direction but kept her distance.

"When was that?"

"Oh, about five years ago. She was just a kitten."

My mind was doing cartwheels, once again racing through the *Is it true? Could it be?* scenario. But the timing was right and the place as well. And besides, I didn't think there could be more than a handful of cats with that unique coat. I'd been working with cats for most of my life, and in all that time, I'd seen only one.

The black of her markings had become diluted as she grew, and some of the speckles had coalesced into stripes, but this was the same cat, I was sure of it. This was Spot.

I'd found her in a gym bag in an abandoned warehouse half a decade ago. I'd nearly been killed by an unknown assailant who wanted the bag which had turned out to contain—besides the kitten—money and drugs. The stuff had been handed over to the police, and once I'd made my statement, I never heard another word about the case.

As a longtime Friends of Felines volunteer, I'd relinquished the kitten into their loving care. I'd thought about adopting her myself, but since I was already housing a clowder of older cats, introducing a kitten into the mix was out of the question.

Besides, Spot was attached to the investigation of the drugs and money and therefore couldn't be adopted out until the case was resolved. I was never told what happened to her, but I trusted FOF would find her a good home when the time came.

So how did Carry keep tabs on Spot when I could not? I wondered. *How had she learned of the little cat in the first place?* I knew just about everything that went on at the shelter, yet Spot's fate had remained dark. The only plausible explanation was that Carry must have friends in high places.

Once more I questioned whether I could be mistaken, and this wasn't Spot at all. It had been five years—no longer the fuzzy little kitten but a sleek and beautiful full-grown cat. I'd since relegated the horrific incident to memory, yet in spite of the passage of time, I hadn't forgotten a whisker on that distinctive face. I never dreamed I would see her again, but there she was.

I reached out to touch the marbled fur. The cat hesitated, then smoothed her cheek against my hand with a welcoming purr.

Carry gave me an odd look.

"Is something wrong?" I asked, continuing the caress.

"She's not usually so forthcoming with strangers,"

Carry remarked with a sudden frown. She leaned closer, scrutinizing both me and the cat. "Why, it's almost as if... as if she knows you."

* * *

The veranda grew even quieter, the only sound Hermione's rumbling purr. I took a sip of tea, making a noise like a cow at a trough in the echoing silence. Quickly I set the cup down on its saucer, but even that simple motion crashed and rattled through the hush. When a sharp ping came from my vest pocket, it seemed as loud as the toll of a church bell.

"My phone," I apologized. "Sorry."

The woman's frown gave way to an elusive smile as she relaxed into her chair, once again concentrating on her beverage.

I retrieved the phone and looked at the screen. It was a text from Patty, an answer to my own, so I put the instrument away again.

"Well, I really should be getting back to my people," I said. "Thank you for the tea."

"Of course," Carry replied, the perfect hostess.

I rose, hefting Harry onto my shoulder. I gave Hermione a final pet, lingering over her soft beauty. She stared at me, then offered a love blink. Her eyes were the bluest of blue—just as I remembered them.

Carry stayed where she was, watching me quizzically.

"What?" I asked.

"Nothing," she countered, but her lips maintained the Madonna smile. "I enjoyed our little chat, Lynley. Please come again."

"Alright," I replied automatically, though I couldn't quite envision a reason for my return... *Except maybe to see that amazing cat just one more time,* I admitted to myself.

I started to leave but turned back to take another look: the odd little woman, the beautiful paisley cat, the wicker table, the tea service, the journal. I couldn't quite make out the cover of the book—something abstract in red and gold.

"Goodbye, Lynley."

I jumped. Was it a dismissal? "Yes, goodbye, Carry. It was nice to meet you."

"And you."

Heading along the path, my footfalls crunching on the volcanic gravel, I let Harry down to walk at his own pace, which was a fast trot interspersed with pauses at significant spots: a mouse hole, a mulberry bush, a discarded cat toy which presumably belonged to Hermione. The stops gave me time to take a closer look at the red garden. With its old trees and established fauna, it wasn't something that had sprung up overnight. I wondered how long it had been there, hidden in the heart of Mt. Tabor Park. Who had planted it? Was it Carry or someone before her? She had been less than forthcoming about the length of time she had owned the place.

Like her garden, Carry was an enigma. Though I'd only just met her, only been in her presence for a short space of time, I was very sure she was a singular entity, distinct from anyone I'd ever known.

I glanced back at the bungalow. Carry was standing on the stoop with Hermione draped across her shoulder. Carry waved, and so did I.

Then she called after me, "Be sure to close the gate on your way out."

Chapter 3

Do your cats greet you at the front door when you come home, ready to hear all about your excursion into the outside world? Some cats are very social and want to know your every move, while others could not care less.

When I reached my house, a large Victorian holdover common to the inner-city neighborhood, Patty was seated on the front steps waiting for me. She was catless, so she must have already dropped her adventure cat Kitty at her apartment next door. Kitty, the elderly gray and white matron, had a strong aversion to other cats, and though she managed to put it aside during her adventure walks, once back on her home turf, she reverted to a small attack monster with rippy claws and bitey teeth, to say nothing of a banshee yowl that could easily bring down the SWAT team if one didn't understand its feline origin.

"Hey, Lynley," the young woman saluted. "Where did you get off to? Tea with a friend? I didn't know you had friends who lived in the park."

"Harry led me astray," I replied as I hefted his carrier up the stairs to the front door. "Come on in."

"I'd kill for coffee," Patty responded, springing up and joining me on the porch.

As I unclipped the house keys from my belt, she leaned over and picked something up off the mat. I glanced at the slip of glossy blue and gave an abrupt harrumph.

"Flyer," I said. "I get them all the time. Everything

from Jehovah's Witnesses to two-for-one tire deals."

I glanced at Patty who had begun to read the leaflet. It held her attention with such interest, I was compelled to look.

"It's Dr. Craven," she said dreamily. "He's coming to Portland to give a reading from his new book, *Cats in the Catacombs*."

"Doctor who?"

"Dr. Wil Craven," she said as if I should recognize the name. When I just stared, she added, "The famous feline archaeologist."

"The feline what?" I peered closer at the tall, attractive man pictured on the page.

"Feline archaeologist. I'm surprised you haven't heard of him, Lynley, being the cat lady that you are. He's a leading expert."

"On what?" I asked, not bothering to conceal my skepticism. Doctors who advertise always seemed questionable to me.

"Feline archaeology, of course," she said bluntly.

I shook my head. I loved Patty like family, but sometimes her simplified view of the world left much to be desired. In her early thirties with pixie features and soft brown bob, she reminded me of a kitten, and her propensity to trust everyone, no matter what sort of snake oil they were selling, seemed a bit kittenish as well.

Patty and her husband Jim had lived in the apartments next door to me for quite some time, though I'd only come to know her as a friend after she rescued my missing cat a few years ago. Turned out she and Jim loved cats but couldn't have one of their own due to housing restrictions. When those restrictions were lifted, she adopted senior cat Kitty and had been lavishing the old girl with love and devotion ever since.

I finished unlocking the door and gestured Patty inside. "Let's get that coffee, shall we?"

"Yes, please." She handed me the flyer which I discarded on the side table to go out with the recycle. *A feline archaeologist? What will they think of next?*

We were met in the front hall by Little, my sturdy black shorthair who liked to oversee all comings and goings in the house. It was up to her whether a visitor passed muster. If Little didn't like someone, she'd been known to snub them, harass them, or in one extreme case, give the intruder a feral growl. If she deemed a guest worthy, which was most often the case, then she instantly became the official welcome committee, greeting the newcomer with a friendly, chatty *prrrow*.

Patty paused to give the cat a rub under the chin. Purring, Little lifted her head, revealing a pendant of white on her ebony breast.

I set the carrier down on the carpet and unlatched the gate. Harry stalked out, pausing only long enough for me to undo his harness, then in two quick moves, he shrugged off the purple straps and headed for his food bowl. Patty and I followed with Little padding along beside us.

"So where did you get off to?" Patty asked, taking a seat at the antique mission oak table.

I went straight for the Keurig machine and popped in a biodegradable pod. Grabbing a pair of brightly colored Fiesta mugs from the cupboard, I pondered just how I was going to respond to her query.

"It all began when Harry slipped his harness about halfway up Mt. Tabor."

"Oh, no!" Patty gasped. "But you obviously caught up with him."

We both looked at the big cat sitting at his food station solemnly awaiting his post-trek treat. I complied with a sprinkling of kibble in his bowl, and he began to munch.

"Yes, but only after he gave me a run for my money."

"You were gone a long time. We were wondering if you'd left for home."

"Well, you know how it is with the adventure club. We all start out together, but after a while, our cats choose different directions, and off we go."

Patty laughed. "That seems to be the way of it. Kitty leads me all over the place. I'm just along for the ride."

Then we both laughed, thinking of the antics of our cats.

I had been very much enjoying the club since its inception. It was such fun to get our felines safely out to the wilderness of nature—or at least to the wilds of a beautiful park—so they could run and jump and play like their big cat ancestors. A few of the members even allowed their cats off-leash, but I was quite content to keep Harry connected to me at all times.

Returning to the task at hand, I saw the first cup was done percolating. I passed it to Patty and put a second mug under the spout.

"A little milk, right?"

"Sure, thanks."

I retrieved a small carton from the fridge and placed it on the table.

"That's not milk," she observed. "It's half-and-half."

"Sorry. I have almond milk too if you'd rather."

"No, I love half-and-half," she exclaimed, pouring a large dollop. "I just don't get it very often. I don't buy such tempting treats with Jim's lactose intolerance."

My coffee had finished its final splutter and drip, and I

joined Patty at the table. Violet, the rotund shorthair, and her tiny Siamese buddy Mab had come in to see what was shaking. Big Red, my shy tabby boy, was lurking around the perimeter, giving me the eye. Harry was still busy with his kibble, and Little had draped herself across my lap the minute I sat down.

"So tell me more about Dirty Harry's big adventure," Patty said between sips.

"He gave me a real chase," I sighed. "I wondered if I'd ever catch up with him. Then finally he made for a house over on the far side of the park." I paused to reflect on Carry and her unique property. "I'd never noticed the place before. It had the strangest garden, all red-leafed plants. I felt like I was on some alien planet. How about you? Did you know there was a house up there?"

Patty frowned. "No, I don't think so."

"Well, you'd remember if you had." I took a swig of coffee, hot and energizing as it went down. "Actually, there's a brick wall around the perimeter, so all you can see from outside are the tops of the trees—the *red* trees. You don't get the full impact until you go in."

"And you went in?"

"Uh-huh," I snorted through my coffee. "That's where Harry was, hanging out with the owner. We got to talking, and she invited me for tea. But the garden wasn't the strangest part. The woman, Carry, has a cat too, a gray cat with white stripes and spots. Or maybe she's white with gray markings—I don't know, they're pretty equally distributed. And I swear she looks just like the kitten I rescued some years ago in an abandoned warehouse. Did I ever tell you the story of Spot?"

"Spot the cat?" She giggled. "What a funny name for a kitty."

"I take it you've never watched *Star Trek, the Next Generation* then."

She gave me a blank look. "What does an old sci-fi show have to do with this cat you rescued? I'm afraid you've lost me, Lynley."

"Never mind about that." Patty, for all her sweetness and enthusiasm, could only concentrate on one thing at a time. My mention of Star Trek was a mistake I needed to rectify by getting back on my original track as quickly as possible. "It was about five years ago, in the summer. I'd been taking a walk on the Eastside Esplanade and was cutting through the warehouse district on the way to my bus stop when I heard a cat cry. It came from one of the buildings, an unusual place for a cat. Me being the queen of curiosity, I went to check it out."

I gazed out the window as I recalled the scene—the sepia gloom of the immense room, the smell of dust in the heated air. "The door was unlocked but the place was empty, at least I thought so at the time. In the middle of the floor was a duffle bag—you know, the type people use for sports or to go to the gym—and the cries were coming from there. It was a kitten. I tried to get her out, but the zipper was stuck. Then..."

I paused. Even five years after the event, just the thought of what happened next made my breath catch in my throat. "While I was fussing with it," I pressed on, "out of the blue someone... well, they... they started shooting at me."

Patty's naturally-round eyes grew even wider. "Shooting at you? Like with a gun?"

I nodded. "Needless to say, I grabbed the bag and ran." I thought back to that perilous chase, a man dressed all in black dogging my heels as I scrambled to get away. The

19

relentless tattoo of my heartbeat, so strong I thought it would burst out of my chest. The explosion of adrenaline through my system that kept me going even when I felt like I'd fall flat on my face. The absolute, unbridled fear...

"I tried to shelter in Webster's Bistro, but they made me leave when they found out I had the kitten. Health restrictions," I scoffed. "When I got back onto the street, the man who was chasing me had been joined by another man. Two against one, my odds were plummeting with every passing moment."

Patty sat frozen, her cup held in mid-air. "Oh no! You must have been terrified!"

"You've got that right. I don't think I've ever been so scared in my life."

"What did you do?"

"I just kept going—I had to. Finally I got to a place I could hide and make a phone call.

"You called the police?"

"I should have. That would have been the smart thing to do, but I wasn't thinking straight. I called my best friend instead." I snickered, thinking back. "I guess God was looking out for me because Frannie grabbed Denny— Special Agent Paris, the humane investigator—and the two of them showed up in his truck just in the nick of time. By then, a second shooter had joined the party and was busy targeting the first guys. Can you believe it? I was lucky to make it out in one piece."

"Oh My Cat! A shootout over a little kitten, you say?"

"Well, actually there were a few other things in that duffle bag besides the cat. A baggie of white capsules and a bunch of money. I doubt they cared about the kitten at all. Who knows how she'd got stuck there in the first place?"

"Well, that explains it." Patty's coffee cup landed

rather loudly on the table. "You must have accidently intercepted a drug buy or something. Did they ever catch the men?"

"I never heard. You know how the police are—once I'd given my statement and turned in the bag, I was done. They don't call you back to say, 'Oh by the way, here is the rest of the story, since I know you're so interested.'"

"No, that's true—of course they don't. Though I really think they should. Call it a *human right to know*. There was nothing in the news about the incident?"

"No, nothing that I could find. And I looked."

"Well, that's disappointing."

"Yes, it was," I readily agreed. "It's not often an average citizen, let alone a cat lady of a certain age, gets embroiled in something newsworthy, and I thought it only fair that I should have been apprised of the outcome."

"Like a television show that wraps up all the details in the end," Patty commented.

"Exactly."

Big Red had conquered some of his shyness in favor of pets and took that moment to hop on my lap. Little gave him a dirty look as he snuggled in beside her, then she jumped down, dashing from the room in a kitty huff.

Harry had finished his snack and was sauntering into the living room for a much-deserved rest. Tinkerbelle, my other black female, made an appearance in the kitchen, only to turn and go out the cat door into the cat-fenced afternoon warmth.

"So what does the gym bag kitten have to do with the cat you saw at the house of the red garden?" asked Patty.

"I think—no, I'm certain—they are one and the same. Spot, even as a kitten, had unmistakable markings, a mottle of black and white speckles and dots like nothing

I'd ever seen before—or since, for that matter, until today. Carry's cat, no longer a kitten of course—well, she wouldn't be, would she—has exactly the same coat, except now the black has faded to a deep gray, and some of the spots have merged into stripes and swirls."

"But Lynley, that doesn't sound the same at all."

"I asked Carry about her history, and it fits. It's her, alright. I'm certain." I shook my head. "To see Spot again after all these years… It's amazing!"

"Do they still call her Spot?"

"No, Carry named her Hermione. I must say it suits her. She's grown into a ravishing beauty."

"Wow, that's quite a tale. Do you think you'll see her again?"

"I don't know," I equivocated. "I'd like to, but I'm not sure on what pretext. Carry invited me back, but… well, I got a strange vibe from her."

Suddenly my eye lit on something in the catchall basket sitting atop the kitchen counter, a plastic cat toy.

"Wait!" I exclaimed, getting up to retrieve the plaything. "This was hers, Spot's—I mean, Hermione's. It was in the gym bag along with the other stuff."

I held it out to Patty as I recalled the morning after the chase. "Spot was here for a short time before we relinquished her to the shelter. Frannie found the toy in the bag and gave it to her to play with. I remember her batting it around for a while, but by the time we were ready to leave, it had disappeared. A fifty-cent cat toy was the last thing on my mind, and I thought no more about it."

Patty studied the bauble. "You kept it for all this time?"

"Not intentionally. My granddaughter discovered it a few months ago when we were getting the new refrigerator. Seleia found a whole slew of toys under the old fridge—more than you can imagine!" I laughed, recalling the lineup of items that had been lost under the big appliance over the years. "But I recognized this one right away."

I brought it up to my eye. Though similar to other cat balls, it was slightly larger and heavier than those I bought at the Pet Pantry. Its blue and yellow plastic outside was pristine, not like my clowder's mauled, scratched, and scraped collection. I shook it and it rattled, though it didn't sound like a bell but something more solid and enticing to a cat.

Before I knew it, a red-striped paw whipped up and slapped the thing out of my hand. The rest of the red cat leapt after it, flowing smooth as water to pounce and play with the new toy.

"Someone likes it," Patty observed.

Big Red was going at the toy with a vengeance, batting it from paw to paw, then slamming it into the wall in a move that would make a hockey player proud. I decided I'd better rescue it before it went back under the refrigerator for another five years. The playful cat glared at me. I tossed him a catnip mouse as compensation, and he was off again in a flurry of paws, claws, and stripes.

As I wiped off the kitty-spittle with a napkin, I studied the toy once more. Something inside the plastic weave caught the light, glittering for a millisecond like sunshine. I tried to make it shimmer again, moving it up and down and rolling it in my palm, but whatever that sparkle had been, it was gone.

Tossing the ball up in the air. I caught it with a smile.

"I guess I do have a reason to visit Hermione after all."

Chapter 4

Tortoiseshell-patterned cats have a reputation for being feisty. They are said to have particularly sensitive hair follicles, so after a point, your tender petting can become painful to them.

I'd considered taking the long-lost cat toy back to Spot-slash-Hermione a little later that same day but got busy and decided to put it off. As intrigued as I was with the return of the prodigal cat, I had other things to do. Though retired from a "real job" ages ago, I now found myself busier than ever. If sixty is the new forty, then it all makes sense. Family, friends, and volunteering opportunities were just a part of it. Sights to see, books to read, films to watch, new recipes to try, new shops to peruse—the list was endless. And since most of my cats were seniors or had special needs, their care and well-being was time-consuming in itself. No, Hermione would have to wait a little longer to be reunited with her property. Since she hadn't missed it in the last five years, I doubted she would mind.

The weather was lovely so I spent the rest of the afternoon working in my garden and chatting with folks who strolled by on their Saturday walks. Though it was only the first week in May, the air was already beginning to have the velvet feel of early summer. Granted, in the Pacific Northwest one could never tell whether it would last or be usurped by another month of torrential rains, but for now, the forecast was all good.

After getting three beds weeded and ready to plant with early vegetables, I took a break to stretch my back and enjoy my surroundings. The deep aqua blue of the sky was strewn with poofs of whitest cloud like something out of a children's storybook. The irises were in bud, and a profusion of forget-me-nots dotted the edgings with their tiny blue-violet blooms. My daffodils were over now, and only a few stray red tulips persevered, but the wisteria that arched above my gateway and ran wild down the fence line was proving to be especially gorgeous this year.

"Yo, Lynley," came a voice from up the block.

An elderly woman wearing purple designer sweats and sporting a lavender jelly bell in each sinewy fist was making her way up the sidewalk at a clip. She pulled to a halt in front of me and leaned on the fence with a sigh.

"Hi, Olive. I see you're out and about again."

"That darned flu isn't going to keep me down," Olive declared. "But it's taking a bit of work to get back to speed." She huffed. "Don't ever get old," she added vehemently.

I laughed. Only a nonagenarian would consider sixty-one young. *Nearly sixty-two*, I reminded myself. My birthday was coming up in a matter of days. Time marches on. If I kept myself in as good a shape as Olive for the next couple of decades, I had nothing to worry about.

"Hey, I saw you earlier today, up in the park." She gave a great guffaw. "You were a sight, all you folks with your animals on pretty little leashes. At first I thought they were little doggies, but darned if they weren't a bunch of kitty cats! What's with that?"

I laughed. "I don't suppose you've heard of adventure cats," I posed.

"Can't say as I have. Is that some new club?"

"It's more of a worldwide movement. The term refers to cats who've been trained to wear a harness and leash so they can go on outdoor trips with their people. It can be walks or rides, hiking or boating, any type of excursion. We just started a local group, mostly Friends of Felines folks. We pick somewhere different to go each weekend, weather permitting. At least that's the plan—so far we've only been on two outings, one last Saturday to Laurelhurst Park and the one today up on Mt. Tabor. With summer coming, we're hoping to do a lot more."

Again Olive cackled her basso chortle. "I can't imagine! But good for you, Lynley. Whatever gets you out and about." She did a few pumps of her baby bells. "Well, I'd better keep moving. Don't want the heart rate to slow down too much. Good luck with your adventurous kitties." She gave a wink and began off down the street.

I was just about to crouch back onto my weeding stool to finish up under the roses when my phone rang. Pulling off my garden gloves, I sprinted to the porch and grabbed it off the railing.

"Hello, Alani," I said a little breathlessly, sprinting not being my strong point.

"How did you...?" she began. "Oh, I keep forgetting. You're on your mobile."

"It's the only phone I have anymore," I replied. "My landline was getting too many robocalls, so I finally let it go the way of the dinosaurs and the eight-track tape."

"The what?" queried the young woman.

"Never mind. Not something you need to worry about. What's up?"

There was a pause on the other end of the line. "I was wondering if you'd heard from Frannie lately?"

Both Alani and Frannie were fellow volunteers at

Friends of Felines cat shelter. I'd only gotten to know Alani in the past a year or so, but Frannie DeSoto was one of my closest friends. I frowned, trying to remember the last time I'd talked to her. It had been a while.

"No, come to think of it. Why?"

Again the hesitation. "It's probably nothing."

A shiver of apprehension coursed up my spine. "What? What's nothing?"

"Well, she and I were supposed to get together at the shelter this morning. We had a meeting scheduled with Blossom from the behavior department to discuss Torta, the feisty little tortie in B-Mod."

"I know Torta. She's a difficult case, shy and aggressive at the same time."

"Then you know Frannie's been working with her for weeks, trying to help socialize her so she can go up for adoption."

"Yes, she's come a long way. I heard she might even be transferred from the behavior modification unit into the general population soon."

"Correct. That was why we were meeting. That, and to set the plans for Frannie's vacation."

Now it was my turn to pause. "What vacation?"

"Well, see, that's the thing. It seemed strange to me, too, that she would suddenly decide to pick up and take off like that."

"Wait, Alani. I don't know anything about a vacation. In fact, just the opposite. Frannie and I have a date coming up for my birthday."

"Oh, well, maybe she'll be back by then."

"But what's she doing? Where is she going?" *And why the dill pickles didn't she tell me about it?*

Silence from the line, then Alani began, "It was a few

days ago, Lynley. Frannie called me to say she'd be out for a week or so. She asked if I would take over with Torta while she was gone. Of course I agreed, and we made arrangements to get together to discuss the case, but she didn't come. I waited all morning, but she never even checked in to the shelter. I've tried phoning, but there's no answer. I've left messages. I'm probably overreacting, but I'm worried. I don't know what to do. I figured if anyone knew what was up with Frannie, it would be you."

My mind reeled. Nothing Alani had said made sense. Frannie out for a week? Abandoning Torta, her special little ward? Missing my birthday? I could understand her not answering her phone—she, like me, preferred to text or email. But she always picked up for her FOF friends or got back to them as quickly as possible.

Maybe she was busy, or out, or...? No, no matter how I spun Alani's report, this was not normal Frannie behavior. And the fact that she had planned some sort of holiday without ever letting me in on it rankled. I was her kitty pal, her confidant, her trusted friend, for goodness' sake! She was supposed to tell me *everything*.

"I'm sure she's fine," I said for no good reason. Reassurance? And if so, was it aimed at Alani or myself?

"Yes, of course. I knew you would have an answer. I'm sorry to have bothered you."

"No, Alani." I sunk into a lawn chair that had seen better days. "I'm glad you called. And in fact, I really don't know what might be up with Frannie. She certainly never mentioned a getaway to me. And it isn't like her to ditch one of her project kitties." Again the whisker-tickle of doubt. "Let me look into it and get back to you."

"Sure. Yeah. Will you be coming to the shelter later on?"

28

I looked at the time readout on my phone—nearly four o'clock. "Not tonight, but I have an early shift tomorrow morning to clean kennels before the Sunday rush. How about you?"

"I'll be working on a mailing project for the director tomorrow, but I'm not sure what time I'm coming in. I like to have breakfast with my husband and the kids."

"Look me up when you get there. I'll be in the cattery. And I'll make sure to check on Torta."

"Okay, see you then. And Lynley..." She faltered. "I hope everything's okay with Frannie."

Me too, I lamented to myself.

The moment Alani rang off, I punched up Frannie's number. Frannie and I went way back, to the beginning of our volunteering career, in fact. At a similar, older age among a youthful contingency of new volunteers, we instantly gravitated toward one another and quickly found we had much in common. Love of cats topped the list, but there were other things as well—history, music, art, and an unmistakable *joie de vivre.* We'd both had adventurous youths in the throes of the hippie era, though we didn't often discuss it. *What happened in the sixties should stay in the sixties,* as they say with good reason. Still, it provided one more area of common ground.

Yes, Frannie DeSoto and I were sisters under the skin. Outwardly, however, we couldn't have been more different. Where I still held onto a few of the hippie fashion statements, such as long hair and a minimum of makeup, Frannie had gone the opposite direction. I pictured the platinum curls that ringed her perfectly-painted face like a halo, the manicured nails matching her current shade of eyeshadow. She accentuated an already-charming figure with the discrete use of undergarments and fashionable

29

dress, even on her trips to the shelter to clean litter pans and do laundry. I myself couldn't be bothered. My clothes were clean but old, and comfort was the deciding factor. You wouldn't catch me squeezing into a set of Spanx, no matter what the occasion!

Frannie and I had been through a lot over the years, confiding our deepest secrets and helping each other through times of trouble with loyal devotion. So why hadn't she told me about her trip? Then again, when was the last time I'd communicated with her? Was I the one who had been remiss, too busy with my own life to give her a call?

But I was calling now. When the line went to voicemail, I clicked off and tried again, thinking she might answer on the second attempt, but she didn't.

"Hey, Frannie," I said to her recording system, "just checking in. I talked to Alani, and she said you missed an appointment at the shelter this morning. Just wondering if you're okay. Call when you get this. I'm sure everything's fine, but you know me—I worry."

I rang off but held onto the phone in case she might call right back. No such luck. Behind me, I heard a muffled meow and turned to see a trio of faces pressed up to the window watching me with somber fascination—my three black cats Tinkerbelle, Little, and Emilio. The three pairs of gem-like eyes, all focused my way, reminded me of the three witches from Shakespeare's Scottish Play. I had the strangest feeling they were trying to tell me something. Something about Frannie? About her unexpected absence? But then the meows started up again, an unmistakable reminder that dinnertime was at hand.

* * *

I made a few more attempts to get hold of the wayward Frannie later that evening. I texted and emailed, just in case those might yield better results. After a few hours without a response, I tagged her on Facebook with an irresistible picture of a cute kitty saying, "Why haven't you called me?" in a pink thought balloon. Short of going over to her apartment and banging on the door, that was about all I could do. Alani's story of the missed meeting and the strange, sudden vacation had me worried, but Frannie was a down-to-earth, intelligent—to say nothing of grown— woman. There had to be some very reasonable explanation for her absence. I just wished she would call and tell me what it was.

With the help of a few mental meditation techniques, I put my curiosity aside—I'd done what I could for the moment, and worry wasn't going to help. If I didn't hear back by tomorrow, I would pull out all the stops and go to her place, but for now, all I could do was have faith in a good outcome, if only for my own peace of mind.

I enjoyed a nice dinner of cold roasted root vegetables in vinaigrette, a slice of fresh vegan rye bread from the bakery, and a glass of iced saffron tea. Some think eating by one's self is the epitome of pathos, but I like it. Besides, with a contingency of cats, I'm never really alone.

After dinner, I spent a few hours on the computer tracing my Scottish ancestry back into the heathered highlands, then another hour watching an old episode of *Doctor Who*. By the end, I was nodding and decided it was time for bed.

I checked that my doors were locked, but before I set the alarm, I stepped out onto the back porch to look at the stars. It was a disappointing few compared with what I knew to be out there in the universe, but still they were lovely. Planes blinked red in the west, and I noted a bright, steady pinpoint of light crossing the blackness—the International Space Station.

"Hi, guys," I waved to the astronauts some two hundred plus miles away. Space was endlessly fascinating to me. In spite of all the doom and gloom scenarios put forth by a dystopian film industry, I dreamed of wise and empathic aliens who would come to Earth and make everything right.

Once back in the house, I attended to the alarm, turned out the lights, and trundled off to bed with a number of cats in tow. Big Red had already found his place of repose, curling into a striped circle on the patchwork quilt. Little hopped up beside him, making a nest in my pillows. Violet, who was fairly overweight, didn't care for the bed, preferring her cushion by the open window. She was there now with Mab stretched beside her.

Elizabeth, the newest member of the family, came wobbling into the room. The young cat had feline cerebellar hypoplasia, a condition that affected her mobility though it didn't slow her down one bit. With diligent use of her front claws, she clambered up the pet steps and tumbled down beside Red. That left Tinkerbelle, Emilio, and Dirty Harry. They would be along in good time.

I looked at the bed covered with cats and wondered, as I often did, how I'd got so lucky.

"Scooch over," I said as I climbed under the covers, setting off a general repositioning as we settled in for the night.

I picked up my book and read a few pages but gave up when the lines began to swim. Setting my glasses on the nightstand and clicking off the light, I let my eyes slip closed, but in spite of my drowsiness, I couldn't sleep.

I thought about Frannie. Where was she? What was she doing?

I thought about Spot. Such a marvel to have reconnected with my miracle kitten after all these years!

I thought about Carry and her red garden. The images of that strange place and its enigmatic occupant still held a fairytale impression, as if the whole experience wasn't entirely real.

As my thoughts drifted among the red undergrowth and through the lush, vermillion trees, I suddenly heard my grandmother's voice—something she'd told me when we were about to begin reading one of the darker stories.

"You must remember, dear," she would say in the most somber of tones, "that not all fairytales have happy endings."

Chapter 5

Most cats coming into the shelter system are either picked up as stray or relinquished by an owner. These cats are understandably disoriented by the huge change to their lives, and their confusion may manifest through behavior such as aggression, timidity, or shutting down. It's the shelter's responsibility to help them transition as gently as possible.

I arrived at the shelter before it opened and jumped straight into my cleaning job. It was Sunday, and I had a little over an hour to finish before the potential adopters, cat fanciers, and lookie-loos would be storming the doors to visit the cats. Each of Friends of Felines' forty-some kennels got a spot-clean every day and a thorough scouring every three. The paper that lined the kennel floor was replaced, along with any blankets or pads. The litter box was swapped out, and the water bowl washed and refilled with fresh water. The bed was left alone unless soiled, since cats favored a bed to which they'd become accustomed. Same with the bell balls, kicker pillows, and other favorite toys. During the cleaning, the cat was let out to roam the office where they could stretch their legs and interact with volunteers and staff.

Spencer, a seventeen-year-old Maine Coon male, was making his rounds while I had my head deep inside his kennel, spraying down the walls with pet-safe cleanser. As I absentmindedly listened in on the chatter from the room, I inadvertently picked out a voice, a familiar one. I pulled out of the kennel so fast my hair caught on the door, but I barely felt the yank as I turned to confirm.

"Frannie!" I exclaimed, starting toward my friend who was conversing with one of the animal care technicians.

Frannie turned slowly, shooting me a look of complete blankness. No, even worse—there was annoyance in her squint-eyed stare, as if my salutation was a bother.

"Sorry to interrupt," I apologized, a polite formality I'd never before felt necessary with my close friend, but now I did. "It's just that I've been trying to get hold of you, Frannie. Didn't you get my messages?"

"Pardon me," Frannie pointedly told the ACT. "Yes, Lynley, I got them. What do you want?"

Something in the flatness of her voice, the clipped words that bordered on rudeness, made me hesitate. Had I done something wrong? Was she mad at me for a reason I didn't comprehend?

"Hey," I placated. "It's nothing really. Just that Alani called me. She said you missed an appointment with her. About Torta."

Frannie's cold gaze roamed the room—the sink, the kennels, the desk—anywhere but me. "I'm here now."

"Right. Yeah." I hesitated. "Alani said you were going on vacation?"

Again the expressionless glare.

"And I just wondered what was up," I added.

The staff girl had moved away from the uncomfortable conversation and was attending to Spencer who was still cruising the room. He'd caught the notice of another cat, a yellow tabby who was new in the shelter and meowing up a storm. Between those frightened yowls and my friend's icy demeanor, my stress level was increasing exponentially.

"Let's get out of here," I told Frannie. "Go upstairs for a cup of tea and a catch-up."

"I can't. I'm busy." There was a pause, then Frannie blurted, "I'm sorry, Lynley. I just can't!"

With that, she pushed out of the office. I watched in amazement as she swept across the cattery into the lobby and straight through the front door. I thought I saw her glance back just as the door swung shut, but I couldn't be sure.

I turned to the staff girl who had the poor tabby in her arms with his head curled into her shoulder, quiet now.

"What was that about?" she asked me, a pierced eyebrow raised in concern.

"I'm not sure. Frannie's not usually so..." I couldn't finish. *Disinterested? Flaky? Rude?* "What were you two talking about, if you don't mind my asking?"

"It was strange." The girl tucked the tabby back in his kennel. Much calmed by her touch, he sank into a loaf on his fleece pad. "She was asking about getting a replacement for her behavior work."

"A replacement? For her vacation?"

"No, for good."

I gasped. "When? Why?"

"Right away, was what she said. I don't know her very well I'm afraid, but she sounded..."

"What? She sounded what?"

The girl thought for a minute, then shrugged. "If anything, I'd say she sounded desperate."

* * *

The incident with Frannie loomed over my morning like a storm cloud ready to burst its cold, drenching rain down upon me at any moment. It wasn't like her to go off that way. It wasn't like her to be so distant. In fact, the behavior she'd displayed in the cattery just plain wasn't like her at all. It was obvious something was on her mind. Why wouldn't she tell me? We'd always confided in each other before—why not now?

I thought about trying to phone her again, about going to her place and confronting her in person, but I wavered. Whatever was happening with Frannie DeSoto was her business, and she'd made it abundantly clear she didn't want my help. I decided the best thing to do was to put it out of my mind for now. I would tackle the problem again later, when my thoughts had cleared. I'd seen Frannie in the flesh and assessed she had not fallen off the face of the planet or been eaten by zombies, in spite of not returning my calls. She was walking and talking and seemed fine, at least physically. I'd voiced my concern and let her know I was there for her; maybe she would call *me*.

I finished with the kennels, and once the shelter had opened its doors to the Sunday throng, spent the next few hours helping with adoptions. An older couple was looking for a senior cat that would enjoy a pampered but quiet life in their West Hills apartment. A mom and teenage daughter enthusiastically browsed for a new kitten. A single man lurked around the perimeter until I asked him if he could use some help. He quickly agreed, describing his desire for one of the shy, stressed cats that were often overlooked in the shelter system, saying he was willing to work with them, *whatever it took*. I hooked him up with three potentials, including the nervous yellow tabby. It was love at first sight, and the tabby went home without a single yowl.

My shift ended at one o'clock, but I was showing a cat when the hour rolled around, so I didn't get away until after one-thirty. Since I had yet to connect with Alani, I decided to give a quick look around the shelter before I left for the day.

I took the private elevator to the second floor and proceeded down the hallway, poking my head into the offices and workrooms. Most were empty, their usual tenants spending Sunday doing weekend things, such as caring for their own cats. I found no sign of my friend but located a woman sitting at a table busily stuffing envelopes. She looked up and smiled as I came in.

"Have you seen Alani?" I asked. "She told me she'd be around here somewhere."

"Sure. She was helping me with this batch." The woman nodded proudly at a full box of finished mailings. "But she went home a little while ago. She said she had an obligation of some kind."

"Oh, okay," I replied, a little disappointed. After my strange run-in with Frannie, I was keener than ever to talk it out with someone who knew the score. But apparently it was not to be. "Thanks," I mumbled as I headed back downstairs.

I gathered my things from the locker in the volunteer room, but instead of going out to my car, I sat on the bench and checked my cell. Since phone calls were frowned upon while working with the public, I often left the potentially offending instrument in my purse. I'm not sure what I expected to find. A voicemail from Frannie telling me she was sorry and wanted to get together after all? Nice idea, but unlikely since she'd just brushed me off as if I were cat litter on the bottom of her shoe.

I had received a text, however, not from Frannie but from Alani. Again I felt a pinprick of hope that her communication might clear up some of the confusion, but all it said was, "Sorry I had to leave. Something came up. I'll call you later."

So much for working out the Frannie conundrum, but now I was free to do whatever I pleased until Alani's phone call. Only one problem: what did I please to do with the rest of my sunny Sunday?

I thought through my list of need-to-do's and want-to-do's. There was always housecleaning, and I could use a few items from the store. Since it was another nice day, yard work beckoned—I wouldn't mind planting those snapdragon starts in the front bed. Of course Sunday was supposed to be a day of rest and my time was my own—I could always go home and take a nap or sit in the back yard and catch up on my reading. Still, none of those inspired me.

Then I remembered Spot's—*Hermione's*—toy. This was the perfect opportunity to take a little walk up to Mt. Tabor and return the long-lost bauble to its rightful owner. I'd enjoy seeing Carry again and learning a bit more about what the paisley cat had been doing for the last five years. Yes, that idea brought a little scamper of excitement. As I headed for my car, I felt lighter with each step.

Chapter 6

Ringworm, though unpleasant and highly contagious, is not a worm but a fungus.

Once home, I changed out of my shelter outfit, throwing the clothes in the laundry to make sure I didn't inadvertently contaminate anything with strange cat germs. There was little possibility of that really, since most feline illnesses were short-lived once out of the cat, but better safe than sorry. The most common feline ailment transmittable to humans was ringworm, and no one wants to get that.

As I bade farewell to the clowder and headed for my car with Hermione's little toy packed neatly into my bag, I noticed a white sedan parked across the street. I couldn't see much of the man inside the tinted window, but he seemed to be watching me. I waved, just to be Portland-polite, and he immediately turned his face in the other direction. *So much for friendliness,* I thought to myself as I took a glance at his out-of-state license plate. Then I shoved the encounter to the back of my mind and enjoyed the drive through the blooming community.

Since I had no idea how to get to Carry's bungalow from the front, I took the back way through the park. As I got out of the car, I couldn't help but linger to take in the view.

Mt. Tabor was one of Portland's great anomalies. Not only was the tiny mountain an extinct volcanic vent, but it also housed a historic open reservoir that had once supplied water to much of the southeast area. Past the artificial lake, the neighborhoods stretched in a green-fringed grid to the sparkling Willamette. On the far side of the river, skyscrapers reflected the early afternoon sun, and beyond, the West Hills crouched like sentinels keeping watch on their urban ward. If one were standing on those hills looking back, one would see the whole thing in reverse—downtown, river, neighborhoods, and Mt. Tabor itself—with one remarkable difference. On the eastern horizon loomed a real mountain, complete with snow-capped peak and glaciered sides—Mt. Hood.

Portland really is a beautiful city, I reminded myself. Being Portland-born, I often took it for granted.

As I began up the hill, following the trail Dirty Harry had chosen the day before, I was overcome with the strangest sensation. I feared the little house would be gone, a Shangri-La, appearing and disappearing at will. Could I have dreamed the whole thing or made it up in my mind? But as I came over the rolling rise, there it was, the brick wall with its cascades of crimson roses, the wrought-iron gate through which I glimpsed the red garden beyond. A bit of that fairytale feeling still lingered, but now it felt more exciting than creepy. I didn't know what it was about this place, this woman, this cat, but it all seemed slightly magical, as if anything might happen with just a twitch of a whisker, a blink of an eye.

I paused when I got to the gate, hesitant about charging in uninvited. Still, unless Carry happened to be wandering in my direction, there really was no other way. Peering through the grill, I saw Hermione sunning herself on the stoop of the veranda. She was on her back, paws in the air, white belly to the sky in complete feline abandon. Before I

41

could stop myself, I was through the gate and heading up the path toward her irresistible form.

I knew better than to reach out and rub her presented underside, despite how inviting it might seem, so I stopped a few feet away and caressed her with my eyes. A sound came from within the covered porch, and Carry materialized out of the shadows, her journal clutched against her breast like a shield.

"Beautiful, isn't she?" Carry attested.

"Yes, absolutely. I hope you don't mind my barging in. The gate wasn't locked."

Carry stared at me intently. "Why would it be?"

"Oh, I don't know," I faltered. "All this..." I gestured around the fantastical garden, "It seems so private. I didn't want to disturb."

The small woman stepped past Hermione, who had righted herself and was watching me with one bright blue eye.

"It's not a problem, Lynley. But it's true, I don't often entertain. Possibly the solitude is reflected in the atmosphere. But come, let's relax under the trees and enjoy the nice weather while we have it."

Without another word, she turned and disappeared down a trail edged with purple hellebore. Again I hesitated but then followed since that was why I had come.

The path made a few twists and turns before I caught up with the small woman as she stood waiting for me by a pair of wooden chairs set in the shade of a huge Japanese maple.

"Please, sit," she commanded, brushing a few stray leaves from the oilcloth cushion.

I eased into a chair, and Carry took the other. Setting the journal on a mosaic-tiled table between us, she folded her legs underneath her in a lotus position. She was wearing a quilted raw silk tunic and striped silk pants that were drawn tight at the ankles. The colors were variants of dark orange with accents of deep teal blue and emerald green that brought out the turquoise of her eyes. With her pale skin and ruddy, blunt-cut hair, she looked like a piece of art against the backdrop of the crimson.

"This is a beautiful garden," I remarked, gazing up into the maple, its filigree foliage rustling in the breeze. "And very unusual. Did you plant it yourself?"

"Not the trees, no. They were here long before I acquired this home, but that's where the concept began. I had the original grass and shrubberies removed and replaced with their warm-hued equivalents." She looked around with a clear sense of pride. "And voila!"

"It's extraordinary. All you need are a few fairies and a nymph or two to complete the tableau."

Carry laughed and nodded to Hermione who, as if on cue, was wandering down the path toward us. "Who needs fairies when one has a cat?"

The paisley feline moved with the epitome of nonchalance, as if her decision to be there was a whim of her own, having nothing whatsoever to do with our human presence.

"Hermione likes the garden," Carry continued. "The reds show off her lovely coat."

"And her pretty red collar," I added, noting the quilted brocade band hadn't come off any rack I knew of. "Was it specially made?"

Carry gave a sly smile. "You could say that."

We both watched as the graceful cat sauntered and sashayed, then hopped onto the little table between us, quickly settling in for a bath and groom atop Carrie's book.

Her movements were fluid and ultimately distracting, but I hadn't forgotten my mission.

Reaching for my bag which I'd set on the ground at my feet, I retrieved the blue and yellow cat toy. Looking up, I was surprised to see Carry staring at the bauble. She had a strange, shocked look on her face, as if I were holding a grenade instead of a plastic ball. Then the look was gone, and she turned her stare on me.

I held the toy out to her. "This has a story to it."

"Oh?" she said, her tone indecipherable.

"The fact is, yesterday wasn't the first time I'd met your Hermione."

"Oh?" she repeated, her brow beginning to furrow.

I recited the story of the kitten in the gym bag, though I omitted a significant part of the shooting and chasing. "Before we took her to Friends of Felines, she was at my house for a few hours. I'm not sure if she knew the toy was hers or if she just enjoyed playing with it—she was a kitten, after all—but she had so much fun! She batted this little thing all over the kitchen. It finally went under the fridge, where it stayed all these past years."

Carry was silent for a good minute. I let her digest these new details about the cat she called her own.

"Is this true?" she said finally.

"Yes, of course. Why shouldn't it be?" For a moment, I felt offended.

But then I wavered. It was a fantastical tale, and I could understand how it might take a leap of faith to accept it without question from a virtual stranger.

I handed the ball to Carry who studied it thoughtfully. "How did you come upon it now," she asked, "coincidental to your rediscovery of the cat?"

"We recently replaced the old refrigerator. We

44

unearthed several lost toys in the process—balls, bells, catnip mice. I remembered this one because it's a little different than the others. Bigger, and a bit heavier than most of the ones they sell. When my granddaughter showed it to me, I knew exactly what it was. I put it away in a basket so the other cats wouldn't get it, I'm not sure why."

"Fortune?" Carry pondered, "or fate?"

For a while, she examined it, rolling the ball between her fingers and peering into the plastic weave. Hermione jumped into her lap, then onto her shoulder for a better view.

"Do you think she remembers it?" I asked, watching the cat study the item with singular interest. "But no, how could she? She was only a baby."

A white paw came up and gently touched the surface. She clearly wanted to play, though Carry seemed reluctant to let the toy go.

"Are you going to give it to her?" I asked

Carry wavered, then tossed it to the ground. Hermione was on it instantly, slinging it into the bushes and racing after.

This continued for a few rounds, then Carry uncurled and retrieved the bauble. "I think that's enough for now, sweetheart," she said to the cat, "or it will again be lost. We can play with something else, yes?"

She held Hermione's toy up to the sun, eliciting just the hint of a sparkle from inside, then placed it in her pocket. Under her breath, she mumbled what sounded like murder hornets.

"Pardon?"

"Nothing. Just a call I need to make."

Hermione gave a little *purrumph* which could have

denoted either agreement or frustration and hopped back onto the table.

I rose. "Well, I'd better get going. I just wanted to give Hermione back her goods." I laughed. "I think they call it closure."

"Oh, must you leave so soon?" Carry's voice held a note of lament with an overtone of urgency.

"Well, yes. I still need to stop by the library before it closes, and I'm meeting my granddaughter at the bakery at four."

Carry's face lit. "Would you mind some company, Lynley? I haven't been to town for oh-so long."

I started. "I'm just going to Belmont Street, only a few blocks away."

Carry grinned. "Lovely. Then it's settled. Let me put this someplace safe. You wait here while I get my things."

With that command, she scooped up Hermione and trotted into the house. A minute later she reappeared wearing a broad-brimmed sun hat and a tapestry cross-body bag slung over her flat chest. She shoved her journal into the bag, and I had to wonder if she took it everywhere she went. I'd certainly never seen it farther than an arms-length.

"Ready?" she asked.

I was slightly stunned by the turn of events, but I managed to smile and stutter, "Well, yes, I guess I am."

As I began toward the back gate, Carry stopped me. "Where are you going?"

I paused. "I left my car in the Tabor lot. I'm afraid it's the only way I know of to get to your house."

Carry gave me an odd look. "Yes, of course. You followed your adventure cat up the back way. Here." She rummaged in her bag and pulled out a little notebook of the same design as the journal. Finding a red pen, she scribbled her address on the page, tore it out, and handed it to me. "This might be more convenient next time you come."

I looked at the paper, a street I'd never heard of, but that was no surprise in the maze-like warren of little roads that skirted the inner-city hill.

"Now yours," she said bluntly.

"My address?"

"No, I don't need that, but I wouldn't mind having your phone number in case I need to reach you."

I wasn't in the habit of handing out my number to near-strangers since everyone knew it was a bad idea, to say nothing of the fact I had a minor phobia of talking on the phone. Yet I found myself jotting it down anyway.

"I rarely answer though," I grumbled. "It's better if you text."

Carry said something as she began walking down the hill toward the reservoir. I wasn't certain, but it sounded like *piffle*.

Chapter 7

Cat Cafés have sprung up all over the world, people quickly taking to the idea of a place they could spend time relaxing and socializing with cats. Most cat cafés are partnered with a cat shelter, so if you fall in love over tea and crumpets, you can make that affair a permanent adoption.

Belmont was bustling with Sunday afternoon business. Over the past century, the old Southeast Portland district had gone through several incarnations, from fashionable to rundown and now back to retro chic. With the arrival of trendy, eclectic shops to complement a few longstanding businesses, it was becoming the go-to place for anything from books to flowers to local craft beer to tattoos. It also housed, at least in my opinion, the best bakery in town, Cupcake City.

I do have to admit I'm biased because my lovely eighteen-year-old granddaughter works there. Even though Seleia was just finishing up her freshman year at Portland State, she'd managed to keep her job and was looking forward to more hours and a raise come summer. I was so proud of her. Though highly intelligent and heading for an eventual major in astrophysics, she had no problem buckling down to unskilled labor and seemed to enjoy both the hard work and the friendly clientele of the bake shop.

But Cupcake City was to be the last stop on my jaunt so Seleia and I would have time to sit and chat. My mother

Carol would be joining us to discuss my upcoming birthday—three generations of strong women. The only one missing would be my daughter Lisa. Sadly, as much as I loved Lisa, she and I suffered a strained relationship. There had been no great argument or falling out—the rift had just happened over time. I chalked some of it up to her creative nature. Lisa was an artist, a successful one and not prone to compromise. I had great respect for her and hoped she could make it to the party, but I knew if she were in on the planning, she wouldn't be happy until she was running the show, regardless of anything I might want.

"Where first?" my unexpected companion asked, pulling me from my contemplations.

I swerved into a vacant space on thirty-sixth and parked the car. Carry was sitting straight in the passenger seat, hands clutched around her bag, a big smile on her face. Her eyes sparkled with anticipation, like a kid at a fair, an incongruous look for what I guessed to be a woman of middle-age.

"Is there somewhere you need to go?" I asked.

"Anywhere. Everywhere! Wherever you're going. I'll just tag along, if that's alright with you. As I said, it's been a long time."

I still couldn't fathom how a trip of less than a mile from her house could be such a big event, but maybe she didn't get out much. I could relate. As a dyed-in-the-wool introvert who spent a major amount of time at home, I sometimes got a feeling of wonder from a simple trip to the grocery store.

"The library is a few blocks from here. We could start..."

"Can we go *there*?" Carry interrupted, staring at

something across the street. "It's a bookshop. I remember loving bookshops. The smell of the books, the solitude…"

Without waiting for an answer, she stepped off the curb and began to cross against the light. A car screeched to a halt with a flurry of shouts and honks, but Carry paid it no mind. Looking both ways and making an apologetic sign to the irate driver, I rushed after her, hustling her the rest of the way before she could be run over by traffic coming from the opposite direction. She seemed to have no concept of what she had done or how close she had come to being flattened into a Carry pancake.

Oblivious, she strolled into the bookstore with me trailing along behind like a nanny after a spoiled child. The Read Nook, formerly known as Belmont's Books, had changed its name with a new set of owners, but most everything else about the spacious, book-filled room had remained the same. I was happy to note they'd retained their employees as I nodded hello to an older man in the well-worn wool sweater, Mr. Cunningham.

One addition implemented by the new management was a small lounge area called "Agatha's" for the great mystery writer Agatha Christie. In Agatha's, store clientele could buy a coffee, tea, or soda, then take it to one of the tables or overstuffed chairs to sip and read their purchased books. For those who hadn't bought or brought reading material of their own, a special shelf of used books was provided. Carry was absorbed in a thorough examination of those offerings.

I sighed and went after her. "Would you like to get something to drink?"

"No, I don't think so," she replied, totally zeroed in on the spines of the paperbacks. One by one, she pulled them out to take a closer look.

Suddenly she stopped, turned, and nipped back into the store-proper, heading for a sale table set up by the front window. Again I followed, unsure what to do with this enigma of a woman. I had no intention of traipsing after her all over Belmont, but then again I felt disinclined to abandon her. I decided the best course was to wait and see what happened next. Maybe she would settle down and act like a normal human being instead of a wayward kitten, and the problem would solve itself.

"Are you looking for anything in particular?" asked Mr. Cunningham as Carry flew past his desk.

She stopped mid-stride and peered up at the lanky man. "No. Well, yes."

"What's the name?"

"Carry, with a C."

"No, ma'am, I meant the name of the book. The book you're wanting."

"Well, let me think. I could use a new volume. My current one is nearly full."

Mr. Cunningham cocked his head in confusion until she withdrew the big journal from her bag. Then with a knowing smile and a satisfied "A-ha," he guided her to a collection of bound and blank notebooks where she happily proceeded to examine each one, just as she had with the Agatha's shelf.

I watched for a few moments to make sure she wasn't going to run off again, but she seemed intent on her work. I took the reprieve to check out a display of cat mysteries, my preferred genre of light reading, and was excited to find the latest from a favored author, Angela T. Moore. Carry picked out a large ledger with an abstract red cover, identical to her current one, and we purchased our items together.

"Where next?" I asked as we pushed out the door into the afternoon sunshine.

She glanced to the right, then wordlessly turned left. I tailed along, weaving through the pedestrians and hoping wherever she was headed would be on this side of the street—I didn't want to deal with another near-miss traffic accident.

The sidewalk was crowded with Sunday shoppers, and I soon got held up, first behind a group of tourists gathered around a map of the area and then a team of kids on scooters. When I finally broke free, I thought I'd lost her. But there she was, half a block up, ducking into a Tibetan shop. I scurried after and was about to go in when she came back out again, on her way elsewhere.

Carry led me through several more shops and stores, never staying more than the time it took to give a cursory look around. I had no idea if she was after something in particular or just sightseeing. Her choices seemed random, yet there was something unmistakably methodical about her actions.

After a half hour and a good five-thousand steps, I was ready to call a halt. We had visited the florist, the jewelers, and the Asian grocery, and even climbed the chartreuse staircase to the cat café. I would have been perfectly content to stay, order a beverage, and relax with a cat on my lap, but she barely made it through the lobby before she turned on her heel and headed back down to the sidewalk.

I had other things to do, and to be honest, though intrigued by this woman and her eccentric ways, I'd come to the point where I really didn't care anymore. I opened my mouth to announce it was time to go home when she came to a dead halt in front of me.

Nearly bumping into her, I stopped too. Carry was glaring up the street with the concentration of a cat about to pounce. Or maybe it was a cat who was about to be *pounced upon*, because though her turquoise gaze was predatory, it also held a glint of another emotion. Anger? Sorrow? *Fear?*

I followed her stare to a tall woman wearing a gray silk suit and spike heels. Among the casual jeans, tee shirts, and sportswear that prevailed on the eclectic boulevard, this mode of dress seemed as incongruous as a purebred Siamese in a colony of ferals. But that wasn't what set her apart. Everything about her pegged her as alien. The made-up face, powdered white with blood-red lips and black pencil-thin eyebrows, seemed more of a mask than a visage. The long, pewter hair that cascaded in perfect ribbons down her shoulders and back resembled the cultured mane of an albino pony. Her ice-green eyes were a shade not seen in nature. They were locked on Carry, and Carry's were locked on hers.

"Carry," drawled the woman as she approached.

"Datura," Carry replied succinctly, as if she had just downed a swig of sour milk.

Datura's full lips curled into a cat-who-stole-the-cream smirk. "And who is your friend?" she said, taking me in with those creature eyes.

"She's no one," Carry shot back. "Leave her be." To me she said, "Would you excuse us, Lynley? I need to talk to my old associate. Alone."

"Um, of course," I murmured. "Will you be able to get home okay? Or would you like to meet later?"

"Thank you for your kindness." Carry reached out and touched my hand. "I'll be fine."

She said something more, but I couldn't make it out.

Harley... or possibly *Charlie...* or even *barley, homie,* or *rocket.* None of them made sense, and I was about to ask her to repeat herself, but she had already moved her full attention to the woman. I had been dismissed.

As I turned to go, I saw a figure lurking in the shadows of an old brick storefront and was caught for the second time with the intense and uncomfortable impression that someone was watching me.

Chapter 8

Cat-themed events are extremely popular. Googling those words netted me some twenty-million results. Whatever the event, a kitty theme will be a welcome treat.

As I sat alone at Cupcake City's window table watching the passersby, I breathed a sigh of relief. Carry was an enigma, there were no two ways about it. I kept reminding myself I barely knew the woman and had absolutely no obligation toward her, yet I worried. That Datura person had acted in what I considered to be a suspicious manner—not exactly aggressive, but confrontational without a doubt. I would wager she and Carry had history, and go so far as to make a side bet that it hadn't always been a good one.

A small, elderly woman suddenly loomed into my line of sight, her wrinkled face smiling through the glass. She tapped twice with a bony finger, then she was gone.

My mother reappeared in the doorway, and I rose to greet her, once again amazed at the vitality exuded by the eighty-five-year-old matron. Yes, Carol Mackey had the wizened hide and white, wispy hair of an octogenarian, but her eyes sparkled with a youth never forgotten—nor left behind.

"How are you, dear?" she asked, planting a lipstick kiss on my cheek.

"Good, and you? Did you have any trouble getting here?"

Carol seated herself with a sigh. "Just because I don't drive doesn't mean I'm housebound." She gave a little sniff at my silliness. "I can get anywhere I want to go in this city. I've got a *network*." She said the word as if it were new to her, and very profound.

"I'm sure you do," I laughed.

"Opal brought me," she admitted. "I'm meeting her at the bus stop up the street at five-thirty." She looked around at the cozy shop with its teahouse décor and old-fashioned oak showcase of goodies. "Speaking of time," she went on, "where is our little girl? I want some tea."

"I'll get it," I offered. "What kind would you like?"

Carol thought for a moment. "Earl Grey, if that's alright with you."

"Earl Grey it is."

I headed for the back of the room where a tea service was set up on a vintage sideboard.

"And a cookie," she called after me.

I returned to the table with a steaming pot and two mugs, and was about to go order the goodies when a stunning young woman in a white dress and a pink embroidered apron swept out the door from the kitchen. As if by magic, she was carrying a tray of colorful, bite-size cupcakes.

"Oh," she said when she saw us. "I'll be right with you guys."

"Hello, sweetheart. No hurry. Your great-grandmother and I were just thinking of a cookie, but those look awfully good too."

Seleia deftly tucked her load into the cabinet, withdrawing an assortment of the luscious confections and placing them on a platter. Grabbing a set of napkins and a coffee mug from behind the counter, she pulled off her apron, hung it on a peg, and came to join us at the table.

Again there was a round of greeting kisses and hugs, then Seleia pushed the plate front and center.

"Mini-cakes, our new best sellers," she boasted.

"These look wonderful!" I picked up a light-colored cake with white icing drizzled in deep golden syrup.

"Butterscotch," said Seleia, choosing a chocolate on chocolate one for herself. "Missy's just began making them."

"What a good idea!" Carol bit into her bright pink strawberry-topped sweet with a groan of delight. "I like cupcakes but rarely buy them because the regular ones are a bit too much for me. These are just right."

As we dug into the treats, each beautifully decorated in a different style, I gazed at the two women, my closest family. In spite of the near-seven decades between them, there was an unmistakable resemblance. The eyes shone with the same light; the mouths in spite of the different textures, curved into the same smile. I didn't see it in myself, nor did I find any hint of it in Seleia's mother Lisa, but there, across the table from me, the familial similarities were inescapable.

"So you're having a birthday, Grandmother," Seleia said to me, shaking back her red-gold hair.

"It rolls around every year at about this time," I answered evasively.

"And how old will you be?" Carol put in.

"You know very well how old I am, Mum. At least you should. You were there, after all."

Carol fluttered a hand, the one not involved in the consumption of the cupcake. "Yes, but it was so long ago I've nearly forgotten."

"Granna!" Seleia barked at Carol. "That's cruel!"

"I'll be..." I announced, "...old enough to know better. Now can we please move on to the party plans? At my age, who knows how much longer I have?"

Carol sniffed, muttering something under her breath.

"What did you say, Mum?"

"I said," she enunciated, "spring chicken. You're nothing but an insolent little spring chicken. Wait until you get to be my age."

With that, we all laughed and were ready to get down to the business of my celebration.

"I don't want anything fancy. Or big," I added.

"That's why we didn't invite Mother to this planning session," Seleia said bluntly. "She would have turned it into an all-out gala."

"Yes, she's good at that," I admitted, "but she got her chance to shine for my sixtieth. Renting that hall and inviting everyone I'd ever met in my entire life—including my dentist and the boy next door from when I was ten! I can only handle an event like that once a decade."

"Let's start with a theme," Seleia offered.

"Cats!" both Carol and I said at the same time.

"Yes, of course. I should have known."

"Maybe we could have it at Friends of Felines, and the guests could take a tour of the shelter as the entertainment."

"We could get them to clean litter boxes and sweep up kibble as part of the experience." I laughed, thinking of a bunch of ladies in party dresses scooping kitty poo.

"Okay, a cat theme, but maybe not quite so hands-on," Seleia mused. "If we had it at your house, we could dress your cats up in little outfits."

"You must be joking," I scoffed. "Elizabeth might stand for it, and Violet would probably allow a silly hat, but Big Red would go crazy and so would Emilio. Besides, I don't want it at my house. I'm supposed to be the guest of honor, which means I shouldn't have to clean up after everyone leaves."

"We'll help," Seleia volunteered. "Won't we, Granna?"

"Okay, not at Lynley's," said Carol, no keener to spend her time cleaning a big Victorian homestead than I was. "We can always have it at the Terrace."

Seleia got up to fetch herself another cup of coffee. "Do you think your condo would hold all Lynley's friends?" she asked over her shoulder.

"The facility has a lovely day room for that sort of thing," Carol replied as Seleia returned with her cup full and steaming. "As long as it's not already spoken for... Here, give me a second." She whipped out her cell phone, and with a gnarled finger, efficiently typed in a text. Placing the instrument face down on the table, she said, "There, that should do it. We'll know shortly if the day room is an option. What else do we need to discuss?"

"I have the guest list right here." Seleia also pulled out her phone and busily scrolled. "I've contacted everyone already, giving them the date and time and telling them the place is TBA. They all said they can come except for your friend Rhonda. She has..." Seleia frowned at her notes. "It says here she has a cat job?" Seleia looked up at me. "Does that mean she's doing a show with her actor cats?"

"Yes, she and the cats got signed on for a new production filming here in town, though I don't remember the name. Her twin kitties are all set to play a recurring part."

"Oh, that's exciting!" Seleia exclaimed. "Her cats are so amazing and beautiful! And she says she'll try to make it if she doesn't get called."

"Well, this is coming along nicely, Carol remarked, bobbing her head like a pigeon.

"Once we finalize all the details," said Seleia, "I'll send out a mass email. I'm so glad all your friends communicate that way. It's so much easier than note cards and snail mail."

"Snail mail has its place," I cautioned my grand-daughter. "I would have sent handwritten invitation notes if I'd got it together in time. But you're right, this is much simpler. And simpler yet because you're doing it for me. Thank you dear. I do appreciate it."

"I know social contact isn't your thing, Lynley. And I don't mind at all."

"Every introvert needs an extrovert advocate in the family for times like these," I told her with an across-the-table hug.

Carol lifted the tea pot, then put it down again and looked inside. "Nearly empty. Seleia, would you mind getting another?"

"Of course not. That's my job!" Seleia gave a smile of genuine pride, so cute on her young face. "What kind is it?"

"Earl Grey. You can just add one more bag to what's there."

As Seleia rushed off to collect the tea, I turned to the window. With its view right onto the busy street, there were always interesting sights to be seen. A trio of folks with rainbow hair and mismatched clothing were at the bus stop all talking at once; a man in a Utilikilt and a Darth Vader helmet cruised by on a unicycle playing the bagpipes; keeping hold of six leashes, a dogwalker maneuvered the crowded sidewalk like a pro.

Then I picked something else out of the melee and gave a gasp. Carol's eagle eye instantly followed my gaze.

"Oh, dear," she exclaimed. "That poor woman! It looks like she's in trouble."

I recognized the little figure who was being hauled along by a tall, well-dressed lady and a hefty young man. From the angry look now set on her elfin face, I judged that none of it was her idea.

"It's Carry!" I burst out haplessly.

"You know her?" Carol exclaimed.

I nodded. "I do. A little."

"Then we must help!"

My mother was right—I couldn't sit there like a lump of cookie dough when Carry was very obviously being hijacked against her will. Before I'd thought twice, I was up and out the door after the jostling threesome.

"Carry!" I yelled as I pushed through the street press to catch up. "Hey, you there—Datura! Let that woman go!"

Datura stopped and turned, all the while keeping a tight grip on Carry's thin arm.

"Oh, it's you." Her voice was the hiss of an angered snake.

"Where are you taking her?" Then to Carry, I asked, "Are you alright? Have they hurt you?"

For a moment, all three were silent as dead stone. Then Carry breathed a huge sigh. "I'm fine, Lynley."

"You don't look fine. Do you want me to call the police?"

"No!" she admonished, then again in a softer tone, "No, it's alright, really. They are just helping me..."

"Yeah, we're helping," said the man, giving me an unconvincing smile. I stared at the glum face, the dark eyes. He reminded me of someone, but I couldn't place him. Maybe it was just his type, the Rock-wannabes, all muscle and glare. A bully, for sure. And now he was bullying my friend.

But again I had to remind myself Carry was not a friend but someone I'd only recently met. She seemed nice enough and was good with her beautiful cat which meant a lot to me, but as far as her life story, she was a mystery. She could be a schoolteacher, a firefighter, an artist, a pirate, a crook, or even a serial killer for all I knew.

She could also be a pathological liar. Was she lying now or telling the truth? She had just declared she was fine—twice!—and though instinct told me otherwise, who was I to argue? Maybe the man and woman really were merely helping her along; maybe their pushing and herding actions weren't malicious and pointed after all. I had Carry's word for it. What more did I need?

I looked at Carry, slumped between her two attendants, more enigmatic than ever. I looked at Datura, tall and straight, almost exotic in her gray silk suit. I looked at the man—his smile had receded, and now his face resembled unpolished granite.

One last time I caught Carry's eye. "I'm sorry if I was mistaken, but it seemed as if these people were intimidating you. If that's not the case..."

"It's not!" Carry exclaimed, far too loudly.

"...then I'll leave you to it."

I waited for a reply, a wink, a hand signal that she really did need extricating, but nothing came. In the end I shrugged and walked away, back to the bakery, back to my family. I felt deflated, embarrassed, and a bit angry for no special reason aside from the fact that my well-intentioned help had been snubbed. As I passed through the door, I caught a glimpse of a shiny blue poster depicting a handsome young man with an inscrutable grin—Dr. Wil Craven. His placid look of absolute privilege angered me even more.

I sat down at the table with a harrumph and turned to the window, but the unlikely threesome had disappeared from view. Seleia and Carol, who had been watching my every move, asked in unison, "What happened?" and "Is she okay?"

"I don't know," I replied to both questions. "I honestly don't have a clue."

* * *

Carol, Seleia, and I sat for a while longer at the little window table discussing party plans, but after the null confrontation with Carry and her "helpers," I felt my energy fading. I reiterated my request for nothing fancy—I hoped they got the picture. Carol had heard back from the Terrace, affirming we had the room; quick as a cheetah, Seleia sent word to the guests. As to the particulars of the proposed cat theme, she promised with a self-satisfied smirk it would be a surprise but a nice one. Then she excused herself because she had a date with Fredric, her beau, and no matter how pleasant it was to hang around with Grandma and Great Grandma, spending time with her young man would prove far more fun.

Carol took off to do a little shopping before Opal picked her up at the bus stop, and I headed home. I kept an eye out for Carry as I drove through the neighborhood, but it was a long shot, and one that didn't pan out.

On the drive, I again ran through my need-to-do list, but when I arrived at the house, Little had other plans. Beckoning me to the couch, she plopped herself on top of me. I kicked off my shoes and succumbed to a nap.

Sometime later I awoke with a jolt, rousing both Little and Emilio who had joined her. Looking at the clock, I saw I'd been asleep only a short while and now felt more tired than I had when I drifted off. It was a different sort of tired, a bone-heavy exhaustion that was rare for me. Was it because I'd been sleeping with two large cats on my chest, or had it been a more cerebral concern?

Shaking off a very disgruntled Emilio and letting Little jump down on her own, I pulled myself into a sitting position. I glanced at the window, only to find a square of darkening shade—the onset of night.

Two individuals popped into my thoughts as I went to the kitchen for a drink of water: Frannie and Carry.

What was Frannie hiding behind her gruff dismissal? What dire circumstance could make her give up her much-loved work as cat a behavior councilor?

As for Carry, the scene of her being dragged down the street by a former associate and a thug kept replaying itself in my mind. Who does that? And why would someone think that sort of conduct was okay?

Two women. Two sets of concerns. Two secrets. Were there two dangers as well?

I felt certain Carry was in trouble; Frannie was another matter. But the fear I'd seen flash across her face just before she ran out of the shelter couldn't be denied. *Rats!* Too many questions, and not one good answer for any of them.

Without more information, those worries would drive me crazy, pulling my mind in every direction with dreaded *what ifs?* I made a decision to leave the Carry business until the morning, then give her a call to make sure she was alright. As for Frannie, if I hadn't heard anything by then, I would go to her apartment and confront her personally and privately. She was my buddy—she had to have more to say to me than "leave me alone!"

I didn't exactly feel better after making those plans, but there was a sense of relief. I knew what I was going to do and could go about my evening with some vague peace of mind. Banishing the final remnants of disquiet, I headed for the kitchen to feed the cats.

Chapter 9

Caring for senior and special-needs cats isn't for everyone. It requires time, money, skill, commitment, and most of all, unconditional love.

The following morning dawned beautiful and sunny. Light blazed in through my uncurtained windows and warmed me like a blessing. I stretched, petted Harry who was curled against my hip, listened to Big Red tell me it was breakfast time, and felt ready to begin my day.

I shrugged on a fuzzy bathrobe—the sun might have been shining, but the house still held the night's chill—and headed downstairs for morning coffee. As a retiree who lived without other human company, I'd developed my own routine: make a cup of French roast in the handy and slightly decadent Keurig coffee maker, then sit down to enjoy my first cup. Once fortified with caffeine, I'd fix breakfast for the cats. Some were on special diets, and a few required morning meds, so their care took time, concentration, and effort. In my opinion, they could hold off for an extra ten minutes before I jumped to do their bidding.

Carrying my mug and phone out onto the covered porch, I sat down on the cushioned bench. The light through the tracery of grape leaves that twined across the latticework was lovely, and the early morning silence, broken only by a few twittering sparrows, was balm for my overactive mind.

But alas, nothing lasts. I was jerked from my quietude by the buzz of my phone. The ringer had been silenced for the night, but that vibration, resounding through the little metal table like a Skilsaw, was alarming all on its own.

The call showed only a number—no name. That meant whoever was bothering me at six-thirty in the morning was not someone I knew. *Probably a crank call from out east where it was three hours later*, I thought to myself. I received the usual run of advertising calls, spoof calls, and downright illegal calls—*the warranty on your car has run out; your social security number has been compromised*. There was another possibility, however. It could be important.

Curiosity being my middle name, I gritted my teeth and answered, ready to hang up if the call proved to be something distasteful.

"Yes?"

"Lynley Cannon?" A woman.

"Yes," I cautiously admitted. "Who is this?"

"It's Carry. I need to talk to you. I have to explain about yesterday."

"Carry?" A prickle of concern shot through me. "What's up? Are you alright?"

She didn't answer.

"Carry," I prompted.

"Can you come to my house?"

"I guess, but… What time…"

She didn't let me finish, saying only, "Good. Thank you so much. I will see you soon then." Was I mistaken, or did that slight waver in her voice bespeak fear?

I waited but there was only silence from the other end of the line. I checked my display; sure enough, she had rung off. Short, sweet, and pointed. Whatever did she want that could only be discussed face to face?

I continued to stare at the phone as if it might ring again and give me the answers I required, but of course it didn't. Then I noticed a little numeral next to my voicemail icon. I touched it, wondering if Carry had somehow managed to leave a message following her call. As I brought up the screen and read the name, I experienced a second frisson of shock—not Carry but Frannie!

Frannie had called me and I'd missed it. I looked at the time—four-twenty-five in the morning. Why was Frannie trying to get hold of me at that wee hour? She must have known I'd be sound asleep.

Quickly I punched playback and listened to the familiar voice of my dear, strangely-acting friend.

"Hi, Lynley, I know it's late and you probably won't get this right away. That's okay, it's nothing urgent. I just wanted to... well, needed to talk to you... about what's been going on with me. You're my best friend and you deserve to know. But it's complicated. It's hard, and I... I..." The voice, though flat and unrevealing, faltered. "Just call me when you get this, okay? I'll be home all day."

I hung up and immediately tried her number. My heart was racing. Her tone had been so hesitant, so uncertain. I'd never heard Frannie sound like that before. And even though she claimed it was nothing pressing, I had the distinct feeling she was only saying that for my peace of mind.

I listened to the hollow buzz as the call rang down the line—once, twice—after which it cut off to voicemail. Disappointed, I mumbled something about playing phone tag and asked her to call back as soon as she could—or anytime. I added how glad I'd been to hear from her, then set the phone back on the table with a sigh.

The cats, impatient about their breakfast, had begun to join me on the porch and tell me all about it. According to them, I'd used up my allotted ten minutes, and they didn't care that it hadn't been spent in coffee contemplation.

"I'm coming," I told the clowder as I went back inside.

I shuffled through the swirling tide of fur, trying not to kick anyone or fall flat on my face. It took some time, but eventually they were settled at their stations. I always felt a sense of pride and accomplishment when the breakfast ritual was done. Not everyone would bother, I thought, patting myself on the back. Not everyone had the time or knowhow, let alone the financial capability to afford all their requirements, I amended, bringing myself back down a peg or two. Tending eight special cats wasn't for the faint of heart. It took dedication and skill. To be there for them, every day and night; to chauffeur them to their routine vet visits as well as the urgent ones when I'd cower in fear wondering if this were the end; to give them not only food, but affection and an environment where they could play hard, sleep safely, and get to act like the little wildcats they were—I loved doing it all, but I would never tell anyone it was easy.

As I sat musing on all things cat, Elizabeth wobbled up to me.

"Are you done, little one?"

She gave a tiny meow, indicating that she was and now she wanted some lap time. I picked her up, and she snuggled into the fuzz of my bathrobe, her silver tabby markings blending with the blue-gray fabric. The love in her eyes as she stared up at me was soul-healing.

As I stroked the soft fur, my thoughts shifted from the needs of the clowder to the needs of my human fellows. The fact that Carry had phoned me was as mystifying as the woman herself. At first I'd wondered how she'd got my number, but then I recalled the abrupt exchange of information we'd made the day before—her street address for my phone number. She said she wanted it—how had she put it? In case she *needed to reach me.* Did she know even then she might need an ally?

But was I an ally? Even that was speculation since she had brushed off my aid in no uncertain terms and gone off with Datura. Could Datura have threatened her in some way I didn't detect, causing her to lie? I'd given Carry every opportunity to make a sign or signal that she needed help, but she hadn't. No, when I left Carry with her so-called helpers, I was convinced she'd made her choice. If there was more to it that I hadn't picked up on at the time, it must have been incredibly subtle.

Now she wanted me. In person. What was it she felt compelled to explain? Did she wish to enlighten me on why being forcibly escorted was somehow okay? Clarify why she hadn't accepted my help? Had she been in trouble after all? Was she still? Maybe she had needed assistance and only now was able to call.

Then a wild thought popped into my mind. Maybe it was a trap.

I shook my head, unsure where that little chunk of melodrama had come from—television, most likely—and turned my thoughts to my other conundrum, Frannie and the midnight message.

Though it wasn't unheard of for people our age to be up and around at four-thirty a.m., it usually signified a bout of insomnia or a nagging arthritic pain that made sleep difficult. Neither of those scenarios required reaching out via telephone to people who were more than likely fast asleep themselves. Granted I'd all but begged Frannie to get in touch, but evening or morning would have been just as good if not better. It went without saying I would have picked up day or night had I'd known she was calling, but it was my habit to turn off the ringer when I went to bed. I might need to rethink that routine, since in reality, night was when all the crises came.

"Two women," I mused to Elizabeth, who had settled into my lap like a warm, furry donut. "Two completely different people in completely different circumstances, yet both suddenly want to talk to me. Both insist it's nothing pressing. And I have the strongest feeling that both of them are lying."

Chapter 10

Unlike humans, cats display a remarkable natural sense of direction. Whether it's a feature of their superior senses or an ability to detect the Earth's magnetic fields, cats have been known to find their way home over incredible distances.

Now that I had Carry's street address, all I needed to do was figure out where in the maze of obscure Mt. Tabor cul-de-sacs that might be. I had no idea what to expect once I got there. Carry in trouble? Carry sitting at her table on the veranda sipping tea? Maybe the strange trio, Carry, Datura, and the henchman, would be enjoying a beverage together. Realistically, that seemed more likely than the possibility something calamitous had befallen the little recluse.

Likely Carry's summons had been nothing more than a whim—she had certainly proven herself a creature of caprice on our chaotic outing. I considered turning back to focus on Frannie instead—after all, Frannie was closer to my heart, and I was genuinely concerned about her. Still, I'd tried calling her and had left a message; there was little more I could do now but worry and wait. Then I thought of Hermione. If Carry were in some sort of danger, where would that leave the paisley cat?

It took me a little while to locate Carry's street, but with the help of Mr. Google Maps, I managed without making too many wrong turns. The road itself was tiny and narrow, a winding, wooded lane curving gently up the hill. The houses tended to be small and varied in style. Interspersed throughout were tall Douglas firs, a holdover from before gentrification, when Mt. Tabor was nothing but parkland.

As I edged upward, pausing to look for address numbers, I noticed more than one person watching my progress. A woman pulled back an inch of gauze curtain, eyes trained on my red Toyota. A man out pushing a mower across his lawn stopped to watch me go by. A jogger with a dog quickly bustled inside a gate, only to turn back and stare. I noted that the dog, a husky malamute type, stared too. None of them smiled, nodded, or in any way made me feel welcome to their private little world.

Or maybe their surliness was all in my mind. I'd already been feeling strangely about Carry's abrupt and cryptic call—maybe the Twilight Zone aura exuded by the locals was only an extension of that sense, a figment of my overactive imagination.

Still, what if there was something to it? As a woman alone in the world, instinct was often my safest guide. Again I thought of quitting and going home. I could call Carry, let her know I couldn't come right now, ask her to tell me over the phone whatever she thought was so important.

Then I spied her number and curiosity drew me like a cat to an open cupboard door. Shoving my doubts aside, I pulled into the drive and parked. Granted I still didn't know what I was in for, but how bad could it be? If nothing else, I reminded myself, I'd get to see Hermione again.

Carry's place butted up against the Mt. Tabor hillside, as nondescript in appearance as a house could be. The bungalow itself was painted drab gray, the shade of a rainy day in Portland—not an inch of the ruddy brick that adorned the walls at the back. The fenced yard displayed only a plain green lawn and a few sparse shrubberies—not a flower or berry, not a single hint of exotic red.

This made no sense to me, since Carry had blatantly shown her penchant for red, not just in her garden, but with everything that surrounded her. The binding of her journal, the print of her clothing, even Hermione's beautiful collar were all saturated with that warm, primary hue.

In fact, I found this flat, soulless layout so divergent from what I knew of Carry that I paused to check the address again just to make sure. But there it was in rouge scrawl across the little page. Unless Carry herself had written it down wrong, or even more unlikely, had deliberately misled me, this was it.

I stared at the plain façade for a few moments longer. Bay windows on either side of the front door were curtained, the left in a beigey tan and the right in light blue. Again no red. But then I saw the front door, shaded within the tiny covered porch—a bright enameled crimson. It wasn't much but it was something.

As I got out of my car and started for the gate, I noted how quiet it seemed. I could count the sounds on one hand: the laughter of kids; the wind in the fir trees; a single singing bird. Then someone called out, breaking the magic with their grating, angry tone.

"You there," yelled a man who stood fists on hips in the adjacent yard. "Can I help you?"

I looked over at the well-dressed gentleman of an indeterminate age. His slightly graying hair contrasted his youthful cheeks and face, but in spite of his cherubic features, his expression was dour.

"No thank you," I countered, suddenly on the defensive. "I'm visiting someone here."

"That *woman*?"

"I..." I stuttered, shocked by the annoyance in his voice. "Her name is Carry."

The man glared at me for a moment longer, then turned away and stalked into his house. Was everyone on this cute little street as hostile as tomcats defending their turf?

I waited to see if anyone else was going to come out and confront me for my intrusion into their sphere, but things seemed to have reverted to the former chorus of dogs, kids, trees, and bird. With a final glare at the neighbor who was now staring at me through the blinds, I straightened my back, held my head high, and proceeded through Carry's gate with all the bravado I could muster.

As I followed the short, curved walkway leading to the house, I saw the front door had been left ajar. After the overt unfriendliness of the community, this sign of welcome was reassuring.

I climbed the steps to the porch and called through the gap, "Carry? It's Lynley."

I waited, but the only answer came in the form of a robin's tweet from a nearby apple tree. Surely Carry must have heard me. In the quiet, my voice was as loud as a lion's roar.

I tapped lightly on the door jamb, expecting the small woman to appear at any minute. Or possibly Hermione would poke her marbled head out to usher me inside. When neither of those things happened, I tapped harder.

"Carry? Are you home?"

Again no reply, which put me in a quandary—go in or go away? Being essentially a polite person, barging in on people without invitation went against my grain. *But I do have an invitation,* I reminded myself. Carry had called me, told me to come right over. She would be expecting me. She was the one who made the date.

I peered through the door but could see little of the dark interior. There was movement though, so someone was home. I heard footsteps going around the room, though they didn't seem to be heading for the door.

Suddenly there was a scuffling, then a clatter, as if something had been dropped and broken.

"Carry?" I repeated more urgently. Now the open door didn't seem as much a welcome sign as a bad one.

"Carry's busy," came a muffled, asexual voice. "Go away."

"Hello?" I countered. "It's Lynley. Carry asked me to come by..."

"Go away!" the voice reiterated. "She doesn't want to see anyone."

I paused. "Well, okay but, I'd really rather hear it from her..."

"Get the heck out!" the voice shouted angrily.

Like an enraged cat, my hackles rose. Not only did I dislike being talked to in such a rude manner, but the more this unknown entity insisted I leave, the more I was set on staying.

Without thinking further, I pushed the door open and stepped inside. It took a few seconds for my eyes to adapt to the lightless room and another few to fully comprehend what I saw. When I did, I drew back with a gasp.

Furniture was overturned; books and knickknacks were strewn across the floor; wall art swung at odd angles. Pillows had been ripped apart, leaving a windfall of feathers cast across the scene like winter frost. Unless

Carry was the worst housekeeper ever, there was only one conclusion I could draw—the place had been tossed.

I almost bolted, the smart thing to do when an illegal activity has been discovered, but what of the mysterious voice? What of Carry? What of Hermione? My mind ran to dark places, places of violence and mayhem. I imagined the worst. Then it was no longer my imagination as, in the gloom, I picked out Carry's small form.

Barely a shadow, she was crumpled on the floor by the desk. "Carry!" I cried, running to where she lay. I crouched to check her vitals. I admit I'm not good at pulse detection, usually ending up feeling only the throb of my own heart, but no matter where I tried on the little body, I could find none.

Yet I did feel something, not from Carry, but coming up from behind me—a shudder in the floorboards. Rats! In my haste, I'd totally forgotten about the other person, the one who had so desperately wanted me to leave.

I rose as quickly as I could, hauling myself up with the help of the table. As I faced the intruder, I realized I really should have taken their advice, should have gone away when they told me to and called the police from a safe distance. Now it was too late.

A shape loomed out of the darkness, and a pair of huge, gloved hands struck out at me like twin battering rams. The shove sent me reeling backwards, stumbling on the debris strewn across the floor. As I fell, my shoulder caught the edge of the desk, eliciting a lightning bolt of pain and sending books, papers, and a priceless set of China teacups raining down on top of Carry.

A split second later, I landed among the flotsam. I lay for a moment, dazed, but aside from the throbbing shoulder, basically unhurt. My impulse was to rise, but I forced myself to stay down—confronting the individual who had jumped me would likely not end well. If they thought I'd passed out, perhaps then they would leave me alone.

I squinted one eye open, saw a shoe next to my head, and closed it fast. Slowing my breath, I willed my muscles to unclench as they would do if I were unconscious. Finally after what seemed like an eternity, the shoe moved off across the room.

Opening my eyes, I tried to gather as much information as I could about the attacker. My glasses had spun off in the fall, so the details were fuzzy, but I got the basics. Black Nikes, black jeans, long black raincoat like the one Neo wore in *The Matrix*. Without moving my head, I wasn't able to see the face or know if they were wearing a hat, and I still couldn't gauge a gender. Sadly, my eye-witness description wasn't going to be much help in apprehending this perp.

The person, whom I dubbed Neo-X for lack of a better designation, had begun rooting around the room again, looking for something. They must not have found it, because after a great tantrum of throwing and kicking, Neo-X gave up and slammed out the front door.

I waited a few minutes longer to make sure they weren't going to return and kill me after all, then squirmed into a sitting position. When I'd fallen, I'd landed on something hard which had been poking me in the ribs. Now as I probed the sore place, I found a small tear in my shirt. From it protruded a shard from the broken cup. Wincing, I pulled it free. A dot of blood soaked into the fabric making a dime-sized circle of red, but it grew no bigger. I was lucky it hadn't been worse.

I peered around for my glasses, found them nearby,

and put them on. The fall had knocked them a bit out of balance, but at least they hadn't broken.

I adjusted them as well as I could, then slipped them on. The first thing I saw was Carry, lying face down, unmoving. Was she dead? I couldn't tell. I shivered when I realized how close I'd come to falling on top of her. The weight of my big body landing on hers would have done her no favors.

Suddenly I noticed the edge of something red protruding from underneath her torso, the corner of her journal. Her fingers clenched around its edge as if, even in those final moments, she'd meant to keep it safe. I stared, bedazzled by the intricate design, the gold ornamentation glinting out of the crimson, brought afire by some obscure light source. then my eye returned to the body.

Terror surged through me. *What the heck am I still doing here?* In a rush of abhorrence, I slipped Carry's journal from its human hiding place, shoved it in my bag, and ran from the house like a cat from a catastrophe.

Chapter 11

If your cat has become lost, you're bound to hear the suggestion to put their (dirty) litterbox outside so they can be guided home by its familiar scent. Though this may work in some instances, pet recovery experts advise against it since the box can attract predators who will chase your cat even farther away.

I already knew what came next. This wasn't my first rodeo—I mean, my first dead body. The police would come, then the detectives. The coroner's van. An ambulance or two. Maybe a firetruck. I would be detained for hours giving statements, answering questions. *How did you know the victim? What were you doing at her house? Where were you...* (insert suspicious look) *...at the time of the murder?*

There was no way I wanted to go through that right now, but I had no choice. Every minute I wasted feeling sorry for myself, Carry's killer was getting away.

Sitting on the stoop of the veranda, I made the call. I was shaking so hard it took a couple of tries just to dial the three simple numbers but finally I got through. The 911 operator asked me to stay on the line until the police came, so I set the phone down beside me and listened for the sirens. It didn't take long before that all-to-familiar wail rung through the morning air.

I had yet to see any sign of Hermione. It was no wonder she didn't hang around while Neo-X trashed the house, but where had she got off to? Was she hiding somewhere in the garden or had she run farther afield? Was she alright? Was she lost? What would happen to her now that Carry was gone?

"Hermione? Kitty, kitty!" I called softly. "Hermione — Spot. Please come out and show yourself."

I moved to rise, then gave a cry as a stab of pain radiated down my arm, torso, neck, back, with even a few piercing jabs into my legs and feet. Stopping to catch my breath, I touched my shoulder and groaned again. I'd wrenched it for sure when I'd fallen into the desk. The adrenaline had kept the pain at bay, but now it was back with a vengeance.

With the help of the railing, I hauled myself to my feet and stood gasping, trying to get a handle on my nerves. I considered going back into the house, then thought better of it. I shouldn't disturb the scene; besides, the chances Hermione had returned to the crazy chaos of the bungalow were slim. It was far more likely she'd run off when the crockery began to fly, then decided to stay in her hidey-hole until things returned to normal. I had bad news for the little cat — normal would never be the same.

I was just about to check the garden when I heard a vehicle screech up out front. Make that *vehicles.* A round of heavy car doors thunked, and the next moment I found myself surrounded by police. While the bulk of the contingent covered the house and yard, one officer zeroed his attention in on me. Though well into middle age, he was rugged and well-built, with broad shoulders, leaving no doubt he could still wrangle the bad guys with the best of them.

"Are you Lynley Cannon?" he asked, straight-faced and reminiscent of Caesar's bust.

"Yes. I'm the one who called you." Grasping my

injured shoulder which was beginning to hurt with every little movement, I bent down to pick my phone from the stoop. Disconnecting from 911, I dropped it into my pocket, then stood aside, glaring at the door. "She's... in the house."

"Please step over there." The cop gestured to another cop, a portly fellow who had taken up residence by the back gate, feet apart and thumbs tucked into his utility belt. "Officer Timmons will take your statement." He turned to his fellows who were setting up a perimeter around the bungalow. I was of no further interest to him.

As I stared after him, the trembling returned. Was this really happening? Could I bear it if it was? Then noticed a familiar face in the team.

"Hugh!" I called out, my shakes abating some. "I mean, Officer Burgdorf."

The young man turned, smiling when he saw me. The smile was brief, however, being that the gregarious cop was on the scene of a serious crime.

"Lynley Cannon," he said, heading my way, all business now. "What are you doing here? Are you okay?"

"I guess so." I took a deep breath. "I'm the one who found her... on the floor... In there..." I added, nodding in the general direction of the bungalow.

"Oh, lucky you," he remarked, then said to Timmons, "I'll take this one, Jack. Lynley and I go way back."

I liked Hugh Burgdorf. The tall, curly-haired officer had a naturally gracious and optimistic character that went a long way to making people feel comfortable, even in the face of a tragedy such as this. Originally friends of a friend, we had gotten to know each other better through a case involving a charismatic serial killer. I liked his partner Stacy as well. To their credit, the young couple had three cats.

Burgdorf peered around, then escorted me to a handy garden bench. "This looks good. Might as well get out of everyone's way while we do this, right?"

"It's nice to see you again, Officer Burgdorf, but I wish it were under different circumstances."

"No kidding!" he sighed. "And since it's just us, call me Hugh."

"Okay, Hugh. Do you know if she's..." I couldn't make myself say the word, dead, but he understood what I meant.

"We only just got here, Lynley," he deferred as he took out a tablet. "Nothing's been established yet. But let's get on with the interview. You know the victim?"

"Yes, her name is Carry. With a C, not a K," I added solemnly, as I knew she would have wanted me to.

Burgdorf tapped on his tablet. "Carry with a C. Is that short for something? What's her last name?"

"She never said. We'd only just met."

"Go ahead and tell me what happened."

I pulled myself together and went through it again in my mind, trying to recall the details so as not leave anything out. I remembered it all with stark clarity—the open door, the vulgar person within, the body on the floor, the rough shove. The only thing I couldn't figure out was where to start the tale.

"I came to see if Carry was alright," I put forth.

"Hold on," Burgdorf stopped me. "What made you think she might not have been?"

Right. I had to go back some. "She called me this morning. She said she wanted to explain about what happened."

"Something else happened?"

I hesitated, realizing I needed to rewind even further. "Well, that's a story in itself. And I don't really understand it all."

"So tell me, and we can work it out together," Burgdorf encouraged, gently guiding me back to the beginning of the strange sequence.

"Last Saturday I was walking my cat in the park..." I paused to see if Burgdorf would require more explanation —by now I'd come to expect questions when I brought up my adventuring cats—but he nodded me on. "Harry got off his leash and hightailed it here. Carry caught him. When I came to get him, she invited me for tea on the veranda."

I thought about filling Burgdorf in on the Hermione side-story but decided against it since the paisley cat had no bearing on the crime. I was trying to keep things brief, succinct, and to the point, as much as could be expected from someone who had just witnessed something terrifying.

"Yesterday—was that only yesterday...?" I queried as time did one of its little flip-flops, making the hours stretch into days, month, years. "I guess it was. Anyway, yesterday I came by to drop something off and ended up driving Carry down to Belmont to look at the shops." I explained how we'd run into her ex-associate, and how sometime after that, Carry and I had parted company. "Then, when I was at the bakery with my mother and granddaughter, I saw Carry through the window being dragged down the street by that associate woman and a man."

"Dragged?" Burgdorf interrupted.

"Well, maybe more like firmly escorted. Carry wasn't exactly fighting it, but she didn't look happy with the treatment. I went out to ask what was going on, if she needed help. She assured me everything was fine." I harrumphed. "There really wasn't much I could do besides let her go on her way, but the whole thing looked iffy to me. Then she phoned around six-thirty this morning. She insinuated there had been a problem after all and asked me to come see her. I thought she sounded scared."

More taps on the tablet. "What happened then?"

"I came as quickly as I could, but I had to finish feeding the cats first." This brought a smile to the young man's face. "And she didn't say it was urgent," I justified. "Only that she wanted to talk. If I'd come sooner, maybe she wouldn't be…"

"I know what you're thinking, Lynley, but fact is, if you'd been here during whatever conflict occurred, you could easily have been hurt as well." I was thankful he said *hurt* and not *killed*, but I got the message.

"Besides," Burgdorf continued, "we don't know for sure that she was murdered. She may have had a heart attack or stroke."

"But what about the intruder? Have you seen the place?"

He shook his head.

"Someone made a huge mess, looking for something. And they were strong. They pushed me down as if I were nothing. I suppose the confrontation could have triggered a heart attack, but don't you think it's more likely she was assaulted?"

Burgdorf evaded the question as police are so adept at doing. "Can you describe this assailant?"

I went through my unsatisfactory description of black Nikes, pants, and the Neo-like coat. "Sorry, that's all I could see from the floor."

"You say this person pushed you down? Are you alright?" Burgdorf didn't wait for an answer. "Come on," he commanded, helping me to my feet as if I were an invalid.

"Where are we going?"

"Let's get you checked out by the EMTs. We can continue our conversation once we know you're unhurt."

Burgdorf propelled me along the garden path and around to the front of the house where the police cars and emergency vehicles were parked. "Ferd," he addressed a skinny youth in lavender scrubs standing by a boxy ambulance. "Ms. Cannon here had a fall..." He looked to me for conformation.

"Somebody pushed me. I landed against the edge of a desk." I pointed to my shoulder, already feeling the swelling there. "I'm sure it's nothing."

"Let me be the judge of that," said Ferd with a sweet smile. "Here, let's have a look."

I dutifully sat in the little ambulance chair and proffered my left arm. The young man gently inspected the area, then moved the arm back and forth checking my range of motion.

"Ouch!" I exclaimed when he shifted it toward the back.

Instantly he stopped, returning it to a more normal position. "The shoulder's bruised for sure, but you may also have injured your rotator cuff. It's not life-threatening, but you should get to your doctor right away. Rotator cuff issues can develop into worse afflictions if ignored."

I nodded, having no intention of disregarding such intense discomfort.

"Do you have pain anywhere else?"

"No, not really. Maybe a bit where I fell on the teacup."

I touched the place on my lower ribs and felt the sting where the china shard had pushed through my shirt.

"May I check?" I nodded and Ferd repeated the gentle inspection process. "A small cut, but nothing broken or cracked, glad to say. I'll swab it and give you a Band-Aid. Change the Band-Aid after you bathe and watch for redness or infection. When did you have your last tetanus shot?"

"I don't remember. My doctor has the records."

"Make sure you're current on that, will you?" He finished applying the little bandage and let my shirt drop back over top.

"Did you hit your head when you fell?" Ferd asked.

"Was pushed," I grumbled. "No, it was just the shoulder. It wasn't that bad, really. But I pretended to be knocked out so the intruder would ignore me."

"Did he?" Burgdorf asked.

"Yes. I think he'd been looking for something, and he went back to it once I was down. He threw a few more things around, then left in a huff."

Suddenly I recalled Carry's journal, so well-hidden beneath her body. Was that what he had been searching for? It made sense; if Carry had been keeping secrets, they would be in there, the big red book she took with her everywhere.

I was about to mention my revelation when something stopped me. If I told Burgdorf I had Carry's diary, he would be obliged to confiscate it as evidence. I really wanted to have a look at it first. I made a flash decision to hold back for now. If it contained anything that highlighted Carry's demise, I would turn it over straight away.

"Then what happened?" Burgdorf prompted.

I looked up, suddenly aware I'd gone silent. "As soon as I was sure the guy had left, I got out of there and phoned 911."

I couldn't decide when I had started thinking of Neo-X as a man, but it made sense. Hugh Burgdorf had used the pronoun first; I had just followed along. But there was still a question in my mind. The stature, the stance, the androgynous voice. For some reason it reminded me of Datura. What had gone on between the big woman and Carry? Could their dispute have ended in murder?

The paramedics were rolling Carry out on a gurney, draped in a sheet. No body bag, nor had they covered her face. That meant she wasn't dead after all.

"Is she going to be alright?" I called as they passed on the way to a second ambulance.

The EMT, a woman built like a teddy bear, looked to Burgdorf with soft, doe eyes. He nodded.

"She's alive, but critical. She sustained a nasty bump on her head. Now we gotta get going."

"Of course. What hospital?"

"Providence General," the EMT called back as she trundled Carry to the emergency vehicle and hefted her inside.

"Should I go with them?" I asked Burgdorf. "Be there when she wakes up?"

"I can't advise you on that." He sighed. I knew what he was thinking—that I might have a very long wait. "Let me wind up this interview, and then you can be on your way, wherever you decide."

"I'm not sure what else I can tell you."

Burgdorf checked his tablet. "Did the victim have friends or family?"

I shook my head. "I don't know, but she gave the

impression she was a loner. Still…" I added pensively, "I suggest you look into this Datura person."

"You think she might be involved?"

I paused. "It's just a feeling."

But it was more than a feeling. When I pictured the tall woman in her gray silk suit, her stern features as cold as stone, I couldn't help but sense danger. I had no idea why that would be—it just *was*. The pewter hair, the ice-green eyes, the ghost-white face and shocking red lips.

Then suddenly I remembered something else about Datura's appearance. She had worn an amulet on a cord around her neck. It had been partially obscured by her blouse, so I hadn't put it together at the time—just jewelry, just a random design.

Now I realized I'd been mistaken. Thinking back, I could see it as clearly as if it were in front of me. A gold disk about an inch across, inlaid with silver and teal. The central design, carefully wrought with bits of moonstone and pearl, was that of a cat. A paisley cat.

Chapter 12

It may not be listed in the medical books, but cat people know that time spent napping with cats is extremely relaxing.

"Okay, Ms. Cannon," said Detective Washburn, the surly investigator who had taken over my interview from Officer Burgdorf. "You're cleared to go now."

The detective had run me though all the same questions as Burgdorf, though not posed nearly so politely. I'd done my best to answer briefly, succinctly, and to the point. I knew there was only one way to get beyond his authoritative scrutiny, and that was to comply with his every command. This last one was no exception. I turned to leave, ready to put that scene of violence behind me, but Washburn called out once more—one final mandate in that gruff, official tone. "Be aware, we may need to talk to you again."

I waved my consent and continued walking. I almost expected to hear him add, "Don't leave town, little missy." His attitude rattled me, but I guess I should have been glad they didn't consider me a suspect and take me to the station for the third degree.

As I mentioned, I was truly ready to go, to get home to my cats and comfort, a hot bath, a cup of tea, and some mindless television until I could think through the events of the morning. But there was something I needed to do first. I had to find Hermione.

Instead of going to my car, I slipped into the red

garden. Watching out for police presence, I headed up the volcanic gravel path, past the little retreat where Carry and I had sat that first day.

Was it only yesterday? I asked myself without comprehension. So much had changed in a short twenty-four hours.

The way twisted and turned, circling back on itself, then going off at a different angle. Every so often I'd come to a dead end and have to retrace my steps. I walked slowly, called softly. I found traces of Hermione in the form of a cat toy or a nested bed, but no cat. Could she have escaped into the park and run away? I had no idea how much Carry let her roam, but I'd got the impression the huge forest park was off limits.

I tuned my ears for the slightest sound, a rustling in the bushes or a soft mew, but there was nothing. The more I searched, the more I worried. If I didn't find her, she could be in danger. Even in the park, cars frequented the web of roads at all hours. There were coyotes, dogs, and some very nasty city raccoons that would hurt a cat without thinking twice. People could be predators as well, and a unique cat like Hermione would be especially vulnerable. If she managed to escape those hazards, she would still be left with the basic struggle to find food and water. Other cats, ones more streetwise than Hermione, would have their territories staked out. The slim pickings would go to whoever won that catfight.

"Hey, you there," a man called out. "What do you think you're doing?"

I sighed and glanced back at Officer Timmons. "It's just me, Lynley Cannon," I said innocently. "Looking for a cat."

"Oh, Ms. Cannon. But you shouldn't be here. This is a

crime scene. You say you're looking for a what?"

"A cat. Carry—the victim—had a cat. She must have run off during the kerfuffle. I need to find her."

"Huh?" He raked off his police cap and shook his balding head. "You say the victim ran off? I don't think so, ma'am."

"No, the cat. Her name is Hermione. She's dark gray and white with stripes and spots. Have you seen her?"

"No, ma'am. And now I must insist you go wait out front."

"The detective said I could leave."

"Then that's okay too." He cleared his throat. "It's just, you need to be out of this area until forensics have had a chance to look it over. You may be messing up an important clue."

"But what about Hermione?" I asked in my most plaintive, old-lady tone. "If I don't find her she could get lost or hurt."

"You still here, Lynley?" It was Officer Burgdorf, walking up to join us.

"Something about a cat," Timmons muttered.

"It's Carry's cat," I said, turning to Burgdorf. "Carry lived alone, and there's no one to care for Hermione now that she's gone... to the hospital, I mean."

Burgdorf glanced around. "Where is the cat?"

"Missing. I was looking for her when Officer Timmons told me the garden was off limits."

"I'm afraid he's right. We need everyone out of this area for now. Don't worry though, I'll keep an eye out for cats."

I knew I was fighting a losing battle. There was no way I'd be allowed to search the garden until the police were finished with it, and even then they would probably string up their yellow tape with its big black printed command, *Do Not Cross!*

"Will you call me if you find her?"

"Any animals we find will be taken to Multnomah County," Timmons grumbled.

"But Hermione used to be my cat," I blurted. It was true, for about five minutes. "Please Hugh. No need to bother MCAS. It would be so much better for Hermione to come to me rather than a noisy shelter. She'll be grieving after losing her person. Besides, Carry would want it that way."

Burgdorf was a cat lover, and yes, I was playing on it. The ploy must have worked because he nodded. "We can do that, I think. Give me your number and a description of the cat. I'll call you if we find her."

There were flaws to the plan, such as, what if it wasn't Burgdorf who found Hermione, or what if no one found her at all, but I knew it was the best deal I was going to get.

I agreed, and with a last anxious look around, departed down the path, through the red garden, and out to the street. I watched for the lost, scared puss, but there was no sign. Before I left, I'd described Hermione and her unique markings. What I had failed to mention was that Hugh Burgdorf had seen this cat before.

Officer Burgdorf had been on duty when I'd found the kitten Spot at that other infraction all those years ago. There hadn't been a reason to remind him of the event, but there'd been none to keep it a secret either.

* * *

Once back home I began to feel sane again, but it didn't last. I couldn't keep from reflecting on the previous hours: the body, the shove, the questions. For a while, I puttered around the house and garden, starting tasks, then moving on to something else before they were complete. I swapped out all the litter boxes for clean ones with new litter but left the soiled pans in a pile soaking in the basement sink. I read my emails but didn't answer them. I made a lunch of Greek salad and roasted vegetables, then put it back in the fridge, uneaten. I never did take that hot bath or drink that calming tea, and though at one point I sat down on the couch and turned on the television, even my go-to cozy mysteries couldn't hold my interest so I turned it off again. I was in shock. I'd found someone near-dead, laid out on the floor like so much rubbish. I couldn't get the image out of my mind.

Time to call my therapist. I rang her office, got her voicemail, and hung up before leaving a message.

The Motrin the EMT had given me all those hours ago was beginning to wear off, and it was time to take another. I probably shouldn't have pushed it by carting around those heavy litter pans, but the physical labor had felt good at the time. Now I was exhausted and hurting everywhere. Grabbing an ice pack and Dirty Harry, I retired to my bedroom for a nap.

When I woke a few hours later, I felt refreshed. Sometimes sleep with a cat or two really is the best medicine. My mind had relegated the morning's horror to that part of the brain which protects us from matters too raw to handle, leaving my thoughts clear. There were three things I needed to do: check on Carry, call Frannie, and find Hermione. Simple as that.

I didn't want to risk running into the police again, so I put off the Hermione hunt for later in the day. Fairly certain the hospital would be less than forthcoming with information about Carry's condition to anyone who couldn't prove themselves a family member, and equally sure the injured woman was beyond caring at this point, I put that off too. Which left Frannie, my longtime friend.

I replayed her voicemail—her flat, emotionless tone revealed nothing, but at least she'd called and said she wanted to talk. That had to be a good sign.

Optimistically I punched her contact icon, a pretty brown cat, but as I listened to it ring on the other end—one, two, six, ten times—with no result, my hopes faded. When the call just kept up the hollow chiming, hope turned to dread.

Why hadn't she gotten back to me? What had happened in those intervening hours that would make her turn off her voicemail?

I went over the events in my head. Frannie had called me at the ungodly hour of four-twenty-five in the morning—the hour of the wolf, if you believe in such things. Since I hadn't picked up, she'd left a message. Because I was asleep, I didn't know anything about the call until I got up a little after six. I'd phoned back right away, but my call had gone to voicemail. I'd left my own message asking her to get back to me soon.

Then, without further ado, I'd gone about my day. I should have tried again. Tried again and again until I got through. What had I been thinking?

I'd been thinking about Carry, I reminded myself. The strange little woman who had showed up in my life with her paisley cat, only to be snuffed out a few days later. *Nearly snuffed*, I amended. Carry was still, as far as I knew, alive.

Suddenly I remembered the journal I'd surreptitiously removed from the scene of the crime. I'd shoved it in my bag, and what with the other distractions, forgotten all about it. It could be important. It could hold a clue as to why someone would want to hurt her.

I located my bag on the stand beside the front door where I'd dumped it when I came home. There was a black cat upon it now, asleep and making tiny snore noises. I paused, knowing I was at fault for leaving it on Little's favorite perch. I hated to disturb her, but I really wanted to see that journal!

Gently lifting the sleeping girl, removing the bag, and redepositing her on the table, I tiptoed from the room. Upon glancing back, I saw one golden eye opened wide, staring at me.

I gave her a love blink. "Go back to sleep, sweetheart. I won't bother you again."

She heaved a kitty sigh, then the eye closed, and I sensed I was forgiven.

Sitting on the loveseat by the window, I pulled out the large volume and laid it flat on the ottoman. The red, swirly cover was well-worn, emanating a loving dog-earedness, as if Carry had owned it for a very long time. I flipped it open with the anticipation of a child with a new book. The first page was blank. When I turned to the next, I fell back against the couch with a gasp.

This was not a journal at all; it was a sketchbook. The minutely detailed drawing had been done in Prisma pencil, the soft leads blending into an artist's interpretation of the red garden. As I explored the subsequent pages, I found more: the secluded bench, the rose-hung wall. Some were impressionistic farscapes, and others, close-ups, drawn with great intricacy. Hermione was present in most but not all.

When I finally finished going through the book for the third time and closed the back cover, I glanced out the window onto my own meager yard. How dull it seemed in comparison with the flamboyant reds and purples portrayed by Carry's artwork.

I found myself feeling uplifted yet let down at the same time. Carry was an exceptional artist, and viewing this very private work was a gift, but as lovely as those pictures were, they gave no hint as to why someone would want to harm her.

Reluctantly, I put the sketchbook back in my bag to give over to the police next time I had a chance. I should never have taken it, a move tantamount to breaking the law, but I was glad I did. It may not have revealed the secrets I'd been hoping for, but it offered an insight into Carry's heart.

And her heart was in that garden. What would happen to it if she were gone?

What would happen to Hermione?

That second question was a more imminent one, and I decided to go back and look for her soon, but right now, I had another priority—Frannie.

I tried Frannie's number again without luck. Her voicemail was off, period, and I resigned myself to the fact I wasn't going to make further headway with that approach.

Since I was getting nothing from Frannie, I called Alani instead. She answered on the first ring.

"Have you heard something?" she asked before I'd spoken more than my name. Her breathless anxiety told the whole story.

"Not really," I replied with a sigh. "I was hoping you had."

"No, not a thing. I'm so worried I'm going out of my mind."

"She called me in the middle of the night," I said. "It was about four-thirty and I was asleep. I feel terrible for not picking up. The ringer was off. I didn't know anything about it until this morning."

"Oh, dear! How sad, but you couldn't have known," the young woman soothed. "Who answers the phone at that hour?"

"I always figured if it were important, they would call again," I justified weakly. "In this case, I was wrong."

"But at least she called," sighed Alani, always the optimist. "What did she say?"

I went through the cryptic, toneless dispatch. There was silence on the line as Alani processed the information.

"Of course you tried her back," she said finally.

"Several times. The first time I managed to leave my own message, but now the voicemail is off. My plan is to call the shelter and see if anyone there has been in touch, and if not, then I'll go over to her place. If she's hiding out, I'll find her, talk to her through the door if I have to."

"Let me make the call to FOF, and I can try a few of the other volunteers who are friends with Frannie."

"Thank you. I... I..." I stuttered. "That would be very helpful.

"Is everything okay, Lynley?" Alani asked. "Aside from your close friend's weird behavior, I mean."

Was it that obvious? "It's been a long morning."

"Lynley, it's three in the afternoon."

"Okay, a long day then. But I can't really talk about it. It has nothing to do with Frannie though, and she's my priority now."

"Alright, but you know you can talk to me. We're cat sisters. We can tell each other anything."

I chuckled at her words. "That we can!"

"Call me if you get any news."

"I will, and you too."

"We'll find her," Alani assured me.

"I know," I replied and hung up.

What Alani said was true. I had no doubt we would locate Frannie Desoto at some point. My greater fear was what would happen when we did.

I had one more call to make before setting out to Frannie's place. The afternoon was indeed wearing on as Alani had informed me, but it wasn't too late to ring my doctor's office and make an appointment for my shoulder injury. After a couple of short holds and transfers, I was all set for tomorrow morning and advised in the meantime to continue the Motrin and try not to do anything strenuous. No more litter lifting, I promised as I rang off.

For a few moments, I sat at the kitchen table with my head in my hands. Everything hurt in spite of the painkillers, and it wasn't yet time to take another. Maybe getting out would do me good. It was still a beautiful day—the fresh air, scented with spring flowers, would surely raise my spirits.

I pulled myself together and grabbed my coat and bag. Little accompanied me to the front door and watched from the window as I trudged down the steps. When I reached my car, I turned and waved to her. She did not wave back. She is, after all, a cat. Cats do not wave.

But then she did. She lifted her black paw to the window and ran it down the glass—once, twice, thrice. I'd only seen her do that a few times before. Those times, it had been a forewarning of things to come.

Chapter 13

Life is unpredictable. I always keep a spare cat carrier in the trunk of my car just in case. Once there were kittens on the side of the freeway, and another time a friend needed to take her kitty to emergency and had no carrier of her own. It's easy to be prepared.

Frannie lived in a classic brick and stone neo-Renaissance apartment building near the Park Blocks in the heart of downtown. Built sometime in the 1940s, it had been one of Portland's most prestigious addresses, but now it showed its age. The new crop of upscale executives preferred the glass and steel condos, which left the elegant old landmark to people like Frannie—retired and of somewhat limited means.

Frannie's was a lovely suite on the sixth floor with a fantastic view of the city, the Willamette River, and on a clear day, Mt. Hood looming like a snowcapped pyramid on the horizon. She and I had spent many an evening after our shifts at the shelter gazing out upon that view and discussing cats. As I now peered up at the dated façade, I felt a pang of regret. What if something really were wrong? What if those innocent days of cats and laughter would never come again?

I chided myself for being melodramatic and got down to the business of getting inside. As with most of those older complexes, the main entrance was locked, and only an okay from a resident would allow passage. There was an old-fashioned call box with a black Bakelite handset and a brass plate containing a row of bronze pins, one for each apartment. Some had names beside them in type or pen and others had been left blank by residents who preferred to remain anonymous.

I pressed the button beside the calligraphed "DeSoto" and waited for a response. None came, and I can't say I was surprised. I took a breath and tried again, then again. By that time, I'd lost patience and held my finger on the knob far longer than was proper. I could almost hear the obnoxious buzz exploding through Frannie's little abode. Either she wasn't there, or she would be climbing the walls by now.

Then I had a third thought: What if she were there but *couldn't* answer? What if she were sick or hurt? It's one of the curses of the single person living alone—no one knows if something's happened to us until it's far too late.

Frannie had shown me the very secret workaround for getting into the lobby. There was one button in the left-hand corner that if pressed three times in a row would release the door. With worry making me clumsy, it took a second try to get it right, but finally I was inside and on my way up.

The elevator came to a jerky stop at the sixth floor, and I stepped out onto plush carpet. Turning left, I proceeded down the hallway to Frannie's, number 617. She had installed a little cat-shaped knocker, and I softly tapped with the tail. Waiting a long minute for an answer, I tapped again, louder this time. My second attempt brought the next door neighbor, an elderly woman in a housedress and a knitted toque, out of 616.

"Wondered what the racket was," the woman grumbled. "Was it you making that infernal buzz?"

"Sorry," I said. "I'm looking for Frannie. Have you

101

seen her?"

The neighbor thought a bit. "Now that you mention it, no. Not since, oh, maybe it was last week. But she's been home. I hear her bumping around. Walls are thin as paper."

"When was that?"

"Last night. And again today. I didn't hear her go out, but I guess she must have since she's not answering your noisy knocking."

"Might something have happened to her?" I choked.

The woman sniffed and pulled a Kleenex from her pocket. "Like what?"

"Oh, I don't know. Something. Anything."

"I doubt it. Now I'd better get back to work." She gave me a coy smile. "I work from home, ya know," she announced proudly. "And do you mind keeping it down a little? Throws off my concentration."

She went back inside and closed the door. I wondered what sort of work she did that required such high focus. The woman was ninety years old if she was a day.

I returned my attention to Frannie. According to 616, Frannie had been home earlier in the afternoon. Maybe she was still there. Maybe she just wasn't responding.

I knocked again, this time softly on the old panel itself. "Frannie, it's me, Lynley. Open up. Please?"

I placed an ear against the warm wood and listened. Nothing. I knew there was no point in checking the deadbolt key slot—gone were the days when keyholes went straight through, providing a peek into the private world on the other side—but it looked like there might be a tiny crack between the bottom of the door and the threshold. After checking the hallway to make sure no one was watching, I got down on my knees to take a closer look.

Yes, there was a hair's breadth gap, but all I could see was the tiniest glimpse of parquet flooring. I watched for a moment anyway. No sign of movement, no shift to the light. I was about to pull away when I sensed a change. I refocused my eye on the miniscule vantage point. Nothing now, but I swear for an instant it had grown darker as if crossed by a shadow. As if someone had walked close by.

"Frannie!" I sat back on my feet and knocked rapidly. "I know you're in there! Come on. Open the door. Or call me. Talk to me. Tell me what's going on!"

I gave a cautious glance at 616, but no repercussions were coming from the working girl. "Okay, Frannie," I said to the door, "if you don't want to open up to your best friend who's over the top worried about you, I'll just sit here and wait until you do."

I slumped down onto the carpet, stretched out my legs, and sat back against the door jamb. For a little while, I played with my phone, checking messages in case Frannie and I had crossed paths and she really wasn't in her apartment avoiding me. I looked at her Facebook page—maybe she had posted there. I got distracted by some cute cat videos and then by some clothes from a company that prided themselves for making women's dresses with pockets. The atmosphere in the hall was quiet and a bit stuffy. Every so often I would look up to see if anything in my environment had changed. It hadn't.

After a while, the light through the window began to fade into dusk. I was getting nowhere. Either Frannie was there but not answering, or she wasn't and I'd been mistaken about the shadow. Either way, it was time to move on.

Searching in my bag for a piece of paper on which to

leave a note, I realized with sudden annoyance I'd used up my little purse-sized cat-print notepad and forgotten to buy another. There had to be something—a receipt, a bookmark, a scrap—but I'd recently cleaned everything out. That left only Carry's sketchbook.

I pulled out the big journal and glanced through it, again marveling upon the detail of the botanical drawings. Every page had been filled to the corners with the exception of the very last one. This bore only a tiny preliminary sketch; I figured I could sacrifice it without too much harm to the collection. I hated the idea—after all it wasn't even my book—but I didn't know what else to do. I needed to leave Frannie a note, tangible proof that I had been there in person. I supposed I could go in search of a stationary store, but that would take time. Since I was at a loss to come up with another alternative, I gritted my teeth and tore.

The big page came away intact. Rummaging up a pen, I thought about what I wanted to write.

Dear Frannie...

No, too formal.

Frannie, Please contact me as soon as possible...

Please get hold of me ASAP...

Call me!

Finally I gave up on thinking and began to scribble. Here's what I wrote:

Frannie, you are my friend and I miss you. I'm so worried, and I'm not the only one. I don't know what's going on with you, but I want to. We've been friends too long for you to just disappear out of my life without telling me what I did wrong...

That wasn't the direction I'd intended to go, but as I stared at the hasty words, I figured maybe if nothing else, they would play on her sympathy. I signed a quick *Lynley*, made a little cat face cartoon, folded the page in half, and squeezed it under the door. I waited a few minutes more in case this might spur her into action, but all was as before. Finally I got to my feet, stretched out the cramp in my back from sitting on the ground, and headed for the elevator. I'd been so sure she was there, that if she knew it was me, knew how much I cared, she'd open up. But maybe I'd been wrong.

I was saddened, but in another way, I felt relief. If I chose to believe Frannie hadn't been home after all, I could also console myself with the prospect that once she returned and read my letter, she would be inspired to call. The theory was somewhat arbitrary, based on hope rather than fact, but I could live with it, at least until new evidence came to light.

* * *

There were still a few hours of daylight left, so instead of going straight home, I decided to swing by Carry's bungalow and see if I could find Hermione. It was iffy — for all I knew the police were still there, fussing with their crime scene. They probably wouldn't be happy to see me. Or possibly they'd finished up but had plastered the place with *Do not enter under penalty of arrest* signs. Either way, my search would end before it began.

But I had to try. The thought of Hermione disoriented, hungry, and alone broke my heart.

I'd try, I decided.

I'd call out.

I'd search as far as I could without breaking too many laws and pray the poor kit would show up.

I entered through the park so if the police did happen to be there, they might not catch on to my presence as quickly. I needn't have bothered—the garden was empty and the house locked up tight with only a single ribbon of police tape strung across the back door.

Once more I traveled Carry's winding paths, beneath the crimson boughs and through the red foliage, calling Hermione's name. After striking out in the garden, I moved on to the house. I peered through the windows in case she'd got stuck inside but saw no sign of her there either. Finally I sat down on the veranda stoop, quiet and still, hoping she might come to me. The feelings of expectation and regret were reminiscent of my recent wait at Frannie's doorstep, and the act produced the same sad results.

As the shadows lengthened and the sun sank lower over the West Hills, I figured it was time to give up. Hermione—and Frannie, for that matter—were on their own for the night.

I trudged back to my car and grabbed out the cat carrier I keep in the trunk just in case I run into a cat-related emergency. I located a collapsing water bowl and a bottle of water, plus a few sample packs of kibble and a plastic yogurt tub. Carting the supplies back to the veranda, I set up a feeding station on the stoop near the back door. Removing the grid gate from the carrier, I added a fluffy blanket, transforming it into a makeshift refuge.

"Well, Hermione, sweetie," I said out loud in case she was listening. "That's all I can do for now. Food and water, though you may have to share it with a stray or two. I'll be back tomorrow morning. It would be in your best interest to show yourself, or you're likely to end up with more alone-time than you might want."

In the darkening evening, the air felt like silk, though

the temperature was cooling quickly. I stopped and listened, gave one more look around, eagerly wishing for a dramatic, last-minute entrance by her majesty the cat, but there was none.

Suddenly I saw something in the bushes beside the house—a man-shaped shadow! For a moment, I stared transfixed at the shape, then fear took over and I hustled through the gate, slamming it shut behind me. Without a look back, I raced away and down the hill as fast as I could go.

Chapter 14

Though microchipping your cat can avert tragedy because it holds important registry information should your cat become lost, be aware that a microchip is not a tracking device and cannot be used to track the cat or establish their location. Its success also relies on you keeping your information up to date with the microchip registry.

The next morning, as I let myself into the red garden through the back gate, I couldn't fathom what had frightened me so badly the night before. A shadow? A reflection? Wind rustling through the leaves? Those were certainly more likely than a strange man lurking in the bushes with nefarious intent. Since first we were human, we've harbored a deep-seated fear of things that go bump in the night. The unknown, the unseen—the dark itself. Now, with the crisp, early sun beaming down like a promise, the place couldn't have seemed more innocent.

I paused to scan the area, just in case, but nothing was disturbed. If any monsters had been creeping around in the dusk, they were tidy ones.

I started for the house, listening to the crunch of the red stone beneath my sandals. Birds sang in the trees and a lawnmower whined from somewhere down the hill, but I didn't hear the one sound I was praying for: Hermione's meow.

Coming upon the stoop where I'd left the food station, my heart fell. The kibble was untouched, as was the water.

I didn't need to check the blanket in the carrier to know it would be stone cold.

"Was this you?" came a sonorous voice from within the shade of the covered veranda.

I froze as a tall woman moved into the light with the elegant stealth of a cobra—Datura.

"What are you doing here?" I stuttered.

"I might ask you the same." She looked down on me, green eyes boring into mine. Tall as she was, plus the extra height of the stoop, I felt diminished, like a naughty child. Then she smiled. "But you're Lynley Cannon, aren't you?"

"How did you know?"

"Why, Carry of course. She told me all about you. You and your strange connection with our cat."

"*Our* cat?" I echoed.

"Hermione. Carry and I have shared her since the day of her birth. Though her true name is Maftet, the Goddess of Execution, First Kingdom."

Oh my goodness, poor kitten, I thought to myself. Who would inflict such a cruel designation on a sweet baby cat?

"Maftet was born the single kit of a breed called the Egyptian Mau," Datura went on, oblivious of my disgust. "Though Mau's are known for their distinctive spotted coat, Maftet's markings were deviant, original. I immediately recognized her as an old soul, the reincarnation of the goddess herself."

Datura shook her head. "I could never understand why Carry insisted on calling her Hermione. A most common appellation, unsuited for such a royal creature. But we have our differences, Carry and I."

Datura seated herself in Carry's antique chair where she proceeded to arrange her legs underneath her in a feline-esque manner. She had foregone the formal business suit for a light sea-green tunic and bleach white pants. The tunic's neckline dipped low across the front revealing not only a goodly amount of cleavage but the pendant of the paisley cat.

"You're looking at my amulet," Datura observed. "Yes, it is she."

"Is that a reproduction? It's nicely done."

"It is original, forged millennia ago, by the hand of a worshiper, I would think."

"Really?" *Who would wear a genuine Egyptian artifact with a tunic?* I wondered, but only to myself.

Datura's appearance at Carry's home had caught me by surprise, but maybe I could use it to my advantage. I had questions, and not just about her odd amulet.

For a moment I hesitated, pondering if it was a good idea to engage this person further, or whether it might be smarter to cut and run. In my opinion, Datura was a prime suspect in Carry's assault. She might not have wielded the weapon, but based on her rough treatment of Carry on Belmont Street, she could well be in on the misdeed.

At least that's what I'd been thinking, but now, face to face, I considered the possibility I'd been wrong. Granted Datura was a bit obnoxious and had lousy taste in cat names, but she didn't seem outwardly dangerous. Besides, if Carry had taken the time to tell her my story, then their relationship was unlikely to have been a murderous one.

"Datura..."

"Call me Dee," said the woman, trailing her fingers through her platinum hair. "And please, come and sit down. Maybe our little diva will make an appearance if she hears us having a friendly chat."

She had a point, and her insight into the feline psyche made me feel just a bit more comfortable.

I moved the wicker chair to where I had a good view of the garden. "Okay, Dee. You have me at a disadvantage. I barely know Carry. She mentioned you were an associate, but that was all she said."

"Oh, we were much more than associates. Carry was my dear friend." Datura gave a little sound that might have been the wisp of a sob, but she quickly recovered. "We were partners."

Partners? I tried to envision the tall, cultured Datura and the tiny, bohemian Carry as a couple and failed.

"We ran a business together," Datura clarified.

"What sort of business, if I may ask?"

"We were quite successful," she evaded, "but we had a falling-out. Until the other day, I had not seen her for a very long time."

"And now she's in the hospital in critical condition," I commented.

Datura sat up with a jerk. "What are you implying?"

"Nothing! Nothing." Rats, I'd moved too fast. "Just that you must be very concerned for her," I backpeddled.

"Yes, I am." She relaxed slightly, but the flash in her ice-green eyes didn't completely disappear.

"Have you heard anything?" I asked. "About her condition?"

"She is no better. It is concussion, and she is not responding. The prognosis looks grim."

"I'm sorry," I said, offering the benefit of the doubt. If Carry really was Datura's BFF, she must be miserable, knowing she'd waited too long to reunite.

We both fell silent, and I took the time to gaze around the garden for signs of Hermione.

"You're looking for her?"

"She has to be out there somewhere."

"You're worried. But then of course you would be. You and Maftet had a special relationship."

I studied Datura's face, but the thick white makeup and kohl-lined eyes gave nothing away.

"What did Carry tell you?" I queried. "How much do you know?"

"Why, everything. It is part of Maftet's saga now. Maftet was stolen from us when she was but a few months old. Someone found her and took her to a shelter. That someone was you."

"Yes, that's right... basically." She had omitted the shooting chase, the drugs and money. Did she not know that part of the story or was she being cagey? I decided that if she didn't mention them, then neither would I.

"The shelter reunited Maftet with Carry through her microchip. But it was at that point that Carry and I made our split." Datura paused, her brows drawn. "I never saw my dear Maftet again until now."

I noticed a definite discrepancy between Datura's story and the one Carry had offered. Carry had denied knowing Hermione before adopting her from Friends of Felines; now Datura said they'd owned the kitten from birth, but that she had been stolen from them. Someone was lying, and though I tended to believe in Carry's honesty, Datura had a few good points too.

I was about to remark on it when Datura reached out and grabbed my hand.

"She is mine now! If you find her, you must bring her to me."

I pulled back, wrenching my bad shoulder in my haste. Hearing my cry of pain, Datura instantly let go.

"I apologize for my abruptness," she said, bowing her head. "It's just that... I need her."

112

"Well, I don't have her," I huffed, massaging my aching arm, "or why would I be here setting up a food station?"

"Of course. Again I am sorry. But you must understand that she is mine by all rights. I do have papers to prove it."

The more she insisted on her ownership, the more alarm bells went off in my head. "First we need to find her," I hedged.

"Yes, of course."

I rose, ready to put more than an arm's length between myself and the unpredictable Datura. "I think I'll take a look around the garden."

"I will come with you," Datura said, unwinding from her chair and following me down the steps. So much for my discreet getaway.

For a time, we walked in quiet, only calling out for the cat—*Hermione* from me, and *Maftet* from Datura. With the rhythm of movement, I felt my apprehension begin to slip away.

The tall woman paused at a bench under a plum tree. Wiping off a few late petals, she took a seat and retrieved something from the ground—Hermione's cat toy, the one I had brought by. Was that just the other day? It seemed so long ago now.

For a moment, Datura studied the blue and yellow weave. "Carry never explained to me how you two met."

I leaned against the tree trunk, listening to the hypnotic buzz of bees. "It was really by chance. I belong to an adventure cat club, and my cat got off his leash in the park. He ran away and long story short, he led me here."

"Adventure cat? What type of cat is that?"

"It's not a type—it's something we do. You've not

113

heard of the adventure cat movement?" She shook her head. "A bunch of us get together to take our cats out for walks."

Datura raised a painted eyebrow. "And you have one of these adventure cats, Lynley?"

"I have three who are leash-trained: Dirty Harry, Tinkerbelle, and Elizabeth. I don't take them all at the same time of course." I chuckled, envisioning my trio pulling me in separate directions. No, one was more than enough when it came to walking the cat.

"Oh, but that sounds like so much fun! I have a cat. May I join your adventure group?"

This caught me completely off guard. "Sure, but…"

"She is well-trained and already walks with me on many occasions."

"Not all cats take to the program," I hemmed. "Walking with others is different than outings alone.

"She will love it. As will I. What should I do?"

I hesitated. I found myself reluctant to give Datura the information, though I couldn't say why. "Well, actually there's a meetup this afternoon at the Rhododendron Gardens," I confessed. "If you're interested. You could check it out, see if it's something you think your cat would enjoy."

"Then it is settled," she said with a satisfied grin.

She slipped the little cat toy into the pocket of her tunic, and we circled back to the veranda where I wrote down the particulars for her. She seemed genuinely happy with the prospect.

"I need to get back home, Dee. I'm sorry we didn't find Hermione."

"As am I," she sighed. "I will stay a bit longer, just in case."

"Would you like me to leave the food station?"

"If you don't mind. She may be lured by it."

"Then goodbye."

"One last thing," she said as I was about to go. "Carry had a book, a journal. You don't happen to know where it is?"

I stiffened. Could she read my mind? Did she know I'd taken it home with me?

"It contained nothing of importance," Datura went on, "but as her partner, I need to make sure there was no sensitive information that could fall into the wrong hands. It might mean a lawsuit, and we want to avoid those at all cost." She smiled, guileless eyes staring into mine.

"I remember the book," I said truthfully, picturing the red sketchbook as it now lay on my coffee table at home. Thankfully I'd taken it out of my bag last night when I'd got back from Frannie's. I was a bad liar at the best of times, and I was sure she would have caught my evasion had I been carrying it on my person.

She waited for me to elaborate, but I didn't.

"Oh, well," she said finally. "It probably doesn't matter. I will see you this afternoon."

I started to leave when I thought of something.

"You didn't happen to be here last night when I was setting up the food station, did you? It would have been right around sunset."

"No, why?"

"I just wondered. I thought I saw someone, but it was probably my imagination."

"I was in meetings for most of the day. That's what comes of owning a business. Maybe it was a murder hornet."

"No, I don't think so," I replied, pondering how she

could imagine I'd mistake an insect, no matter how large, for a full-grown human. Besides, wasn't May a little early for hornets? Carry had mentioned hornets as well. What was it with these people and their fixation on eusocial wasps?

No matter. I'd got my answer. Datura had not been the shadow lurking in Carry's bushes. Which meant it must have been someone else.

"'Bye then," I said, walking away as quickly as I could without looking suspicious. Even so, I felt Datura's ice-green stare bite into my back like fangs.

Chapter 15

Play with your cat, and I don't mean just twirling a birdie as you watch TV. Doing things together is a bonding action that can benefit both your little wildcat and you.

My appointment with the doctor went smoothly. She ordered x-rays, told me to ice the area, gave me a prescription for extra-strength Ibuprofen, and sent me on my way. The shoulder joint had hurt in the night when I lay on it wrong, but otherwise the pain had been relatively mild.

After the doctor, I had a few errands to run: a trip to the grocery store for black beans and kale; a quick check-in with Seleia to pick out my birthday cupcakes. As I passed the bookstore on my way to the bakery, I had a sudden thought and popped inside. Moving directly to the display of journals, I picked out one identical to Carry's, and on a whim, I bought it. As I was leaving, my eye caught another of the blue posters advertising Dr. Wil Craven, eminent whatever. Two women were huddled around it, one of whom was copying it onto her phone. The guy obviously had a following. I didn't know why I was so skeptical about his verity, but I was.

Seleia was still finishing up when I got to Cupcake City, so I grabbed a glass of water from a frosty pitcher on the self-serve sideboard and sat down at the window table to wait. I retrieved the big journal from my bag, along with a pen, and opened it to the first blank page. I sat for a moment in contemplation, then began.

I made a line across the top of the page and another down the center. *Carry*, I headed one column, and *Datura*, the other—though she had insisted I call her Dee, in my mind the appellation, reminiscent of an actress from a 1960s surfing movie, just didn't fit.

Datura said she and Carry were friends. No, that was wrong—Datura's exact words were, "Carry *was* my dear friend." *Was*, as in *those were the good old days*, or *was*, as in *used to be but isn't any longer*? Not the same thing at all.

In the Datura column, I wrote, "Carry *was* dear friend."

Datura also said she and Carry were partners but had experienced a falling-out. She hadn't elaborated on the circumstances. I wrote "Partners" but then I hesitated. "Falling-out" could mean anything from a personality clash to a disagreement to a full-on lawsuit. I wrote "Dissolved" next to "Partners," and then the note, "Less than five years ago," an extrapolation I made from Hermione's age, since according to Datura, she and Carry had shared the kitten before the breakup.

Carry had told a different story, however. She'd not once mentioned Datura when she spoke of her past. Only when confronted with the woman did she admit, and then with a decidedly hostile tone, that Datura was an associate. As far as my understanding went, associate and partner were two different matters, and neither touched anywhere near the dear friends category. I wrote "Old associate—hostile?" in Carry's column.

Carry had said nothing about the co-owning of Hermione either. In fact, she'd given the impression she and Hermione had a singular relationship, and it was obvious they loved each other deeply. Carry had even gone so far as to rename the cat, replacing the awful Maftet, *Goddess of Execution*, with Hermione, which held the more optimistic meaning of *Earthly Messenger*. Datura, on the other hand, had not seen the cat for some years. That didn't seem like much of a relationship to me.

I wrote "Hermione" under Carry's column and "Maftet" under Datura's. I drew an arrow between the words, "dissolved," and "Maftet."

"What are you doing, Grandmother?" Seleia asked as she pulled up a chair.

"Nothing really. Just a bit of journaling."

"Oh? I didn't know you kept a journal." She laughed. "And here I thought I knew all your deep, dark secrets."

"I haven't done it for years—not since long before you were born—but I thought I'd try again," I fudged. "See if it helps me collect my thoughts."

"Is there anything in there about your birthday party?" Seleia asked, trying to read my scribbles upside down.

"No, not yet." I closed the book. "But we should get on that, shouldn't we?"

"Yes, we should."

She whipped out a pink three-ring binder and opened it onto a set of glossy photographs displaying various cupcake delicacies. With gorgeous goodies such as Truffle Pie, Vanilla Delight, and Maple Syrup Maple, I ceased all thought of the Carry-Datura puzzle. I should say, nearly all thought. Still buzzing around in my head was Datura's final, offhand question about Carry's sketchbook. Her excuse of needing to check for confidential material didn't add up. In fact, if anything, it proved she had no idea what the red book contained.

* * *

From the bakery, I went straight home. After unpacking my groceries and tidying up the kitchen, I settled down for a play session with the cats. They have plenty of interactive toys with which to occupy their time, from fancy battery-operated mouse chasers to a funky wine cork that hung from the doorframe by a string, but as famous cat behaviorist Jackson Galaxy says, none of those can replace one-on-one playtime with their cohabitor.

I chose a teaser wand with feathers and a bell, casting it across the living room to see who I might catch. Dirty Harry was the first up, materializing from out of nowhere to run and jump like a kitten. When Harry began to tire, Little and Red took over, and then Emilio. Mab was late on the scene, but as the youngest of the clowder, made up for lost time with amazing sprints and leaps. Tinkerbelle and Violet were content to watch from the couch, and Elizabeth played solemnly by herself with her favorite treat ball, batting and falling, batting and falling. Once over on her side, she would eat the treat, so all was good.

Finally we were played out and went our separate ways. All that flipping of the wand had set my shoulder to hurting again, so I made a cup of tea, took a painkiller, and lay down on the couch. I was just beginning to drift off when I heard someone at my back door.

"Anybody home?"

It was a rhetorical question since the door was standing wide open, but I answered anyway. "Hi, Patty, come on in."

My neighbor let herself through the screen door, closed it, and stopped dead.

"You're not ready!" she exclaimed. That was an understatement since I was lying down with a lavender bag over my eyes and Tinkerbelle ensconced on my abdomen. "Lynley, what's wrong?"

I pulled the lavender off my face and sat up, much to Tinkerbelle's disgust. Donning my glasses and taking a sip of lukewarm tea, I said, "Shoulder ache," as if that explained the mysteries of the universe.

"Oh, I'm sorry," Patty said as she came to sit in the easy chair. "Is there anything I can do? Something I can get you?"

"No, actually it's pretty much gone now. I took a pill. That's why I was lying down. But I don't think I can make it to the adventure cat meetup."

I was lying. Granted my shoulder had been throbbing, but the pain had diminished some time ago. Fact was, I was worried about Datura and the possibility she would be there. I didn't know what it was about her—she seemed friendly enough, and she had exhibited a good, working knowledge of cats—but something felt off. Maybe I couldn't shake that first impression of her and her henchman dragging Carry down the street. Maybe it was because I knew she had lied about the sketchbook—what else might she be lying about? Or was it something more furtive and internal? She held an aura of mystery, epitomized by the ancient artifact she wore so casually around her neck, to say nothing of her insistence Hermione was the reincarnation of an Egyptian goddess.

"But you have to go!" Patty was saying. "The lady from the newspaper is coming to do an article on us. You need to be there."

Oh, rats, I'd forgotten all about Evie Ester and the adventure cat feature she was planning to write. It was important to get the word out that cats don't need to sit at home, bored and lonely. The enrichment of the outdoors was a proven cure for behavior disorders such as clawing furniture and hostility toward their fellows. Many housecats could be leash- and harness-trained, and whether one took them into the back yard, around the block, to the park, or across the country, the exposure did their spirits a world of good.

"Okay, right," I conceded. "Can you give me a minute?"

"Sure, take your time. Kitty's all ready. I just need to grab her when we go."

I went upstairs to change my clothes and splash water on my face. Hopefully Datura was just being polite about attending the meetup and would not actually come. And if she did, I would deal. Who knows? Maybe we would even become pals.

When I got back downstairs, garbed in jeans and a tee shirt, I found Patty looking through Carry's sketchbook.

"These are beautiful!" she remarked. "I didn't know you were an artist."

"They're not my work. They were done by the woman who lives on Mt. Tabor, the one I met when Harry ran away in the park." I went about gathering the things I would need for the outing: a bag of treats, a portable water bowl. I filled a bottle from the tap, then loaded everything in a tote. It didn't take long to locate Elizabeth, my adventure cat of the day, and slip on the little vest harness. She knew what was coming next and eagerly hobbled into the carrier for transport.

Though Elizabeth's condition made her wobbly on her feet, she could still walk, climb, and even jump a bit. Since she tended to fall over if she stood in one position, she had developed her own fast-walking gait to compensate. Walking her was fun as she raced from place to place like a guided missile. She truly loved the freedom.

Patty picked up her pack and began to rummage around in it. "Aha!" she exclaimed as she withdrew a pair of heavy paper rectangles, shiny blue. She held them up in the air like a prize. "Guess who's going to Dr. Craven's book launch tonight?"

"Oh? You?" was all I could manage.

She nodded vigorously. "And guess who's coming with me?"

"Jim?" I guessed, her husband being the obvious choice.

"No, he's got something else on. Besides, he thinks Dr. Craven is a bit of a sham."

Smart man, I thought to myself.

"No, Lynley. You! You're coming with me to see the doctor speak."

"Me?" I stuttered. "Oh, I don't know…"

"I realize this is short notice," Patty said, "but it's a chance of a lifetime. I doubt Dr. Craven will be coming back to Portland any time soon."

"He will if it pays," I grumbled.

"Pardon?"

"Nothing. It's just that…" I was all set to give her my uncensored thoughts on the matter—how I believed the good doctor to be a charlatan; how those expensive tickets she held in her hand were most likely funding Rolls Royces, not research—but I stopped myself. In reality, I had no idea what the deal was with Dr. Wil Craven, feline archaeologist. Feeling, not fact, had brought me to the conclusion he wasn't on the up and up.

"It's just that I'll be tired after the adventure meet."

"The lecture isn't until eight. You'll have plenty of time to rest."

"Oh, well…" I was about to say I had something else to

do but knew I'd get caught out in the lie. "The shoulder," I fudged. "It will probably start hurting again. The physical therapist said to take it easy."

Patty stuffed the tickets back into her purse. "If you don't want to go, just say so."

"I don't want to go," I said before I could stop myself. "I'm sorry, Patty. It's just I don't think I'd enjoy it."

"Why? Feline archaeology? I thought it would be right up your alley. You're usually so interested in anything to do with cats."

I sat down on the couch with an *oof*. She was right. My reluctance made no sense, not even to me.

Patty came over and sat beside me. "What's going on, Lynley? You're not acting yourself today."

"I have a lot on my mind, that's all. That woman who lives on Mt. Tabor, the artist who did the sketchbook drawings—she nearly got murdered yesterday, and I was there. The perp knocked me down. That's how I hurt my shoulder."

"Oh my goodness!" Patty exclaimed.

"And Frannie is avoiding me, and I'm sure something's terribly wrong, but she won't talk to me so I have no idea what."

"Oh, dear," she appropriately announced.

"Plus that cat Hermione whom I hadn't seen for five years has gone missing, and a strange woman is claiming that she, not Carry, is the rightful owner, but I don't trust her. I don't feel she has the best of intentions. And now she said she might show up at the adventure cat meet. Oh, Patty, I'm just overwhelmed. I think you should find someone else to go with you tonight."

Patty put a hand on my knee. "I get it. No problem. It sounds like you've had quite a time of it. A murder, you say?"

"Near-murder, thankfully."

Suddenly a long, wailing *yeow* broke through our conversation. Elizabeth could not care less about murder and mayhem. To her mind, it was high time for her walk!

Chapter 16

Feline Cerebellar Hypoplasia, also called Wobbly Cat Syndrome, is described as a non-progressive, non-contagious neurological condition that causes problems with balance and walking. Cats with moderate FCH like Elizabeth still learn to function quite well.

I grabbed Elizabeth's carrier while Patty went next door to collect Kitty. We met at my Toyota, piled in with our cats, and headed for the Rhododendron Gardens. As promised, I filled Patty in on the recent goings-on. She ooh-ed and ah-ed at all the appropriate places.

Then she said quite bluntly, "What an ordeal! But now you need to forget about it for a while so you and Elizabeth can enjoy your walk. You'll feel better afterward, and maybe you'll be able to think more clearly."

I looked at Patty as we pulled into the lot and parked. How did such a young, outwardly-naive woman get to be so wise? Not only was Patty's advice good, it was inevitable—before we'd even got the cats out of the car, two other members joined us, and then two more. With the pleasant chatter and cat talk, I felt better already.

En masse, we carted our carriers and accoutrement bags to the little check-in kiosk. There was a bit of friendly chaos as we got our kitties readied for the jaunt, but soon everyone was set, cats harnessed or in front packs or strollers, and their people equipped with water and treats for breaks.

Three more folks had joined us, making seven humans and eight cats since Paula had brought both her Persians which she rolled in a bright pink stroller. Though we all started from the same place, we soon began to fan out in an autonomous way befitting a gathering of cats. The cats were the leaders, and their humans just along for the ride.

Patty and Kitty headed off with Paula, while Elizabeth and I started down the path that led across the little stream into the park proper. It couldn't have been a better time for it, with both the grand old rhododendrons and the perky azaleas in full bloom on every side. The air was fresh with ozone, and birdsong blended with the tinkle of the brook to drown out all but the loudest of the city sounds.

Suddenly I heard someone call my name. I looked back to see Datura at the check-in kiosk waving madly.

"Lynley!" she shouted like a long-lost friend.

Sweeping a spotted cat into her arms, she approached me with the smooth assurance of a tiger. Careful to face her feline's eyes away from Elizabeth, she paused a few feet from us and smiled.

"Datura. You made it." I smiled back but could do little to sound enthusiastic.

"It's Dee, remember? Yes, and I apologize for being late. But I am here now. Please tell me what to do."

"There's not much to it." I gestured toward the others who were making their ways along the winding paths, some together and others alone with their feline companion. "We just walk around and enjoy the scenery."

"Alright. May I walk with you?"

I hesitated. "Elizabeth's okay with other cats. How about yours?"

So far I'd only seen Datura's feline from the back, a bronze-colored beauty with a constellation of black spots in varying sizes. Now the long face turned toward me, displaying a pair of vivid green eyes. With a slow blink, my heart melted.

"She is Mut, Egyptian Mau," said Datura, "though nothing so special as our Maftet. The Mau are typically a shy breed, but I have trained her. She is well-mannered with felines and humans alike."

"Mutt?" I grimaced. "Like a dog?"

Datura laughed. "No, of course not. Mut was the mother goddess worshipped in ancient Egypt. One of her many aspects was that of a cat or a human in the company of a cat."

Datura set Mut down some way from Elizabeth. Crouching to her knees, she petted the spotted cat and spoke to her in low purrs. Mut rubbed her face along Datura's leg with obvious affection, then turned into the path and began to walk.

Elizabeth watched Mut's every move with fascination. When Mut started down the hill, Elizabeth did too.

"That's our cue," I commented, following Elizabeth as she wobbled along. Datura did the same, allowing Mut to stop or go as she pleased. Whatever else this strange woman might or might not be, she had a caring and sympathetic understanding of her cat.

For a while, we walked together as a foursome. Datura and I talked about nothing in particular and definitely not about Carry. The cats sniffed at bushes and dabbled their paws in the little stream. We finally met up with others of our group. Datura went off with them, while Elizabeth and I found a grassy area and watched the ducks. There were ducklings, all cute and fuzzy, and Elizabeth really wanted to play with them, but I said no—cat cohabitors have to draw the line somewhere. To compensate, I sat down at a picnic table and let out her leash so she could totter back and forth without getting too close to the baby ducks.

I took a few pictures with my phone and was busy posting them on Facebook, *hashtag-adventurecat,* when Blake and Evie Ester found me. Our fearless leader had already given Evie the rundown on the adventure cat movement, and now she was introducing the individual members. We chatted for a few minutes, and I found the journalist likable and easy to talk to. She asked basic questions: How did you get involved with the club? Did your cat require any special training? What's it like to take a cat for a walk in the middle of a city? She was especially interested in Elizabeth's condition and how FCH affected her ability as a walking partner. I gave her the nutshell version of what it was like to care for a special needs cat, and how the practice of walking actually helped Elizabeth's symptoms by strengthening her muscles.

When Evie had all the material she wanted, she thanked me and said she'd be sending a copy of the article to Blake for review by the club. Then the pair set off across the grass in search of someone else for an interview. A few minutes later, Patty came by with Kitty, and we decided we were both ready to call it a day.

"I saw your friend made it," said Patty as we strolled across the foot bridge on our way back to the parking lot.

"She's not a friend," I countered. "I don't really know what she is. It's all balled up with the thing I was telling you about earlier."

"The cat thing?" Patty commented.

"Yeah, that, and the murder thing. Attempted murder," I amended. "Carry's still alive." *As far as I know,* I thought, but only to myself. "That woman—Datura is her name—was partners with the victim a long time ago. Now she shows up out of the blue, right when Carry's ambushed? I'm sorry but I'd call that suspicious. And on top of it all, she claims Hermione belongs to her." I sighed, shaking my head. "Really, I don't know what to think. A few days ago, I'd never even met these people—now one of them is in the hospital and the other is on my home turf walking her cat. How did that happen?"

"It's because you're a nice person, Lynley. Datura is probably very upset about her partner. You did a good thing, inviting her to the meetup. She looked like she was having a nice time."

"You're right." I conceded. "She and Mut did seem to be having fun, and I found her interesting to talk to. She didn't bring up Carry or Hermione even once."

We came to the hill leading up to the front gate. Kitty paused by a wooden bench to lick a back paw, and Elizabeth was chasing a bug, basically by tumbling on top of it, so Patty and I took a seat. I gazed around at the layer upon layer of bright pinks, purples, and reds. With its glossy green background, the scene reminded me of a Monet painting.

"This place is so beautiful!" Patty exclaimed.

"Yes, it is. I remember coming here as a kid. The bushes were smaller then, but otherwise it's exactly the same."

"That must have been wonderful. What a lovely way to grow up."

"The admittance was free back then. No entrance kiosk."

We both automatically turned to look at the shingled building with its cash box and display of souvenirs. Visitors were coming and going through the gate, the normal crowd for a weekend in May. Then my eye caught something unexpected. Standing off to the side were

Datura and Mut. Datura was engaged in an intense conversation with a tall man, and by the looks of it, she wasn't happy. The man was looming over her, quite a feat since they were both of the same tall stature, but it was more body language than actual height that told the story. I couldn't see his face, but the stiff stance, the squared shoulders, the way he leaned in until the pair was nearly nose to nose, conveyed nothing short of hostility. I could see Datura's face, red blotches rising on her whitened cheeks. Her kohl-lined eyes were squinted into black slits. Her crimson mouth was partly open even though she wasn't the one doing the talking.

"Isn't that your friend there?" asked Patty, following my gaze. "Oh, my goodness! Do you see who she's with?" Patty turned away, her face flushed and her eyes alight.

"Who?" I asked, not recognizing the handsome fellow, though I did find him familiar.

"I can't believe it! It's him! It's Dr. Craven!"

"*The* Dr. Craven? The one who's giving a reading tonight?"

"Yes! And doesn't he look casual in his ecru linen jacket!"

"Hmmm," I muttered, wondering at his connection with Datura.

"Do you think he'd be mad if I asked for an autograph?" Patty put forth breathlessly.

"I wouldn't bother him right now..." I began, but she was already off, Kitty in tow, scrounging in her bag for paper and pen. *Ah, well, such is fame,* I thought as she brazenly approached the arguing couple.

It took barely a second for the good doctor to morph from anger to celebrity-style cordiality. Datura required a little longer, but she, too, managed to don a perfect, noncommittal smile. Next I knew, Craven was signing Patty's notebook and giving her his card with Datura laughing coyly at something someone said.

I watched a few minutes longer as the threesome continued to chat like old friends. Elizabeth was getting tired, and since Patty gave no sign she was ever coming back to us ordinary folks now that she had the ear of the great doctor, I decided it was time to go.

As I made my way out, I paused. "Goodbye, Dee, Patty," I said stiffly. "We're taking off now. Do you need a ride, Patty, or can you find your own way home?"

She gazed over at me, her eyes still glassy and star-struck. "I'm fine, Lynley. I can go with Blakie."

I started out the gate, then hesitated. Briefly I'd caught the eye of Dr. Craven and found something hypnotic in his pensive stare. It hadn't been what I'd expected, the conceited look of a superstar. The gray eyes were soulful and a bit sad, holding not ego but a well of experience and a surprising depth of perspective.

"Hey, Patty," I remarked. "I've been thinking. I'd like to go with you tonight after all. If the offer's still open."

"Really, Lynley? That would be great! Pick you up at seven-thirty?"

I nodded but she'd already turned back to her idol.

I couldn't pinpoint what it was that had prompted my change of heart, but I was willing to run with it.

Chapter 17

Treats are a valuable teaching tool. Giving treats for good behavior creates a habit that goes beyond reward or bribery. A treat when traveling in a carrier, administering medication, or doing other things cats may not instinctively enjoy can result in a favorable memory that will make that event easier the next time.

I couldn't get the image of Datura and Dr. Craven out of my head. They were definitely having a disagreement about something. I couldn't even begin to guess what. Maybe he'd offended her in some way as they passed on the path. Maybe she'd offended him. Maybe they were lovers having a tiff. There was a plethora of possible ties, and I had no information to corroborate any of them. So why did I think it had something to do with Carry, the sketchbook, Hermione, and the attempted murder?

Once home, I let Elizabeth out of her carrier and gave her a treat. She munched it with relish, then wobbled off to her bed where she tipped over and immediately fell asleep. Though only mid-afternoon, the other cats were beginning to wonder about dinner, or at least why Elizabeth had gotten something when they had not. Obligingly I pulled out the treat basket, chose the packages to correspond with their differing wants, needs, and diets, and set about doing their bidding.

While everyone concentrated on their goodies, I went upstairs to change out of my jeans into something more comfortable. As I shrugged on a loose, sleeveless dress and dug through my closet for a sweater since the weather wasn't quite up to summer speed, I thought about the evening ahead. What does one wear to a reading given by a feline archaeologist? The pink, glittery cat-ear headband I often don for cat-related events might not be appropriate in the lecture hall. Something more professional, more somber. Maybe something black.

I shut the closet door with a bang and sat down on my bed. Why did I feel such trepidation? What was it about Wil Craven that flustered me so? My initial bad reaction to the man was now confused and compounded by the incident in the park. I thought back, trying to remember every move, every nuance of his and Datura's confrontation. I couldn't hear the words, of course, but the intentions were clear. I'd wager big bucks the pair were anything but friends.

Something round, furry, and weighing about seventeen pounds landed on my lap with a *purrumph*. My hand automatically stroked down the red back, eliciting a rumbling purr and a slightly slimy mouth-caress on my arm.

"What am I doing, Red?" I asked the cat. "Why do I care?"

A red ringtail twitched in answer.

"You're right," I replied to the gesture, "I shouldn't care. I'll go to the reading because Patty asked me and learn what I can about cat archaeology. It does sound interesting, doesn't it?"

Another flick of the tail told me it did.

"Yes, I'll go and keep an open mind. Whatever happened between Datura and Craven at the rhodie garden has nothing to do with tonight, and nothing to do with me.

"I wonder if she will be there?" This was a new idea, and I wasn't sure where to put it in my box of random thoughts about the Carry incident, of which Datura was very much a key player.

Big Red had tired of my introspection and hopped to the floor. Tail in the air, he headed back downstairs. I was about to follow when my phone rang. I looked at the caller ID and my heart leapt.

"Frannie!" I cried, almost before I'd answered. "Where are you? How are you? I'm so glad you called!"

"Hi, Lynley," Frannie said in a bleak monotone, so softly I could barely hear her. "I'm sorry I haven't got back to you." There was a pause, and it took all my willpower not to jump in with a load of questions. "You're right. I've been avoiding you." Another pause. "I've been avoiding everyone."

Then she fell silent. After thirty seconds of dead air, I ventured, "Why?"

"Oh, Lynley, I..." Now she sounded like she might break into tears. "I do love you."

The endearment, one we'd shared on multiple occasions, now seemed anxious and woeful.

"I love you too, dear," I replied, trying to keep the trepidation out of my voice. "But let's get together and talk face to face. You know you can tell me anything."

I was afraid she would shine me on again, but to my surprise, she agreed. With sudden perfunctory thoroughness, she gave me a time and place, then rang off without a goodbye. For a full minute, I sat with the lifeless device in my hand, unable to do more than breathe.

Finally I got up and went downstairs. Ignoring the cats, I moved zombie-like through the living room, through the kitchen, and out onto the patio. I didn't stop there but followed the grassy path to the plum tree where I fell like a leaden weight into the old Adirondack chair.

My thoughts were all over the place: Frannie was okay—she had called me! Frannie *wasn't* okay—by her tone I could tell something was very wrong. I closed my eyes in an attempt to corral my worry. She had promised to meet—hopefully then all would be revealed.

But there was one thing I had to do first. I needed to call Patty and tell her I wasn't going to make it to the reading after all.

"Hey, Lynley!" came Patty's exuberant voice on the line. "What's up?"

"Bad news, I'm afraid. Or actually it's good news—Frannie called. She wants to get together to talk about what's been going on with her."

"That's wonderful! Did she tell you what happened?"

"No. I still have no idea, but she did admit she's been avoiding me." *Avoiding everyone* was what she had said, and for a moment, my blood ran cold remembering the dullness of the statement. "But thing is, she wants to meet at eight, so I'm going to have to miss Dr. Craven's talk."

"Oh," Patty sighed.

"I'm so sorry. It's just that this is the first chance..."

"Lynley, I totally understand. Of course helping your friend is more important than entertainment, no matter how educational it might be. I'll miss you though. I really wanted you to see how amazing Dr. Craven is."

"Maybe he'll come around again sometime."

"That may be." Her tone brightened. "When I was talking to him earlier today," she began with obvious pride, "he was saying how much he loves the Pacific Northwest, so who knows?"

"Then you had a nice chat? Did you get your

autograph?"

"Better!" she exclaimed. "He asked me to come backstage after the show tonight, and he'll give me a signed copy of *Cats in the Catacombs*. He even mentioned taking a selfie with me!"

"Well, good for you," I said honestly. It wasn't in my nature to be so bold, but her impetuous action had turned out nicely. "You'll have to let me read the book."

Patty laughed. "You can borrow it the moment I'm done."

"How did you get on with Datura?" I asked on an impulse.

"Dee? She's quite lovely, really," Patty said. "In fact she and I hit it off. We have a lot in common, you know."

"Oh?" I prompted, since I couldn't imagine what that might be.

"Yes, after Dr. Craven left, she and I did another round of the park with Kitty and Muttie. Dee was great fun to talk to, and a good listener as well."

"What did you talk about?"

"Why, you, of course!" Patty giggled conspiratorially. "Nothing personal—mostly cats and your work at Friends of Felines. Dee loves cats, and she knew about FOF. She even adopted one from there once, about five years ago."

"Really?" Was this yet another version of the Spot/ Hermione/Maftet saga?

"She talked a lot about her friend in the hospital, Carry. It seems they were more than just partners, they were besties. Then something happened, but she didn't go into what. I was curious as anything, but I didn't want to pry."

This part basically correlated with what Datura had told me, and I was mulling it over when Patty caught me by surprise.

"Dee was excited to hear you have Carry's sketchbook," she said with absolute innocence.

"What?" I spluttered. "You told her about the sketchbook?"

There was a silence, then Patty countered, "I didn't know it was a secret, Lynley. I figured since you were the one who found Carry after she was attacked…"

"You told Datura I was the one who found Carry?"

Immediately I knew I'd messed up. Naturally in Patty's blameless mind, my role in Carry's discovery would seem a logical topic of conversation, and the news of the sketchbook would be of special interest. Why I hadn't told Datura myself was more the mystery. The fact that I'd found the book underneath Carry's comatose body; the fact that Datura had pointedly asked about it, though at the time she'd thought it was a journal; the fact that her excuse for wanting the book, to make sure it revealed no confidential business records, was flimsy at best, if not a total fabrication—these all added up to doubt. The bottom line was, I didn't trust Datura, and no amount of cat walks in the park could make me change my mind.

"I'm sorry, Patty. I didn't mean to be abrupt."

"Oh, that's okay. Dee told me your relationship was a little strained because of the Carry factor."

"The Carry factor?"

"Apparently Carry is a bit unstable, if you know what I mean. Dee wasn't sure what she might have told you about her, things that could have caused your mistrust."

The only thing that caused my mistrust was Datura herself, beginning with that strange and obviously forcible removal of Carry from Belmont Street, but I refrained from pointing that out. Instead I pursued the other matter.

"Unstable?" I repeated. "Carry seemed quite stable to

me."

"Well, she would, wouldn't she? That's the problem."

"I don't understand."

"Dee said she has a mental health condition that makes her believe her own lies. A pathological liar, I think she called it."

"Oh, nonsense!" I pronounced before I could stop myself. "I'm sorry but I don't accept that. I talked to Carry on different occasions, and she seemed fine."

"I'm only telling you what Dee told me. Of course, I've never met the woman. But Dee's known her for a long time…"

Patty let the implications hang in the air, and I realized the conversation was going nowhere. Carry? A pathological liar? Datura the sane one with Carry's best interest at heart? I suppose it wasn't altogether impossible, I begrudgingly admitted. I would need to consider it further, but right now I had more important business.

"I'm sorry, Patty. I didn't mean to argue. You're right, I really don't know Carry that well. Or Datura, for that matter. I'm glad you made friends. And I'm sad to miss the lecture. Now I'd better go and get ready to meet Frannie."

"That's okay, Lynley. I understand." She paused. "I admit Dee is a little… different. I enjoyed our conversation, but after talking to you, I guess I have a few things to think about. I hope everything goes well with Frannie."

"Thanks," I said and rang off, the mention of my troubled friend eclipsing all thoughts of Datura and the Carry Factor from my mind.

Chapter 18

Cats' whiskers are amazing, but did you know that the face is not the only place whiskers grow? Cats also have whiskers on the back side of their front legs.

I walked in the door of Webster's Bistro and stared around at the cozy decor. I hadn't been there for a while, but nothing had changed—to one side was the dining room where candles flickered on intimate tables; to the other, through an archway, was the cocktail lounge. I headed into the lounge and found a vacant table. As I gazed around at the painted mural of an Italian street scene and the high ceilings strung with fairy lights, I remembered my first time there. It was the night I found Hermione in a nearby warehouse, the night I was pursued by a man with a gun who wasn't shy about using it. I'd ducked into the bistro to hide but had been kicked out by staff when they found I was harboring a kitten. They put me back on the street to face my foe alone. Frannie knew every detail of that encounter. Why on Earth had she chosen this meeting place now?

I'd arrived about ten minutes early, and not surprisingly, there was as yet no sign of my friend. I ordered a ginger ale, then waited, counting the seconds, wondering if Frannie would really show. As eight o'clock came and went, my heart fell. Frannie was usually so punctual, and she would never have stood me up without calling to let me know—but that was the old Frannie, my kindhearted, thoughtful, compassionate ally. I had no idea what to expect from this Frannie, the one with the flat tone of voice and cryptic words; the one who had barked at me at the shelter; the one who'd been sidestepping me at every turn. I feared the new Frannie might be capable of anything.

"Penny for your thoughts," came a familiar voice over my shoulder as the woman in question swept into the bench opposite, dumping her bag down beside her.

"Frannie! You came! I was beginning to worry."

Frannie gave an almost-smile, then looked around for the server. Summoning him over, she ordered a glass of water, no ice, then got busy in her purse as if looking for something.

A million questions ran through my head, but I pushed them aside to let her make the first move. I didn't remember when last I'd seen Frannie face to face, but it couldn't have been more than a couple of weeks ago. Yet in that short time, changes had taken place, noticeable differences in both her appearance and demeanor.

Frannie had lost weight, and underneath her makeup which seemed heavier than usual, her cheeks were sallow. The day dress she wore may have been Vera Wang, but it no longer fit right, giving a disheveled look that didn't suit someone usually meticulous about their clothing. The cracked fingernail polish and moons showing where the color had grown out proved she'd not been keeping up her routine. And beyond the obvious, she carried, like a weight on her shoulders, an undeniable air of woe.

As she continued digging in her bag, I wondered what could be so elusive in that ten-by-twelve pouch. Finally she gave up and turned to me. Of all the changes, her hollow, haunted stare startled me the most.

Automatically I reached out to take her hand, but she pulled away as if burnt.

"You might not want to be doing that."

"What? Why?"

Because..." she began, and then so did the tears.

I don't think I'd ever seen Frannie cry before, and it was a shock. Mascara running down her cheeks, carving rivulets through the blush, she hung her head like someone ashamed.

My heart was pounding faster than a cornered cat, but I didn't speak. I didn't move. I don't think I even drew a breath.

"I have a disease," she finally whispered. "It's... bad."

"Oh, no!" Again I reached for her; again she drew back. I put two and two together. "It's something contagious?"

"Yes, no. Yes, it is. Oh, I don't know. There's so much conflicting information, I'm not sure what to think."

I took a deep breath. "Start from the beginning. What is it you have?"

Again the look of shame. Again the whisper. "It's hepatitis. Hepatitis C."

I sat back in my chair and breathed a sigh of relief. "Oh, my stars, is that all?"

Frannie gave me a look of utter surprise. The look turned to disappointment, then to rage.

"I'm sorry," I cried. "That was a terrible thing to say. I know that's bad, honey. It's just that I was imagining so much worse."

"Worse?" she retorted. "Worse than a chronic, life-threatening, shameful disease, common to degenerates, drug addicts, and lowlifes? I can't think of anything worse than that."

"Oh, Frannie..." I started but she interrupted me.

142

"I had a friend with... *that disease*," she blurted. "She got it from a blood transfusion in the hospital—not the *other* way, the shameful way. Still, she was shunned by her friends and family. No one wanted to come near her, scared they'd get it too. She wasted away, lonely and alone."

"Did she receive treatment?"

"Sure. Her doctors gave her a round of horrible medications. It took a year, and she was sick and miserable every single day. And it didn't work. When it was finally over, she still had the virus. It had all been for nothing. The next step was a liver transplant. She died of complications soon after."

Frannie stared at me, the tears starting up again. I wanted to take her in my arms and hold her, but I knew the gesture would not be welcomed.

The server picked that moment to cruise by with our drinks. Frannie turned her ravaged face away as she mumbled a thank you. *That's my Frannie*, I thought tenderly. *Courteous to others, no matter how bad she's feeling herself.*

"What does your hepatologist say?" I asked when the server was gone.

"I haven't been to one. My doctor gave me the name of a gastroenterologist, but..."

"You mean you haven't consulted a specialist yet? Oh Frannie, you need to do that as soon as possible."

"Why?" she spat. "I just don't see the point. What good can they do besides offer meds that don't work? I don't need someone to tell me I'm going to die."

"Frannie," I said with every ounce of calm I could muster. "Take a drink of your water, then go in the bathroom and wash your face. When you come back, I'll tell you a story that I promise will make you feel better."

She peered at me questioningly but did as I asked. While she was gone, I gathered my thoughts.

Frannie returned some ten minutes later, noticeably improved. Though maybe not up to her normally flawless standards, at least her platinum curls were combed and her makeup reapplied. No amount of concealer could have hidden the dark bags under her eyes, but the tears were gone, at least for the moment.

"Lynley, I trust you, but there's nothing you could say that can change what is."

"That's true, but I think I can change how you feel about it. Will you listen?"

She nodded slowly, and I began.

"I also have a friend, Owen, with hep C—it's quite common, you know, though like you, most people don't want to talk about it. When Owen was diagnosed, he was scared too, but he went to a hepatologist and found out there is now a cure. The regimen only took two months, and the pharmaceutical company covered most of the cost. The new drug has very few side effects—Owen suffered none at all. And in the end he was cured—not just in remission, but the virus had been eradicated from his system. Gone. His liver damage resolved, and now he's in perfect health. That could be you, if you'd quit hiding away and let yourself get help."

Frannie was staring at me like I was crazy, but I caught a tiny glint of hope in her eyes. "A quick fix? You're putting me on."

"No, I'm not." I dug out my phone and pulled up the internet. After a few tries, I found what I was looking for, an article by the American Liver Foundation and another from the CDC. Both collaborated what I'd told her, adding

144

even more encouraging information on top of it.

I punched a few more pages. "And while you're at it, here's a site that tells how hep C is transmitted. It's actually very difficult to catch."

I handed her my phone and sat back, pondering how Frannie could have missed the news about the recent breakthroughs in treatment. It had been in the papers and magazines, and the drug commercials were all over the television, showing happy people doing exciting things once they took the cure. If nothing else, her doctor should have told her, should have anticipated the psychological turmoil the diagnosis would cause. Frannie needed real information, not just a hand-off to some other medical professional.

As I thought about the hell Frannie must have been going through, believing she had no recourse but misery and death, I was getting madder and madder at her care team. But I knew it wasn't entirely their fault. Frannie had exacerbated their deficiency by going into hiding, clinging to rumors and data from an outdated source.

As she finished the articles, she looked up at me, her face filled with confusion.

"You poor, sweet thing," I burst out. "You've spent so long thinking you'd lost everything."

For a third time, I reached for her hand. Slowly, timidly she allowed the touch.

"Is this true? The cure?" she asked in a near-whisper, as if speaking of it might make it disappear like so much fairy dust.

"Yes, it's true. Go to a hepatologist. Ask them. I think you'll be amazed."

"I'll go tomorrow," she declared, a bit of color flushing back into her face. Pulling a tablet from her purse, she made a note. "And I'm going to have a talk with Dr. Clooney too. I admit I was in shock when she told me, but if she'd just walked me through it..."

"You would have been spared all this anxiety."

"Yes, or at least some of it. I've been spending my days in my apartment, afraid to go out, afraid I'd accidently infect someone. I didn't want to see the doctors because I was scared of what they'd tell me. I didn't even look on the internet. I just couldn't take any more bad news. I've missed so much..."

Abruptly she sat forward. "Oh, no! Torta! I resigned from her case at the shelter! They must hate me for being so irresponsible."

"No one hates you—they've been worried, that's all. And Alani's been taking good care of Torta, keeping up the behavior work you started. But she'll be pleased as punch for you to come back to it yourself. You and Torta have a special bond."

"Yes," Frannie asserted. "I'll do that tomorrow too. I still can't believe I've been so stupid!"

"Not stupid," I soothed. "Terrified. And you have every right to be. A health concern at our age is nothing to joke about, but there's every chance you'll be fine. Just take it one day at a time."

"From now on," she vowed, "that's exactly what I'm going to do."

Chapter 19

2021 AAHA/AAFP Feline Life Stage Guidelines have recently been updated to include four distinct age-related stages (kitten, young adult, mature adult, and senior) as well as an end-of-life stage.

For a while longer, Frannie and I sat in quiet companionship, sipping our drinks and watching the people come and go. As the hour advanced, the jean-clad, after-work folks began to give way to the dressed-up, out-to-dinner-and-drinks crowd. When a group of rowdy twenty-somethings took the table next to us, all loudness and laughter, I'd had enough.

"Want to get out of here?" I asked Frannie. "We could take a walk on the esplanade and look at the city lights."

Stuffing cash into the plastic check folder the server had dropped on one of her whirlwind trips around the busy room, we headed outside. I had nothing against fun and wildness, but once we'd left the noise behind, I felt a definite sense of relief.

The May evening was clear as could be, and the Eastside Esplanade, a pedestrian and bicycle path that ran along the shore of the Willamette River, seemed especially gorgeous. The public walk went all the way from the Hawthorne Bridge to the Steel Bridge with a few miscellaneous bridges in between. They call Portland the City of Bridges for a reason, and tonight the curving structures silhouetted against the urban brilliance and defined by the red and white lights of passing cars were nothing short of spectacular. The air was crisp, still sweater weather but with that hint of warmth that promised summer was close at hand.

"Which way, north or south?" I asked Frannie.

"If you don't mind, Lynley, could we go to your place instead? I'm feeling a little shaky."

"Of course." I took her arm. "Where are you parked?"

"I came in an Uber."

"Good. That means only one car."

We rounded back to where I'd left my ancient Toyota, and ten minutes later were pulling up in front of my house. Little greeted us at the door and followed Frannie and me into the kitchen where she proceeded to plop herself onto Frannie's lap the moment she sat down at the table. Frannie cuddled her, exhaling a sigh of pleasure.

"I've missed this so much!" Frannie exclaimed, then looked at me. "I missed you too, of course. But there's something about cats. I just love the way I feel when I'm around them."

"I know what you mean. You must have been doubly lonely without your trips to the shelter."

"I haven't felt the loss of Teasel so acutely since right after she crossed the Bridge. I always had the shelter kitties to keep me occupied."

While Frannie and Little relished each other's company, I made a pot of tea, lemon chamomile for relaxation. Bringing the teapot to the table, along with a tub of local honey, I sat.

Still rubbing Little's ebony sideburn, Frannie looked up at me. "I was there, you know."

"Pardon?"

"I was at home when you came by." Frannie sighed. "I

kept waiting for you to go away but you just stayed and stayed. You are a stubborn thing, aren't you?"

"I thought I saw movement under the door. There's a gap."

"You were peering under my door?" She laughed. "I would like to have seen that, you down on all fours, sniffing around like a cat."

"I may have been on all fours, but I wasn't sniffing, I promise you."

She gave a little giggle, then sobered. "I really wanted to answer, to let you in and tell you everything, but I just couldn't. Now I wish I had."

"Me too, but it's going to be okay. I promise."

She huffed but with a smile. "That's a promise you can't make, dear, but I appreciate your optimism. By the way," she added, "I loved the sketch on the back of your note. Was that something you did?"

"No, not me. They're done by a…" I was about to say "friend," but that was the wrong word. As I searched for a better one, I found myself pulled once again into that dark world of intrigue, mystery, and attempted murder that was the Carry factor. For the past hour, I'd put it aside, concentrating on Frannie's needs. Now, like a douse of ice water, it all came rushing back.

For a moment, I felt overwhelmed. Then I realized I now had an ally at hand. I'd done what I could to help Frannie with her issue; now maybe she could help me.

"There's a sketchbook. Here, let me get it." I retrieved the big red volume and laid it out on the table. Frannie opened it and gasped.

I watched as, fascinated, she moved from page to page, picture to picture. While she perused the book, I filled her in on the story behind it.

149

"These are wonderful," she said as she reached the final illustration and closed the back cover. "What an imagination! And the way she identifies the focal point in each of the different views is nothing short of genius."

"Focal point? What focal point?"

Frannie's penciled eyebrows rose as she stared at me with incredulity. "Didn't you notice?"

"Notice what?"

"Why, the pattern, of course. In spite of all the different angles and perspectives, each of these drawings are telling the same story." She tapped thoughtfully on the cover. "If only we knew what that story might be. What are they? Illustrations for a fantasy book?"

"They're of a real place, Carry's garden. She planted the whole thing in shades of red." Suddenly I wished I'd thought to take photos and decided next time I went to look for Hermione, I would do just that.

Frannie opened the journal and began to examine it for a second time. She went through slowly and methodically, sometimes turning it horizontally or even upside down.

"You know what they remind me of?" she mused. "One of those find-the-treasure stories."

"Find the..." I stopped dead.

"You know. Where there's a mystery to solve and the pictures give the clues. Are you sure they're not meant to be book plates?"

"I don't think so. She never mentioned anything about writing a book. She always kept this volume close at hand, never let it out of her sight. That's why until I looked inside I thought it was a diary."

"Well, she's definitely saying something through this artwork. If only we could guess what."

I pulled my chair around next to hers. "Here, show

150

me."

Frannie pointed to one of the drawings, a spot within the intricate patterns of foliage. "There." She turned the page and pointed again. "And there. And this one's really obvious," she said, flipping the page once more. She fanned the remainder. "Every single one of these sketches focuses on the same exact place."

I gasped. She was right. I hadn't seen it, but Frannie got it immediately. "Frannie, I could kiss you!"

For a moment, she looked appalled.

"In fact, I think I will." I kissed her lightly on the cheek. "Remember what we talked about. Nothing about you is outwardly contagious."

She sighed and put her hand on mine. "It's going to take some getting used to. I'd always believed that people like me were pariahs."

"That's what they used to think, but it's not true. And soon you'll be well again."

"I'm calling the doctor the moment the clinic opens in the morning!" she swore.

This time we really hugged, no holding back. I could feel the fear and tension ebb out of her as I held her in my arms. *How cruel*, I thought to myself, *the old attitudes that set people apart when they needed each other the most.* But now she knew the truth, and things would get better from here on in.

I heard a *me-row* as Emilio launched his hunky self into my lap, then laid down, half on me and half on Frannie. Little looked up from her place, gave Emilio a lick on his backside, then went back to sleep. As we untangled from our hug, we both laughed for a very long time.

* * *

Once Frannie left, I gave the cats their night treats and went to bed. I was exhausted, but even so, I lay awake staring at the ceiling and thinking about everything that had happened in the past twenty-four hours.

The day had started with me at Carry's place looking for Hermione. I'd found no sign of the paisley cat, but I had met up with Carry's partner-slash-dear friend Datura—Dee—who was looking for the cat as well. Dee then somehow invited herself into my life, and now she and Patty were adventure cat buddies. Chatty Patty had told Datura everything I'd told her: how I'd discovered Carry unconscious; how I'd then been assaulted myself; and finally, how I had absconded with Carry's sketchbook. I couldn't blame Patty—it had never crossed my mind to ask her to keep it to herself.

But my crazy day hadn't stopped there. Frannie was back, which was great, but she had a chronic disease which was bad. I'd been able to give her some hope in the form of recent advancements in HCV treatment and the fact that she could now be cured. Frannie had come over to my place, where she discovered a pattern in Carry's sketches indicating a single point. A treasure hunt, she had called it. But what was the treasure?

I turned onto my side with a huff, displacing Tinkerbelle who had been sleeping on my chest. The little black fluff slipped in next to me without a sound and was back napping before I'd even settled into the pillow.

Treasure, I contemplated. A romantic idea. Frannie always was a romantic. But there was no denying the drawings did have a common feature. It was so obvious once she brought it to my attention, I didn't know how I'd missed it. Still, to conclude that's where they hid something valuable seemed a leap. It could be anything: a meaningful place, a special memory, or just one of Carry's whims. Maybe she was obsessive. Maybe she was trying to get the drawing just right. Maybe it was an assignment for an art class or an entry in a competition.

The possibilities were endless, and as I drifted toward sleep, my theories became increasingly bizarre.

Maybe that's where the fairies lived.

Or the ley lines lay.

Or the aliens landed.

Maybe that's where the body was buried…

I sat bolt upright, displacing Tinkerbelle for a second time. She'd had enough and hopped off the bed. I could hear her stalk across the floor in the dark. How such a tiny cat could clop, clop, clop like a draft horse I could never understand.

But the echo of her footfalls was the last thing on my mind. I knew I was being silly, that the likelihood the sketches revealed the location of a gravesite was ludicrous and melodramatic, yet I couldn't get it out of my head. If it had been anywhere else, anyone else, I would have passed the idea off as total fantasy. Too much mystery television before bed, or perhaps the garbanzo-arugula sandwich I'd eaten for dinner hadn't set quite right. But this was Carry. This was the woman who cohabited with Spot. This was the partner of the mysterious Datura, whom I didn't trust for a minute.

Suddenly, as clear as the blast of a gunshot, I remembered. That unforgettable night when I'd found a tiny kitten in a gym bag, I'd been chased, shot at, and nearly killed. With a shock that resonated throughout my whole body, I suddenly knew where I'd seen Datura's henchman before. He was the one who had taken shots at Spot and me in that fated warehouse. The Man in Black!

It was finally coming together. The trepidation I felt around Datura and the sense that all was not right with Carry—those instincts were not merely my imagination but connected to that long-ago event. There had been drugs and money involved, things people kill for. And now through a total quirk of fate, I was involved again as well. Was I in danger? Was that obscure incident coming back to haunt me after all this time?

For a full minute, I sat staring into the darkness, then I grabbed my phone. By the clock, it was only ten-thirty, but even had it been midnight, I would have sent the text.

As quick as my fear-clumsy fingers would move, I typed, *Are you still up? If so, call me. Now.*

I slumped onto the pillows and gazed around the room as I awaited an answer. The soft radiance of the phone highlighted only the closest objects, giving them a magical glow. The side table with my glass of water and pile of books to be read. The wooden bedframe, and the quilt with three cats curled on top. Most times I found comfort in the almost-dark, felt safe in the shadows, but not now. I wasn't sure I'd ever feel safe again.

When the phone buzzed I jumped even though I was expecting it.

"Frannie!" I exclaimed. "I'm so glad you got back to me. I need to talk."

Chapter 20

Cats are primarily nocturnal like their wildcat cousins who hunt for food under the cover of night. A housecat that sleeps with their cohabitor, however, may adopt a diurnal routine, coming to bed and staying in the same spot until the wee hours.

"Lynley what is it? What's happened? Are you alright?"

"Yes, I'm fine. I'm sorry if I worried you, but I just thought of something, and you're the only one who can help me reason it out. I hope I didn't wake you," I added as an afterthought.

"No, I was just watching a movie on streaming. Nothing special—I can see it later. Our talk gave me a lot to think about. I looked up more hep C information online when I got home. You're right, of course—I was completely out of line. My antisocial behavior only made things worse. But I've got a plan now. It's still scary, but I feel more positive than I have since I got the news."

"I'm glad. I know it isn't a walk in the park, but it will be okay. If there's anything I can do, just ask."

"I will, dear, but right now this is about you. What's up?"

I took a breath. "I've been thinking about the patterns in Carry's sketches. You suggested they might point to a treasure, but what if..." I hesitated. Would what I was about to postulate sound as farfetched to Frannie as it did to me? I said it anyway. "What if it's not treasure but something more macabre, like a body?"

There was silence on the other end of the line, but I didn't want to wait for her to tell me I was crazy, so I plowed ahead.

"Carry and Datura were business partners and maybe friends, depending on which one you talk to. They owned Spot, aka Hermione, aka Maftet together."

"Yeah, huh?" Frannie muttered.

"After we relinquished little Spot to FOF—again depending on whose story you believe—she was either adopted by both Carry and Datura, *or* by Carry alone, *or* FOF located Carry through the microchip, meaning she had been Carry's kitten all along. But none of that matters. What's important is that it all ties back to that night at the warehouse when I found Spot in the gym bag."

"Hold up, hon. You've lost me."

"You were there, Frannie, that night. You and Denny came and pulled me out of a shooting war."

"Yes, I remember—how could I forget?—but what has that to do with…"

"When Carry and I ran into Datura down on Belmont," I broke in, "she was with a man, a thug. I thought he looked familiar but couldn't place him at the time. Just now I remembered! He was the Man in Black, from that night—I'm certain of it. I don't know what it means, but it must mean something."

"Are you sure it's the same man?" Frannie questioned. "Don't all those muscle men look a bit alike? And it has been five years."

"It's him. I know it."

"Okay, I believe you. But it's got to be a coincidence."

"Does it? Carry hasn't seen her old partner for years, then Datura suddenly shows up again, and not in a nice way. The very next day, Carry is mugged and her place tossed. Whoever did it must have been looking for something, and I think it was the sketchbook. I think Datura figures it holds some sort of information she wants. Maybe this focal point you discovered is the key."

"Wow!" Frannie exclaimed. "Are you saying Datura was the one who tackled Carry?"

"She, or her thug."

"Are you sure?"

"Not completely, no."

"Okay then. Let's slow down and think about this logically."

I grunted in frustration, but Frannie was right. That was why I'd called her, to get her levelheaded insight balancing conjecture with fact.

"There's no way to know if the break-in at Carry's was a random act or a deliberate attack by Datura and her man, but if it was as you say, with connections to that old crime..." She took a deep breath. "...then this could be bad. People who traffic in drugs are dangerous, and chances are if they were successful at it five years ago, they're still doing it now. Whatever else, you're right to be concerned."

"But...?" I pressed when she was quiet for what I considered to be far too long.

"Well, Lynley—a body buried in the garden? Pinpointed by Carry's beautiful drawings? I suppose it's not impossible, but who would it be? Why were they killed? How does it fit with the other pieces of the puzzle?" She paused again. "No, it seems more likely that if there is something there, it would be a thing of value, something Datura wants. If it were a dead person from her past, I'd imagine she'd prefer to leave it buried."

"Good point," I admitted. "Like I said, it's late and I've

been watching far too many Nordic mysteries lately. On TV, if there isn't a murder in the first fifteen minutes, it just doesn't seem right."

Frannie thought for a moment. "That man wearing black, the one that shot at you—wasn't there another man as well?"

"Yes, Man in White. Another big brute who was chasing me around the block trying to get the gym bag."

"Man in Black and Man in White, and now you know they were associated with this Datura person. Have you seen the man in white as well?

"No, no sign of him. Unless..."

"Unless what?"

"Well, a couple of times lately I've had the feeling I was being watched. It wasn't Man in Black, so maybe..." I didn't finish. This latest layer to the convoluted onion would need some further reflection, and I wasn't up to it right now.

"And what about the other shooters?" Frannie asked. "Who were they?"

The other shooters! I'd forgotten all about them. When Datura's thugs were zeroing in on me, just before Frannie and Special Agent Paris came to my rescue, there had been more gunfire, a second gunman aiming for the first.

"That's right! It had all but slipped my mind. At the time I assumed it was the police, though thinking back, it seemed like they didn't arrive until later."

"But what if it wasn't the police? What if someone else was after that bag as well?"

"Oh, goodness, Frannie. I call you for comfort, and you offer up a whole new can of cat food."

"I'm sorry, but this is serious. If it all ties back to drug dealers, you could be in danger."

I thought about Carry lying comatose on the floor of her bungalow. I thought about the person who had knocked me down on top of her. That experience was traumatic, but I was beginning to realize it might have been so much worse.

"I've done it again, haven't I? Stumbled upon something that could get me into more trouble than a cat in catnip. Dirty Harry's mad dash into Carry's garden was a total fluke, but what if everything that happened afterward has been carefully orchestrated? Carry's battering, Datura's search for Hermione, her presence at the adventure cat meet? And if that's the case, what comes next?"

Frannie considered for a minute. "She will want to get the sketchbook. She may contact you, make some excuse to visit. Does she have your information?"

"I didn't give it to her, but Patty may have. Since Datura came to the adventure cat meet, Patty naturally assumes we're friends."

"You don't think Datura would use force to get the book, do you?"

"You mean send her thugs to steal it? I wouldn't put it past her. What are thugs for if not to do the dirty work?"

I fell silent as a thought hit me. If Datura were behind Carry's beating, had she meant for her agent to incapacitate the small woman or was murder the intention all along? If murder, then Carry was still in danger.

My mind raced to darker places: *Could I be in danger too?*

"Lynley," Frannie broke into my musing. "Are you still there?"

"Still here, but my head is buzzing. I'm going to get to bed. Talk tomorrow?"

"Anytime. And don't worry. I'm sure things will seem brighter in the morning."

I rang off but continued to sit pondering our conversation. If I'd hoped talking to Frannie would help resolve my confusion, I'd been dead wrong—I now had more to think about than ever.

* * *

At four o'clock, I gave up on sleep. No amount of reading, playing games on my phone, listening to soothing music, or counting the proverbial sheep was going to get my mind off these new revelations.

One thing was clear—as long as I associated with the players in this scenario, I was putting myself at risk. The logical thing to do was drop the whole thing flat. It shouldn't be hard. Though I'd formed a precarious friendship with Carry, we were still basically strangers to one another. She could get along without me and I without her. As for Datura, if all she wanted was the sketchbook, then no problem. I wasn't about to hand it over to her, but I could return it to Carry. The hospital could take care of it until she recovered; then it would be up to the two of them to duke it out. I guessed that Datura would quit the adventure cat club as soon as the sketchbook was no longer in my possession. I'd warn Patty not to communicate with her anymore, and that would be that.

There was only one problem: Hermione. As long as the cat was missing, I was still involved. I needed to find her. Mt. Tabor wasn't a good place for a cat on its own. No, I had to make sure Hermione was safe before I turned my back on the situation.

A little giddy from lack of sleep, I got up and began to dress. A few cats raised a drowsy eye to watch the process.

"How are my kitties..." I started, then suddenly remembered. "Hey, guys, today's my birthday! What did you get me?"

Their unanimous reply was *meow*, not that I expected any different.

I went downstairs and made a coffee in a to-go cup. Only my panther girl Little bothered to accompany me, the others considering the black of four a.m. a ridiculous time to be up. Cats may be inherently nocturnal but seems my clowder had evolved to a more civilized routine.

"I'll be back in time for your breakfast," I told Little who silently followed me to the door. As headed for my car, I failed to notice her jump up to the window, nor did I see her raise her paw to the glass.

Chapter 21

Your cat has a lot more to say than meow. Be sure to watch eyes, ears, whiskers, tail, and other body language to learn what your cat is thinking and feeling.

The idea behind my pre-dawn Hermione search was that the likelihood of encountering Datura was small. She'd never expect me to go at that insanely early hour. At least that was the theory. When I pulled up and parked in front of the bungalow, I wasn't so sure. It seemed like everyone on the block was already up and moving. The jogger was out with his dog; the mower guy was now doing his edging. As I got out of my car, the lights came on next door and the rude neighbor man gave me a dirty look through the window. Carry's place was dark as a Bombay cat, but that was to be expected. I knew better than anyone she wouldn't be home.

I slipped through the gate and took the path that skirted the house but stopped in awe at the edge of the red garden. I'd never seen it in the dark before, lit up like an enchanted forest with fairy lights spun through the trees and solar-generated garden torches set among the plants. Most were in the red tones, but others, ones shaped like butterflies, dragonflies, and hummingbirds, shifted colors from orange to sunburst to turquoise to green. If I'd thought the place magical in the daylight, this took it to a whole new level. I could imagine elves, sprites, and tiny child-like creatures with mushroom cap hats running down the paths and dancing in the branches.

A rustling in the bushes brought me out of my fantasy like a splash of cold water. I started, blasting the beam of my flashlight onto the place. My heart erupted in a flurry of fear-beats as I eyed the shaking leaves of the anemone shrub. Then there was a plop. The bush gave one last shiver, and out hopped a cat.

"Hermione!" I cried, sinking into a crouch as she padded straight toward me. Though my initial thought was to grab her and stuff her in a carrier right then and there, I resisted. The last thing I wanted to do was to spook her and have her run away again. No, she was coming to me of her own accord. I would let her take her time—*then* I'd stuff her into the carrier.

"Hermione, sweetheart..."

I began the litany of soft cat-speak, meaningless words in a soothing tone to let her know she was safe. It took her a few minutes, but she came. I settled onto the ground right where I was, and after a general inspection, she stepped into my lap. Curling into a circle, she looked up at me, her eyes reflecting her adventures, and her fears.

"What have you been doing, sweetie?" I stroked the marbled back, noticing seeds and burrs lodged in her silky fur. Her backbone felt spiny—she was already beginning to lose weight. "You must be hungry. Did you eat the food I left you?" I performed a gentle check for other indications of trauma, wounds or scratches, but besides needing dinner and a good brushing, she seemed fine.

She had dropped her head into my lap as if she were exhausted by her ordeal. I let her be. The sky was lightening, first to gray, then to an unearthly purple, and finally to crimson as dawn broke. Still, we sat. The solar lights winked out one by one. The fairy lights in the branches above me shut off, leaving a sudden shadow. Then the sun itself rose into view, casting blazing tendrils. The red-making haze burnt away to a sky of perfect blue. Hermione continued the sleep of the innocent and the very, very tired.

I couldn't say how long I sat there with the cat in my lap, but eventually my foot fell asleep and my bad shoulder began to ache from its unsupported position. A pebble was poking into my backside, and with the advent of the new day, insects were awakening. When a large ant ran across my ankle, I deemed it time to move someplace more suited for human comfort than the middle of the volcanic rock path.

Cradling the napping cat, I hefted myself upright but stumbled the moment I tried to put weight on the sleeping foot. In that instant of insecurity, Hermione tensed and pushed away. Before I could stop her, she'd bolted out of my grasp like a rocket.

"Hermione!" I couldn't help but cry. The sharp sound of my voice just made her run faster.

Rats! Rats, rats, *rats*! Hermione was gone again, back into the bushes, and it was all my fault. I wanted to run after her, but I knew that would scare her even more, so hobbling like the grandmother that I was, I made for the porch instead. Slumping onto the stoop, I rubbed the feeling back into my foot and settled in to wait.

* * *

Hermione had come out once; she would do it again. Wouldn't she?

That was the question I asked as the morning worked itself toward noon. I called. I rattled the kibbles in the food bowl. When my foot was once again in working order, I went around the garden looking for any sign of the paisley cat. Then I went around again. All the time I blamed myself. I'd had her in my arms! Now, due to my clumsiness, she was lost once more.

The garden was eerily quiet, just as it had been on my previous visits. The silence had made perfect sense in the pre-dawn morning, but now that the day was coming into full swing, it seemed spooky and wrong. I didn't understand what could insulate the place from the outside world in such a way. Was it the brick wall? The preponderance of trees? It could have been invisible alien tech for all its weirdness. Anywhere else, I would have heard trucks, airplanes, emergency sirens, and the ever-present blare of the city, but even as I tuned my ears to listen, all I picked up were bees in the flowers and birds in the trees.

Then I did hear something, a rustling of leaves. My heart leapt—this time I was not afraid. The sound was coming from around the corner of the house, the shaded side of the bungalow. I rose slowly, determined not to spook the elusive Hermione with my blundering, human moves. Proceeding cautiously, I took a few steps, then paused.

All had gone quiet again.

"Hermione, kitty kitty."

Nothing.

"Hermione, please come out," I bantered softly, hoping the sound of my voice would reassure her. "It's for your own good, you know. I'm so sorry your person has gone away. It wasn't her idea, believe me. I'm sure she'd much rather be here with you than in a hospital bed." I edged a few feet closer to where I'd last heard the rustle. "This is a lovely garden, and you seem to be doing alright on your own, but you really don't want to spend another night in the…"

Suddenly the sound took up again, but this time it was louder, and there was something else as well—footfalls. I sighed. Had Datura found me after all?

I considered running away, but I stopped myself. How would that look? As it stood, Datura's and my relationship was at least cordial. If Datura really was involved in Carry's misfortune, it would better for me if it stayed that way, which meant not apprising her of my mistrust. Of course if this convoluted web of intrigue was all in my head, and Datura was innocent, then there was no need to run in the first place.

No, better to face her and get it over with. How bad could it be? Another lecture on the cat gods of ancient Egypt? Another claim that she owned the marbled Maftet?

Taking a breath, I straightened my back and stepped boldly around the corner. The sun was in my eyes, but the area beyond was in deep shadow. At first I could see nothing, then a shape split from the darkness, neither cat nor woman but that of a huge man.

I gave an inadvertent cry as he loomed toward me.

I didn't think twice but took off at a run.

* * *

I ran to my car, jumped inside, and locked all the doors. Even then I wasted no time starting the engine and gunning it back down the hill toward home. I kept glancing in the rearview mirror, afraid that the big man had followed me, but the street remained empty. By the time I made it to my house, I'd begun to wonder if I had been overreacting.

I pulled up and parked, but I didn't get out of the car

right away. Instead I thought the whole business through one more time.

Granted it was a man, and granted he had come toward me, but for goodness sake, that in itself meant very little. Wouldn't it be more likely that, rather than someone harboring nefarious intent, he was the gas meter guy or even a police officer sent to recheck the scene?

In the few seconds before I turned tail and fled, I hadn't been able to distinguish anything about him, his clothing, his features. All I knew was that he was a big—very big—man. *Man in Black?* I flashed suddenly. But no, I didn't think so. Even in silhouette, this one hadn't carried himself with the same dodgy swagger as Datura's thug.

I sat a few minutes longer, letting the panic recede, then with a sigh, headed inside to attend to the cats.

Chapter 22

There is a common misconception that a house cat can survive just fine if suddenly dropped into the wild. It's true that all cats are resourceful, but a cat raised in a home will not have developed the skills to lead an out-of-doors life.

It may have been my birthday, but I had stuff to do. My party was set to start at four, and it was already nearing noon. As I rushed through my simple chores, the horror of my encounter in Carry's garden began to abate. One good thing had come of the morning's adventure—I had seen Hermione. I'd held her and gauged that she was essentially okay. Best of all, she had come to me. If she did it once, she would do it again.

Meanwhile, it was high time I visited Carry in the hospital. I could give her the good news that Hermione was alright and deliver the sketchbook into her hands. I'd already determined that getting the red journal back where it belonged was my best hope of distancing myself from this convoluted drama. Now I just had to do it. Maybe Carry would be awake and the doctors ready to release her. They hadn't done it yet, I surmised, or she would have come home. But whatever condition she was in, the sketchbook would be her problem, not mine.

After a hearty brunch of vegan lasagna and a fruit and ice smoothie, I changed my clothes, grabbed the sketchbook, and was on my way. Providence General was only a mile or so from my house, and I considered walking, but for some reason, I felt time was of the essence and ended up driving instead.

It took longer for me to locate an open place in the old parking structure than it did to get there, but finally I found one on the very top. Taking the elevator to the sky bridge, my mind jumped ahead. What would I find once I arrived? Would Carry want to see me? Would I even be allowed in since I wasn't a family member? I thought about sneaking by the admitting desk and heading straight up, but that would leave me essentially going on a door-to-door search through a warren of floors and rooms. Rejecting that idea, I went to check in like a good girl. There was really no reason they shouldn't admit me as a friend. And if I ran into a snag, I could always assert my senior status to persuade them to give me the information I required.

When I reached the desk, I found all my worry to have been for nothing, since aside from a guy in scrubs rummaging behind the counter, the place was unattended. He really didn't look like admittance staff, but I figured I'd couldn't hurt to try.

"Excuse me, but could you help me find a patient?"

The young man looked up from his crouching position, brown eyes peeking over the top of the counter. "I don't work in this department, ma'am."

"I'm sorry, but I really need to see her. When will the attendant be back?"

The guy rose—Mark, according to his ID tag—and cocked his head. "Gee, I really don't know. 'Cuz I don't work..."

"...in this department. Yes, you mentioned. But do you think you could look anyway?" I gave my best granny smile and nodded to the computer terminal. "She's been very ill and must see me as soon as possible. I'm her aunt."

Yes, I lied. And though I'm not good at it, poor Mark seemed content to take me at my word. He was a compassionate soul, and after a few moments deliberation, he gave a sympathetic smile and logged into the system.

"What's the name?"

"Carry, with a C."

I realized the problem instantly—I didn't know Carry's surname. Oops! An aunt really should know her niece's last name, shouldn't she?

"I'm not sure what she's going by now. We've been estranged...

"And she got married...

"And then she got divorced...

"And she may have changed it. Several times..." I knew I was over-explaining, a sure sign of a fib, but Mark didn't seem to notice.

"Looks like there is a Carry here." He peered closer at the screen. "That's funny."

"What?" I gasped, fearing the worst.

"Oh, nothing bad, ma'am," he soothed when he saw the look of terror on my face. "It's just that she's listed as 'Carry Doe,' like in 'John Doe.' I've never actually seen someone whose name really is Doe, is all."

I gave a sigh of relief. "Can you tell me her room number?"

"She's in ICU, second floor, unit sixteen. Take the blue elevator. Do you know where the blue elevator is?"

"I think so. Thanks so much. I really appreciate it."

"No problem, ma'am. Glad to help. I hope she's doing better."

I went in search of the blue elevator, past the gift shop with its colorful knickknacks, through the atrium hallway, and into the bowels of the hospital proper. I took a few wrong turns, but then I found a sign pointing to my destination and made it up to the second floor with no further delays.

As I counted the unit numbers down the sterile hallway—one, three, five, seven—I realized Carry's should be around the corner. I hurried toward the L-turn, more anxious with every step. A new worry raised its ugly head: What if Datura were there with her? What if she demanded I give her the sketchbook instead of leaving it with her partner?

Then I rounded the bend, and all my concerns were eclipsed by the big one: was Carry okay? An orderly was coming out of the room I guessed to be number sixteen. I watched as he deposited a roll of soiled bedding into a laundry hamper, then picked up a plastic cleaning caddy and headed back inside. There was a gurney sitting catawampus by the door, its tissue covering rumpled as if recently used. I had no reason to believe these things had anything to do with Carry, herself, or that even if they did, they boded ill, but still I shivered as I rushed ahead. Unit ten, twelve, fourteen—sure enough, the room in question was indeed hers.

I brushed past the orderly, hoping against hope to see Carry lying in a newly made bed, looking all bright and cheerful. Yes, the bed was newly made, but the rest of the scenario was a no-go. The unit was empty.

"Where is she?" I gasped.

A flash of emotion crossed the man's face as he fidgeted with a roll of paper towels. Then his expression went deadpan. "You need to ask at the nurses' station. Go back down the hallway the way you came..."

"I know where it is!" I snapped even as I ran out the

171

door, headed for it.

Though the cubicle with its computer stations, file cabinets, and white cupboards fixed with shiny silver locks was only a short distance, I was breathing heavily by the time I arrived. I felt like I had run a marathon, and moreover, that the ordeal had taken equally as long. It was anxiety, a disorder I knew all too well, that can distort time and warp the senses. The bane of my existence, anxiety turned everything around me terrifying and tragic. *Oh, no!* I screamed inwardly as I felt myself slipping into its paralyzing maw.

But panic attack or no, I couldn't let it deter me from my objective. "Where is the woman who was in unit sixteen? Carry?" I blurted to any one of the several people stationed at the desks. "Where is she?" I repeated when none of them gave an instant reply.

A young nurse at the workstation closest to me turned to an older woman standing at the back talking with a man in a doctor's coat. The older woman's face fell. She gave a sigh as she approached.

"Are you a friend or relative of Carry Doe's?" she asked guardedly.

"Yes! What's going on. They told me downstairs she would be here."

The woman gave a huff, then sighed again. "My name is Glorie. If you'll just come with me please."

She turned and started down the hallway. I followed.

"In here please." She gestured to a room with no number on the door. Once inside, I saw it was a tiny chapel.

"Please sit down."

I sat, just to get her to stop saying please, since her overt courtesy was beginning to scare me.

Glorie seated herself beside me on the wooden pew, pulled at the knife-like crease in her scrubs pants, then turned to me, her round face filled with the unmistakable sympathy that accompanies dreadful news.

"Where's Carry?" I repeated, but my voice had dwindled into a whisper. I already knew what she was about to say.

"What's your name, dear?"

"Lynley," I barely managed. "Lynley Cannon."

"Are you related to Carry?"

"Yes. No. Not really—I'm a friend, perhaps her only one."

"I'm afraid I have very bad news for you, Lynley," she said in the most solemn of tones, as if she had done this many times before.

"Carry Doe is dead."

* * *

"Dead?" I stuttered.

"Yes, dear. I'm afraid she never recovered from her injuries which were quite extensive. I can get the doctor to go over that with you if you wish."

"Dead?" I repeated. I needed to wrap my mind around that fact before it would allow me to move on to anything else. Carry dead. What did that mean?

"Yes, dear," Glorie was saying. "Would you like a few minutes alone?"

"Did she ever come out of the coma? Did she say anything?"

"Not that I know of. I can check."

"Would you please? It might be important."

A thought had begun to creep into my mind, black as a raven and lethal as a snake. "Did Carry have any other visitors this morning?"

"A couple came earlier. The woman said she was her partner. Her companion said nothing at all."

The snake began to curl python-like around my heart. "And Carry died sometime later?"

Glorie nodded but frowned, picking up on my trepidation. How was I going to word my fears?

"Are the doctors certain her cause of death was the head injury, and not... something else?"

"What are you asking?"

"Oh, nothing." I was being paranoid. Even Datura wouldn't walk brazenly into a hospital and kill someone. Would she? "Thanks so much for your kindness. And yes, if you could give me a minute, that would be..."

"Take as long as you need. Come by the desk when you're ready. I'll check with the staff to see if Carry had any last words, but as far as I know, it's doubtful."

"Thank you."

"You're welcome, Lynley. I'm sorry for your loss."

Glorie rose and left the room, left me to digest this new transpiration. Carry's death changed everything. Whether it stemmed from the original battering or something more heinous, the result was the same: Carry had been murdered!

For a moment, I sat in shock. Then strangely, my mind cleared and my anxiety lifted. I knew what was required of me now.

Chapter 23

Cats can change moods in the blink of an eye, but if you learn to watch their body language and heed the signs they give you, they're not nearly so apt to catch you off guard. A slow blink is a friendly sign, where a flicking tail can be a sign of discontent. In most cases, a hiss means leave me alone, though cats with sight or hearing impairment may hiss when surprised.

Carry was dead. Whoever had lashed into her had caused her death, which made it murder—manslaughter at the very least. But that wasn't my problem—the police would be handling the legal side of things. My problem was soft and spotted and alive—Hermione. Since I still laid my bets on either Datura or her Man in Black being the killer, it was more important than ever that Hermione not fall into their hands.

I drove directly from the hospital to the bungalow, praying the whole way that Hermione would be there napping in her carrier-slash-cubbie or chomping the kibbles on the veranda. I tried to picture her in my mind, coming to me, tail in the air, speaking little *purrumphs* of welcome. Positive thinking—my father had believed in it wholeheartedly, and right now I chose to believe as well.

I parked, pulled on the emergency brake, and was out of the car in one fluid move. I didn't bother to see if the neighbors were watching but hightailed it through the gate and around to the back garden. Once there, I consciously slowed my step—I didn't want to spook the poor cat again.

Moving along the red gravel path, I called her name.

And there she was, sitting tall on the veranda stoop like a little marbled statue of Bast, the Egyptian cat goddess. I couldn't believe my luck as I thanked both the Powers that Be who had heard my prayer and my father who had taught me that optimism carried a strength of its own.

"Hermione, sweetie, I'm so glad to see you. Be calm. Everything's alright now. You're going to be coming home with me."

The cat rose, stretching first her front legs, then her back, one at a time. She uttered a little meow and came straight for me, giving me a look which seemed to say, "Where have you been? I was waiting."

I crouched down to her, slowly. I was still wary of scaring her, but I needn't have worried. She smoothed her face along my hand, then rose and put her front paws on my leg. I lifted her into my arms and she cuddled, purring contentedly. For a few moments, I just held her, then I began to calculate.

I'd taken the gate off the carrier to use it as a shelter box, and I hadn't thought to bring another one, so the only way to transport her to my car was in my arms. If I went carefully, would she allow it? I knew it was a gamble. A loud noise, a barking dog, or that lawn mower down the street could send her scrambling. I could scruff her and tuck her under my arm like a football as we did in the shelter, but at the shelter, the hold was only required for a few steps; this distance was much farther.

Rats! I told myself. Though my goal of the day had been to recover Hermione, now that I had her, I was completely unprepared.

Meanwhile the cat in question was snuggling deeper

into my arms. She seemed happy and content where she was, so I decided to roll with it and head for the car. If I felt her tense, I could scruff her then. Hopefully she would stay calm and the ordeal would be over.

I began to head back down the path when I heard a sound behind me.

"I see you have found her," came Datura's honeyed voice. "Our goddess has come back to us."

As I turned, Hermione lifted her head. With one look at Datura, she gave a hiss.

"Oh, my darling Maftet!" Datura crooned as she closed on the cat without regard for the feline warning. "Give her to me," was the vehement command.

"I think she's happy right where she is," I countered. "She doesn't seem to like you much, or did you not notice?"

"It is nothing. The scent of my other cat."

"I have eight cats, and she doesn't mind their smell on me. No, Datura, I think I should hold onto her. That's what Carry would have wanted... now that she's dead."

I'd put that out there to gage Datura's reaction, but there was none.

"You've already heard?" I pressed.

Still nothing.

"Did you kill her?" I blurted, though I hadn't meant to go down that road.

Datura glared at me with those kohl-lined eyes, emerald orbs shooting fire. Then she blinked innocently.

"Of course I didn't kill her. I thought we had already discussed this. I would never hurt Carry. Besides, I was in business meetings. I can prove it if you wish."

"What about this morning?"

"What about it?"

"I know you were at the hospital."

Datura winced. "You know a lot of things, don't you, Lynley? But your imagination is overactive. I did not wish any harm on Carry, before or now."

"If not you, then your man."

"Kurt?" She laughed. "Don't be ridiculous. Why would he hurt Carry?"

"Because you told him to," I answered bluntly.

"I did nothing of the sort." Datura gave a shrug. "You have this all wrong. I held no resentments toward Carry, even though she double-crossed me and cost me a lot of money. That is the chance one takes when doing business. I suggested that she make things right, that's all."

"*Suggested*? At the hands of your thug?"

Datura scoffed. "Believe me or don't."

"Okay, but you can't deny you sent him to the bungalow to get that sketchbook—the journal. I was there, remember? I saw him."

That got Datura's interest, and she gave me a startled look.

"Yes," I reiterated. "I wasn't passed out like he thought. I saw the whole thing."

Okay, so I was fudging a bit. I really had no idea who the large person in the black Neo coat might have been, but Datura didn't know that. She would now either continue to deny her involvement or admit to it.

"You saw who hurt Carry?" she burst out, taking neither path. "Who? Who was it?"

This caught me off guard. She sounded angry as well as amazed. Could I be wrong in thinking she was the one who instigated the assault?

I looked away. Hermione was getting heavy in my arms, but at least she was making no move to jump down.

"I didn't see the face. He was big, like your guy. Dressed in black." I paused. "But if you weren't behind it, who was?"

For a moment, Datura looked confused. Then she muttered something under her breath that sounded like a swear. "But none of that matters now. Just the cat. Here, Lynley, you must at least let me hold her."

We were back to that again, Datura's claim on Hermione. She took a step toward me, and I pulled away.

"Have it your way." She paused, then stretched out her hand, the blood tips of her fingernails glinting in the sun. "A caress, then. What can it hurt?"

Without waiting for my approval, Datura swooped in, but instead of a simple pet, she grabbed Hermione around the torso. Momentarily I held on, but knowing a tussle could injure the cat, I relinquished her into Datura's grasp.

Hermione had other plans, however. With a quick and lethal swipe across Datura's chalk-pale face, she twisted away and vaulted to the ground. Datura cried out in rage and pain, pressing a hand to the parallel scratches that were beginning to bleed red on the white.

"Get it!" she yelled. "Get that cat now!"

For a moment, I didn't understand, then a figure materialized out of the shadows—Man in Black.

In spite of his muscled bulk, he was quick to corner the angry cat. He had no qualms about grabbing her by the scruff, and within seconds, had her tucked tightly under his arm. She struggled for a moment, then went limp.

"Stop that!" I yelled, "You let that poor cat go!"

I stepped toward the man and raised my fists, ready to...

Ready to, what? Beat up this brute who was twice my size? Again, playing tug of war was out of the question.

Datura approached Hermione, a little more cautiously

than before but with the same rude intent.

"Don't hurt her!"

Datura ignored me as she cautiously reached out. "Forgive me, my goddess," she said to the cat. Then with a deft move, she snatched the red collar. The break-away clasp came apart. Datura whirled away, holding the prize in her hand.

Hermione was struggling again in spite of the scruffing.

"Yeow!" Man in Black shrieked as sharp claws raked his arm and dagger teeth ripped into the flesh of his hand.

"Don't be such a wuss, Kurt," Datura said to the whimpering henchman.

"She's a devil, this cat!"

"Let her go if you must. We do not need her anymore."

The man dropped Hermione like a hot potato, and she raced away, hightailing it into the garden with a hiss.

"No!" I cried as I watched the angry cat disappear once again. Would she ever come out after the rough treatment she had received at the hands of that vicious goon?

There was nothing to be done about that now, so I turned my attention to Datura who was examining the cat collar with a mix of awe and purpose.

"Why the…?" I began.

Datura snapped her fingers, and without hesitation, Man in Black was upon me. Though he didn't actually touch me, the threat was palpable. Forcing myself to be still, I waited to see what would come next.

Datura was fiddling with Hermione's collar. I had noticed before that it wasn't the standard style one found at the pet stores. This was wider, bulkier, and sewn from fine silk brocade. I'd thought maybe it contained some calming herbs, or even flea repellent, but as she pulled the stitching, the article unrolled like a scroll, revealing nothing so commonplace.

Datura sighed like a lover as she plucked something from the folds. She turned and held it out to me. A tiny, gold and lapis cat face with a short, metal shaft descending like a tongue. No bigger than a beetle, it looked ancient—and arcane.

"The key!" Datura exclaimed, wrapping her fist possessively around it. "Now I shall have what is due me."

"And what would that be?"

Datura's gaze became clouded, as if she were looking inward. "There is an artifact, the most precious in the known world. For a time, Carry and I possessed it together. Then it was lost." Her vision cleared and her stare fixed on me, hatred sparking from her eyes. "You took it. Five years ago. There was a duffle, a drop at a warehouse. Do you remember it?"

"Of course I remember. Who could forget dodging bullets?"

"But still you held onto the duffle. If you had just let it go, none of that would have happened."

"Hermione was inside," I said flatly. "I couldn't leave her. And the zipper was stuck so I couldn't get her out. I had no choice."

Datura grunted. "Maftet had crawled inside. We did not know until much later how profound was our loss."

I thought back, going over the scene once again. It seemed like I'd been doing that a lot lately, but I always came up with the same scenario.

"Drugs, money, Hermione and her toy. I don't recall anything close to an artifact in the bag."

Datura was silent, raging.

"The cat toy?" That was the only thing that made

sense.

"The ball, yes, and a very distinctive one. You may have noticed." Her look soured even more. "Carry taunted me, told me how you had delivered it to her intact. After all these years, it was a miracle."

With a flash, I remembered! "I saw you pocket it last time you were here, but I couldn't figure out why."

"It was wishful thinking. Of course Carry had removed the artifact. The toy was empty."

"Smart," I commented.

"Smart but not smart enough, since I knew how Carry's mind worked. There is a vault, and a key." She held up the tiny mechanism. "I guessed the location of the key—she had used that hiding place before, when we were still partners. Even then she sought to evade me," Datura added with a grimace.

She turned her gaze upward, seemingly lost in the blue of the sky, then her eyes snapped back to me. "I need only one thing more, and you, Lynley, have possession of that as well."

"What?" I asked though I feared I already knew.

Confirming my suspicion, she took my chin between her long fingers.

"The journal. I need Carry's journal."

Chapter 24

Cat scratch fever isn't just the title of a song from the seventies. If a cat scratches you, immediately wash the area with soap and water, and for the next two weeks, watch for signs of infection such as a red bump or blister, a low-grade fever, headache, fatigue, or poor appetite.

"I need that journal," Datura spat. "It tells where in this chaos of a garden the vault can be found."

I thought back on Carry's detailed drawings. In none had I seen anything that resembled a vault.

"I know you have it," Datura went on. "Your little friend Patty told me." She sighed, nodding toward the bungalow. "Yes, I admit I did send Kurt for the journal, but only that. He had nothing to do with the violence."

"So Carry just gave herself a fatal blow to the head?" I muttered.

"I do not know what happened. Only that Kurt did not do it."

"He told you that? And you trust him?"

"I do."

I had to admit she sounded like she was telling the truth, her version of it at least.

"Well, too bad he didn't find what he was looking for," I commented.

"Oh, he found it." She turned a withering look on her henchman. "Just not the right one. The book he brought to me was empty."

I laughed in spite of myself. "She'd just bought a new one. Oops."

At first, Datura looked angry, and I realized I should be careful about pushing her buttons with Kurt still hovering way too close. I could easily become his prisoner in a snap of Datura's long fingers. But then her face went blank and she waved a hand in the air.

"No matter now, a short delay to a long plan, a plan that has taken years to come to its fruition. First I needed to locate Carry," she explained, as if to a child. "She had done a superb job of disappearing after our breakup. She eluded me for years, until that day on the street with you."

"I told you, I barely know her. It was a coincidence we met at all."

"Enough!" Datura shouted. "Kurt, take her to get the book. I will see you back here once it is in your hands."

"What about her?" Kurt asked, eyeing me doubtfully.

"Do what you will. No, wait," Datura countered. "Best bring her back with you. I wouldn't want her alerting anyone of what we are about to do."

Kurt nodded perfunctorily, and I was almost surprised he didn't salute as well. It was clear Datura had all the power and then some.

Without warning, the big man grabbed me by the wrists. Pinning my hands behind my back, he began to propel me toward the gate.

"Let me go!" I cried impotently.

"I'm not hurting you," he snapped back, "and I won't, if you do as she says."

"What makes you think I'll tell you where I live?" I snapped.

He gave a grunt. "Oh, you'll tell me. I have no doubt."

"No need." A man stepped out from the shadow of a

beech tree. I didn't recognize him, but Datura did.

"Craven!" She exclaimed, turning all sorts of red underneath her pancake makeup. "What do you think you're doing here?"

"The same thing as you, I'd wager," the man said obliquely.

Dr. Wil Craven—I remembered now! The good-looking, well-put-together gentleman doctor pictured on the blue flyers that had cropped up all over town. Wearing a casual suit, he looked more like the man I'd seen at the rhododendron gardens than the model in the picture. Again I wondered at his relationship with the strange Datura.

"My goodness, Dee," Craven said, peering at the tall woman. "What happened to you?"

Datura gave him a questioning stare, then touched her face where the three long marks scarred the white cheek.

"It's nothing," she grumbled. "A cat scratch."

Craven's eyebrows rose. "I must say, it becomes you, dear. Have you ever considered an eye patch? To show people the pirate you really are."

Craven was smiling that charming little-boy grin as Datura's face grew angrier by the second. She began to signal her henchman, but Craven held something up in his hand.

"I wouldn't do that if I were you," he snickered, waving the object with obvious glee—Carry's sketchbook!

"How did you...?" I gasped.

Craven looked at me, the smile growing even wider. "You left it in your bag in the car, Lynley. It is Lynley isn't it? We haven't met, though I've heard a lot about you. You should have locked the doors. You never know who might decide to rummage through your things."

"It was here all the time?" Datura gasped.

She gave me a black look, then turned her hatred on Craven. Even as she crossed the distance between them, her hand darted out to grab for the book.

"Give it to me!"

"I don't think so, Dee," he teased, holding it just out of her reach.

"Give it!"

"Not a chance."

Craven was obviously enjoying their game of keep-away, but Datura tired of it quickly and kicked him hard in the shins with her pointy-toed Gianvito Rossis. Craven grunted with pain; the sketchbook fell to the ground.

"You didn't have to do that, Dee," he said, rubbing his leg. "I was just teasing."

"Shut up, Wil. You're not nearly as funny as you think you are."

He turned to me, eyebrows raised in mock surprise. "What do you think, Lynley?" The doctor approached me, that salesman smile never wavering. "Let her go, will you, Kurt? For goodness' sake, don't be so rude."

I glanced up at my captor. Man in Black seemed confused. He shot a look to Datura, but she just shrugged. The big hands loosened, then dropped from my wrists. I jumped back, putting as much distance between myself and the ogre as I could without actually running away.

Run away—that was what I should have done, but the string of thoughts that fast-flashed through my mind kept me riveted: Datura and Kurt hauling Carry down Belmont Street; Carry as I had first seen her, holding Dirty Harry in her arms; a distant but still-distinct memory of a kitten in a gym bag—Hermione.

Somewhere in this strange red garden, Hermione was hiding. I couldn't leave her as long as these people were present and could do her harm.

Besides, things were just getting interesting.

Chapter 25

From the First Dynasty of Egypt, Cats were praised for killing venomous snakes and protecting the Pharaoh. Skeletal remains of cats were found among funerary goods dating to the 12th Dynasty.

Datura had the sketchbook open and was poring over the pages. Dr. Craven stared across her shoulder, then pushed in beside her to get a better look. At first I thought there would be another scuffle, but she seemed past that. Now all that mattered was interpreting the meaning of Carry's drawings.

"I've got it," he cried, pulling the book from Datura's hands. Turning until he was facing the direction indicated by one of the sketches, he studied the scene. After a few moments' contemplation, he flipped the page, moved to another spot, and did the same thing. One more go and he closed the book with a snap.

"Well?" Datura hissed. "You have figured it out?"

"Yes," he said with all the pride of a male lion after a meal provided by his queen. "If I'm not mistaken—" He paused, flashing that grin again. "...and I'm not—what we're looking for will be right..." He took a few paces toward the brick wall that surrounded Carry's garden. "...here!"

He began to push aside a thick patch of dwarf barberry but pulled back with a cry.

"Youch!" he yelped. "Those things have thorns."

"You are sure that's the place?" Datura replied without sympathy.

"As sure as I can be. Go ahead. Take a look."

Datura stepped forward and peered down at the red bush. "Kurt," she commanded.

The henchman swaggered over, and without hesitation, swept the shrubbery aside. The sharp briars raised welts among the cat scratches on his forearm, but his stoicism never wavered

Datura crouched down to inspect something near to the ground, and so did Craven. I was more than satisfied to assess their discovery from afar.

"The vault!" Datura cried. "We have discovered Carry's vault." She jumped up. "Now get this stupid bush out of my way."

Kurt withdrew a huge tactical knife from a sheath in his boot and began to whack. After a few minutes of snapping twigs and pulling roots, the shrub was gone, revealing a rusted metal plate with a circumference about the size of a large cantaloupe. Kurt brushed away the dirt and leaves with the tail of his black tee shirt.

Shoving the thug aside, Datura and Craven jostled like a pair of comedians doing an act to get a better look. Though curious as a kitten with a new toy, I was loath to move any closer for fear I would end up a prisoner again. I couldn't see details from where I stood, but the thing looked old. Very old.

"The key," Craven stuttered. "Try the key!"

"That is what I'm doing, you imbecile," Datura retorted.

"Come now, dear Dee," Craven scolded. "No need for vulgarity among friends."

Datura gave him a look of pure hatred. "You are not

my friend."

"Your loss," said the handsome doctor. The words were innocent enough but carried an ominous undertone.

Datura held his stare a moment longer, then with the little cat-face key gripped between her fingers, she moved her hand toward the plate. Metal touched metal, but there she stopped.

"This is mine," she said to Craven. "I'll kill you before I let you take it from me."

Glancing at the henchman who stood ready to do his mistress's bidding, the doctor threw up his hands in surrender. "I get it. It's yours. I just want to see it. You can't begrudge me that after all we've been through to come to this point."

Her stare lingered on the man, then dismissing him, she got busy with the key.

Datura's back was to me, but judging from her body language, she was having trouble with the mechanism. There was swearing going on, and sweat was beginning to stain her silk tunic.

Suddenly something changed. She jumped back with a cry. There was a grating sound and a pop, then the metal lid sprang open. As one, Datura and Craven leaned over the hole and peered inside.

"Well, well," Craven muttered.

"It's empty!" Datura screamed. "All for nothing!"

"No, wait. Look at this."

Craven reached in. I watched his arm disappear up to the elbow. There was another pop and more grating, but this time it was far louder and not coming from the plate but from the nearby brick wall.

The sound became deafening as a cloud of gray dust began to roil. The climbing rose tore apart in a flurry of leaves and petals and a shadow appeared, breaking the continuity of the brick. The shadow became a gap, and the gap, a fissure.

"What the hay?" Craven gasped.

"Carry's vault!" Datura cried. "This must be the entrance. The other is merely the releasing device."

"But so big...?" Craven began. "Why, she could have a whole museum down there."

Datura wasn't listening. As soon as the gap was wide enough for a body to pass, she ran for it. I fully expected her to forge on in, but instead she paused at the threshold.

Turning to Craven, her face even paler than usual if that were possible, she said in a whisper, "What does it mean?"

"That's not for you to know, Datura," came a slow, slightly asexual drawl from behind me.

I recognized that voice instantly—the person who'd been so insistent I leave Carry's house, right before he attacked.

Whipping around, I saw him looming in the gateway—pale skin and hair so blond as to be nearly white. Though the black Neo coat had been swapped for a white skin-tight tee shirt and white pants, he was definitely the same man. And not just any man—this was Man in White—Datura's second thug!

While his steel-blue gaze was fixed on Datura, I started to back away—no treasure was intriguing enough for me to face off with both Datura's henchmen—but before I could slip around the corner and disappear into the proverbial sunset, the gaze latched onto me.

"Where do you think you're going?" he barked.

I froze. "Just... getting out of the way. I really have nothing to do with this."

He seemed to think about it. "Okay, but I'll be watching you."

Watching me. The words sparked something in my memory. The man who'd been watching my house from his car, the shadow watching from the bushes, the guy who'd come at me from the side of the bungalow. Again I studied the henchman. It fit. "Was that you?"

"I had to take care of Carry, didn't I?"

"Take care of her?" I gasped. "You mean kill her?"

The big man turned away, declining an answer, but that was answer enough. And now it was time for me to leave. Before, when he'd told me to get out, I hadn't complied. If I had, I could have saved myself a whole lot of grief. This time I had every intention of taking that advice.

I'd only made it a few steps however when a new exchange caught me by surprise.

"You shouldn't have come back, Datura. Back to the scene of your crime."

"Harley!" she spat. "I have committed no crime, but you... you are another story."

"You killed Carry." The tone was flat and accusing, leaving no doubt that Man in White—Harley—meant what he said.

My gaze moved to Datura. To my amazement, his words had her flustered.

"She had nothing to do with it," Kurt defended, stepping between Datura and his pale counterpart.

Harley's blue stare shot to the darker man. "I see you're still loyal as ever, Kurtis. Willing to fall on your sword for your mistress."

"At one time, she was your mistress too, Harley. But you betrayed her."

"Carry was always my commander. When she broke

from her thieving partner, naturally I went with her. I've been with her ever since... when she would allow it."

"Then you've failed your mission, brother," Kurt mocked. "Carry is dead."

Harley gave a grunt that on a lesser man might have been a sob. "When Carry broke from your Lady and went into hiding, she dismissed me, assuming my services were no longer needed. But I knew better. I continued to work in secrecy. But you're right. I did fail."

"Fail or kill?" Kurt pressed. "I was there, Harley. Carry was alive when I left the bungalow. Can you say the same?"

"Why, you!" Harley spat, his temper flaring. "I'm done talking to the servant when it's the master who is to blame."

With long strides, Harley began to close on Datura, fierce intention blazing in his rage-filled face. He'd only made it a few steps when Kurt lunged into him with the force of a power shovel. The two big men began to brawl, throwing and landing blows like a pair of cage fighters.

For a moment, Datura stood, watching them go at each other, Hercules and the Cretan Bull; then she turned to the gap in the wall and ran on in.

Or more accurately, she ran *down*. I watched as she stepped ever lower until she disappeared into the ground. Craven hesitated only a moment before following. I glanced at the thugs who were still fighting like dogs, then I, being more cat than canine, zipped around them. Running full tilt after the Lady and the doctor, I headed into the unknown.

Chapter 26

Because the ancient Egyptians worshiped cats, many cat relics have been found in that area, but cats were revered in other places as well. Many paintings from the Middle Age depict cats, often catching mice.

I rushed to get past Man in Black and Man in White as they duked it out in the garden, but once through the dark maw in the wall, I lingered. A rough stone staircase led straight down to blackness, broken only by the twin blue-white glows—Craven's and Datura's cell phones. Suddenly I wondered what I was doing, running into an enclosed space with the enemy.

I looked back at the fighters who were circling each other, coming closer every second. Both now sported battle wounds—a torn tee shirt, a split lip, a blackened eye. Kurt was holding his big knife front and center, and Harley had picked up a garden spade which he was brandishing like a club. As the two loomed toward me with the ferocity of an oncoming tornado, I decided I'd be better off taking my chances in the vault. Datura might be vile, but I doubted she carried out her aggression with her own hands. Dr. Craven was certainly involved in ways I had yet to discover, but I didn't see him as the violent type.

Besides, I was curious. A hidden key to a hidden device that opened a hidden door to a hidden cave? Who wouldn't be?

Just then Harley thwacked Kurt with the shovel. As

Kurt came reeling straight for me with all his two hundred-pound bulk, my decision was made.

Down I went, rushing the first few steps, then slowing when I realized I couldn't see where I was going. The men had veered off now, and I thought briefly about heading back out again. But no, I'd made it this far. I wanted to see what all this fuss was about.

Following the cell phone beams, I felt my way to the bottom without mishap. As my eyes adjusted to the low light in the small cavern, I saw Datura and Dr. Craven busy exploring as if it were the most important thing in the world. To Datura, and possibly Craven as well, it probably was.

Since my bag which contained my own light-giving device was back in the car, I found myself at their mercy. Datura had gone to the left and Craven to the right. I chose to join the doctor, a feline archaeologist seeming safer than an enigmatic, sometimes scary ex-partner of a dead woman.

"What is this place?" I whispered as I approached the tall man.

"Oh, Lynley," the man gasped. "You surprised me." A beam flashed in my face, then dropped to the floor revealing a pattern of brick slates, cracked and dusty but still beautiful in their antiquity. "It was probably a grotto, built around the turn of the century. See the tiles? They were into that sort of thing back then."

The phone light ran along the ground for a few moments more, then began to play up the stone wall. Every so often, the glow revealed a niche in the rock. Each held a wood and Lucite box containing an antique treasure—an urn painted with Greek characters; a Chinese porcelain vase; an Egyptian ankh carved from stone—but

Craven passed them by as if they weren't worth his time.

"What are you looking for?"

"Something fantastic," he said without pausing his search.

I glanced over at Datura. She was doing the same as Craven, safely away on the other side of the room.

Craven's beam bounced across an especially craggy place, then returned to inspect it more carefully. There was a deeper hole, a black void in the stone of the wall. As the doctor moved the light into the niche, a form began to take shape—gaping eye sockets, a glimmer off a white dome of bone.

With a tight scream, I cringed away. Craven had no such qualms; in fact I thought I caught him smiling. He leaned forward for a closer look, then reached a brave hand into the niche. Pulling out the dusty skull, he held it up like a modern-day Hamlet.

"Ugh," I exclaimed in disgust.

He turned it toward me. "It's not real. Polished clay, by the feel of it. A cat, most likely a jaguar."

I let myself relax a little, but now that I knew these nooks might hold anything, I was much less enthusiastic about getting the first glimpse.

"No box," I remarked as he returned the relic to its hole. "It looks like it's been here for centuries. Do you think it came with the place?"

"It is old, pre-Columbian, but it's not from the Pacific Northwest. My guess would be Mayan. They sculpted many such figures from limestone and volcanic ash"

"Do you think Carry put it here?"

"Yes," he said solemnly, casting his light around the chamber. "This would be her collection, stolen from museums all over the world."

I looked at the doctor, his face intent in the phone's glow. *Carry's collection of stolen goods*, I thought to myself. Another piece in the puzzle that was Carry.

Craven and Datura were progressing around the perimeter of the cavern. Eventually they would meet up with each other, and I wasn't sure I wanted to be there when they did. With the discovery of the skull, real or not, treasure hunting had got a whole lot less appealing for me, and I figured it was time to head back topside while I still had the chance.

"Ahhh," Datura hissed, then snapped her mouth shut. It was too late. Both Craven and I knew she had found what she was looking for.

Turning her kohl-lined eyes wide upon us, she stood stock still.

Craven began toward her. "Here, let me see..."

Datura grabbed a small box from the wall and tore it open, withdrawing something that sparkled wildly, even in the vault's haphazard lighting. For a moment, she cradled the item in her palm, then dropping the container, she popped it into her pocket and was on the run.

Craven lunged after her as she bolted for the exit, but she slipped through his grasp, hightailing it up the steps two at a time. The doctor pursued, but Datura had the advantage of the higher ground and she knew it. Swiveling on her heel, she brought up a booted foot and planted it in the center of his chest. With a gasp, the man toppled backward, down the stairs, and straight into me.

Craven and I fell in a jumble of arms and legs that undid any good results from my shoulder therapy. As I screamed in pain, Datura sped out the door, yelling as she ran.

"Close it! Close it!" she called to her thug.

As the doctor and I worked to disentangle, I heard the grating sound that meant we would soon be on the wrong side of a very thick door. By the time we'd made it to our feet, it was already too late.

"Dee, wait!" Craven called, racing after her. He threw himself at the diminishing exit, but the space was too small and growing smaller all the time.

Just as the door was about to snap shut, I saw a mottled blur streak through the breach. Hermione launched herself at me. I held out my arms, and with the force of something twice her size, she landed. Burrowing her face in my neck, she gave a little mewl. I held her tight, and she embraced me back. Frightened claws dug into my shoulders, but I barely felt them. With a resounding thunk, the brick door slammed tight, leaving Craven, Hermione, and me in absolute dark.

"Nooo...!" Craven wailed.

"Turn on your phone," I gasped, but nothing happened.

Then I heard a clapping sound, an object striking against the palm of a hand.

"Good grief!" he swore. "This old thing! What a time for the batteries to fail."

Something hard, presumably the dead cell phone, hit the floor and skittered across the tiles. After that came a scream of absolute anguish.

"Dr. Craven!" I cried. "What is it?"

The scream died away, but then another sound emerged, a whimper followed by a full-fledged sob.

Though my heartrate was elevated, and anxiety pressed at the edges of my consciousness, I suddenly realized the doctor was much worse off. I had no love for being stuck in a lightless cavern, but his gut reaction was based somewhere far more primal.

"Claustrophobia?" I asked as gently as I could and still have my voice heard over his hysteria. When he didn't react, I continued, "Try to relax your muscles, Dr. Craven. Take a deep breath. In and out, in and out."

The sobs turned to hiccups, then the hiccups grew quieter as he took my advice.

"That's good. Now keep it up. Breathe in-two-three-four. Out-two-three-four."

Hermione, who had been clinging to my neck, loosed herself and hopped down. A few seconds later, there was another scream.

"Something's in here with us!" Craven yelled.

"It's only Hermione, Dr. Craven. It's the cat."

"Call... me... Wil..." he managed, though his voice was strained and hollow. "Oh, yes, sweet Hermione," he crooned, and as his breathing evened, I assumed the cat was working her feline magic on the frightened man.

"I'm usually okay with it," Wil whispered shakily. "I've done desensitization work. It's just that... It's just this..."

"I know. This is extreme."

"I can handle it. Just give me a minute."

I waited, listening to Hermione's rhythmic purr. "Better?" I finally asked.

"Better. A little. But I think enough."

Now that Wil's phobia was in check, I found that mine was ramping up. *No way out,* I fretted. *Would there be enough air? What if we were stuck for days? Would we starve? Were there bugs? —I don't like bugs. Would someone come and find us? Ever?*

The temperature had plummeted in the underground room, and I shivered in my thin sweater. I felt a tear trickle down my cheek. Rats! If I succumbed to anxiety, I'd be lost.

Breathe, I told myself this time. *In-out, in-out...*

The rhythm helped me as it had the doctor, and as I calmed, I tried to focus on other things. In a dark room, however, the possibilities were limited.

Adjusting my next-to-useless glasses and opening my eyes, owl-like, I peered around for something—anything—for my sight to latch onto. At first there was only black on black, but as my gaze moved past the doorway, a point caught my peripheral vision. I glanced back and saw a tiny spot of light coming through a dime-sized hole in the door. Immediately I dashed up the stairs and put my eye to it. All I could see was the patterned leaves of the rose tree, but it was enough.

"There's a hole here," I called back to the doctor. "At least we won't die of asphyxiation. And maybe someone will be able to hear our cry for help if they come close enough."

I turned away, shoulders sagging. *If they come close...* The only people in the red garden were the two warring thugs and the vile harpy that put us there in the first place. Who else would be dropping by a dead woman's yard?

"Well, it's better than nothing, isn't it?" I said impotently as I felt my way back, sinking down onto the bottom step. A useless observation.

Something bumped into my thigh, and I cried out.

"Sorry, Lynley. Just me," said Wil, his foot on the tread.

"Oh, right. I'm a bit jumpy, I guess."

"I'm going to see if I can open the door from inside. Here, come help me."

I rose and followed up the short stairs once more. Together we threw our full weight against the rough brick. I pushed with all my not-considerable might, said a fervent prayer, and pushed some more. I guessed by his grunts Wil was doing the same, yet there was not even the slightest shift to the unforgiving stone, not a single sound of the rough door beginning to budge.

"It's no use," I said. "The thing opens inward. There's no way we could push it out."

I stood back, still balanced on the top step. I could feel Wil's warmth beside me as he muttered, "We had to try."

In the tiny glow from the hole, I watched him begin running his hands along the seal. "Find anything?" I asked.

"I was hoping there might be a mechanism, some sort of spring latch, but so far, it's just brick and more brick."

"Let's keep looking," I said, drawing my fingertips along the walls as I descended the stairs. "I'll check down here."

We worked away at it, hands caressing every inch of the terracotta, until it became clear that whoever built the grotto all those decades ago had not meant for it to be opened from within.

Sinking to my knees, I collapsed on the dusty tile.

"You're giving up?" Wil asked winsomely.

"Yeah. You?"

"For now. I need to think. I've read about these grottos, and it seems to me there was something… some way… Oh, fiddlesticks, I wish I had an eidetic memory like some of my colleagues."

Suddenly I burst into a fit of completely inappropriate laughter. "You know, Wil, when I first heard of you, I questioned whether you were a real doctor at all."

"Why?" he squeaked, taken off guard.

"I don't know. I guess I'd never run across a feline archaeologist before."

"And you refuse to accept anything you don't already know?" he scoffed. "That seems terribly narrow-minded, Lynley."

"Maybe it was the brochure," I mused. "Like those iffy dentists you see on late night television commercials. Or the doctors who promise to suck out all your fat cells for less cost than the other guy. I don't trust physicians that advertise."

"You didn't like my flyer?" His voice was peevish, a little boy lilt.

"It's not that I didn't like it," I said, feeling a pang of guilt at my insult. "It was nice..."

"My publisher hired a team of very expensive media experts to come up with the brand."

"Your publisher?"

"Yes, of course, to promote my book. You don't think I'd bother to do that for myself, do you?"

"I have no idea. I just assumed."

"Well, I wouldn't. I wrote the book, and I want people to read it. The ad team said this was the way—the book tour, the presentations and in-person signings. The only thing I care about is the science."

I'd never considered that Craven, the man, and Craven, the celebrity pictured on the shiny blue brochure, might be two different personas. I'd been quick to judge, and as Wil said, I'd been narrow-minded as well.

Accepting the possibility I'd been wrong about the doctor, I asked in a more sympathetic tone, "How are you doing? Is your claustrophobia settling down?"

"Cat's in my lap," he said softly. "Cures all ills."

"So you like cats?"

"Very much," he answered gently. "That's why I chose to study their influence on our oldest cultures."

"That does sound interesting," I acquiesced. "I guess I'll have to catch your lecture after all."

Then something completely different crossed my mind.

"Datura and Carry—what on Earth is your connection there?"

Chapter 27

The ancient Egyptians worshiped many zoomorphic deities. Bast, daughter of the sun god Re, was given the form of a lioness and later, a cat.

Craven was silent. As my eyes adapted to the smattering of photons coming through the hole in the door, I could see his outline. He seemed pensive.

"Carry and Dee," he said finally. "Long ago and far away, as they say in the movies. It seems like something out of a movie," he added, "as I look back on it now."

My mind filled with questions, but I squelched them so as not to break his concentration, a fragile thing in our dubious state.

He turned to face me. "How much do you know about those two and their trafficking business?"

"Next to nothing. I only met Carry a few days ago, then Datura after that. It never crossed my mind they were criminals."

Then I reconsidered. "No, that's not entirely true. I sensed something iffy, especially from Datura. But smugglers? That wouldn't have been my first guess."

"Yes, rare pieces from South America, Africa, and Asia. Sometimes they set themselves up as legitimate archaeologists, other times as Canadian buyers. They got their henchmen to steal the articles that would bring the most value in illegal sales."

"Kurt and Harley?"

"They're the ones. A nasty pair of brutes for sure."

"I know. I had a little run in with them myself, five years ago while they were still working together."

"Oh? But I thought you said..."

"That I didn't know Carry and Datura before this week? That's true, but I'd met their thugs, and it wasn't pretty."

"Tell me about it."

I wanted to hear his story, not relive mine, but I supposed it couldn't hurt to give a brief outline. Anything to keep the darkness from closing in.

"I'd found something of theirs—a gym bag that turned out to contain money and drugs, and a kitten. The kitten was Hermione." I petted the cat who had settled on the step between Wil and me. "Then someone began shooting, and I ran." I felt my heart beat faster, as if I were running now, running for my life. "At the time I couldn't think of why they would pursue me for a kitten. It was only later that I learned about the other stuff in the bag."

"You got away," Wil posed, "since you're here to tell the tale."

"Yeah, I got away, but only because someone else started shooting at the thug brothers. My friends came and got me out of there, me and Hermione. That was the last I knew until I ran into Carry the other day. I recognized Hermione immediately. Even five years later, her unique markings are unmistakable."

Wil was silent—thinking or succumbing to his phobia again?

"I know this story. Carry told me when we became friends."

I turned in surprise. "What?" I stuttered. "What did she say?"

"There was something else in that bag, Lynley, besides the cat and the contraband. Something of utmost importance to both partners."

"The artifact," I said quietly.

"That's right. You see, Carry and Dee were already on the angry cusp of their partnership breakup. They knew the separation was inevitable, and each wanted to get away with as much of their plunder as they could. This artifact was the prize above all measure, and both women wanted it for their own. Dee got hold of it first and instructed Kurt to hide it, which he did, in the cat's toy. But Harley knew about the trick and told Carry. She went after it with a vengeance. She was the one who was shooting at the boys that day."

"Carry was the second shooter?"

"Yes, and she's a crack shot, too. If she had wanted to hit someone, she would have. She was just trying to scare them away from her treasure."

"I thought Harley was her man."

"Harley hadn't cemented his loyalty at that time. Up until then, the two bodyguards had worked for the women in tandem. But when Carry made her final break, he went with her."

I thought about this sad scenario of partner fighting partner. "But I took the bag and turned it over to the police, so neither party got what they wanted." I sighed. "Funny. I had that thingy all along. I only just returned it to Carry the other day. Of course I never thought of it as anything special. I just wanted to give a cat her toy."

"Carry must have been astounded when you came up with it after all these years. Finally her collection would be complete."

"So what is this amazing artifact?"

Wil laughed. "Just the most coveted relic in the known world, now and ever after."

"It must be very small to fit into the ball like that."

"Tiny but precious," Wil said. "It's called the Mafdet, a carving of a cat from the First Period, ancient Egypt. The Mafdet was discovered by Harold Carter during one of his historic digs. In spite of accepted protocol, he kept it as his own personal possession for some time."

"Mafdet? That's Datura's name for Hermione, except she pronounces it 'Maftet.'"

"Hum. Interesting, though not surprising when you consider how much influence that piece must have had on her life."

"Is it very valuable? I mean, to others besides archeologists and thieves?"

"One similar sold years back at auction for upwards of two million dollars, and that one was broken. This Mafdet, smaller and cut from a single great diamond, is in perfect condition. To the ancient Egyptians, diamonds represented light, the sun, and the source of life itself. Before it was lost during World War II, it was said to be priceless."

"Wow," I commented, wrapping my arms around myself. The chill of the cavern was beginning to creep into my bones. Hermione had crawled up into Wil's lap again—I really wished she'd come sit on mine.

"Wow is right," Wil agreed.

"And what was your connection to this fabulous piece?" I went on quickly.

"The Mafdet had been the focus of my study. I traced it to a small village on the Nile where I ran across Carry and Dee who were also researching the relic. They were posing as fellow archaeologists, and I had no reason to disbelieve them. Actually, I got on quite well with them, especially

Carry whom I found to be both intelligent and informed. There was something about her," he mused. "Something fay-like…"

"I know what you mean. She struck me that way too."

He was silent for a moment before continuing. "Anyway, they knew their stuff. We met again in Cairo and worked together for several weeks cataloging items housed at the great museum there. Then one day they were up and gone, disappeared into the desert taking a crate of relics with them."

"The Mafdet?"

"Yes, that too. Their theft threatened the whole of my study, not to mention my belief that I was a good judge of character."

"So you went after them?"

"In a fashion. I'm no detective, but I am a terrier when it comes to my work. Through a few of my contacts, I managed to discover where they'd got off to. After that, it wasn't hard to keep an eye on what they were doing. About five years ago, I was ready to step in and demand they hand over the Mafdet, but that's when the split hit the fan. Carry suddenly withdrew from the partnership, called the authorities on the business in exchange for immunity and relocation, and went into hiding, never to be seen again."

"Until this week," I commented.

"Until this week," Craven agreed.

"I didn't know an artifact smuggling tipoff qualifies for witness protection."

"It wasn't just the artifacts. There were large shipments of drugs involved as well. Carry and Dee had started out small, interested only in acquiring seed money to finance their business. But the trade grew larger as Dee came to like the extra cash. When Carry gave Dee up, a few drug kingpins went down too."

"So Carry ratted out Datura," I mused. "No wonder Datura has issues. Did she get prison time?"

"No, she was found innocent of the drug connections, though she had to pay a hefty fine for the trafficking."

"What happened to the artifacts?"

"Many of them had already been sold; the rest were returned, except for the Mafdet. That piece had disappeared without a trace. I assumed Dee had squirreled it away, but when she kept up her search for Carry with a vengeance, I realized it must be the other way around—Carry had kept it for herself. Turns out I was wrong on both counts," he added. "You had it all along."

"I didn't know. The toy rolled under my fridge when I rescued the kitten and stayed there until we got the new fridge a few months ago."

"Fate," he sighed. "A strange mistress."

"I think the quote is 'a cruel mistress,' but it still may apply."

"And now the Mafdet is lost again," he proclaimed as I felt the heat of his anger radiate off of him. "Dee will take it and disappear into thin air! Or maybe if I'm lucky," he added sarcastically, "it'll turn up on the black market for some illegal goods mogul to purchase at an ungodly price."

"I'm sorry, Wil. This must be terribly frustrating for you."

Wil uttered a growl in reply, and I decided it was time to change the subject.

"How did you know about the sketchbook?" I blurted off the top of my head.

"Carry told me," Wil said after a few seconds, his voice

shaky at first but beginning to calm. "I couldn't have been happier when she contacted me earlier this week. She'd got one of my flyers in the mail and knew I was going to be in town. We met at her place and it was just like old times. "She was a tease, that one," he went on. I could sense his smile even if I couldn't see it. "She never committed to being in possession of the Mafdet, but she alluded to other items of great price. She showed me her book, said it held the clue to the location of what she referred to as her vault. But she wouldn't let me see the pictures or tell me how to extrapolate their significance. She just said that when the time was right, I would know."

"And you did. But what do you think she meant? Did she foresee something happening to her?"

"Hmm," Wil considered. "It almost seems like it, doesn't it?"

"Do you think Datura killed Carry after all?" I posed.

I awaited an answer, but when one didn't come, I forged ahead, "I know she denied it, for both herself and Kurt. But Man in White—I mean Harley—seemed to think differently. He straight out accused Datura of being the killer, didn't he? It sounded like that to me."

Wil had fallen silent. I could hear the rumble of Hermione's purr as he petted her faster and faster. Were the walls closing in on him again? I couldn't have that.

"And who," I went on quickly in hopes of distracting him, "was the guy who pushed me down—Kurt or Harley? It had to be one or the other of them. I figured it was Kurt at the time, though it crossed my mind it might have been Datura herself. But now we know Harley was there too. Everybody was accusing everybody. I can't make up my mind what really happened in there."

I took another break in what was turning into a lengthy

monologue, but the black hush was too much for me. "Datura admitted Kurt was looking for the sketchbook," I ruminated. "The place was a mess. Carry was on the floor. She didn't just decide to hit her head on the table and die—it had to have been Kurt, since Harley's supposedly Carry's man. He wouldn't hurt her, would he? Though he did say something about having failed his mission to protect her.

"Wil?" I pressed. "Please. Answer me."

"I'm sorry," Wil said after a time. "I don't know who killed Carry."

He hunched forward, embracing Hermione and mumbling something into her fur.

"Pardon? I didn't catch that."

The doctor straightened up again. Then he uttered the very words I did not want to hear.

"Right now, Lynley," he intoned, "I'm more concerned with whether someone is killing *us*.

Chapter 28

Cats' ability to squeeze through the smallest of places may seem a bit like magic, but it actually has to do with their anatomy. Cats do not have rigid collarbones, so as long as their head and neck fit, the rest of the cat can follow.

"Do you think we should try calling once more?"

The conversation had been on-again-off-again, spanning the hours as Wil and I sat helplessly locked in the vault. There were lapses of silence, getting longer all the time. As the surreal dark took on a personality of its own, Wil did his best to keep his panic at bay. Sometimes he talked to me, sometimes Hermione, and sometimes to the darkness itself.

Every so often, one of us would go up to the entrance and scream our little heads off, hoping someone might hear—what else could we do? As the hours stretched and our hopes dwindled, the screaming sessions grew further and further apart. This time, when the doctor put forth the idea of giving it another shot, neither of us could summon the motivation to try.

"Wil? Where are you?" I shock ran through me as I touched the step where he had been sitting and found him gone. "Are you alright?"

"Yes, I'm fine," he said from the far end of the cavern. "I'm looking for Hermione. She seems to have disappeared."

I stood quickly. "Hermione? She couldn't have. We're

stuck in here, remember?"

"But she's so much smaller than we are. Maybe she found a hole.

"Hermione," he called, his voice moving around the grotto. "Hermione, where did you go, little one?"

Suddenly a light blazed and a tinny rumble sounded.

"What…"

"It's my phone!" Wil cried with glee. "I found my phone. And it's not out of power after all." In its tiny glow, I could see his face smiling like a Cheshire cat. "It does that sometimes. It's old, so when I use certain apps for too long, it turns itself off without warning."

"Certain apps, such as the flashlight?"

"Yes, that's one of them. Gosh, I don't know why I didn't think of it sooner. Look! It still has a good fifteen percent charge."

"Well, don't push it. That light is precious. Do you think you can call out?"

"Already trying."

I watched him poke at the little screen, then look up at me triumphantly. "It's ringing! I called 911 and it's ringing."

Suddenly the room went dark again. "No!" he cried. "No! Curse this outdated technology! I swear when I get out of here, I'm going to buy a brand new, state of the art…"

His voice dwindled into nothing. I knew what he was thinking.

"*If* we get out," I finished for him. "Do you think you got through to the emergency line before it died?"

"No, no way."

"Try turning it on again…"

"I'm trying!" he snapped. "But it's no use. It's really

gone for good this time."

Then there was silence—dark, depressed silence. Neither of us had the energy to keep up the chat. It was over. I could see the headlines now: *Three found dead in underground grotto. Dr. Wil Craven, cat lady Lynley Cannon, and Hermione...*

"Hey wait a minute!" I exclaimed. "Did you ever locate Hermione?"

"What good's that going to do now? If she discovered a way out of here, more power to her. I doubt she'll pull a Lassie and bring back the troops to save our sorry behinds."

"*Your* behind may be sorry, Wil, but mine's still hoping for a good outcome. If Hermione found a way, maybe we can too."

"But we've looked."

"I know, but just for fun, let's look again. Hermione," I began in my most inviting tone. A few moments later, Wil took up the call.

"Hermione!"

"Hermione, sweetheart? Where did you go?"

There was a tiny *purrumph* from the very farthest corner of the vault, a part that had been in shadow even when the entrance door was open and there was light. Hermione meowed again—in fact, suddenly she wouldn't stop meowing. I knew she meant for us to follow her. I just knew it.

I edged toward the meows, feeling my way along. Sure enough, the wall didn't turn but kept on going. I shuffled a few steps forward. As I did so, the pinhole of door light winked out of my view.

"I think it's a tunnel! Ouch," I added as my head knocked on an overhanging rock. "Or maybe it isn't.

I moved ahead another few inches when my foot hit stone. I tried to feel my way around it, then over it, but without luck. I reached with both hands to gauge the breadth of the obstacle, but everywhere I touched was rock. Or to be more accurate, square-sided objects I guessed to be bricks. The passage, now clogged with debris, may once have led to a second exit, but not anymore.

Rats! I swore to myself. *What I wouldn't give for a good working flashlight!* In the dark, each brick felt like a boulder, an impossible, immovable barrier to our escape.

"It's no good. The way's blocked." I kicked at the brick pile in frustration, a move that hurt no one but myself.

"But that makes sense," Wil said, coming up beside me. "Carry didn't build this grotto herself. She must have discovered it when she acquired her property—or maybe she bought the place because she knew it was here."

"You figure it out," I huffed. I had no patience for an analytical debate.

"But for her to use it as a vault," he went on, oblivious of my annoyance, "the place needed to be secure. And for that to happen, any ingress besides the one in her garden would have to be sealed."

I was done. I dropped to the ground, and falling back against the jagged stone, began to weep. Hermione climbed into my lap and put her paws on my shoulder to comfort me.

"Sweet kitty," I snuffled.

I went to embrace her, but she slipped right through my arms. Hopping onto my shoulder, I felt her back feet press into me as she made a leap. She didn't jump down however—she jumped up!

Whipping around, I tried to figure out where she had

gone. I couldn't feel the cat anymore, but I did find something even better.

"There's a gap in the rubble!" I exclaimed. "Hermione found a gap!"

"Is it big enough for us to get through?"

"I don't know, but I'm surely going to try."

A fluffy tail whipped against my face, then moved away. I wasted no time crawling after my feline guide.

"Be careful! It might not be safe."

I faltered. He was right. If the wall had broken once, likely its stability hadn't improved with time.

I considered going back, but returning would be as risky as continuing forward. I'd made it this far—I might as well go for the goal.

The space was tight and getting tighter. I realized with a shock that I couldn't turn back now, even if I'd wanted to. Panic spiked through my system, adrenaline heating my skin. I opened my mouth to cry out but all that came was a pathetic moan. Then a warm nose touched my face. I gave one more squirm. The rocks fell away, and I was through.

"Come on!" I called back. "It's narrow but I made it. I'm on the other side."

There was a pause. "I don't know... don't know if I can..."

"You can! You have to!" When there was no response, I added, "Just think about Hermione. Imagine yourself as a cat—a brave, stoic, unflappable cat.""

I heard a big sigh, then the rain of gravel that let me know Wil was on his way.

"Talk to me, Lynley," he whispered, his voice trembling with unguarded fear.

My mind went blank. "What should I say?"

"Anything. Whatever you think of. Tell me about your cats."

"My cats," I mused. "Dirty Harry, Little, Big Red, Tinkerbelle, Violet, Mab, Emilio, Elizabeth. Dirty Harry is the oldest..."

As I droned on about the clowder, one cat at a time, I listened for signs of Wil's progress. I'd made it to Violet and her kitten buddy Mab when a tumble of rocks and some mad scuffling indicated he was through.

"Well, that was pretty terrible," he blustered.

"But you did it!" I cheered, thinking how much courage it must have taken for the claustrophobic man to traverse that close, dark space. "Where do you think we are now?"

This new place had a different feel than the grotto. Though still shadowed in gloom, the atmosphere seemed less opaque than the vault itself. The floor felt smooth, and the ceiling was high enough to easily pass. Within a few steps, the hand I was using as an antenna touched something slick like tile. Instinctively I picked up my pace, and a hairpin turn later, I saw the most beautiful sight I could have imagined—light!

Another S-turn and the radiance became so bright I had to shut my eyes, but I was ecstatic. When I opened them again, Wil had caught up with me. Hermione was trotting ahead, not waiting for us slow-moving humans. She had a point. Wil and I sped after her. The short tunnel, the kind built for workmen back in the forties, was no more than ten feet long. At the end was a set of stairs, the civilized sort with treads and a railing, leading to an exit door. A few more feet, and we were there.

"Locked," Will grumbled as he shook and rattled the handle.

"I supposed it would have been too much to ask for the fates to have left it open for us, but still, it's a new hope. Wherever this leads, it has to be better-traveled than Carry's secret garden."

I began banging on the metal. Wil followed suit.

"Help!" we cried in unison.

I picked up a chunk of brick and hit it hard against the door. On the third try, it broke up in my hand, but it had done the trick—I could hear voices on the other side.

"Help," Wil called. "We're locked in."

"We'll get you out," someone said. "Stand back."

I scooped up Hermione, then held my breath, already anticipating the absolute joy of freedom.

The door swung outward with a clang, revealing a big man standing in the threshold. For a frightened moment, I thought it was Kurt or Harley, but then the face turned toward me—a stranger.

He was one of four persons who stood in a military-style row, grim expressions on their faces. They were dressed in matching black uniforms with flack vests, full utility belts, and guns in holsters. The gold insignias on their shoulders were foreign to me, but I didn't care. *Private security*, was my first impression. Again, it didn't matter. I was free!

I rushed outside, only slightly behind Wil who was gulping air like a feral cat with a bowl of kibble.

"Thank you so much. I'm so glad you're here. We were locked down there, it must have been hours. What time is it? Today's my birthday. There's a party for me and it should be starting soon."

I don't know what wild hair made me think about my birthday all of a sudden when there were so many other, more pressing considerations, like telling the police all about Datura and the thug boys. Then the man said something that stopped me dead.

"You're going to miss it," he barked. "We've got somewhere else to be."

His statement didn't make sense. We were free. We'd given Datura the slip. We could do anything we darned pleased...

"Wait. What?"

I felt a hand clamp onto my bicep and looked up into a pair of coal-black eyes.

"Let go of me or I'll call the police."

"Maybe later," he said, "but right now we want you to quietly start walking. Don't even think about calling for help, not if you want what's good for you."

I wasn't sure what he meant, but it didn't sound pleasant. I looked to Wil, but he was being held by another of the men. This one had something shoved into his back.

Wil's eyes were wild and his face devoid of color.

Silently he mouthed one word: *Gun!*

Chapter 29

Some cats enjoy being held or carried, where others abhor even being picked up.

We began to walk, ushered by two of our black-clad escorts, the other two taking up guard, one ahead and one behind. After the long, strange time in the lightless vault, this new predicament seemed surreal. I couldn't understand what was happening, and so began to wonder if it were happening at all. Were these soldiers a figment of my imagination? Was I still in the cavern, passed out and waiting to die?

But no, this was real. I could smell the stuffy Portland air overlaid with the acrid scent of the fir trees around me. I could hear the hum of the city, the roar of cars from down the hill, children playing, a woman laughing, a jet overhead, the howl of a dog. I could taste the sour, dry thirst on my tongue from hours without water. This panorama of senses was far too detailed to be a dream.

Where was I then? I gazed down the asphalt pathway, the wide, black trail twisting through the cultivated forest. A steep, grassy slope to one side, and to the other, a stretch of water shimmered in the late afternoon sun. That tunnel, I realized, had brought us back into the park. There were only a few people present, a man walking his dog and a couple making whoopie on a bench overlooking the city. I was surprised to see the sun so low to the horizon. Wil and I had been in that forsaken vault for hours! And now what? I really couldn't take much more.

"I have to go to the bathroom," I said flatly. "There's a public toilet over there. I suggest you let me use it."

Our escorts paused to look at each other, then one nodded, a woman. "Let her go."

"Thanks..."

"Don't mention it. I'll go with you."

Though I did indeed need the facilities after all that time underground, I'd also thought the trip might provide an opportunity for escape, or at least to let someone know we were in trouble. That possibility, however, was quashed by my companion who stood outside the stall until I had finished and flushed. All I'd managed by my ploy was to create a pause in whatever plans the troops had for us.

Once done and back on the walking path, I felt a bit clearer and soon realized where we were headed. Hermione, who so far had been content to let me carry her, even in the bathroom, now sprang from my arms and hightailed it across the grass toward her home territory. This was the way Dirty Harry had guided me that first day I'd met Carry. How I wished things had gone differently then: that I'd used the better harness; that Harry had headed down the hill instead of up; that the minute I saw the small woman standing in her gateway, I'd grabbed the cat and run like the wind in the other direction.

"You're taking us back to Carry's place. But why? Are the police there?" I asked, hoping against hope these military types were on the right side of the law after all.

There was no answer from our escorts, and another scenario came to mind.

"Datura? You're not taking us back to Datura, are you? But that makes no sense," I went on. "If Datura were

221

smart, she'd be far away by now, not wasting time on Wil and me. After all, she got what she wanted."

"Datura got what she deserved," the man holding Wil mumbled.

"Pardon?"

"Quiet," said the woman. "We're almost there."

The escorts herded us through the gate and into the red garden. The lights in the trees were just beginning to wink on, and the solar lamps twinkled their colorful hues. In spite of my exhaustion and fear, I registered the beauty of the still surroundings. Or maybe it was *because* of it. I'd lost all clue as to what was transpiring—I'd lost all hope. The only thing that remained in my uncertain heart was this moment of pure splendor.

The grip on my arm loosened. I looked up into the man's face—craggy, clean-shaven, a stoic stare that gave nothing away. Eyes that had seen too much, reminding me of warriors I'd known.

"Up yonder." He cocked his chin toward the veranda. There was something in the shadows but couldn't quite make it out. A figure in a chair, sitting very straight. Then I got it.

"Datura!" I hissed.

"Go on," said the man. "She can't hurt you now."

Again I glanced at my captor, but his face was shaded. Looking back at Wil, the doctor seemed calm, or maybe just resigned. He was standing on his own, no sign of the threatening weapon. In the gathering dusk, I wasn't sure, but I thought he might have been smiling.

"I know who you are," he said quietly.

"Oh?" countered the woman.

"Yes. At least I think I do." He walked over to me and put a protective arm around my shoulder. None of the crew made to stop him. "If I'm correct, Lynley, then we're in no danger."

From the veranda came a muffled grunt and a string of stifled gibberish. As my eyes adjusted to the darkness, I saw why. It was Datura alright, but she was bound to Carry's antique chair, her wrists ziptied to the barley-twist arms. Her mouth was gagged with a professional-looking muzzle. Her eyes were crazy.

"What's going on?" was all I could think to say.

"May I introduce the Murder Hornets," Wil announced with obvious glee. "That's right, isn't it, ma'am?"

"That's correct," said the woman. She stepped forward and offered her hand. "Major Hannah González. And these are Lieutenants Aubrey, Finn, and Maloney."

Wil gave a brief but enthusiastic handshake to the Major. "You're Carry's estate guards, aren't you? I've heard about you, though I was never really sure you existed."

Hornets? Not that again! Both Carry and Datura had spoken of hornets. I'd never figured out the reference. Now it seemed it wasn't about bugs at all.

"We exist alright," said González, "though we prefer not to use the tag. We have no plans to murder anyone."

"But your client was murdered." Wil commented.

"Correct again, Dr. Craven."

She turned a black look to the veranda. I followed her gaze. Datura was not alone—sitting backs to the wall, bound, gagged, and defeated were the two thugs, Man in Black and Man in White.

"I thought you Hornets only worked for the aristocracy," the doctor pondered. "Where does our Carry fit into that model?"

Major González glanced at her troops. "Have you

heard of the Klatten empire?"

"Klatten?" I repeated. "The name sounds familiar."

"It should," said Wil. "They're one of the wealthiest families in the world."

"Correct. And the person you knew as Carry was in fact Karla Klatten. Like many of the idle rich, she rebelled against her heritage and ran for a short period with criminals like Datura, but she grew tired of it. She saw how it hurt others, and she got out. Her revelation was due to the advent of a very special cat."

"Hermione?" I asked.

As if summoned, the paisley cat appeared from out of the hedgerow, winding her velvet softness around my legs with a *purrumph*. I picked her up, and she settled across my shoulder as if she had always been there.

González reached out to gently stroke the spotted fur. "Yes, Hermione. After Ms. Klatten's spree and the subsequent turning over of her partner to the authorities, Ms. Klatten became a recluse. She persevered in her complete anonymity for five years, then a few days ago, she contacted Mr. Craven and forged a friendship with you, Ms. Cannon. We don't know what triggered her desire to step back into society, but it was her downfall. Datura found her, and shortly after, she was dead."

"If you were her bodyguards, why didn't you protect her?"

"We're not bodyguards; we are *estate* guards. Our job only begins after our client's passing.

"What is your job?" I asked. "What is an estate guard anyhow?"

"We make sure the client's property is distributed to their unique specifications."

"I thought lawyers did that. Wills, living trusts, and

such."

"They do, for the most part. But sometimes a client may have possessions that cannot be passed through normal channels."

"You mean illegal things—like Carry's stolen artifact collection?"

"You get the idea," González confirmed.

Wil frowned. "Are you saying you're going to redistribute the items in Carry's vault? But most of those were never hers to give."

"We're only concerned with one, and that artifact, hidden for so many years, must be placed directly into rightful hands."

González reached into the pocket of her flak vest and withdrew the Mafdet. She held it for a moment, captivated by its sparkling facets, then stepped close to Craven and placed it gently in his upturned palm. Though the item weighed less than an ounce, he staggered as if he'd been given a great weight.

"The Mafdet! To me?"

"Ms. Klatten knew you would do right by it. She couldn't bring herself to turn it over while she was alive, but now that she's dead, she wants it to go where it belongs."

"The Museum of Egyptian Antiquities," the doctor said without hesitation.

"Correct. Not many people could be trusted with such a treasure. If it has to pass through the legal chain of custody—police, FBI, and the inevitable assortment of museum curators—something so small and so valuable could be waylaid. People are greedy and easily tempted. Ms. Klatten was confident you would have no such failings."

"Alright," I observed. "I see why you want Wil here, but what about me?"

"There's another entrustment we must convey. Ms. Klatten cared about three things in her life: her garden, the artifact, and Hermione." Again she touched the cat's marbled cheek. "This unique feline meant everything to Ms. Klatten. Now you must take her. You must give her a home."

"But... But Carry and I just met."

"Still, she was very determined it was to be you."

"Thank you, I guess," I stuttered, pushing aside the fact I already had a full house. Hey, what's one more?

Then I thought of something. "But that arrangement could only have been made within the last couple of days. Did Carry—Karla—know something was going to happen to her?"

"It's possible, probable even. That's not for me to say. As I told you, we only enter the scenario once the client has passed."

I shook my head. "Why all the subterfuge? You nearly scared me to death when you dragged us here at gunpoint. I thought we were being abducted. Again."

"Apologies. We needed to be sure we were alone while handing over the bequests. And that wasn't a firearm." She gave a sly look at her fellow. "Finn just wanted you to think it was."

Finn held up a short leather baton and gave a sly smile. "Sorry about that."

"You could have just asked," I grumbled.

Major González declined to answer, but I thought I saw a flash of sympathy cross her face.

"What happens to them?" Wil nodded to the threesome on the veranda.

"That's part of our job as well, to make sure all aspects of her death are accounted for. In this case, the killers must be brought to justice. They," she nodded toward Datura and the henchmen, "have signed confessions which the authorities will find adequate."

"Confessions?" I gasped. "To Carry's murder?"

González nodded.

"How did you get them to do that? No, wait," I blurted. "Who did it? Which one?"

"All three are guilty. All three had a hand in Ms. Klatten's death."

Wil looked at her with uncertainty. "How does that work? Datura and Kurt I get, but Harley. Where does he fit in?"

"Why don't I let them tell you for themselves?" She moved to the bound men. "Who wants to 'fess up to their crimes?" She thumped both men smartly on the forehead. "It's the least you can do for these good people."

González slipped off the gags. After wiping his mouth on his shoulder as best he could with his hands tied behind his back, Kurt began the tale.

Chapter 30

Don't forget to make arrangements for your cats when you draw up a will or living trust. What happens to your little family after you're gone is in your hands.

Kurt had his orders. He was to find the red journal. His mistress the Lady Datura said it contained the necessary information for her to carry out her objective of locating the precious Mafdet. She had given no other instructions, which meant Kurt was to get the book by any means necessary. He had no problem with that. Kurt had been with Datura for a very long time and knew her to be utterly devoid of a conscience.

Breaking into the little bungalow was a snap, but once inside, he wasn't sure where to start. *Where do girls keep their journals?* he wondered to himself. Bedroom? Beside the TV? It could be in the commode for all he knew of the habits of normal women. But Datura had described this journal as large with a bright red cover. It shouldn't be hard to find.

He began with the bedside table, then moved under the bed, under the mattress, the closet, the chest of drawers, the wardrobe. He searched methodically, pulling things from their places and scattering them on the floor to make sure he didn't miss anything.

When the bedroom came up empty, he proceeded to the living room in the same ruthless manner. Tearing couch pillows and bolsters, he let loose a flurry of stuffing that swirled through the air like choking snow. He sneezed, then sneezed again. "Blast!" he swore as he stopped to blow the cotton out of his nose.

Kurt was getting antsy, and careless. Where he had started out quietly for fear of being overheard, he now swept objects from their place with no thought about noise. A vase crashed to the floor in a shower of shards; a collection of pottery was swept from its shelf to reveal what was behind—nothing. He moved on to a bookcase, a desk, an antique cabinet. He knew he had to get that journal, or his life would be worthless.

Suddenly he heard a sound, then silence.

He waited a moment, but when nothing materialized to account for it, he went back to his work.

"What do you think you are doing, Kurt?" came a soft voice from close behind him. He whirled to see Carry in all her five-foot glory, staring at him with angry, turquoise eyes.

"Ca... Carry!" he stuttered.

"Yes, Kurt. Who else would it be, since this is my home? I assume my former associate sent you."

"Uh-huh," he said. This little woman scared him almost as much as his mistress. Almost.

"What does she want from me now?"

"A book, ma'am," he answered honestly.

"And what book would that be? *War and Peace*? *To Kill a Mockingbird*? *The Cat Who Wasn't There*?"

"No, ma'am."

"A sketchbook, perhaps?"

"Is that like a journal? Big and red?"

"Maybe."

"Then yeah, that's what she wants."

Pulling together, Kurt made himself look the small

woman in the eye. He set his face in a grimace and took a step toward her. If it was meant to seem menacing, it had no effect. Carry stood her ground with a smile.

"Kurt, dear, you know I can't give you my sketchbook. It's mine and no one else's business."

"That's not what the Lady says. She says it's hers, and she wants it. She says you owe her, after all these years gone by."

Kurt took another step, and as he did so, he noticed something under a pile of books on the dining table. Something big. Something red.

"Is that the one?"

He reached out a hand, but before he could touch it, Carry grabbed the book and scurried behind the table, putting the antique cherrywood between herself and the henchman.

Without hesitation, he pursued.

"Stop right there!" Though the voice was gender-neutral, there was no mistaking the hostile tone.

Kurt spun to find a man outlined in the doorway. Blond hair, light skin, wearing a black coat that failed to obscure his brawny torso—Kurt's old accomplice Harley!

"Hey, buddy," Kurt said. "Long time. What you been up to since you betrayed the Lady and went over to the dark side?"

"Not much, Kurtis. Just trying to keep things copacetic. Which brings me to the fact that it's time for you to leave." Harley stepped into the room and peered around with disgust. "You've done enough damage here. I should make you clean it up, but I think I'd rather just see the back of you. Go on—git!"

"You know I can't do that. Datura will have my head if I don't bring her what she wants."

Harley tsked. "Not my problem, brother. Go on, before I make you."

Kurt guffawed. "You couldn't if you tried."

Harley's blond brow furrowed. As the two thugs stared daggers at each other, Carry gripped the book flat to her chest, anticipating what was to come.

With a battle cry, Kurt jumped Harley, or maybe it was the other way around. Neither was sure of anything except that the fight was on.

There was no preliminary circling or posturing between these two, nor was there mercy. They had known each other from way back and were familiar with the moves. As they pounded with hammer fists and kicked out with feet like cement blocks, what bits of Carry's room not destroyed by Kurt's search fell to their grotesque dance.

Carry cried as the skirmish flared and waned, flared and waned. The contest went on hard and long, but even heavies get tired, and the opponents were weakening. With a final blow, Kurt sent Harley flying into the wall where he lay stunned. Kurt stood for a moment to make sure he didn't get up again, then stumbled to the table where he had seen the book. To his consternation, it was no longer there, but then he found it close by. Seizing it, he ran for the door and was gone before Harley could recover.

Harley shook off the daze and pulled himself to his feet. Dumbly, he stared around at the destruction their warring had done to the beautiful room. Then something else caught his eye. Carry! The small woman lay face-down by the table, covered with shards of broken China. She wasn't moving.

Harley started toward her, stumbling across the debris-strewn floor. Then he heard a sound. Someone new had entered the room.

231

* * *

"That was you, Lynley," said Major González. "Harley pushed you down, then while you were passed out, he searched for Ms. Klatten's sketchbook, which he thought to contain secrets she wouldn't want to get out. But here's where the confusion lies: there were two books, one with the drawings that revealed the location of her vault and a newer one that contained nothing at all. The book Kurt absconded with was the new one and absolutely worthless."

"Carry must have been holding the old sketchbook when she fell," I mused, "because it was lodged underneath her. I took it."

"Yes, you did. You were more observant than poor Harley. Since he couldn't find it right off, he ran. In the meantime, Ms. Klatten's contusion, sustained when the fighters ploughed into her and sent her hurtling into the corner of the table, had already begun to cause bleeding into her brain.

"Two big brutes, tussling, not watching what they were doing," she huffed. "Neither noticed her at all as she lay on the ground. Only after Kurt left did Harley realize what had come about. He might have saved her had he acted quickly, but when you came on the scene, he panicked, thinking only of himself."

She gave a hateful look at the man in white, then turned her back.

"We'll be taking our leave now. The police are on their way."

"You're not staying?" Wil exclaimed.

"No, we'd rather not have to disclose our part in this. You two would be smart to make your departure as well."

"Really?" I asked. "Won't the police want us to wait

and give a statement?"

"I'm sure that's what they would prefer, but it won't gain them anything. On the other hand, it may lose you quite a bit. The Mafdet will surely be taken as evidence, and from there where it goes will be at the whim of a judge. Hermione will fare little better in an investigations cage at the county shelter. You are their custodians now, officially if not legally. You must do what's best for those things Ms. Klatten loved."

"She's right," Wil said. "The Mafdet must be handed over to the museum directly. If the cops get hold of it, who knows where it might end up?"

"I'd hate for Hermione to be confiscated," I agreed. "No, as much as I'm for following the rules, this might be the exception. My car's out front."

"Mine too," said Wil. "But won't it look suspicious if we run off just as the police arrive? This isn't going to work if they come after us later for fleeing the scene."

"Don't concern yourself," said González. "We have that covered."

"If you say so." He paused to look at me, then he smiled. "It was nice meeting you, Lynley Cannon."

"I'm not sure the term *nice* quite fits, but yes, it was good. Look me up if you're ever back in Portland."

"And if you see me on tour somewhere, there's a front row seat reserved just for you."

The sirens were getting louder. It sounded like they were coming up through the park instead of the street.

"No time for long goodbyes," González urged as she and her troops began to slip away. "Take care of Hermione and the Mafdet. We will be watching."

I started for my car, then turned back as something came to me. "Major, you said Carry loved three things: the

Mafdet, Hermione, and her garden. Who will take care of the garden now?"

"It's been bequeathed to the Portland Parks Foundation, to become a part of Mt. Tabor Park. In addition, Ms. Klatten left an endowment to finance the venture and make sure it's kept up in perpetuity. The bungalow is to be remodeled into a teahouse, with proceeds benefiting a local cat shelter—Friends of Felines if you want to look it up."

"Friends of Felines," I laughed as I hurried to make my getaway, Hermione held close in my arms. "Yes, I know them well."

Chapter 31

In ancient times, cats were worshipped as gods; they have not forgotten this." —Terry Pratchett

My car clock read ten-thirty-two p.m. as I pulled into the underground parking lot of the Terrace, the senior living complex where my mother Carol lived and the location of my sixty-second birthday party. The festivities had been set to start at an easy four-o'clock. I was six and a half hours late.

"Better late than never," I said to Hermione who was curled up on the passenger seat. She blinked at me with her beautiful blue eyes as if she surely agreed.

Since I hadn't bothered to recover my gateless carrier from the bungalow, I was in a bit of a quandary. I didn't want to leave Hermione in the open car, so I decided to take her in with me. The building allowed cats, so there shouldn't be a problem with me walking her through the lobby and up the elevator to the Commons. I just hoped Hermione would agree with that conclusion.

I retrieved the leash and harness I kept in the glove box just in case. In case of what?—I'd always wondered. Now I knew. In case a contingent of estate soldiers placed a precious cat into my waiting arms, and I didn't have a carrier.

I slipped the harness over Hermione's back and neck, clipped on the leash, and we headed into the building. Aside from the woman behind the front desk and an old man reading a book in the corner easy chair, the big room was deserted. Hermione didn't seem at all perturbed by the strange space, nor did she shy at riding the elevator. No balking or playing dead, she just trotted at my side as if she were going someplace special.

And indeed she was.

The first thing I'd done once I left the red garden was to call Carol. She'd started to chastise me in a motherly fashion about missing my own party, but once she heard my story—the run-in with Datura, the Mafdet and the secret vault, confinement in said vault with Dr. Wil Craven, the estate guards and their unique final bequests—she changed her tune. She had halted me mid-tale to put my call on speaker phone for the whole group to hear. I didn't know who all was there, so I kept the details vague and the parts that skirted the letter of the law even vaguer.

Now that I was there in person, though, I knew the whole truth would come out. Before I'd even exited the elevator, Carol and Seleia were rushing toward me with Frannie only a short way behind. After my ordeal, I was ecstatic to see them too.

I opened my arms for a group hug, but to my surprise, they ignored me, moving straight for Hermione. Greeting her gently with a slow touch to her cheek and a stroke to the top of her head, next I knew they were having a four-way pet fest right there on the carpet.

Seleia glanced up at me, love glowing in her sweet brown eyes. "Oh, Grandmother, what a beautiful cat! Those blue eyes—just like one of those Egyptian cat goddesses. And she's yours now?"

"Apparently so. I hope she gets along with all the others."

"She will," Seleia assured me. "I just know she will."

"Give us a boost up, will you, dear?" said Carol, holding out a hand. "The old bones need a little help these days."

With Seleia's assistance, the octogenarian grunted to her feet and straightened her little lace jacket. She looked me in the eye and said, "You're late."

"We've been over that, Mum," I told her.

"Yes, but it bears repeating," Carol huffed.

"I drove straight here once I was let go," I mumbled.

She acknowledged the less than pristine state of my informal dress with a harrumph. "Most of your guests have already left. You missed your entire party."

"She means to say we were worried," Seleia translated, "and that we're glad you're here now, no matter what you're wearing."

"It sounds like you had quite an adventure," said Frannie.

I sighed. "That's one way to describe it."

"So does that make Hermione your new adventure cat?" Seleia chuckled.

The four of us gazed at the paisley puss who in turn was peering up at us. With a little *meow*, she began pulling me toward the Commons.

"Maybe so," I called back as I trundled along after.

The room had been beautifully decorated, courtesy of Seleia. Black, white, orange, and gold streamers fell from the ceiling, the colors of a calico cat. The tables were draped in gold linen and topped by tiny floral arrangements with stems of fresh catnip as greenery. The walls were hung with posters of cats—*my cats!* I realized in surprise.

"How did you...?" I uttered as I admired her

237

handiwork.

"Isn't it wonderful?" exclaimed Frannie. "Seleia did an outstanding job."

"That she did." I looked proudly at the young woman I was honored to call my granddaughter. She smiled and glanced away, still young enough to blush.

There were a few guests remaining, and Hermione insisted we greet every one. When she had made the rounds to her feline satisfaction, she hopped up onto a linen-draped table and became especially interested in the catnip arrangement. I gave her a sprig, then handed Seleia the vase which she moved to a sideboard out of sight. Hermione chewed daintily on the spray, then curled up in between the coffee cups and empty cake plates for a nap.

I sank back in my chair with a groan, very glad to be among friends, very glad to be safe. Others came and sat nearby, and for a while, we talked and chatted. I received a few gifts, mostly of a cat-related nature, and everyone had seconds of coconut cream birthday cake while I enjoyed my first. One by one, they said their goodbyes and departed, until finally it was only Carol, Seleia, Frannie, and me.

"You missed a lot of people," said Carol. "Special Agent Paris, Halle and her wife, your friend with the Bengal cat."

"I am sorry," I reiterated honestly.

"Mother was here," Seleia said softly, "but she had to leave. She wanted me to tell you happy birthday and to give you this."

She passed me an oversized envelope with a shiny cobalt seal across the flap. I prized it open to find a hand-printed card depicting a little girl with a bouquet of flowers.

"Is this hers?" I asked of the print.

"She made it for you. Limited edition of one."

Though executed in Lisa's abstract style, the result was breathtaking, and the gift hit me like a revelation. I felt tears well in my eyes. My daughter, so often estranged from me, had reached out with her artwork in a way she found impossible in real life.

"It's probably valuable," Carol quipped to dispel my melancholy. "You should keep it."

I blinked back the mist and laughed. "If you say so, Mum. Seleia, please tell her thank you. I'll call her tomorrow."

"She'd like that," Seleia said.

There was a brief lull in the conversation, then all eyes turned to me.

"You know we want all the gritty details," Carol said matter-of-factly. "The grotto and the treasure and the smuggling ring…"

"And the killers," Seleia put in.

Carol shot her a glare, then returned her gaze to me. "But to be honest, you really don't look up to it."

"You're right, Mum, I'm not. But I will tell you that it all turned out for the best."

"Not for the dead lady," Seleia commented.

"Seleia!" Carol exclaimed.

Seleia shrugged. "Just saying…"

"No, not for Carry." I shook my head, again wondering if Carry sensed the danger she'd invited by revealing her whereabouts after all those years. My instinct told me she must have. "But at least her things were distributed as she'd wished, in spite of the, uh, *irregularities* of the bequests. That amazing red garden will become part of Mt. Tabor Park with her house as a tearoom. The Mafdet, the ancient Egyptian treasure she and her partner stole, will be turned over to the Museum of Cairo. And Hermione comes with me."

I smiled and petted the sleeping cat, marveling at the series of events that led to her return after all these years. In a city the size of Portland with a feline population into the millions, what were the chances? But maybe there was more to it than chance. I remembered the expression on Carry's face that first time I saw her, almost as if she knew.

"The killers are in the hands of the authorities by now," I went on, leaving that mystery for another day. "Their written confessions will help to convict them of their crimes." I sighed. "But I thought you were going give me a break."

"Right," said Carol. "We are. No more murder talk. Agreed?"

Everyone nodded, including me.

"Frannie, you look great," I commented. She had pulled out all the stops in a chartreuse cocktail dress and tiny hat perched upon her platinum coif. "Are you feeling better?"

"Oh, much. I've consulted a specialist and am all set to begin my new meds next week. They don't expect any complications."

"That's wonderful! I'm so happy for you." I grabbed her hand across the table and gave it a squeeze.

"You were the catalyst, Lynley. If it weren't for you, I'd still be hiding in my apartment waiting to die a miserable death."

I glanced at Carol and Seleia, wondering how they would take Frannie's shocking allusion, but Frannie just laughed. "They know all about my hep C. We were discussing it earlier."

That was a turnaround, a positive one. For Frannie to put aside her misplaced shame and confide in her friends was almost as much of a relief as hearing the good prognosis.

"But there is some news I know will interest you," Frannie put in. "I have it on good authority that the shelter is about to receive a huge endowment, an estate from a wealthy supporter."

Carry's bequest of the future Mt. Tabor Tea Room? I wondered. But no, it was far too soon for that to have hit the rumor mill.

"A man—I don't know his name, but he's been described as an eccentric old coot—has been donating anonymously for decades. Now that he has passed, Friends of Felines will be getting something extra specially good."

"That's awesome!" exclaimed Seleia.

"Well deserved," Carol said with a nod.

I frowned, I wasn't sure why. " 'Extra specially good?'—what does that mean?"

"I'm not sure, but it isn't just cash—something else of great value goes along with it. There's a catch though. We have to fulfill the stipulations of the bequest."

"Stipulations? Like what?" I was beginning to get a weird feeling about this *generous* gift.

"Probably some legal hoops to jump through."

Hoops, I thought to myself. That could mean just about anything.

Maybe it was the fact I was coming off twenty-four—no, make that *forty-eight*, or even *sixty*—hours of crazy, but the idea of a secret bequest that required a quid pro quo seemed a bit weird. Perhaps, as Frannie speculated, it was nothing more than the usual legalities. But with an "eccentric old coot" who could tell?

I thought of the classic haunted mansion story. By the terms of the will, the inheritors must spend the night on the property before it comes into their hands. Needless to say, they don't survive to see light of day.

I shook my head. I was being silly. Money for the little cat shelter was always a good thing. This would be too.

Suddenly I felt a weight as Hermione landed in my lap. Using me as a living step, she sprang to the floor and headed for the water bowl Seleia had set out for her. When she reached the end of her leash, she looked back at me with such displeasure that everyone broke down laughing.

"The mistress calls," I said as I stood to escort the little diva to her desired destination. Perhaps she was part goddess after all.

About the Author

Native Oregonian Mollie Hunt has always had an affinity for cats, so it was a short step for her to become a cat writer. Mollie is the author of the award-winning **Crazy Cat Lady Cozy Mystery Series**, featuring Lynley Cannon, a sixty-something cat shelter volunteer who finds more trouble than a cat in catnip. The third in the series, **Cat's Paw**, was a finalist for the 2016 Mystery & Mayhem Book Award. The fifth, **Cat Café**, won the World's Best Cat Litter-ary Award in 2019. The sixth, **Cosmic Cat**, is the winner of the Cat Writers Association Muse Medallion Award for Best Cat Mystery 2019-2020.

Mollie's sci-fantasy, **Cat Summer** (Fire Star Press), also won a Muse Medallion, this time for Best Cat Sci-fi Fantasy. **Cat Summer** is the first in the **Cat Seasons Tetralogy**, followed by **Cat Winter**. Cats saving the world!

Mollie also published a stand-alone mystery, **Placid River Runs Deep**, which delves into murder, obsession, and the challenge of chronic illness in bucolic southwest Washington. Two of her short cat stories have been published in anthologies. She has penned a little book of **Cat Poems** as well.

Mollie is a member of the Oregon Writers' Colony, Sisters in Crime, the Cat Writers' Association, and the Northwest Independent Writers Association (NIWA). She lives in Portland, Oregon with her husband and a varying number of cats. Like Lynley, she is a grateful shelter volunteer.

Visit Mollie's Website: *http://www.lecatts.wordpress.com*

A NOTE FROM THE AUTHOR

Thanks so much for reading my cozy cat mystery, *Adventure Cat*. I hope you enjoyed it. If you did, please consider leaving a review on your favorite book and social media sites. Reviews help indie authors such as myself to gain recognition in the literary jungle. Thank you in advance for your consideration.

Adventure Cat is book eight of the Crazy Cat Lady Cozy Mystery Series. I'm now working on book nine, so be assured that Lynley has not cleaned her last litter box or solved her final mystery.

Want more Crazy Cat Lady escapades? Find the rest of the series (eBook or paperback) on my Amazon Page: http://www.amazon.com/author/molliehunt

For those of you who enjoy cat sci-fantasy, check out the Cat Seasons Tetralogy. Available so far are book one, **Cat Summer** (winner of the Cat Writers Association Muse Medallion Award for best scf-fi/fantasy) and book two, **Cat Winter**, (awarded a Certificate of Excellence by CWA). **Cat Autumn** will be coming soon.

"Mollie weaves a story that blurs the lines of mythology, spiritualism, mysticism, science and reality that took me into another world. With her use of vivid imagery, I wasn't reading about Lise, the human-cum-feline protagonist and the cats fighting evil, I was in the trenches with them. The continuous struggle of good fighting evil, well, it's frightening--not in the least because so many of the things she's written are real."
— Ramona D. Marek MS Ed, CWA Author

"A genre-bending fantasy, Cat Summer carries the flavor of Warriors and the author's own contemporary Cat Mysteries, together with Arthur Clark's 2001..., Tolkein and other dark fantasy. For cat-lovers and earth-lovers, a cool and fascinating tale."
—Sheila Deeth, author

Poetry lovers, check out **Cat Poems: For the Love of Cats**.

"This collection of cat poems touches on the joy of becoming acquainted with a newly adopted friend, the heartbreak of saying goodbye to an old one, viewing life through a cat's eyes, and celebrating those who foster and advocate for cats... Every one will touch your heart." —Mochas, Mysteries, and Meows

Not cat-centric? I've published a stand-alone mystery thriller, **Placid River Runs Deep**.

From the back cover:
"When Ember Mackay learns she has a life-threatening illness, she runs away to her secluded river cabin, but instead of solace, she finds mystery, murder, and a revenge plot that has taken a generation to unfold."

"...A thrilling combination of menace and pastoral beauty. After reading this book you may want to rethink your summer holiday." —Lily Gardner, author of **Betting Blind**

☙

Made in the USA
Middletown, DE
16 October 2021

50177404R00146

The Bucket List

List

Carrie Jacobs

MW01224138

Copyright Notice

This book is a work of fiction. Names, characters, places, and incidents are either the product of the author's imagination or are used fictitiously. Any resemblance to actual persons, living or dead, events, or locales is entirely coincidental.

Copyright © 2022 by Carrie Jacobs

ISBN: 978-1-957117-01-0

All rights reserved. No part of this book may be reproduced, distributed, or used in any manner whatsoever without written permission of the copyright owner except for the use of brief quotations in articles or reviews.

Edited by Court of Spice Editing courtofspice.com
Cover Art from Deposit Photos and/or Canva
Cover Design by Carrie Jacobs
First Edition 2022

Other Books By Carrie Jacobs:

<u>Hickory Hollow series</u>:
Drunk on a Plane
Caller Number Nine
The Boy Next Door
Luck of the Draw
Cat Burglar
Mending Fences

<u>Stand Alone novels</u>:
The Bucket List

To stay informed of upcoming titles, sign up for my newsletter!

Visit carriejacobsauthor.com or scan this QR code with your smartphone:

for Jen Mahoney
and my other favorite former coworkers
at least we didn't have pep rallies

Chapter 1

"Hey, Shasta, it's time." Ellie, my cubicle neighbor announces.

I bang my head lightly on the padded wall of my cell — er, cube. "Huzzah," I reply in the flattest tone I can manage. The first Friday of the month is the *worst*. Yeah, I know everyone is supposed to love Fridays, but PAMECorp forces us to endure these nauseating pep rallies designed to spark our productivity or some shit.

I click to save my spreadsheet. Wouldn't it make more sense to let me, I don't know, *work* instead of making me sit through another multi-hour meeting that's supposed to inspire me to want to work? Whatever. If they want to waste their money, it's on them. And they certainly do. As Senior Accounting Manager, I see the receipts for what they spend on these monthly farces.

Ellie and I ride the cramped elevator to the conference room. Actually, it's the conference *floor*. Floor 17, to be exact. PAMECorp remodeled most of the building with a modern, sleek feel. Technically, PAMECorp only occupies five floors, and in keeping with most corporate decisions that make no sense, none of our floors are together. The rest are rented out as office space to other companies. On Floor 17, they gutted everything and installed retractable walls that can be configured in like a million different ways. On the first Friday, all the walls are open and the most uncomfortable chairs in the world are arranged so the four hundred of us who work on-site can endure these meetings.

All the seats near windows are already taken, so Ellie and I grab two seats in the back row. I set my notebook on my chair and join the line at the snack table. It's the only positive thing about the meeting. I scoop grapes and apple slices into a paper bowl because all the baked goods are picked over so I'm stuck with fruit.

"Look at you, being all health conscious," a deep voice teases from my left. Del Hudson. Ellie jokes that he's my work husband because he hardly talks to anyone else outside of his department. That, and I made the mistake of admitting out loud one time that I think he's cute. He's tall and solid, the perfect example of a "dad bod", with dark hair that's just a little too long and blue eyes that hide behind his black glasses.

"Couldn't make up a suitable IT emergency to get out of this one, huh?"

Del grabs the last raspberry danish — *yuck* — and plops it on his plate. "No. I was stuck on a conference call with one of our security vendors so everyone else got their 'emergencies' lined up."

"I can't feel too bad for you, Del. You've managed to weasel your way out of the last five of these."

"Four. I had to sit through the February one." He shudders.

"That one was the worst." As one would expect, the whole theme of the February pep rally was love. They somehow managed to twist that into how we're supposed to show love for our customers. It was absurd.

I point Del to the seat next to mine. Ellie is on my other side, chatting with Trevor, the smarmy head of the sales team. She adores him. I think he's a little creep. To be fair, he reminds me of my ex-husband, so I might be a little biased.

"Big plans for the Fourth?" Del asks me.

I pop a grape in my mouth. "Meh, nothing exciting. How about you?"

"Family cookout at my parents'. Then we'll spend the evening watching their neighbor's illegal fireworks with 9-1 already dialed, just in case there's another incident."

There's got to be a story there. "*Another* incident? With fireworks?"

"Yeah. Three years ago one of their roman candles set my parents' shed on fire."

I almost drop my grapes. "No way."

"Yeah. Thank goodness it was only the shed and not the house."

"Good afternoon, PAMECorp!" Cecily, VP of Bullshit, flounces onto a small platform at the front of the room and grins. She lifts both arms and wiggles her fingers, waving at all of us. Her manic open-mouthed grin is the icing on the cake.

"Oh, shit," Del grumbles.

I smile, which Cecily wrongly assumes is due to my excitement at her dramatic entrance. She points at me and gives a double thumbs up.

"Are we all excited to be here?" Cecily missed her calling as a televangelist charlatan (not that all tv preachers are charlatans, but she totally would be). Instead, she's here, spreading the One True Message about the joy of corporate devotion.

A few people shout, "Yes!" and I'm convinced they've been given a bonus to do so, because nobody is that happy to be at work on a Friday afternoon before a holiday weekend.

Cecily claps her hands and jumps up and down a few times. "Come on, PAMECorp, you can do better than that! Are we all excited to be here?"

Most of us muster a lukewarm "Yeah," which is good enough for Cecily.

"If you're not excited now, you will be," she threatens.

"I'm too old for this," Del grumbles at my ear.

Me, too. I'm a few months shy of my forty-seventh birthday, old enough to be steeped in cynicism and immune to people like Cecily. (Why yes, I am GenX. Is it that obvious?) Del's fiftyish, cute in a geeky sort of way, with a wicked sense of humor. We've bonded over *Seinfeld* references most of our coworkers are too young to fully appreciate.

Cecily presses on. "I'm sure you've all noticed the gift bags on the floor under the chairs."

I hadn't, actually. I'd noticed two things. The lack of donuts and my proximity to the exit. Priorities, you know.

"Go ahead and grab the gift bag under your chair." She clasps her hands as if she expects to be blown away by our collective reaction.

I lean over, trying not to spill my grapes, and reach back to pick up the bright red gift bag.

"Okay, friends," Cecily shouts. "Open your present!"

Rustling fills the room. I balance my bowl of grapes on my lap and pull the items out of my bag. A thin leather book and a rectangular wooden case. I flatten the bag and open the case. A pen is nestled on foam inside. An expensive pen.

I flip the leather book over. On the front, engraved in gold leaf, are the words, "My Bucket List."

What the heck is this crap?

Chapter 2

"What's this shit?" Del whispers, echoing my thoughts as he inspects his journal and pen.

"I'm sure we're about to find out," I whisper back.

Ellie clasps her book with both hands. "This is awesome," she gushes. "I've always wanted to make a bucket list."

Not me. Bucket lists, vision boards, empowerment dream charts... all that woowoo bullshit is for the birds. No, actually, birds deserve better than this nonsense. My goals are sensible, just like my shoes.

It's casual Friday. Ellie is in an adorable sundress and red heels. Casual Friday, Ellie, *casual*. I'm in jeans and sneakers and a standard-issue gray prison — er, PAMECorp t-shirt. Nobody likes a showoff.

Okay, that's a lie. I adore Ellie. She's in her late 20s, and steeped in all the perky optimism that comes with being that age.

"What are you going to put on your list?" Ellie asks, just as Cecily retakes the stage and saves me from answering.

"Alrighty, friends, let's get down to business with the PAMECorp motto! Ready? Go!"

The crowd mumbles along as Cecily shouts into her headset. She claps her hands on each syllable. I hope she gets a blister.

"People! Action! Motivation! Efficiency! PAMECorp! PAMECorp!"

People actually applaud. Del and I glance at each other, and

I mutter, "If they start rolling in trays of Kool-Aid, I'm out of here."

He snorts.

Cecily beams and holds up her own leather book. "You all know that PAMECorp's number one priority is YOU. Without you, there would be no PAMECorp at all. To show our appreciation, July's theme is all about… can anybody guess?" She cups a hand to one ear and leans toward the audience.

Low, so only I can hear, Del says, "Torture?"

I bite my lip.

"That's right! Independence!" She claps again. "This month's theme is all about YOU — the amazing individuals that make up our amazing team. You all do an amazing job here, and so we want you to make your own bucket list." She holds up a hand in a "stop" gesture. "Now I know you'll all be tempted to put things on your bucket list related to PAMECorp, but we want your bucket list to be full of amazing things for YOU."

"If she says 'amazing' one more time…"

Del whispers, "How dare you mock our Leader."

We look away from each other to keep from laughing out loud.

Ellie is facing forward with rapt attention and I hope I'm not disrupting her magical experience.

Cecily blathers on as I run my finger over the gold leaf title on the journal. I try to stop them, but the thoughts come anyway. When did I become so cynical and stop letting myself have fun goals and dreams?

Oh yeah, I never started. I'm pretty sure I came out of the womb cynical. Probably because my mother was unconscious

— back then the actual woman giving birth was a bit of a nuisance, so it was standard procedure to knock her out, deliver the baby, and then bring her around.

In my case, my mother was unconscious, I was born, and my father was flying high as a kite, thanks to his never-ending love affair with cocaine. Despite this, the doctor asked him what my name was. As legend has it, the only thing he could remember was that someone in the waiting room was drinking a soda. Behold, my name. Shasta. Thank God they weren't drinking a Mr. Pibb.

When my mother came to, she was furious. You're probably on her side right now. Don't be. She wanted to name me Moonflower. No, I'm not shitting you. They compromised. My name is Shasta Moonflower, which went so nicely with my original hippie last name of Rivers. When I got married, I couldn't take his name — DeAngelo — fast enough. And when I got rid of him, I kept it.

The pen is really nice. A Parker pen, to be exact. If I'm not mistaken, these pens run a solid fifty bucks apiece. I glance around the room. About two hundred of us in attendance, plus two hundred smarter employees who are not. So if they got one for everyone, that means the company coughed up twenty grand for pens?! Plus another however much for the journals.

I inspect it more closely. Soft leather cover, thick pages, loop to secure a pen... yeah, these probably cost at least thirty dollars. Twelve grand. Thirty-two thousand dollars on this crap? Not to mention four hundred gift bags? The wastefulness makes me itchy.

I realize Cecily's voice has stopped. I glance around at a sea of bowed heads. Most people are writing in their journals. I look to the front of the room. The giant whiteboard has a helpful suggestion to write "My Bucket List" on top of the first page and then list ten items. Goals. Dreams. Visions. Things to manifest. Whatever.

Fine. I'll play along. Maybe I can manifest a chocolate doughnut.

I smooth the journal open and at the top of the first page, I write, "My Bucket List" and the number one.

It mocks me.

What can I possibly write down? I could write down that I'd like to change my name. No, as much as I fantasize about it, I don't think I'd ever do it.

I poise my pen over the paper and get ready to write. Is the point to make a list of things to waste money on? Fine. It's not like I'm signing a contract. I could splurge on those fancy cotton candy flavored grapes instead of the regular ones. Wow. No way I'm writing that down, because it's the most pathetic, lame, pitiful wish list ever. Grapes? Really? That's the best I can come up with?

Cecily startles me by clapping her hands to get everyone's attention again. "Okay! Let's hear some of the things on your lists. I'll randomly call on a few of you to share. Carol S. Tell us something on your list."

A woman in the front corner of the room stands and says, "I want to hike the Grand Canyon."

Applause.

"Monica D. Your turn."

Monica pops to her feet like a sugared-up whack-a-mole. "I

want to write a book."

Applause follows her, and each of the next ten people who share their big dreams. I politely clap, not paying attention, until Del elbows my arm. "She just called on you."

Cecily looks over the room and repeats, "Shasta? I thought I saw you earlier." Her hand is over her eyes as if she's shielding them from the sun as she searches for me.

Shit. I stand up and mumble, "I, um, want to go to Pamplona for the Running of the Bulls."

I sit to thunderous applause. My face burns because I hate being put on the spot.

"Bull is right," Del says.

"What was I supposed to say?"

He leans over and looks at my closed journal. "What's on your list for real?"

I open it and show him the blank page.

"Wow, really getting in the spirit, eh?"

"What's on your list?"

Sheepish, he opens his book and lets me see the page. His handwriting is small, tight, and neat. His first item is to do ten random acts of kindness. His second? Restore a muscle car. That's way closer to what I expected to see.

Cecily is reading some statistics on goal setting and how writing down your goals makes them eleventy billion times more likely to come to fruition. I look at the clock and sigh. It's only one thirty, which means we're trapped here for at least another hour and a half.

"We have one last surprise for you. If you look inside the back cover of your journal," she says, pausing for everyone to look.

"You've got to be kidding me." I roll my eyes at the crisp twenty-dollar bill.

"We're giving you a little bit of seed money to start fulfilling your bucket list!" Cecily gives a little squeal. Seriously. She squeals in delight, the shrill noise giving me a headache.

"How much you think they spent on this?" Del asks.

"Pfft. Upwards of fifty grand."

He makes a strangled noise. "Are you serious?"

"I'm an accountant. I'm always serious."

"Sheesh."

I share the sentiment. I know I'm supposed to be grateful the company is so "employee oriented" but the level of spending — which I feel is directly proportional to the level of stupidity — puts a bad taste in my mouth. I look down at the pile in my lap. I could have put the hundred bucks they spent on my "gift" into an investment account and turned it into more money. It also irks me that they can lay out this kind of money for nonsense like this, but our department has to jump through a dozen hoops and practically sign blood-oath declarations of need in order to get toner for the five-hundred-year-old copier the "can't afford" to replace.

I slide my finger along the sleek black casing of the pen. It clicks so smoothly and writes like a dream. Fine. I can admit the pen is pretty awesome.

While Cecily continues, I glance over at Del's notebook. "Tell me about the random acts of kindness."

He blushes a little and pushes his glasses up his nose. "It's no big deal. Something I used to do with my mom when I was a kid. It was the first thing I thought of."

Cecily says something about breakout sessions, and a handful of us take advantage of the motion and chaos to cram into the elevator like rats leaping onto the Titanic's last lifeboat.

Del's arm is against mine. The warmth is enough to distract me from the uncomfortable position I'm in. If I shift my weight at all, I'll be pressed against his side, and while the idea isn't offensive, it'd likely be an HR violation. I scarcely breathe until the door opens on the eighth floor. Del and I hop out. He heads right and points back at me. "Get to work on that list."

"I'm on it," I answer sarcastically and hold the gift bag over the trash can. My department is to the left, so we part company with a smile.

At my desk, the red gift bag mocks me. I turn all my attention back to the spreadsheet I was working on, and stifle a curse. I hate being interrupted mid-project, and now I can't remember what formula I was trying to set up. It takes me a good fifteen minutes to work backwards and start that section all over.

The only upside to these pep rallies is moments like this, where everyone else in my cube farm is at the meeting and it's just me, working in a quiet office. Well, me and Carl, who never attends these things, but he's on the far side of the room.

It's almost four when half a dozen accountants spill back into the room. Ellie appears in my cube doorway. "*Ohmygoshyoumissedit,*" she says it like it's one word. "Where'd you disappear to?"

"Bathroom." I feel a little bad about lying, but it's so much easier than telling Ellie that I hate those meetings. She loves them, and bless her heart, she'd probably try to convince me to love them, too. It's better for both of us this way. "What did I miss?"

She's breathless. "Oh. My. Goodness. Cecily had us break into small groups and we workshopped items for our bucket lists. We had general topics, like travel, adventure, personal, all kinds of stuff to get us started."

I'm hard pressed to think of something less appealing than discussing anything private with my coworkers. Ellie is the exception, and I think that's mostly because she reminds me so much of my daughter, Katherine. Kat's a little younger at twenty-five, but they both share that unbridled passion for life generally reserved for the young.

"It was sooo great."

"Awesome," I say.

Her eyes sparkle as she catches my gaze. "Do you really want to go to Spain and see the bulls? That would be so amazing."

I can't lie to her about that. I shake my head. "It was the only thing I could think of when Cecily put me on the spot like that."

She looks slightly disappointed. "Oh. What *do* you want to do?"

"Finish my spreadsheet and go home," I answer with a laugh.

She eyes me just like Kat would. "You should make the list. It'll be good for you."

A moment later I'm alone in my cube. Just me and the stupid blank page mocking me. Well, forget it. There's no way

I'm making a list.

Not now, not ever.

* * *

My Bucket List

1.

Chapter 3

I just finished washing my supper dishes when Kat's call comes in. I check my watch. Eight on the dot. "Hey, sweetheart, I thought it was my turn to call you?"

"It is, but I just got home and Daniel's working late."

There's a two-hour time difference between Pennsylvania and Colorado, so it's six there. "How was your day?"

She yawns and I hear the telltale rustling that lets me know she's flopping onto the couch. Probably already in her pajamas. "Good. Long. I was supposed to get off at two, but I didn't want to hand off my patient. I even had to throw her over-involved mother-in-law out of a delivery room this afternoon. Good times."

"Oh, no." It's just something to say, because I know Kat has zero problem handling troublemakers.

"Oh, yes. The poor mother is in active hard labor, and this woman is badgering her that she's not pushing enough." She sips something. "At one point my patient is crying. She tells her husband to ask his mother to leave. Squirrely little wuss wouldn't do it, so I did." That's my girl, staunch advocate for those in need.

"You go, Kat." I swear she's a superhero.

"Man was she *mad*. I asked if she would prefer to stay in the waiting room or be escorted out of the building. She calmed her ass down after that. Half an hour later we had a healthy baby girl and a tired but happy mama. And how was your day?"

I tell her about the pep rally.

"Mom. You should totally do a bucket list." She sounds far more enthusiastic than I expect. "Seriously. It doesn't have to be big stuff. Just things you never do for yourself. You know, because you *never* do anything for yourself," she scolds.

"That's not true. I…" I can't think of anything except binge-watching Netflix.

"Exactly." There's a pause and something shifts in her tone. "Soooo, part of the reason I called is that I kind of have a bucket list item of my own."

"Oh?" I'm immediately on edge. What is she up to now?

"You know how much I love being in labor & delivery, and that's where my heart is."

"Yes." Ever since she was little, Kat was destined to work with babies in some capacity. When she finished nursing school and had the chance to take the job in L&D, she didn't even hesitate. In fact, her internship in school had been at a birthing center. My girl has always known where she was going.

"I have an amazing opportunity. Now don't freak out."

"Kat." What's the easiest way to get me to freak out? Tell me not to.

"We're moving to Nashville."

Surprising, but hardly the bombshell I was expecting. "I thought you loved living in Fort Collins."

"I do. We do. But."

Oh. I sense something big coming.

"I got a scholarship to get my Master's so I can be a certified midwife."

"That's incredible." My heart surges with pride. "Where?"

"Vanderbilt."

"Holy shit, Kat!" I'm on my feet. I wish she was here because I would bear-hug her so hard. "That's amazing!"

"Here's the part you're not going to like."

I sit back down.

"The scholarship stipulates I have to be a full-time student. Which means I'm not going to be working. Not that I'd have much time anyway. It's an intensive program."

I bite my tongue. She's already heard my lecture a billion times about not relying on a man for support.

"It's a two-year program. Daniel already has a job lined up at Vanderbilt UMC that he's really excited about."

"When are you moving?"

"Three weeks."

I don't expect that answer. "That's really soon. Do you have an apartment lined up? Are you okay for the move?"

"Yes." She sighs. "I wish we could have toured it in person before we signed the lease, but we couldn't afford to fly to Nashville and back and then move."

"Ugh." My risk-averse spirit shudders. Kat's always been bold and adventurous. I envy her sometimes. "What can I do to help? Do you want me to come to Nashville and help you move in?"

She correctly translates my offer. "Mom, you don't have to go check the place out. It'll be fine. We're hiring movers." Before I can comment, she says, "Yes, they're legit, yes, we're getting the extra insurance, and yes, I'm packing our breakables myself. And yes, we'll have our valuables in our cars, and out of sight."

"How long's the drive?"

"Like eighteen hours. We'll stop in the middle and get a hotel somewhere."

I'm nearly bursting with the desire to give her advice and warnings, but I hold my tongue. She's got an amazing head on her shoulders, and I like to think it's because I gave her the right kind of guidance while she was growing up.

"And yes, I promise I will text you when we leave and when we stop. You don't have to worry."

"I might not *have* to, but I will."

"I know you will."

"Tell me more about the scholarship."

"It's amazing. I applied on a whim and never in a million years thought I'd get it. It's practically a full ride. Covers all the tuition and most of the lab fees. I still have to cover books and scrubs and stuff like that."

"That *is* amazing. Let me know what you need. You didn't use all the college money we had set aside. I'm not sure exactly what's left." That's only partially true. I know the principal amount to the penny, but it's earned interest over the two years since she graduated.

"Dad said he's going to buy my books."

"Great." The word flies out of my mouth, a reflex so I don't laugh or tell her not to believe it until his check clears.

Her words are hesitant. "I was hoping you might help with the security deposit for the new place."

"Only if you're on the lease."

"Of course I am." Her answer is a little prickly, which I fully understand, but my priority is making sure she's protected. Daniel's a nice guy, but his feelings aren't even on my radar. "We do have enough in savings, but I don't want to run us short in case we have something unexpected come up during the move. I'll pay you back when we get this security deposit back, but it might be like a month."

"I'm in no hurry. Just let me know what you need and when." No hurry indeed. She doesn't need to pay it back ever.

"Thanks, Mom."

"I'm so proud of you, Kat. I can only imagine how stiff the competition is to get into that program, and to do it with a scholarship is incredible. *You're* incredible."

"You are too. Which is why I think you should do your bucket list. Put some fun stuff on there. Spend some of your moldy money," she laughs.

Joke's on her. I'll use PAMECorp's moldy twenty bucks. "Fine. I'll put something on this stupid list."

"I'm serious. When's the last time you thought about doing something fun?"

I don't like it when my daughter flips the script and sounds like the wise parent. "I'll work on it."

No way she's letting me off that easy. "What's your first thing?"

"I haven't put anything on the list yet. I need to think about it."

She makes an impatient noise. "No, you don't. Right now, right off the top of your head, what's one thing for your list?"

I blurt out, "I want to buy a lottery ticket."

"Yay! Mom, you did it!" Her level of enthusiasm is entirely disproportionate to the task I've chosen.

Then it hits me, like the proverbial ton of bricks. It's probably the most frivolous thing she's seen me do.

"Mom? You still there?"

I hold the phone a little tighter. "Kat, am I boring?"

Her silence answers me before her carefully chosen words do. "You're amazing. I would never call you boring. You're funny and kind and... careful. I do wish you'd do more fun stuff. I know you think a lot of stuff is wasteful, but maybe if you reframe it as paying for the experience?"

I swallow down the lump in my throat.

"Geez, Mom, I'm sorry."

"No." I clear my throat. "No, don't apologize, you're one hundred percent right, and nothing you said was wrong."

"Yeah, but I don't want to hurt your feelings."

I smile. That's my girl, so thoughtful and empathetic. It's what makes her an amazing nurse, and will make her an outstanding midwife. "Kat, you didn't hurt my feelings. At all. I'm just taking stock and it's depressing."

"Eww, it shouldn't be depressing. Go buy your lottery tickets."

On second thought, buying lottery tickets seems stupid. I could easily find something more fun to spend the money on, right?

As if she reads my mind, Kat says, "The fun of lottery tickets is imagining what you'd do if you hit it big. Did you write it down?"

"No, not yet."

"Huh-uh. You said it, now write it down as your first bucket list item."

Guess I'm not getting out of this. I open the journal and write "Buy a lottery ticket" on the first line. "There. I wrote it down. Happy now?"

"Yes. Have fun with it. Hold the ticket in your hand, and until the numbers are called, it's potentially the big winner."

This does make me laugh. "Schrödinger's money?"

"Exactly. The ticket is simultaneously a winner and a loser. Either way, you've had fun imagining the possibilities."

"Okay, I guess I can see that."

"Daniel just pulled in, so I'm going to go."

I hate to hang up. Kat's my favorite person in the whole world. "Okay, sweetheart. I'll cash app you the money for the security deposit. Have a good evening, and congratulations again. I'm so proud of you."

"Thanks, Mom. Love you."

"Love you, too. Say hello to Daniel for me." Despite his low rank on my list of priorities, I do like Daniel. He's good to Kat, and she loves him.

We hang up and before I can change my mind, I put my sneakers on and grab my keys. I drive to the convenience store and park. People are like ants, streaming in and out of the busy store. Are their lives as boring as mine? Probably, if they're spending Friday evening here. A car parks beside mine and I feel the thumping bass in my chest.

Inside the store, it occurs to me that I have no idea how to buy lottery tickets, so I stall by getting a soda from the fountain. No ice.

I pop a lid onto the cup.

From the corner of my eye, I see a man hanging back, waiting for the fountain. I grab my straw and move out of the way.

"Hey, Shasta."

My head jerks. "Del. Hey." It occurs to me that this is the first time I've seen him outside of PAMECorp. He looks different, but it might be the lighting. My heart flutters a little.

"What'cha up to?" He fills his cup to the top with ice and then root beer.

I watch the bubbles foam to the top. "You know you're just paying for ice."

He grins. "I like my soda cold all the way to the end."

Why does that bother me? I drink barely cool beverages all the time. Heck, they don't even use ice in Europe, right? Fine. It might not taste quite as good, but I get a lot more drink for my money.

"Big plans this evening?"

My attention lands on his nicely tanned bare forearms. Does he work out? "Um, no. I came out to buy a lottery ticket and then I'll probably watch television or read a book or something."

A slow grin spreads across his face. "Lottery ticket? That doesn't sound like you."

"It's the first thing on my bucket list."

He laughs. "You're using the PAMECorp seed money, aren't you?"

My cheeks heat a little. "So?"

"So nothing. I like the loophole. You won't spend your hard-earned money on something so frivolous, but you'll use the free money from the company. Smart."

"Yeah? What are you using your seed money on?"

He winks — actually winks! — at me. "Lottery tickets."

"You're making fun of me."

"Not at all. I buy lottery tickets every Friday night."

"Why?" Every Friday? The concept is foreign to me.

"Because it's fun."

Doesn't get simpler than that, does it? We walk toward the cash registers. "But surely you don't win all the time."

He shrugs one shoulder. "No. I break even overall. But the fun part is scratching them off and imagining what I'd do if I hit a big winner."

Wow. Del gets it. Kat gets it. Apparently I'm the only one who doesn't. But that's about to change.

We wait in line, and then Del lightly bumps my arm with his elbow, nudging me toward the far register. "Tickets are over there." I pretend the tingle going up my spine is the anticipation of buying my first lottery ticket and not the warmth of his unexpected touch.

"Oh."

He walks with me and sets his drink on the glass counter. Rows of colorful tickets are lined up under the glass, and I'm suddenly overwhelmed. And then I feel stupid for being overwhelmed by something so simple. Forget it. I'm just going to pay for my soda and go home.

Del taps the glass. "I'd like one of the five-dollar frog tickets, a five-dollar fireworks, one two-dollar dog, a two-dollar jewel, a two-dollar wizard, and one each of these four one-dollar tickets along the front."

I know he spelled it all out for my benefit, and I appreciate it.

He pays for his tickets and drink, and it's my turn. "Can I get the same as him?"

"Sure." The cashier rips off the tickets and scans them.

I hand over PAMECorp's twenty and two bucks to cover my drink. Change rolls down a little chute and I scoop it out.

Del grins at me, and we walk to the sliding door. I'm not paying as much attention as I should, and a man hustles in the door, slamming into me. I yelp and stumble back into Del. We both manage to save our drinks. Mostly. My lid pops off and a blurp of soda sloshes onto my shirt.

Our tickets scatter across the floor.

The man apologizes profusely and scrambles to pick up our tickets and hands them to me in a lump. "Sorry about that. Are you okay?"

I take quick stock. "I'm fine." Other than my wet shirt and embarrassment, I'm fine. I quickly count the tickets. They're all accounted for. Just one problem. We have no way of knowing who bought which ticket.

"Be more careful," Del admonishes the man mildly.

The man scurries away and we exit to the sidewalk. I hand the tickets to Del while I secure my lid back onto my cup.

He steers us over to one of the small tables on the wide sidewalk. "You sure you're okay? He ran into you pretty hard."

"Yeah, I'm fine. I'm just a little upset about the tickets. We don't know which tickets are whose."

"Well, we can do this one of two ways." He sits in one of the uncomfortable molded chairs bolted to the cement.

I take the chair across from him and wait.

"One, we can just split them up and go on our merry way. Or two, we can split them up with the understanding that we split any winnings fifty-fifty since we *could* have each other's tickets."

"Wow, gambling with gambling."

"Exactly. Your call." He spreads the tickets out on the table.

I study the colorful tickets and make my second snap decision of the day. "Let's split them fifty-fifty."

"You divide them up."

Even though we bought the same tickets, it's harder than I expect to decide which one to keep and which one to give him, so it takes me a while. He doesn't seem to mind. Once the tickets are divided, he slides a quarter across the table. "Shall we?"

"Oh. We're scratching them off now?"

"We don't need to," he says, leaning back in his seat. "If you have to go…"

"No." I don't want to go. This is, dare I say it, fun. I pick up his quarter and debate. Do I start with the one-dollar ticket and work my way up, or start with a five-dollar and work my way down? I start small.

"Which one are we doing?"

It gives me a little rush of excitement that we're doing this *together*. I haven't spent any time with an actual man for a couple of years. Wait. Not a couple, seven. *Seven*. Holy shit, that means I haven't been on a date since I was in my thirties. Here I am, more than halfway through my forties, and I haven't been on one single date.

Not that this is a date.

But wow, I really *am* boring.

"Shasta? You in there?"

I jerk back to attention. "Sorry. Let's start with the diamonds."

"You got it." He scratches and little flecks of gray pile up.

I watch him, then scratch my own ticket. I uncover a large diamond. According to the instructions, that's an automatic winner. I look closer to see my prize. "Five bucks!"

Del reaches over for a high five. Our hands smack with a satisfying clap.

"Mine was a loser."

We scratch the next three one-dollar tickets and between us we win a free ticket.

"How's that going to work?" I ask.

"Same way. We'll pick a ticket and split any prize. Deal?"

"Deal." I believe him. Wheee, look at me, taking a man at his word. Of course, it's not life or death stakes here. It's a cheap scratch off ticket. Baby steps, right?

I sip my iceless soda and crack my knuckles before tackling the two-dollar wizard. The wizard does his magic and gives me a twenty-dollar winner. I squeal and stamp my feet on the concrete. "This is awesome." I finally get it. The experience is the fun part. Sitting here scratching off tickets with Del is well worth the twenty bucks.

We scratch off ticket after ticket with no yield. Finally, we're down to the five-dollar frog tickets. Our haul so far: a free ticket and twenty-five bucks.

I scratch off lily pad after lily pad, and on the last one, I win another twenty dollars. Splitting the money, I have officially come out two dollars and fifty cents ahead of where I started. It paid for my tickets and my soda with a dollar to spare. If that's not a win, I don't know what is.

I look over at Del. He seems confused. Or shocked. I can't tell which. "Del?"

He looks up at me and holds the ticket out. "We need to get them to verify this."

I take it and read the instructions, then look at the scratched off lily pads. My breath hitches in my throat. "That can't be right, can it?"

If it is, we just won ten thousand dollars.

* * *

My Bucket List

1. ~~Buy a lottery ticket~~
2.

Chapter 4

It's been two and a half weeks since Del mailed in the forms and the ticket. I'm still skeptical — hello, cynic here — that he'll share the jackpot with me. I have no basis for that assumption, especially considering that we sent the required forms to split the tax liability, and he called the lottery office to see if they'd issue two checks (they won't), and he gave me copies of the ticket as well as a copy of the post office receipt with the tracking number.

The lottery office says it'll take four to six weeks to get a check. I'm taking Kat's advice and using the time to think of it as Schrödinger's money. The real prize is the dream, right?

I sit at a table in the PAMECorp cafeteria with the lunch I brought from home and my bucket list journal. It's still blank except for line one, where I wrote "Buy a Lottery Ticket." I guess I've crossed off my whole list, ha.

The blank page mocks me. I'm a grown-ass woman. Why is it so hard to come up with a handful of things I'd like to try?

I click my Parker pen — seriously, it's the nicest pen I've ever had. Beside the number two, I write, "Go Through Automatic Car Wash."

You can't possibly be surprised that I only wash my car by hand. It was a challenge for me to even spend the handful of quarters use the car wash's power washer, but once I calculated the number of washes with store-bought cleaning supplies, and the fact that I never have to clean out their vacuum, the cost is a downright bargain. I've never been able to take the leap and spend paper money on the automatic wash, though.

I'm staring at the blank number three when Del slides a tray onto the table. "Mind if I join you?" We've had lunch together almost every day since we got the tickets, but he still asks every time. It's been an easy routine to fall into, and look forward to. I can't help but hope it continues after we get the money.

I smile up at him. "Not at all. How's your day going?"

"Ugh." He plops onto the chair and makes a face. "I don't understand why people insist on clicking links in emails. The phishing training could not possibly be any clearer."

"Hey, one of these days a *real* Nigerian prince will be trying to send you five million dollars, and you'll be sorry."

"If only it was that interesting. You saw the email from the fake bank Wednesday afternoon?"

"Yeah, I deleted it."

"Well, seventeen people didn't. I mean, come *on.* 'You've won a Chase Fargo raffle prize, click here to claim?' Half of it wasn't even spelled right, but seven. Teen. People. Clicked. I couldn't have made it sound any faker. So now I have a shitload of paperwork to fill out and forward to the managers."

I sit back and pretend to be shocked. "Trickery! Our own IT department is phishing us. For shame."

He laughs. "I use the same fake bank name every time I send one of those emails, too. You'd think people would catch on. The worst part is that there have been so many there's a new policy, which means I have to personally meet with every single person who clicks any of the links. They don't pay me enough for this."

My phone vibrates. "Sorry, I have to look at this."

He waves his hand in a "don't mention it" gesture and unwraps his sandwich.

I look at my text from Kat and blow out a long, slow breath. I feel the tension drain from my shoulders and neck.

"Everything okay?"

"Yeah. My daughter is moving from Colorado to Nashville. They were supposed to get there yesterday but there were massive storms in Missouri so they decided to stay at a hotel instead of driving through it."

"Good call."

"Definitely." I finish my salad, glad I can relax now that I know Kat and Daniel are safe at their new apartment. Kat texts that it's very nice and promises to send pictures.

He points his fork at my journal. "Finish your list yet?"

"Ha. Not even close." I put my hand on the journal and look at my nails. I'm inspired to add another item to my list. I flip the journal open and in number three, I write, "Get a Real Manicure."

I keep going, and write, "Get Hair Done in Actual Salon" in the number four spot.

Look at that, I'm on a roll.

Del raises an eyebrow, but doesn't ask.

"I get my hair cut at Cheap Chops. I always wear it tied up, so it doesn't matter. But I'd like to splurge and get my hair done in an actual salon. Maybe even get highlights or something." I have no idea why I tell him this.

He nods. "My daughter really likes the Serenity Salon and Spa." He adds, "I know this because I just got her a gift certificate from there. For her birthday. Which is next week."

It occurs to me that we've never really talked about our families except in passing. "Is she your only?"

"Oldest of two. Allie's turning twenty-six, and Ben is twenty-one. You?"

"Just the one. Kat. Katherine. She's twenty-five." I remember that he's divorced, but I don't know if he's seeing anyone. If he is, I wonder how she feels about the lottery ticket.

"And what about a Mr. Shasta?" Apparently he's on the same wavelength.

My cheeks heat. "Divorced him eight years ago. How about Mrs. Del?"

"Divorced her four years ago."

"Oh."

Footsteps clack rapidly up behind me. "Shasta, I need you." Ellie is out of breath and panicked.

"What is it?"

She bursts into tears. "The Brighton payroll is all messed up. I tried to fix it but I think I made it worse." Her shoulders shake as she sobs.

I jump to my feet and grab her upper arms to get her to focus. "Hey. Hey, it's okay." I shove my phone in my back pocket and glance at Del.

"Good luck," he says around a bite of something. He waves at my lunch containers. "I'll grab that for you."

I wave my thanks, grab my purse, abandon my lunch, and usher Ellie to the elevators. "It's okay, Ellie. I promise we'll get it figured out."

Thankfully, the elevator is empty the whole ride to the

eighth floor. She composes herself by the time we step out. At her desk, she shows me a hot mess of a report that doesn't correspond in any way to the payroll software.

"I was verifying the numbers and the first couple were okay, but then nothing was matching up. I don't know what I did wrong." Her eyes shine with tears again.

"Hang on, let me grab my chair." I take the few steps to my cube and roll my chair over to Ellie's desk. We squeeze in. After half a minute, it's clear this report is completely unusable, so I have her close everything and start from scratch. "Import the files again. I'm guessing something got corrupted in the transfer."

It's almost six o'clock when we run the report again, and this time everything is as it should be.

Ellie bonks her head on her desk. "I'm so sorry. I still don't know what I did wrong."

I pat her shoulder. "Don't worry about it. It could have been a typo or corrupted files, or it could have just been because this software is shit." It's true. Brighton is our last client that uses an archaic system that they should have upgraded years ago.

She sits up straight and runs a hand down her face. "I'm really sorry I made you stay late."

Definitely not how I wanted to spend my Friday evening, but it's not Ellie's fault. And it's not like I have a hot date. I give her a hug, even though it's probably inappropriate by HR standards.

She squeezes me tight and sniffles. "Thank you."

"Don't stress about it. It's done, and now you can go enjoy your weekend." I smile and roll my chair back to my cube.

The rest of the office is empty. I listen as Ellie's heels clack down the hall to the elevator, and then I'm alone.

I wake up my computer and glance over the open files. Nothing that can't wait until Monday. That's when I notice my lunchbox and journal on the corner of my desk. Del must have put them here when he was done with his lunch. I'll have to thank him.

The cleaning team rolls a mop bucket past my cube. I stand up and startle the man, whose music thumps out past his ear buds. I lift my hand and say, "Sorry," even though he probably can't hear me. He smiles and touches his chest over his heart, then gives me a thumbs up.

I shove my journal into my purse — a pale pink leather Kate Spade bag I snagged at a Goodwill for six bucks — and grab my insulated lunch bag. I push the buttons to put my computer to sleep and head for home.

It's late, and I have zero desire to make myself something to eat, so I splurge and go through the Wendy's drive-through. At home, I change into yoga pants and eat my dinner while scrolling through my phone.

Kat texts me pictures of the apartment — it's gorgeous — and an apology for not calling, but she's exhausted. I send her back a string of colored heart emojis and then a few dancing hug gifs. She sends a thumbs up and a smile.

I put my phone down and fish the journal out of my purse. Surely I can think of something else to add. I click the Parker pen and open the journal.

A bright orange sticky note greets me. It says, "5. Ask Del out for a date." Below it is his phone number.

* * *

My Bucket List

1. ~~Buy a lottery ticket~~
2. Go through automatic car wash
3. Manicure
4. Get hair done in real salon

Chapter 5

I take a picture of the sticky note and immediately text it to Kat with the message: **WHAT DO I DO????**

She texts back two dozen shocked face emojis, then, **ASK HIM OUT!!!!!!!!!!!!!!!!!**

Easy for her to say. I feel guilty about bothering her when she needs to get some rest, so I just say I'll let her know how it goes.

On the one hand, that takes care of the fear of rejection, doesn't it? On the other hand, that could get messy, going on a date with Del. What if it doesn't work out and I lose his friendship? That would suck beyond all sucking.

As I ponder all the ways this could go wrong, Kat texts me again.

Took a lot of guts for him to leave that note.

Well, crap. It did, didn't it?

My phone dings again.

Don't let fear hold you back.

I text a rather snarky, **Thanks, Dr. Phil.**

She responds with a middle finger and a string of laughing faces.

Is it fear, though, or common sense and experience? If we want to get all psychological, it's pretty clear why I'm not a big fan of the male species. Let's recap, shall we?

We've got my father, the drugged-out hippie who first of all named me after a fricking soda can, then nearly let me die of pneumonia when I was eight. *"Who needs modern medicine, man?*

Nature is the cure to all things." Then, during my last visitation with him, he topped off years of horrific parenting by simply saying it was up to me when one of his commune "brothers" offered me heroin and the opportunity to "experience the joy of physical love" because age is nothing but a social construct. Yeah. I was twelve, and I declined.

My grandparents — my father's parents — took custody of me after the pneumonia incident and put an end to the visitation after the last. My grandfather was angry and bitter because he had to put off retirement for a few extra years to support me. I get it, I do, but I was *eight*. He'd promise me things, like a trip to the mall, or a sleepover with my friends, or a kitten, but he'd always yank those promises away and say it was my fault because I'd been bad. Usually by something so egregious as singing or laughing too loud. I can still see him, shaking his head like I was a huge disappointment, then he'd verbally slap me down by telling me I acted just like my "druggie whore mother." He died when I was sixteen. I wasn't sorry to see him go.

They say women generally either end up with a partner that's exactly like their father, or the complete opposite. I thought I'd gone for the complete opposite, but somehow ended up married to Nick, a soulless tax attorney who cheated on me with my best friend. I found out by walking in on them. You'd think that's what made me divorce him, but no. That came a few months later, when I caught him smoking pot.

Yup, I forgave his wandering dick, but a little recreational weed was a bridge too far. How messed up is that?

In any event, the only good thing that came out of my

marriage to Nick was Kat. She was away at college when it all ended. I always thought it'd end with a big dramatic bang, but it was more of a quiet click that sounds an awful lot like the front door closing.

Nick made one mistake in the divorce. He underestimated my drive to protect myself, my daughter, and our financial future. It's the one time in my life I splurged and went brand-name. I paid for the best divorce attorney in the whole damn state. Maybe even the country.

I was out-earning Nick at that point, so he thought he'd get a windfall. Turned out, he got not one penny from my investments, and had to buy out my half of the house. Real estate was on an upswing, so the appraisal came in hugely in my favor.

Nick called my lawyer a shark and a bitch. I called her worth every penny.

It's been eight years, and I still send her a card at Christmas.

My phone vibrates again, and it's Kat, asking if I've asked him yet. This time, it's me who sends the middle finger emoji and a string of laughing faces, followed up with, **Thought you were going to sleep?**

She responds with, **DO IT!**

I add Del's number as a contact in my phone. Not that I'm actually planning to ask him out.

But I move the sticky note into the number five spot.

Just in case.

* * *

My Bucket List

1. ~~Buy a lottery ticket~~
2. Go through automatic car wash
3. Manicure
4. Get hair done in real salon
5. Ask Del out on a date (!!!!!)

Chapter 6

It's after eight o'clock. Is that too late to send someone a text? I have no clue. That's a lie. I know it's not too late, but I'm a big fat chicken. I like Del. A lot. And now a post-it note has me all in a tizzy because it's tangible proof that maybe, just maybe, he likes me, too. That's a lot of pressure.

Right after the divorce, I went on a few dates. A few *first* dates, and not one single second date. Some of them were real weirdos, like the guy who brought his parakeet. I'm serious. He had some sort of bird cage backpack contraption with a clear window so the bird could see out. He put the backpack right on the table and the bird chirped and waddled back and forth on its perch the whole time. The bird was a gorgeous shade of blue, but I really didn't want to have dinner with it again.

The parakeet was a step up from the guy who brought his mother along. For real.

Then there was the guy who seemed promising, until Kat made me google him and we found out he'd just gotten out of prison. For armed robbery. With hostages.

A couple other dates were barely memorable. I think partly because I was only dating because I felt like I was "supposed" to. I had no real desire to date, and I wasn't invested in the outcome at all. So it was never a blow to my ego when the guy ghosted. And no surprise that I stopped bothering.

But Del? Going on a date with Del and having it not work out would be awful. A little voice that sounds suspiciously like

Kat suggests it might actually be great.

And what about work? We're both department heads. Would we have to disclose our relationship to HR? Eeew, that would be traumatic. And what if we had an ugly breakup, and it made things awkward at work?

In the end, I don't text him. Not tonight. Instead, I eat my weight in Nutter Butters and stare at my phone like I expect it to do the work for me. It doesn't.

* * *

It's Saturday and I'm up at the asscrack of dawn, scrubbing the bathtub and going through the kitchen cabinets, fridge, and freezer, updating my inventory lists. I toss an expired box of pasta and mentally plan out next week's meals.

When the sheet on my clipboard is updated, I write my menu plan on the dry erase board on the front of my fridge.

I'm just sitting down with a bowl of Cheerios when my phone vibrates with an incoming call. I don't even have to look to know it's Kat, so I swipe to connect the call.

"Good morning, sweetheart."

"Sweetheart? Guess we've leveled up, huh?" Del chuckles while I choke on my cereal.

I cough and pound my fist against my sternum. "Shit," I wheeze.

"You okay there?"

The Cheerio dislodges from my throat, and I take a drink of water. I clear my throat and I'm really, really glad this isn't a video call. My face is on fire, half from choking, half from mortification. "Yeah, um, I thought it was Kat calling."

"They really should come up with some way to identify who's calling. Maybe have the number or name light up on the screen somehow."

"Ha, ha, very funny." Nick used to say things like that, trying to make me feel small, which usually worked. But with Del, it's a whole other vibe. Lighthearted teasing is just that — lighthearted teasing. The old adage is so true — it's not always what you say, it's how you say it that matters.

"The reason I'm bothering you on a Saturday morning is that our check came in the mail today."

Our check? I like the way he says that. "Wow." For a second I wonder how he got my number, but I'm pretty sure it was on all the claim forms we had to fill out.

"I don't know where you do your banking. I use First Valley Credit Union."

"Me, too." Of course I do. It's the bank with a branch closest to PAMECorp, so I can do any errands on my lunch break. Efficiency and all that.

"You want to meet at the branch on Winchester? Around ten?"

It's nine thirty now. I touch my scrungy hair and know I'm not going anywhere without a shower. "How about ten thirty?"

"Sure."

As soon as we hang up, I jump in the shower. When I'm finished, I wrap myself in a towel and stand in front of my closet with no clue what to wear. If I'm not at work, I'm in yoga pants and t-shirts with funny sayings on them. That seems just a little too casual. I flip hangers and then I see it. A sleeveless floral shirtdress I bought at a yard sale for a dollar. It was so cute I couldn't resist, even though I had no idea when or where I'd ever wear it.

I bust out my slip shorts (goodbye, chafing) and pull the dress on. I debate the buttons. Too high seems prudish, too low seems desperate. I use a safety pin to end up somewhere in the middle. I do a little twirl in the mirror. Heck, yeah. I look good. On a whim, I keep my hair down. It falls halfway down my back in waves. I know it'll be tied up before lunchtime, though. I can't stand it when it's in my face.

I go for broke and put on a little mascara and lip gloss. My eyeliner begs to be applied, but I don't want to look like I'm trying too hard. I know, too late. I second guess the dress, but when I check the mirror again, there's no way I'm changing. I haven't looked this cute in, well, let's just say a while.

Sandals complete my outfit. I grab my purse and head out the door.

The drive to the bank takes about fifteen minutes. I get there at 10:29. Del is standing on the sidewalk looking at his phone.

When I walk over, he glances up, back down at his phone, and then his head jerks up. "Shas. Dang. Wow. You look great."

His reaction is way better than I'd hoped. "Hey. You don't look so bad yourself."

He's wearing khaki shorts and a short-sleeve button-down shirt. Baby blue. It matches his eyes, even though they're hidden behind his black-frame glasses.

We're probably twenty feet from the front door. When we get closer, Del reaches out to open the door for me. It's a simple gesture, but I appreciate it.

There are four teller windows inside, and three of them are occupied by customers. The fourth window frames the teller, a young man who looks pleasantly approachable. He conducts the transaction, depositing half into my checking account, and half into Del's, and we're on our way back outside.

"That was easier than I thought."

I nod in agreement. "It seems silly that the lottery office can issue multiple W-2Gs for ten grand but not multiple checks unless it's over fifty. That doesn't make a lot of sense."

We're stalling on the sidewalk next to my car. I feel like I should say something about the journal. Or more accurately, about the sticky note in my journal.

"Hungry?" Del asks.

I am. I hadn't finished breakfast because I'd abandoned it after his call in favor of showering. "I could eat."

"Wally's?"

I perk up. "Yes. I haven't been there in ages."

Wally's is amazing. They're pretty much a citified diner. The ambiance is clearly "we're pretending to have small town charm even though none of us have probably ever set foot in a small town" but the food is home-cooked comfort all the way.

We walk almost a block to get to Wally's, which is busy as usual. It's barely eleven o'clock, so we've got the tail end of the breakfast group on top of the early lunch group. We don't say much as we wait in line. We're finally led to a table in a little alcove with six two-seat tables. Four of them are occupied, including ours.

I pick up the menu and set it back down. My hands are

sweaty and I'm not really seeing the words in front of me. Instead, my mind is reeling. Does this count as a date? Probably not, since nobody actually asked anybody to go out. But it's not *not* a date, right?

A waiter comes by and takes our drink orders. Del is sitting patiently, his hands clasped atop his menu, no doubt ready to order. When the waiter comes back, I still haven't decided what I want, so I tell Del to order first.

He orders pancakes with strawberries and whipped topping, along with a side of bacon.

"I'll have the same," I tell the waiter. I hand the menu back with a smile.

Del puts his elbows on the table and rests his chin on fisted hands. "Do you often have breakfast for lunch?"

I spread the napkin across my lap. "Not often enough. You?"

"Every weekend. Well, most weekends. Not so much anymore, but it was something I always did with the kids. We'd sleep in on Saturday and then go out for breakfast."

"Just you and the kids?" Ah, crap, what possessed me to say that? Oh, well. The words are out, so I can't unask the nosy question.

"It's always been important to me for the kids to have separate relationships with their parents and with each other. It just worked out that Saturday morning was my time, and they usually did something with their mom Sunday evening."

"That's really nice." I wish Nick had felt as strongly about forging his own special relationship with Kat. They get along now, but probably only talk every few months. Nick is such a fool for missing out on knowing his daughter better.

"Is Kat getting settled in?"

"She is. Daniel — her boyfriend — started his new job yesterday, so she spent the day unpacking and got her new laptop and lab coat and shoes ordered, then she drove around the university and their new neighborhood so she knows where all the grocery stores are."

"University? What's she studying?"

"She's an RN now, but she got an opportunity to go to Vanderbilt for their midwifery program."

His glass stops halfway to his mouth. "Vanderbilt. That's impressive."

"I'm so obnoxiously proud of her. She's always known she wanted to work with babies, and as she got older and learned more, she shifted her focus slightly toward the expectant moms."

"Sounds confident and driven, like a chip off the old block."

I blush a little. No one has ever called me confident. "As long as she only picked up my good habits. What about your kids?"

"Ben starts his senior year in a few weeks."

"Where's he go?"

"Ohio State."

"Oh, that's nice. It's not too terribly far away. When does he go back?"

Del sits back as the waiter sets our plates of massive pancakes in front of us, followed by orders of what must be a pound of bacon apiece. When he leaves us, Del answers, "He's there full time. He plays football, so he takes courses over the summer." He adds, "His mother lives out there, not too far from the school."

"In-state tuition makes a big difference. What's he studying?"

"FFW."

I give him a raised eyebrow. "Which means what?"

"Forestry, Fisheries, and Wildlife. Kind of a dumb name if you ask me. His plan is to be a wildlife biologist."

"That sounds ambitious." What I mean is that I have no idea what a wildlife biologist does, but I'm not prepared to admit it.

"He has visions of backpacking all over the country, and possibly the world, studying all kinds of animals and their habitats. He's even talked about converting a van to live in so he can move around easily."

It would definitely reduce expenses, but that's a nope for me. "That sounds... okay, I'll just say it. That sounds dangerous. I have enough anxiety with Kat's life. I can't imagine if she was living in a van and backpacking out into the wild." I groan. "Oh, you know what? I can see her doing exactly that. Traveling with something like Doctors Without Borders to deliver babies in third world countries. She would totally do that." I selfishly hope she never does that.

"And no one in the world would be more proud than her mother."

"Proud, yes, but I'd drive myself nuts worrying about her. What about your daughter? Allie, right?"

"Right. She's an aerospace engineer working on something about fuel efficiency for airplanes. It's over my head."

I laugh. "Over your head? Airplanes? You're so good at making dad jokes you don't even have to try."

Del snorts soda and ends up in a coughing fit.

"You going to make it?" I hand him a napkin.

"I think so." He wipes his face and clears his throat. "I'm not sure if I should be impressed with my dad joke game or a little scared by it."

"Both."

He's polished off all of his pancakes and most of his bacon. My stomach is still in knots, so I've only managed one pancake and maybe two pieces of bacon.

He says, "Now that you've got your lottery money, what bucket list items are you going to check off?"

* * *

My Bucket List

1. ~~Buy a lottery ticket~~
2. Go through automatic car wash
3. Manicure
4. Get hair done in real salon
5. Ask Del out on a date (!!!!!)

Chapter 7

I poke gingerly at the second pancake.

"You have no idea, do you?"

"I mean…" I set my fork down and lean back. "I do know some things I want to do."

He leans back in his chair, mirroring my position. "Have you added anything to your list since lunch yesterday?"

"No." Why do I feel defensive? It's my list. My business. I cross my arms. "I suppose your list is done and you've begun checking things off." My tone is sarcastic because I highly doubt he's put *that* much thought into it.

"I have. Look, I know it was a stupid thing for the company to spend so much money on. But it's been fun. I know I get so caught up in just going to work and going home and doing the same thing again the next day that it's been nice to stop and think about things I'd really *like* to do."

Okay, wow. He has put that much thought into it. "I'm not sure I'm the right kind of person for this exercise. I *like* routine. I *like* knowing what every day is going to look like. I *like* being secure and not blowing a bunch of money on things that won't last."

"There's room for both," he says mildly. He swipes a piece of my bacon and pops it in his mouth.

I double down on my position. "I'm just not a frivolous, fancy-free kind of person. I'm not going to change that for some stupid PAMECorp activity."

He seems unmoved by my logic. "You shouldn't change. You're great the way you are. The point isn't to change. It's to intentionally do some things you enjoy. We only get one ride on this merry-go-round."

"What's on your list?" I intend to challenge him, but he's got the answer at the ready. Of course he does.

"Nothing too crazy. You know about the RAKs and the muscle car. I want to go to the Indy 500, visit Alaska — probably with Ben, since that's one of his dream vacations. Deep-sea fishing. I'd like to meet Mike Tyson."

"Mike Tyson?" I'm trying not to smirk, but that is such a *guy* thing to put on a bucket list.

Del shrugs and picks at the edge of his placemat, looking a little self-conscious. "He's the GOAT."

"Goat? What?" What on earth does Mike Tyson have to do with goats? Did I miss some crazy reality show or something?

"G-O-A-T. Greatest of all time."

I mumble, "I'm not sure Evander Holyfield would agree."

"Probably not."

"What else?" This fascinates me. He's really thought about things he'd like to do. And here I sit, with one eye on this exact moment and one eye on retirement. I'm ignoring the whole in-between.

"I think it'd be cool to crush a car with an excavator." He has a little gleam in his eye. "There's a place in Hagerstown called Heavy Metal Playground where you can crush cars and dig holes and pretty much play with all that heavy equipment."

"I concede. That sounds fun." The waiter comes back with the check and Del grabs it before I can. "But you're kind of proving my point. Everything on your list costs money."

"So?"

His response has me taken aback. "So? So it's more responsible to save money and plan for the future."

He gives me a slow half-smile. "Do you honestly believe that taking a vacation or getting ice in your soda signals a complete lack of responsibility? There's a wide range between burning money and being a cheapskate."

Did he just call me a cheapskate?

"I didn't realize you had such a low opinion of me."

I'm very much not enjoying this conversation. "My opinion of you is just fine."

He puts his elbows on the table and leans toward me. "What if I told you I get takeout three or four times a week? Or that I spend three times as much to get the containers of onions that are already chopped up? Heck, Shasta, sometimes I even run the dishwasher when it's only half full."

My hands clench in my lap. "You're mocking me."

"No. I'm just a little annoyed because you're literally saying I'm irresponsible with my money."

"I never said that."

He tilts his head and stares at me.

Okay, so maybe I implied it a little bit. "I don't care what you do with your money."

"You care enough to insult the things on my bucket list."

Ouch. He's right, as much as it pains me to admit. I've been really judgy about his list. "Sorry."

The waiter returns with Del's change, buying me a minute to put my thoughts together. We stand up from the table and

Del follows me through the crowded dining room to the door. With every step, I'm hyper-aware of him behind me, and trying to think of a way to both apologize and explain my position. It's not that I'm judging how he spends his money... oh, shit. I really am judging how he spends his money. Which is not even a little bit of my business. He was open enough to share his bucket list with me, only for me to be really obnoxious about it.

A frazzled waiter rushes across my path, his tray skimming the air just inches in front of my nose. I lurch to a stop and Del bumps into my back.

"Sorry," the waiter gasps, his tray full of food unbalanced and tottering wildly.

"It's okay," I try to reassure him, but I see from his wide eyes that he's shaken.

He turns gracelessly and the already off-balance tray dips a hard right.

"Nooooo!" he cries.

My arm jerks out to grab the tray, but I'm too late and only catch air. A massive salad flies off the tray in comically slow motion and arcs upward, then drops down, landing in the lap of a well-dressed woman. A plate slides off the tray and lands upside down. The tray itself hits the floor with a bonk and rolls under a table several feet away.

The waiter bends to clean up the mess just as the woman moves to stand. Their heads make an audible clunk when they connect. The restaurant is silent, frozen in horrified rapt attention.

"I'm sorry I'm sorry I'm sorry I'm sorry," the poor waiter breathes as he — on his hands and knees — picks chunks of lettuce off the floor. Gravy seeps out from under the upside-down plate.

"Damn it, Kyle!" A man rushes from the kitchen area, pushing a mop bucket.

The woman gives a little laugh as she flicks shredded carrots off her shirt. "At least I didn't order the soup."

Del's hands are still on my upper arms. He gives a gentle squeeze, nudging me to my right. We zig zag through tables and push through the doors to escape to the outside.

On the sidewalk, I press my hand to my chest. "Oh, that poor kid."

"I do *not* miss those days," Del says.

We walk slowly down the sidewalk. "You waited tables?"

"In high school. I worked in this pizza joint that was chronically understaffed, so I'd cook and then deliver food to the tables. One time I had a pizza slide off the tray, just like our friend Kyle here, and it landed cheese-side-down on the table. The man starts screaming at me and grabs ahold of my shirt and raises his fist. So I pushed him and he fell backwards into the booth. I got fired."

"That's bullshit."

He shrugs one shoulder. "Turned out okay. I got a job stocking shelves at the grocery store like two days later. I made twice as much money for half the aggravation."

"I worked in a grocery store, too. Cashier. I did waitress in college for a semester. Hardest job I've ever had."

"Yeah, waiting tables is no joke. It's why I always over-tip."

"Me, too."

He stops walking and looks at me, surprised. "No offense,

but I figured you were probably the person with the calculator figuring out an exact fifteen percent tip."

I purse my lips and scrunch up my nose. "I hate to admit this, but I did that for a long time."

"What made you give up your calculating ways?"

We start walking again and round the corner, back to where our cars are parked near the bank. "Kat waited tables in high school and came home one day with a pocketful of change. She'd waited on a big table of accountants, and all of them calculated their tips to the literal penny. She'd worked hard all day, then had to lug this extra weight home and count it all out. I felt awful. She never complained, mind you, but I realized it was kind of ridiculous."

"Wow."

"Before you get too impressed, I still calculate the tip in my head. I just round up now. And I calculate at least twenty percent."

He chuckles.

"I'm really sorry about earlier. I shouldn't have been so obnoxious and judgmental about things you like to spend money on."

"I accept your apology."

I point to the car we're beside. "This is me."

"Can I ask you a question that's probably inappropriate, and is one hundred percent none of my business?"

I take half a step back and look up at him. He's regarding me curiously. "You can ask. Whether or not I answer is another matter."

"Fair enough." He clears his throat and puts his hands in his pockets. "Do you think it's really about money? Not putting anything on your bucket list? I don't know, you just seem really freaked out by the whole thing, and we both know spending twenty bucks on lottery tickets wouldn't hurt your bottom line at all. So… like I said, not my business, I'm just nosy I guess."

I blink a few times and turn my head to watch a car drive down the street. I'm not sure how to answer.

"Sorry. I didn't mean to upset you or offend you or— "

"No. You didn't. I'm really not sure why this exercise bothers me so much. It frustrates me that I've tried to think of things I'd like to do and I keep coming up empty. I guess I don't like facing the fact that I'm boring."

He squints a little and shakes his head. "Boring? You're definitely not boring, Shas."

"Yes, I am."

"Nobody who's boring would try to convince Cecily to add Festivus to the corporate calendar."

I laugh. I'd all but forgotten about that. "To be fair, I still think witnessing a company-wide Airing of the Grievances would be amazing."

"Don't you mean 'awesome'?" His voice goes up two octaves on the last word, mocking Cecily.

"Okay, but that's one thing, and it was a year and a half ago."

"We always laugh a lot at lunchtime. That's not boring."

That's true. Sitting with Del, making smartassed comments while we eat is for sure one of the best parts of my workdays.

"Maybe you just need to untangle money and fun a little bit."

My skepticism floods over me. "Impossible. There's no way to have fun without spending a ton of money. You can't even go to an amusement park for under a hundred bucks a person."

A huge grin takes center stage on Del's face. "Challenge accepted."

"What?"

"I bet we can go to an amusement park and have a great time for under a hundred bucks for *both* of us."

"Not a chance."

"What are you doing tomorrow?"

My heart skips a little. "Full day. I'm alphabetizing my spices."

"Pssht. Five bucks says your spices are already alphabetized."

"Okay, so are you saying the two of us can do an amusement park tomorrow for under a hundred dollars total?"

"That's exactly what I'm saying." His smile falters a little. "It's just an idea. Throwing it out there. No big deal if you're busy."

I may not be the best at picking up on clues, but even I can see that he's worried about being rejected. By me! He can say it's not a big deal, but I know it is. For both of us. I match his light tone and act like it's no big thing. "I can't wait to see how you pull this off."

His smile widens again. "Pick you up at ten?"

My brain launches into the million ways this could go wrong. But I say, "Perfect."

* * *

My Bucket List

1. ~~Buy a lottery ticket~~
2. Go through automatic car wash
3. Manicure
4. Get hair done in real salon
5. Ask Del out on a date (!!!!!)

Chapter 8

The door is barely shut behind me before I'm dialing Kat.

"Is everything okay?" is how she answers the phone.

"Of course. Why?"

The concern in her voice vanishes. "You're calling me off-schedule, that's all."

I toss my purse onto the chair and sit down to unbuckle my sandals and kick them under the coffee table. "Well, prepare yourself for something even more shocking than my blatant disregard for our carefully set up phone schedule."

"Yeeesss?" She drags the word out and I can tell she's dying of curiosity.

So of course I let her hang a little bit longer. "You know I was telling you about Del."

"The cute IT guy who wants you to ask him out."

"Yeah."

She sucks in a breath. "Did you do it? Did you ask him out?" She's practically giddy at the mere thought.

"Slow down, no."

"Mom." Disappointment drips from the word.

"But wait. Hear me out. He called me this morning to let me know the lottery check came."

"Sweet."

"We met at the bank and split the money." I'm deliberately giving her information in slow pieces.

"Nice."

"And after that, we went to Wally's to eat."

"We? You went together?" I can feel her excitement building again.

"Yes. It was around eleven, but we got breakfast. I was so nervous they could have served me dog food and I wouldn't have noticed."

She laughs. "Go on."

My enthusiasm dips a little bit. "We talked about our bucket lists. Well, *his* bucket list since I still barely have anything on mine. And I ended up insulting him because his list is a lot of big things like trips and restoring a car and stuff like that."

"Stuff that costs money," she wisely interprets.

"Yeah."

She sighs. "Let me guess. You used the word 'irresponsible' somewhere in your reaction."

"Maybe forget being a midwife and try being a psychic." I curl my legs under me and smooth the skirt over my calves. "He totally called me out on it and he was right. I apologized because I really was kind of a jerk. Soooo then we got to talking about how to have fun without spending a lot of money and I said you can't even go to an amusement park and have fun for under a hundred dollars per person." I pause and wait for her to take the bait.

After a beat, she says, "Mom. You're killing me here. What happened?"

"He bet me that we could have a great day at an amusement park for under a hundred bucks for the both of us."

"Whoa."

"You know how I am about being challenged. Long story

short, he's picking me up tomorrow and we're apparently going to see if we can do an amusement park for under a hundred dollars."

"I like this guy."

"Me, too."

"What are you wearing?"

We launch into a discussion of my sad wardrobe, and she tells me exactly what to wear. I won't budge on my Bermuda-length jean shorts, but I let her boss me around about the shirt I should wear. Luckily, my kid knows my taste and insists I wear my plain AC/DC t-shirt and recommends one of my strappy sports bras underneath. Cute, casual, and comfortable.

And because she is *my* daughter, she makes it a point to remind me to take sunscreen and apply it often. "Yes, ma'am," I answer.

We get off the phone and I change into shorts and a tank top and finish cleaning the house.

When evening comes, I microwave some leftover casserole and then decide to treat myself to something I haven't done in ages, even though it's free.

I run my garden tub full of hot water and pour in some lavender-scented bubbles. I pour myself a glass of wine and set the music app on my phone to my favorite 80s monster rock ballads channel.

For a minute, it feels silly to do nothing but soak in the tub. I could be updating my checkbook or planning out next week's meals and grocery list. I tell the anal-retentive voice to shut up and I sink down to my neck in the hot water. It feels amazing.

As my skin prunes, I consider Del's question about whether

my reluctance to make a bucket list has anything to do with money at all.

I suspect it doesn't.

I think back to 8- and 9-year-old me, living with my grandparents. Grandma and I would dance barefoot in the kitchen while she taught me to cook. She'd put old vinyl records on the massive turntable that dominated the living room and crank up the music. We'd sing and do chores. Between chores, she taught me to do the foxtrot and cha cha. I remember her smiling and pretending the feather duster was a microphone as we wiped the blinds.

Then, I remember her smile turning stiff when the clock struck four thirty. That meant Grandpa would be home in half an hour. We'd spend those last thirty minutes frantically finishing dinner and making sure nothing was out of place. My job was to set the table, make sure the newspaper was on the left arm of his La-Z-Boy, and place his slippers right in front of it. He'd often fuss that he couldn't afford a television with a remote control because he had to spend all his money taking care of me, so as atonement for my sin of existing, my evenings were spent shuffling across the shag carpeting to change the channels. Every time I'd reach out for the little metal knob, I'd get a static shock in my finger.

It's taken a lot of years to realize he was just a bitter asshole, but boy oh boy do those negative childhood associations have deep roots that slither down into your very soul and make you think you're unworthy of anything good life has to offer.

Even in school, I was reprimanded on a regular basis for speaking out, being too loud, being a show-off know-it-all. So I learned to drift to the back, keep my mouth shut, and color inside the lines.

The water cools and turns chilly. I turn the hot faucet on with my toes and let it run until the temperature is hot enough again. My wine glass is empty. I recognize that when left to its own devices, my brain drifts into negative thoughts. So I force it to think of positive things. Small things, like the Ratt song that's playing right now. Round and Round. I had a Ratt t-shirt in high school. I wore that thing until it got so threadbare it fell apart. I'd been fourteen and used birthday money to go to the mall and sneak into Spencer's to buy it.

It's probably why I love my retro AC/DC shirt so much. Yes, the one Kat insists I wear tomorrow. It reminds me of those moments with my sponge-foam Walkman headphones (it was bright yellow) blasting music (probably damaging my eardrums) I recorded on blank cassette tapes from the radio.

The lavender bubbles are another positive. Most of them have dissolved by now, but their sweet fragrance clings to my damp skin and hair.

Lunch with Del was a huge positive. Right up until I insulted him.

The $3,646.50 in lottery money sitting in my account, after the feds got their 24% and Pennsylvania took its 3.07%.

The ball of tension in my belly is another positive. It's anxiety and anticipation, but there's no dread. I feel like a kid waiting for Christmas morning.

Little niggling thoughts try to worm their way in and show me all the ways tomorrow could go wrong, but for once I'm able to push them away.

I'm finally pruned enough, so I pop the drain and carefully climb out. I towel off and do a quick pluck of stray eyebrow hairs and one on my jawline. Why the hell are hairs popping up on my chin? And a zit? Seriously? Middle age is bullshit.

My bathroom. That's another positive. It's big and roomy and has lots of counter space and a huge linen closet. I'd paid a fair amount to have it, along with my master bedroom, remodeled when I'd bought the house. Yes, my main thought had been on resale value, but I picked out the granite countertops and brushed nickel fixtures because I liked them. See? I *am* capable of spending money. I just need a good reason for it.

I climb into bed and pull the cover up to my chin. I stare up into the darkness and decide to do my bucket list for real. Del's right. Kat's right. It's not about money.

And even if it is, I've got $3,646.50 in "free" money to use.

I can do this.

* * *

My Bucket List

1. ~~Buy a lottery ticket~~
2. Go through automatic car wash
3. Manicure
4. Get hair done in real salon
5. Ask Del out on a date (!!!!!)

Chapter 9

Sunday morning comes too soon. I tossed and turned all night and got up to pee four times because I'm so nervous and excited. There's a little bit of trepidation because this isn't just any old random date. This is a whole day with Del.

And let's be real. I've been crushing on Del since the first time he crawled under my desk to replace some cables on my computer. Eighteen months ago. Well, actually, seventeen months, three weeks, and four days. Yes, I counted. I *am* an accountant. Numbers are kind of my thing.

It was Friday, January thirty-first. My stupid computer had shut down right in the middle of a massive project. Screen went black. *Poof.* All my data sucked into the ether. One of the new IT guys came over and couldn't figure out the problem. So in walked Del. Tall, shy, and handsome. He popped under my desk, muttered a curse word, apologized for the language, and left.

I sat there, wondering what was up, when he came back with a fistful of cables, crawled back under my desk, did his magic, and restarted my computer.

He stood up, gave me a nod and said, "Should be good now," and left.

A week after that we sat beside each other at the February PAMECorp pep rally. (I totally didn't get there early to get a seat close to him.) Cecily was wearing a poofy white shirt with ruffles and Del quietly said, "But I don't *wanna* be a pirate." I immediately got the *Seinfeld* reference and thought I was going to die holding my laughter in.

I laugh now, remembering that day. He'd looked over at me and we'd shared this eye contact that said we were on the same page. It had been *A Moment.*

And to think I'd been so mad about my computer crapping out.

I whip the cover back and get up to get ready for the day. It's supposed to be sunny and hot. I get dressed and stare in the mirror, debating whether or not to wear makeup. I rarely wear any, but I decide on some eyeliner and mascara. Hopefully, I won't get all sweaty where my eyeliner runs and makes me look like a racoon.

I pull my hair back into a messy bun and clean things that don't need cleaning to burn off the nervous energy I have. I nervous-pee like six times. Middle age is great.

Ten o'clock finally rolls around and I peek out the window until Del's car, a gray Chevy Malibu sedan, a few years old but in really nice shape, pulls in my driveway.

I grab my purse and head outside, pulling the door shut behind me.

Del is out of his car. I walk down the porch steps and smile. "Hey."

"Hey. Love the shirt."

I look down, even though I know what I'm wearing, then I look at his shirt. Slayer. "Yours, too," I say, pointing.

"It was either this or Michael Bolton," he deadpans. He opens the passenger door for me, then closes it when I'm inside.

When he's settled in the driver's seat, he pulls out his wallet. "Just proving that I'm following the rules." He opens his wallet and pulls out some cash. He counts out ninety-seven dollars, then puts his wallet in the center console and closes it. He puts the money in his shorts pocket. "I don't have any other cash on me."

"I believe you."

"You're not allowed to spend any money today, or you forfeit. The deal is to have a great day on less than a hundred dollars. Total."

"Deal." I still have my doubts, but I'll play along. It makes me a little nervous, but I put my purse in the console with his wallet. "As long as nobody breaks into the car, we'll be good."

He grins. "This old thing? Nah."

"Where are we going?"

"Knoebels."

My jaw drops. "Are you serious? I haven't been there in *years*. Oh gosh, I bet Kat was only ten or eleven." Well played, Del. Knoebels is billed as America's largest free admission amusement park.

"You're in for a treat." He backs out of the driveway and heads down the road.

"You go there often?"

"Not really. I was there last year. And probably three or four years before that."

"With the kids?"

"My brother's kids. They were staying with my parents for ten days, so Mom asked me to go along since her and Dad won't go on most of the rides."

"That's nice. How many kids?"

"Four. Two boys, two girls, from eight to sixteen."

"Fun. Do you have other brothers and sisters?" I want to know all the details.

"Two more brothers."

"Four boys? Your poor mom."

He laughs and nods his head. "We were a handful. How about you? Siblings?"

Such a simple question. I should have expected it, but somehow it still catches me a little off guard. I want to talk about his family, not my shitshow. "Funny story. I don't actually know."

He turns his head to look at me, one eyebrow raised in confusion. "Oh?"

"My parents were — still are, I assume — hippies. Not just peace and love, but real, all the way hippies. As in living on a commune and free love and all that."

"Wow."

"I went to live with my grandparents when I was eight, and never saw much of my parents after that. The last time I saw them at all was when I was twelve. I assume there are some siblings and/or half-siblings running around out there, but I don't know for sure."

"That's some heavy stuff. They didn't try to see you?"

I snort and adopt my best stoner impression. "Too much hassle, man." I lift my fingers in a peace sign.

"I'm sorry. Did you have any cousins or aunts and uncles?"

"Nope. I lived with my dad's parents, and he was an only child. There was a sibling who died in infancy, but it was all very hush-hush. My mom's parents had disowned her, and I'm not sure they even know I exist." I shake my head and make a "blah" noise. "That got dark fast. Let's go back to your family. Do the other two brothers have kids?"

"The oldest brother, George, has one daughter who's about thirty. She's married and has two kids. I'm the second to oldest. Number Three, Thomas, is the one with four kids, and Number Four, Dwight, doesn't have any."

"Do they all live close by?"

"No. Dwight lives in Taiwan right now. George is in Wisconsin, although they are in the process of moving back to PA, and Thomas is the closest in Maryland. It's fine, though. We have a standing Sunday night conference call that we're really good about making."

"You're not going to miss tonight, are you?" I can hardly imagine having a whole family to pop onto a weekly conference call. I feel guilty for making him miss it, and guilty for not providing a big, close-knit family for Kat that enjoys each other so much they have such calls. There was nothing to offer her on my side, and Nick's family isn't the warm and fuzzy type.

He shrugs. "I'll probably be late, but it's okay. They're all just excited I have a date." His fingers tighten on the steering wheel. "Or, uh, I mean, not like a *date*, I guess, I mean, they know we're, uh, that I'm going to Knoebels, uh, with, you know, you."

The butterflies in my stomach kick into overdrive. "I was kind of wondering about that myself. Is this a date? Or not a date?" I hope he doesn't hear the uncertain quiver in my voice.

He looks over at me. "Do you want it to be a date?"

What a loaded question. "Do *you* want it to be a date?"

* * *

My Bucket List

1. ~~Buy a lottery ticket~~
2. Go through automatic car wash
3. Manicure
4. Get hair done in real salon
5. Ask Del out on a date (!!!!!)

Chapter 10

I fiddle with the hem of my shirt. "Um… does it change anything depending on what we call it?"

"Probably not," he says.

"I mean… it feels like it's kind of a date, so we can call it that if we want to." Holy shit is this awkward. "Or we could completely change the subject to something that doesn't make me want to break out in hives."

"The idea of dating makes you break out? Or the idea of being on a date with me?"

I suck in a sharp breath. "Definitely not that. I haven't been on a date since my thirties. I am literally more than halfway through my forties and haven't been on a date since I was thirty-nine."

"Why not?"

"How many reasons would you like?"

"Four."

I have to laugh at his deadpan automatic response. "One, I went on a bunch of dates that were complete disasters, so it didn't inspire me to keep kissing frogs. Two, it's a lot of effort for very little payoff. Three, I got busy. Or lazy. Or something, and six months turned into a year, which turned into eight years. Four, I'm a strong, independent woman and I don't need a man."

"It's not about *need*, is it? I mean, dating should be about want. Like wanting to spend time with someone whose company you enjoy, right?"

"That's how I thought it was supposed to be, but times have changed. Now it's all about hooking up with random strangers from an app." Aaaand now I feel even older, referencing the way things "used to be" in the "good old days."

"Cynical."

"Realistic. What about you? Do you date a lot?" I'm not sure I want an answer.

"What's a lot? I've gone on a few dates here and there, but I wouldn't call it a lot."

I don't point out that anything more than zero seems like a lot to me. "When's the last time you were on a date?"

"Probably six months ago."

"Oh. Was it good?" Why do I keep asking questions I don't want the answer to?

"No." It came out fast and sharp. He gives me a side-eye.

"You know I'm dying to know the story."

He sighs and slows down for a yellow light. "She's my sister-in-law's good friend, so they thought it would be great for us to do a double date. We went to a movie and dinner. It started at the movie when she asked me if I thought the main character was attractive. I said I hadn't really thought about it, but that wasn't good enough. She asked if I prefer blondes or brunettes. Now I might be a guy, but I'm not totally stupid. I knew it was a trap, so I just said I don't really have a preference, I'm more interested in personality."

"Oh, no."

"Oh, yes. She took it as a complete insult. Then, at the restaurant, she apologized and told me that her ex used to compare her to other women all the time so she was insecure about it. I said that was awful, and I thought we were done with it."

"Then what?"

"We place our orders and she gets real quiet. Then she goes off about me flirting with the waitress right in front of her. I swear, I gave my order and handed her my menu. I might have smiled or something, but I don't think I even made eye contact. My sister-in-law says she didn't see anything, at which point she accused us of sleeping together, dumped her water in my lap, and stormed out. My sister-in-law followed her and got her calmed down and brought her back in. We ate in pretty much complete silence, and I couldn't wait to get home. Later that night, she texted me that she had a nice time and did I want to go out with her again."

"Oh, my. She sounds unhinged."

"I blocked her number. There was no way I could come out looking like the good guy in any scenario, so I figured I'd just cut my losses and ghost."

"I don't blame you. Many a Dateline special has started that way." I put my finger to my chin. "I do have one question, though."

"Yeah?"

"Yeah. Blondes or brunettes?"

He shakes his head. "No way. You're not turning me into a Dateline special, either."

We spend the rest of the drive trying to top each other's bad date stories. I'm pretty sure I end up winning with my tale of the dude who brought his parakeet on our date. Or losing. I'm not sure which, since that doesn't really feel like a win.

It's just before noon when the park opens, but the parking lot is already more than half-full. Del pulls into a spot and says, "Hungry?"

"A little."

"I brought lunch." He reaches into the back seat and grabs a small cooler. He opens it and pulls out a bag. "Sandwiches, bottled water, chips, and pickles."

I'm impressed with how prepared he is. I tease, "How much was all this?"

He laughs. "I knew you'd ask that. The total for everything in the cooler is three dollars and seventeen cents." He shows me a sticky note breaking down the ingredients, right down to the individual slices of bread.

"I just want to make sure we weren't cheating the hundred dollar limit."

"That's why I took the three dollars out. Do you want me to take out the seventeen cents?"

I shake my head. "That's probably overkill."

"Whoa, are you sure?"

"You make it seem like I'm a complete miser."

He cocks an eyebrow. "I seem to remember a phrase that might be appropriate. Something about shoes fitting? Let's head to the pavilion."

My jaw drops but before I can think of a comeback, he's out of the car and around to my side to open my door. I still haven't thought of a response as we walk across the grassy parking area and settle at a picnic table under one of the pavilions.

He sits across from me and sets the food and water on the table. "This one is turkey, this one is ham. I like them both, so you can choose."

"I'll take the turkey, thanks."

There's another plastic baggie with lettuce and tomato slices. And three mustard packets. He's thought of everything.

Del grins when I take a mustard. "Those came with some takeout so they were free."

"I wasn't going to ask." I tear open the packet and squeeze the mustard on my sandwich, then put some lettuce and tomato on it.

He arranges the rest of the veggies on his own sandwich, and we eat in relative silence. The other picnic tables are filling up, so we're surrounded with the indistinguishable hum of conversation and laughter and children yelling, along with the crunch of gravel as car after car drives into the park and inches along to find a space. When we're finished, he clears up our trash and throws everything in the can. "Ready?"

"Ready."

We walk past the kiddie rides and stop at the ticket booth next to the Ferris wheel. Del buys books of tickets — proudly showing me a coupon from a saver book his niece was selling for a school fundraiser — and picks up a park map. "Where to first?"

I look up, up, up at the giant Impulse ride next to us — part roller coaster, part death machine with a million twists and loops. My stomach flip flops just looking at the beast. "Um…" There's already a long line for this ride, and the park just opened. Yikes. "What kind of rides do you like?"

"All of them. You?" He follows my gaze. "Not into thrill rides, I take it?"

I shake my head. "Not really. Sorry."

"Don't apologize. There are plenty of mild rides."

I have no idea why I'm apologizing. Probably because I don't want to disappoint him or hold him back. "If you want to ride it, go ahead."

"This monster? Nah. Let's start with something a little less dramatic." He nudges me toward the entrance to the Ferris wheel. "We'll get a nice view of the park from up top."

There's only a short line, so we hand over our tickets and the operator opens the bar on the cheerful yellow car and latches it behind us. A minute later we're moving upwards. The butterflies calm down as we smoothly ride toward the sky. The day couldn't be more perfect. It's hot, but there's very little humidity, and a nice breeze to boot. The sky is clear and bright with puffy clouds lazily drifting by. Even better, I'm sitting beside someone incredible.

"Couldn't ask for a better day, huh?" Del says.

"I was just thinking that." The breeze catches my ponytail and strands of hair brush across my face. I sweep them behind my ear.

We go around in circles for a while, just enjoying the ride. The Ferris wheel slows and comes to a stop, then stops again and again as riders get off and new riders get on.

We're at the top again when Del says, "What do you do for fun?"

I think about it for a minute and come up empty. I look over at him. "I feel like that should be an easy question to answer, but I'm drawing a blank. I go home, I watch some television, I read books... I used to knit, but I haven't for a while."

"Why not?"

The car in front of us empties and is immediately reoccupied. Then our car slides to a stop at the platform. We hop out and a family piles in.

"I don't know why I ever stopped knitting." The question burrows deep into my mind, but I try to push it aside. "Where to?" I ask.

"Pirate ship?"

We spend the next several hours riding rides and walking through the park. His question itches at the back of my mind. Why *did* I stop knitting? I never stopped enjoying it. Maybe it was a combination of reasons. Yarn isn't cheap. There have been times I picked up skeins of yarn and put them back down because I couldn't justify the cost. I ran out of people to give knitted gifts to, and at some point I was just too busy taking care of Kat and getting through each day that I let any sort of hobby fall to the wayside.

Good news, I just found another item for my bucket list.

* * *

My Bucket List

1. ~~Buy a lottery ticket~~
2. Go through automatic car wash
3. Manicure
4. Get hair done in real salon
5. Ask Del out on a date (!!!!!)
6. Get back into knitting

Chapter 11

The afternoon starts to fade, and so do I. Del points. "Gift shop."

"Budget."

He clucks his tongue. "Buying souvenirs is part of the deal. Remember? Rides, food, souvenirs. The whole fun experience." He makes a dramatic circle with his hands to encompass it all.

"Fine." Inside, I find a tie-dyed tank top and a magnet for the fridge. Del buys a t-shirt. From there, we stop at the Old Mill Shake Shack and buy the most delicious milkshakes I've ever had. Mine is strawberry, Del's is vanilla. I have to laugh because I would have expected it to be the other way around.

We stroll along the creek and stop on the covered bridge. Del pulls a Sharpie out of his pocket and adds "Del and Shasta were here" to the layers of name graffiti covering the beams.

We haven't talked about it, but we're heading back toward the park entrance. I have a little twinge of guilt that he hasn't gotten on a thrill ride. I ask, "Are you sure you don't want to ride any of the big stuff?"

"Nah, I'm good." He sucks down the last of his milkshake and tosses the cup in a nearby trash can.

Here's the thing. I believe he's perfectly satisfied leaving without going on a thrill ride. But I'm not satisfied knowing this day might not have been everything he'd hoped because I'm too cautious. Time to take one of those steps outside my comfort zone. I imagine Kat will be proud and that gives me the courage I need. "This looks fun." I point to a ride called Downdraft that most definitely does not look fun. It's like county fair swings on steroids. Instead of little individual swings, octopus-like arms hold brightly painted cars that hold several people.

"Really?" He perks up and his hesitant, hopeful smile is just too much, so now I'm stuck.

"Yeah. Totally." I bravely step into the line. Before I can change my mind, the ride stops, the line moves forward, and now we're stuck in the cattle chute part and there's no escape from here unless I'm willing to cause a big scene trying to get around people to get out. I'm not.

I try not to pay attention to the people screaming as the ride runs. Instead, I focus on Del's fingers tapping excitedly on the cattle chute bars. Then I'm out of options as we're herded onto a cheerful yellow car with a flimsy bar across the front to keep us from spilling out and splattering on the pavement below. What was I thinking?!

The ride starts off innocuously enough, spinning in a circle and lifting us off the ground. It definitely feels like the swings at the county fair, only higher budget and marginally safer. I hope.

The ride swoops us down and back up into the air. Down, up, down, up. I clutch the bar in front of us. The people behind us whoop and holler and I'm just hoping I don't barf. Okay, I'm being a little dramatic. The ride has a rhythm and once I let myself relax, I start to enjoy it. There's nothing crazy about this ride. No loops or jump scares or major thrills. The wind feels good on my face, and the downward swoops put a fun dipping sensation in my belly.

The ride slows, bringing us down, and I'm shocked to find I'm quite disappointed. I give Del a side-eye. He's grinning from ear to ear, and now I feel bad. We could have been doing this all day.

Once we're back on the walkway, I say, "Okay, let's do it."

"What?" he asks.

I point to the monster that had scared me when we first walked in.

"Impulse? You want to ride that?" He's incredulous.

"Yes." *Nope.*

"Okay, if you're sure." He doesn't sound confident, but he follows me to the line.

Surprisingly, we don't have to wait long. I'm still running on adrenaline from enjoying the Downdraft ride, so it isn't until we're in the roller coaster car being pulled straight up into the sky that I fully understand that I've made a huge mistake. "Oh, shit. Bad idea. Bad bad *bad* idea." My throat tightens with abject terror. What was I thinking?!

"Too late now." The train is pulled to the top of the coaster where it hesitates just long enough to send me into a complete panic, then I'm screaming as we drop straight down and then we're upside down, right side up, sideways, up, down, being flung in all sorts of unnatural directions the human body has no business going.

I only stop screaming when the last turn sucks the breath out of me. My hands ache from gripping the bar so hard. The coaster is flat now, slowing down, but I'm afraid to open my eyes and see what fresh hell is coming next.

"You did great," Del says.

"Is it over? Please tell me it's over."

He chuckles. "It's over."

The car rolls to a stop and Del has to help me out because my legs are shaking so bad it's like walking on jelly.

"Let's do one more ride," he suggests, putting a strong arm around my waist and lending me support.

I'm too shaky and weak to object, but I seriously wonder what he's thinking until we turn the corner and he nudges me toward the Scenic Skyway. There's a very short line that's moving steadily. We hand over our tickets and settle into the gentle, non-scary chairlift ride that takes us up over the mountain and back. We're about a third of the way up the mountain when my heart rate finally drops back into the normal range and I can breathe again.

Del reaches over to hold my hand. "I'd say we found your limit, eh?"

"Shit."

He laughs. "No, for real, I'm impressed, Shas. You went way out of your comfort zone."

"Yeah, and choked. That was terrifying."

"And now you know. From experience, not from assumption."

"That's pretty deep there, sensei." It is, actually. I'd assumed I would hate riding Downdraft, but I was wrong. I'd assumed I could easily handle the roller coaster, and once again, I was wrong. Del's right. Now I know for sure and can make an informed decision. Would I like one of the other roller coasters that doesn't twist and go upside-down? Yeah, I think I might.

Would I want to try the Impulse again or any coasters like it? Oh, hell no.

The lush green scenery is calming and absolutely beautiful. We reach the top of the mountain and make the turn to go back down. The entire ride is almost fifteen minutes long. Long enough for me to come completely down from my Impulse experience. I'm finally calm, but now I have to pee something awful.

We hop off the ride and head back toward the exit. "Restroom."

"Me, too," Del says, but I'm already rushing into the women's side of the building.

I pee for a thousand hours and finally finish up and wash my hands. I go outside, but I don't see Del.

A minute later, he comes out of the men's room and hands me a bag.

I joke, "You got this in there?"

"Yes. It was stuck in the urinal." He laughs at my horrified expression. "Or perhaps I got it over there." He points to the little gift shop across the walkway, at the corner of the Impulse.

I peer into the bag and pull out a plastic tumbler with the ride stats on it. "Thank you. Now every time I drink out of it, I can be reminded how terrifying it was."

He puts an arm around my shoulders and pulls me against his side as we walk. "Or you can be reminded of that time you went way out of your comfort zone and even though you didn't love it, nothing bad happened."

"Are you sure you should be in IT? I think you missed your calling as a therapist or something."

He chuckles.

We make one last stop to buy kettle corn to take home. On the way out into the parking lot, Del stops a family heading in and says to the dad, "Here's some extra tickets. Enjoy." He hands the unused tickets to the man.

"Hey, thanks a lot. We really appreciate it."

"That was nice of you," I say as soon as we're out of earshot.

He shrugs and reaches out to take my hand. "If I take them home, they'll just get tossed in a drawer. Might as well pass them along to someone who can use them."

"Does that count as one of your random acts of kindness?" I lace my fingers with his.

"Sure."

"This is probably a dumb question, but what qualifies as a random act of kindness?"

We reach the car and Del opens my door. After I'm inside, he puts our bags of popcorn in the back and then gets in and starts the car. "First, it's not a dumb question. And second, I never really thought about it. It's just something nice you do for someone with no expectation of reciprocation."

"You just described a birthday gift."

Shaking his head, he says, "Not quite. Random acts are usually for no reason, and there's no expectation from the recipient. People generally expect birthday gifts. The guy behind you at Starbucks doesn't expect you to buy his latte, and you're under no obligation to do it."

"Ah. That makes more sense, I guess." I still don't quite get the appeal. "What if they don't appreciate it? What if they're a horrible person?"

He shrugs and eases out of the parking space. "Not really my business. I mean, sure, I *hope* I didn't just buy a coffee for a recently escaped serial killer or some parent who beats their kids, but I have no way of knowing. And I have no way of knowing if they appreciate the gesture or feel entitled to it. I just assume I did a nice thing for a regular person who's surprised and it made their day just a little bit better."

I consider this. Why does even this simple thing seem like something outside my comfort zone? It feels like it doesn't serve a *purpose*. "I really feel like this one is actually a stupid question, but what do you get out of it? Or is the point that you don't get anything out of it? You just do it for the sake of doing it?"

"I do get something out of it. I get to feel really good about doing something nice and brightening someone's day." We inch along with the surprising amount of traffic exiting the parking lot and finally get on the main road.

"Why not just send flowers to your mom?" I'm not sure why I'm arguing the point here.

"Because she's my mom. If I send her flowers, she'll feel obligated to call me and thank me or do something in return. When I do something nice for a stranger, they don't know who I am, so there's no expectation of contacting me or doing anything in return. At best, they might feel compelled to pay it forward."

"What if you want to pay for the guy behind you at the Starbucks drive-through and they just ordered coffee for their whole office and their bill is like fifty bucks?"

"It's a risk."

I can feel my eyes bugging. "You'd still pay it?"

"Of course. There's probably not going to be a drive-through order too big to cover."

"Probably?" The thought makes me want to break out in hives. "If you budgeted five dollars, and it's ten times that amount, that could be a problem."

He laughs. "It's fine. Really. If I spend more on one random act than I intended, maybe I skip the next one."

I sigh and look out the window. "Why does everything seem so risky? Look at me. I can't even consider doing a random act of kindness because I'm afraid I'd go over budget."

"Then don't pay for someone's coffee."

"Isn't that kind of what it is, though?"

"It's anything. It's pushing carts back to the store that have been left in the parking lot. Donating blood. Leaving good reviews for businesses you use. Complimenting a stranger or clipping coupons and leaving them with the product in the store. Sending cards to someone serving overseas. It doesn't have to cost anything."

"Oh."

"If you want to buy someone's coffee but you don't want to overspend, you can always order a five or ten dollar gift card and have the cashier give it to the next person. Nice surprise, never goes over budget."

"You do this a lot?" I wonder what his RAK budget is, but I'm definitely not asking. My nosiness does have limits.

"Kind of. I mean, I'd gotten out of the habit of doing it intentionally until the bucket list thing. I'm really glad to be doing it again." He changes lanes. "Do you want to get something to eat?"

"Yes. I'm getting really hungry."

"Any preference?"

"I'm not sure what's around here." We're still almost an hour away from home.

We ride in silence for a few minutes until Del points. "Looks like a diner. Want to try it?"

"Sure."

He pulls into the parking lot and finds a space along the sidewalk.

We go inside and are greeted by a huge dry erase board telling us to wait to be seated. Under this instruction is a list of the day's specials.

A waitress comes by with menus and asks us to follow her. She leads us to a corner booth and takes our drink orders, then leaves us to peruse the menu.

After she brings our drinks and takes our food order, Del pulls a handful of crumpled bills out of his pocket and puts it on the table. He flattens the money and counts it.

"Eight dollars."

I wonder if this is supposed to have significance, then just as quickly I realize this is the money left over from the park. "That can't be right. With the three dollars in the car, that would mean we only spent eighty-nine dollars."

"Yup."

"Oh."

"You know what that means, right?"

"What?"

"It means I was right, you were wrong, and I win."

"Congratulations." I roll my eyes at his triumphant grin.

I'm in trouble. That's a grin that could make me do something stupid. Like lose my heart.

* * *

My Bucket List

1. ~~Buy a lottery ticket~~
2. Go through automatic car wash
3. Manicure
4. Get hair done in real salon
5. Ask Del out on a date (!!!!!)
6. Get back into knitting

Chapter 12

Del won't stop smiling, even after the food arrives. He just sits there, chewing all cocky and basking in his rightness.

"You don't have to be so smug," I grumble.

"I think I do. Admit it. You had an amazing time today."

Amazing is an understatement. "It was okay, I guess."

He laughs. "You can't even say that with a straight face. It was incredible and you know it."

"Fine. I'll concede the point."

He turns his attention back to his food and manages to eat despite his obvious amusement.

I swear I can hear Kat clearing her throat in my mind, waiting for me to do something I should do but I'm kind of nervous to do. "So, um." My throat freezes.

He looks up. "Yeah?"

"Well, I was thinking."

He sets his fork down and focuses on me, which makes me even more nervous.

"We had a good day today, at least I assume you did. It seems like you did. And I already told you I did. Um, I thought maybe, um, you might, I don't know. Oh, this is ridiculous. I was thinking that maybe we could, um, maybe do this again sometime. I mean, not like Knoebels, of course, because that would be a bit much with that drive, but…" Holy rambling, Batman, I can't shut up and I can't spit it out.

A slow grin spreads across Del's face. He's looking at me,

waiting, and I realize he's going to let me flounder out here, beyond my comfort zone, so I can decide if I'm going to run back to safety or take the next step. We both know he's going to say yes, but the ball's in my court.

I pull in a deep breath. "Do you go want to maybe out sometime?" I squeeze my eyes shut. "Gah, that was awful. English, Shasta, English." I reopen my eyes and actually look into his. I'm like six miles outside the boundaries of safety at this point. I carefully enunciate each word. In the right order this time. "Del. Would you like to go out with me sometime?"

I swear the sun and moon and stars and all things bright and wonderful beam from his smile. "I would love to." He reaches across the table and squeezes my hand, which is clenched around my napkin. "I really would."

His warm fingers feel so nice, but only make my heart beat faster. I laugh and suddenly feel like I could cry. Horrified, I look down at my plate and busy myself with arranging my silverware perfectly perpendicular to the table's edge. Excitement? Relief? I have no idea, but I'm a grown-ass woman. This shouldn't be so hard.

As I often do, I downplay my discomfort with humor. "I guess I get to cross that off my bucket list then, huh?"

One eyebrow lifts. "Asking me out was on your list?" He acts so innocent.

"I have to admit I didn't come up with the idea myself. *Someone* put a sticky note in my journal with the suggestion."

"Awfully bold of them, wasn't it?"

"Was it, though? I feel like whoever put it there could have suggested that *you* ask *me* out."

He hides a grin behind his cup. "Maybe they were afraid you wouldn't be interested, so they wanted to put the ball in your court."

"I figured it would have been pretty obvious."

He sets his cup down and looks serious. "Maybe they were afraid it was just wishful thinking, and they thought maybe they were reading too much into things."

"This conversation is getting really complicated." I swallow hard and blurt out, "I'm way outside of my comfort zone right now."

His hand is still atop mine. "I know."

I hurry to clarify. "It's not a bad thing."

"I know."

I haven't loosened my grip on my napkin. "I'm not good at this."

Little crinkles form at the corners of his eyes behind his glasses as he smiles at me. "You're a lot better at it than the parakeet guy."

I laugh. "Not a very high bar, Del."

"You didn't bring your mom. That's a plus." His face goes serious, and he sits up straight. "I'm sorry. That was insensitive."

It actually takes me a second to realize why he's apologizing. "Oh, no, no worries." I wave away his concern. "I knew what you meant since I just told you about the guy who brought his mom."

"Where would you like to go?" He asks.

"I hadn't thought that far ahead."

"How about we go dancing?"

That makes me laugh. "Dancing? I wouldn't even know where to go to dance."

"You know that little café down the street from PAMECorp?"

"Yeah?"

"In the building behind that there's a dance studio that does lessons for like the waltz and tango and salsa. Allie used to take dance lessons there, and they also did adult classes."

I'm suddenly reminded of wonderful times doing the foxtrot and cha cha in my grandma's living room. "Do you... *want* to go dancing?" Don't get me wrong — I can easily see dancing with Del. He's tall and broad enough that I think he'd be the perfect-sized dance partner.

He sips the last of his soda and looks thoughtful. "It could be a lot of fun."

The memories are getting a little too intense for me, so I say, "Yeah, until we end up in the ER because I broke four of your toes. I was thinking something safer like dinner and a movie."

"If you're going to break my toes, dinner and a movie does sound like a better option."

We're definitely back in my comfort zone now. Mostly. "When would you like to go?"

"Tonight." He grins.

I feel my cheeks heat and I know I'm blushing. "We're already having dinner."

"What about second dinner?"

"No time for a movie."

"You got me there."

The waitress brings our check and Del hands her his card

before I can reach for the bill.

"I was going to get that," I say. I half wonder if he's so worried about my cheap streak that I'd fuss about something on the bill.

He lifts one shoulder in a shrug. "You can get the next one."

"I will." Are weeknight dates a thing? Because I don't want to wait until the weekend. All of a sudden, sharing lunchtime together just isn't enough.

* * *

My Bucket List

1. ~~Buy a lottery ticket~~
2. Go through automatic car wash
3. Manicure
4. Get hair done in real salon
5. ~~Ask Del out on a date (!!!!!)~~
6. Get back into knitting

Chapter 13

The drive home is comfortable. "I hope you don't miss your whole family call."

He glances at the clock on the dash. It's eight thirty-two. "I'll catch the tail end. I'm betting most of them will hang on just to hear about how my day went."

"What will you tell them?"

His smile is wide. "The truth."

He's teasing me now, making me sweat a little even though I know we had a good day. "You should make up something exciting. Maybe how the Ferris wheel got stuck, and you had to climb down and rescue fifty stranded people one by one."

"Spending the day with you is plenty exciting."

I swallow hard. Exciting? Spending the day with *me*? Does he seriously mean that? Surely not.

He clears his throat. "It's been a great day. I've looked forward to this for a long time."

I don't even know what to say to that so I barely manage to squeak out an awkward, "Me, too." My brain races. He's been looking forward to this? A long time? How long? What does he consider a long time? A week? A month? Since we got the lottery tickets? Since the day he fixed my computer? No. Definitely not that long. I'm the one who's been infatuated. (For seventeen months, three weeks, and four days. But who's counting?) He told me earlier he'd been on a date just a few months ago. I bet it's been since the tickets. That makes sense.

Well, as much sense as it makes that he'd been looking forward to time with me at all.

In a romantic sense, I mean. I *know* he looks forward to seeing me on a friendly basis. How could he not? No one else in his department knows that the heiress to the Oh Henry! Candybar fortune doesn't wear a bra or that it's unthinkably rude to not spare a square or how "Serenity now!" doesn't work.

He pulls into my driveway and puts the car in park. "Can I walk you to your door?"

"Sure." I don't trust my tongue to get anything else out.

I hop out of the car and meet Del at the front. The car is running, so at least there's no awkward wondering if he's expecting to come in. Although I am ninety-nine percent certain that if I invited him in, he'd turn the car off and come inside. Ninety-eight. Okay, maybe like eighty-five.

Standing in front of my door, he pulls open the screen door and holds it. My hands are a little shaky as I turn the key in the lock and nudge the main door open.

"I had a blast with you today," Del says. His voice is low and rumbly and I feel like we leveled up at some point.

"Me, too." I hold up the plastic bag holding the Impulse cup. "Except for the ride that almost made me lose my guts."

"But you didn't." He pats his Slayer shirt. "Which is great news for my favorite shirt."

"It would have been a shame to throw it away at the park."

He shakes his head vigorously. "Throw it away? Oh, no, I would have rinsed it off in the bathroom and tossed it in the trunk for the ride home."

"Wow. It really is your favorite, huh?"

"Irreplaceable."

We both laugh a little and it gets awkward again. At least for me.

"I'll see you tomorrow at lunch?" he asks.

"Yep, I'll be there with my leftover chicken noodle casserole."

"Sounds good. I'll probably have my usual wilted salad from the salad bar and a sandwich."

"That's really sad. It makes my leftovers sound gourmet."

"To be fair, everything's gourmet compared to the cafeteria."

I gasp. "Don't let PAMECorp hear you disparage the cafeteria."

He ducks his head and looks around suspiciously. "You aren't going to turn me in, are you?"

I pretend to think about it. "No, but if they interrogate me, I won't be able to lie for you."

"I couldn't ask you to."

We laugh and it feels like a good lead-in to saying good night. "Thanks for a great day. Even though you did get a little cocky about being right about the bet."

"I'm not right that often, so I went overboard."

His self-depreciating humor always cracks me up. "Good, then it won't happen again for a while." I reach out to nudge his arm. "You should go catch the end of your family call."

"I will." He shifts a little. "I hate to put an end to the day."

"Me, too."

"Can I give you a hug?"

"Of course." I reach out at the same time he does and our

arms collide in midair. I pull my right arm up, just as he lifts his left, and we're in some weird octopus-like hug that sums up every awkward part of every first date ever.

He pulls back and shakes his head, his palms up. "I'm not sure how that went so wrong. Sorry."

My face burns and I shrug. "Guess it's not like riding a bike." I immediately feel even more blood rush to my face as my brain catches up and realizes how dumb that was.

"If it makes you feel any better, I can't ride a bike."

"Neither can I."

He catches my eye and we're both laughing too hard at something that wasn't all that funny but we're both nervous and it's adorable and this is the exact instant I realize I could fall for Del. For real. Not as a distant crush or "work husband" or *Seinfeld* co-conspirator.

My stomach churns worse than it did on the Impulse, and my fight or flight instinct kicks in. "I should..." I poke my thumb over my shoulder, pointing toward the inside of the house.

"Yeah, me, too. I'll see you tomorrow."

I step backward, up onto the threshold, pushing the door open with my hip. "Thanks again."

He nods and steps back, grabbing the screen door before it can slam and guiding it shut. "Night, Shas."

"Night, Del."

He makes the next move, smiling, giving me a little wave, and turning to head off the porch and to his car.

I slowly slide into the house and close the door. I subtly peek through the slats of the blinds, watching him back out of my driveway and pull away.

I turn off the porch light, lock the door, cross the room, grab the pillow off the couch and press it against my face. I scream into it, letting out a bunch of anxiety, nervous energy, and a heaping cup of fear. This is bad. Bad, bad, bad. I like Del. A lot. I'm not sure I'm up for anything more than that.

It's scary, and I don't do scary.

* * *

My Bucket List

1. ~~Buy a lottery ticket~~
2. Go through automatic car wash
3. Manicure
4. Get hair done in real salon
5. ~~Ask Del out on a date (!!!!!)~~
6. Get back into knitting

Chapter 14

"Mom! That's amazing!"

Kat has zero respect for my caution. "Amazing?" I don't mean to be, but I'm yelling. "I just told you I'm freaking out and all you can say is that it's amazing?"

"Mooooom." She draws the word out in exasperation, like *I'm* the one being unreasonable here. "I'm so happy!"

"I'm not." I try for indignant. "He's at his place right now, talking about me to his family. That's kind of offensive."

Kat snorts. "You're talking about him to your family right now."

I open my mouth but I can't manage to find a suitable retort.

"I'm glad you're freaking out."

"What? Why would you be happy about that?" I shriek. *I'm* certainly not happy about it.

Her voice goes serious. "Because you're getting out of your comfort zone and taking some chances. I know that must be really scary, and I'm really proud of you."

I close my eyes and shake my head, bringing the volume back down to normal levels. It means a lot that Kat is proud of me. I might even be a little bit proud of myself. "Yeah, yeah, yeah. When do classes start?"

"Way to change the subject. August 16. I'm super excited."

"Me, too. I'm so proud of you. Do you have everything you need for school?"

"Yes, I do. I picked my laptop up yesterday and I have all

my clothes and shoes and equipment and all that stuff. Tomorrow I have to get a new crockpot and I'll be all set."

"What happened to yours?"

"Only thing we can figure is that it got damaged in the move. I never saw a crack or anything, but the other night Daniel heard a loud pop from the kitchen. We went in to look and here the crock just snapped in half."

While she's talking, I cash app her a hundred dollars. I know she got the notification when she sucks in a breath. Funny thing that I don't even hesitate when it comes to spending for Kat, but I probably would have gone to four thrift stores to find a replacement slow cooker for myself. Which is kind of ridiculous. No, not kind of. It's fully ridiculous. Is it progress that I at least recognize this?

"Mom! They're not that much."

"Get one of the programmable ones that's a little more expensive. They automatically flip to warm once the cook time is over. And get some of the liners if you don't have any. They're the best thing ever."

She agrees wholeheartedly. "Aren't they amazing? I would seriously kiss whoever came up with those."

We spend a few minutes gushing about the practical brilliance of slow cooker liners.

Kat yawns. "I should get to bed. Thanks for the money, but I wasn't hinting for you to do that."

"I know you weren't. I just want you to have everything you need."

"I miss you, Mom."

"I miss you, too. Good night, Kat."

We hang up and I clutch the phone to my chest. Sometimes I miss her so bad it hurts. This is one of those times.

* * *

Monday is a whirlwind of problems. A brief storm over the weekend knocked out the power and caused a boatload of technical issues. It's annoying enough in our department, where all the computers rebooted into safe mode, but I can only imagine the frenzy in IT.

Carl huffs over to my cubicle. "Do you believe this crap?"

I'm not sure which particular crap has him so irritated since there's plenty to choose from. "You'll have to be more specific."

"I called upstairs to let Edmonds know today's stuff is going to be delayed, and you know what he tells me? To send out an email to all the department heads. An email! When nobody can access their computers. I swear they don't promote anyone with functioning brain cells in their head."

"It pays to have an uncle in high places, I guess." It annoys me, too. A lot of our executives have lost touch with what it's like to work down here in the trenches, but Edmonds (SVP of douchebaggery) is particularly clueless. And annoying. During my last meeting that included him, he told me how he takes his coffee as he came in the room. Needless to say, he remained coffeeless. Jackass.

Carl shakes his head. "I could do his job in my sleep, but he'd never be able to do mine. Yet he makes six times what I do. It's bullshit."

"Believe me, I know." It's odd to see Carl so worked up. He's one who comes in, does his job, and goes home with a minimum of interaction. Nice enough guy, just not interested in mixing his business and personal existence.

"I can't wait for vacation," he grumbles.

"Oh? Where are you going?"

His scowl relaxes. "Taking the entire family on a Caribbean cruise for my fiftieth birthday. Judy's got the whole thing planned out."

I remember meeting his wife a handful of times at various corporate events. "That sounds amazing. When are you going?"

He smiles the biggest smile I've ever seen on his face. "Exactly one month from today."

I vaguely remember approving his PTO request but I don't typically look at the reason for the request. If someone has PTO available, I figure it's none of my business how or why they plan to use it.

Carl tells me a little about the cruise line (Royal Caribbean) and an excursion they're planning (swimming with dolphins). It's the most I've heard the man speak in a decade. Finally he goes off and I poke my head in Ellie's cubicle. "Getting anything done?"

She jumps a mile high, and blushes as she clicks her phone off. "Oh, uh, I was working on… um…" Her eyes flit to the black screen on her computer.

"Ellie. I'm joking. Nobody can do anything right now."

She gives a nervous laugh. "Sorry. Texting with Trevor." I swear her pupils are little cartoon hearts. Barf. He's not worthy of her.

Before she can gush about how great he is, I go back to my own cube and watch the clock until lunchtime. I grab my lunchbox and head for the cafeteria. I'm done with my sandwich and the chapter of the book I'm reading on my phone when a tray clunks down onto the table.

Del flops into the chair and sighs. "This day."

I turn my phone off. "I can only imagine."

He waves a hand and shovels a forkful of salad into his mouth. I barely understand when he says, "Your department is next."

"Good. Does that mean the sales department is back up and running?"

He nods and takes a swig of soda. "Yeah. It wiped out parts of the website and everything. It's been a nightmare. And then that dumbass Wilkinson had the nerve to come down and waste an hour of my time blaming my department for the outage. I told him the backup generators are the maintenance department's responsibility, but he didn't want to hear it." He shakes his head and stabs at his salad. "I thought his head was going to explode when I told him this was on *him* since he voted against having off-site backups. Dumbass. They don't want to spend a buck on things that make good business sense, but they'll drop a mint on their stupid meetings. Do you know what they pay just to cater those pointless board meetings?"

I raise my hand. "Accounting. Yeah, I know. I had to submit a whole freaking written request with prices from three different vendors to get one of my people a sixty-dollar adding machine last month."

"Ugh. And they don't even consider that your wasted time

cost them more than just buying it." He gives his head a grumpy shake.

"Yup." I snap the lid on my container and put it in my lunchbox. "You're not the only one having issues with higher-ups today." I tell him about Carl and the instruction to send an email to the department heads.

Del rolls his eyes, hard. "And they're the ones making the big bucks."

"That's what we said." I watch him wolf down his sandwich. "I didn't figure I'd get to see you today."

He nods a little. "I can't stay long. I needed a break, though, and I wanted to see you." He gestures to his tray. "And eat something. Was starting to get hangry."

"I hope your afternoon goes better than your morning has."

He pauses and grins at me, his entire face relaxing. "It's better already."

My cheeks burn and I can't help but smile.

"I hate to rush, but..." He waves his hand to encompass the current situation.

"I'll talk to you later."

He takes his tray and heads for the trash can, and then he's gone.

I briefly see Del again when he pops into my department to make sure all of our computers are reconnected to the network and no one is having any residual issues. He stops in my cube on his way out. "You up for some really lousy company for dinner tonight?"

* * *

My Bucket List

1. ~~Buy a lottery ticket~~
2. Go through automatic car wash
3. Manicure
4. Get hair done in real salon
5. ~~Ask Del out on a date (!!!!!)~~
6. Get back into knitting

Chapter 15

When I arrive at the pizza place near Del's house, he's already sitting in a booth. He looks up, and it does something funny to my chest when he sees me and his face immediately breaks out in a big smile.

I slide into the seat opposite him. "I hope your afternoon was smoother than your morning."

He leans back, relaxing for probably the first time today. "Much. Except when I got called up to Parson's office."

"Whoa." It was a rare and unpleasant thing to get called all the way up to the CEO's penthouse office. Office *suite*.

"That jackass Wilkinson tried rolling my department under the bus. Luckily I figured that's what it was probably about, so I printed off all the stupid committee minutes showing how many times I fought to get off-site backups done. Then we would have only lost an hour or two and not a whole day for the entire company. Morons. Wilkinson said he'd never been presented with the option, then stuttered and stammered and turned purple when I whipped out that stack of minutes."

In my estimation, Wilkinson is better than Edmonds, but not by much. "I wish I could have seen his face."

Del drops his mouth open and bugs his eyes out. "Something like this, only purple."

I laugh and shove his arm. "Then what happened?"

"Parson kicked him out of the office and asked me a few questions about the backup. Then he asked about the backup generator and I explained that was a building maintenance issue, not an IT issue. He made a few notes, and I left. It was all very anticlimactic."

"Disappointing."

He leans forward and puts his elbows on the table. "I'm glad you gave me a heads up about Edmonds telling Carl to send the email. Holy shit, I got a whole earful when I went over to check Carl's system."

"I'm sure you did. I haven't seen him that mad since they brought in that efficiency expert like four years ago and we had to do those fifteen-minute incremental activity logs."

Del groaned. "Those stupid things were brutal."

"And completely unnecessary. We all know who doesn't get their work done, but instead of having the balls to reprimand those people, we all have to suffer."

"Carl also told me all about his upcoming cruise, which was a much better topic of conversation."

I drop my pizza crust onto my plate and wipe my hands on my napkins. "Yeah, he seems really excited about it. I would be, too. The Caribbean? Sign me up."

Del adjusts his glasses. "I should've done that for my fiftieth last year."

"You can always do it for your fifty-first."

"Too late. My birthday's in February."

"Fifty-second, then. I bet a cruise in February would be amazing." Right up until you have to come back to the cold, crappy winter waiting at home.

He pulls another slice of pizza from the pie and hesitates. "You could go for yours."

"I wouldn't have time to plan for it. My birthday's in like two and a half weeks."

His eyebrows shoot up. "It is? Really?"

I'm a little embarrassed. Birthdays have never been a big deal to me. Probably because half the time, nobody remembers mine. Kat excluded, of course. "Yeah."

"What are you doing for your birthday?" he asks.

I hadn't given it much thought. "It's on a Saturday this year, so I'll probably sleep in late and then splurge on lunch and maybe go see a movie."

"Whoa, slow down there. You're too wild and crazy for my blood." There's a teasing twinkle in his eye.

"Yeah, I know."

"If you could do anything at all, what would you do?"

I sit back as our server drops off drink refills, and I think about it until he leaves. I say, "If I could do anything, like for real, not some wild last minute Caribbean cruise, I'd take a long weekend and go visit Kat. Drive down on Thursday and come back home Sunday. Maybe check out Opryland or take one of those homes of the stars bus tours."

He's put his pizza down and is just staring at me.

I feel stupid for saying it, and more than a little defensive. Apparently even my wildest fantasies are lame. "Yeah, I know. Boring, right?" I sip at my drink so I don't have to see the boredom in his eyes.

"What? No. Not boring at all."

Suspicious, I glance over to see if he's teasing me.

"It sounds amazing, and you should think about doing it." His voice softens. "Shas. You should have seen your face when you were talking about it. I hope you seriously consider actually going."

For real? Could I do that? I fidget with the corner of my napkin. "I don't know. She starts school the Monday right after that, and I'm sure she's busy getting ready." The idea has taken hold, though, and the argument is weak.

"Just think about it."

"I can't spring this on her." It dawns on me that I don't need to crash on her couch like I did in Colorado. I look up at Del. "I mean, it seems kind of silly to spend so much money on a weekend just for myself."

"Kat's getting ready to start a super intensive program. I bet it would do her a world of good to have a friendly and supportive face encouraging her."

"Wow, you're going for the gut, aren't you?"

He grins at me. "Tell me I'm wrong. I've never met her, but I'd bet she'll love the idea." He fumbles with his pocket and then slaps a twenty dollar bill on the table. "Bet."

"What? No, I'm not betting twenty bucks."

"*Bok bok bok bok*." He makes chicken noises at me. "Text her right now. Ask her what she'd think about you coming for a visit."

"You're ridiculous," I say, but I pull out my phone.

He taps his finger on the twenty.

I roll my eyes, but type, **No promises, I'm just thinking, but what would you think if I came to Nashville the weekend of my birthday?**

I put my phone down. "There. Happy now?"

"Yes." He's got that cocky expression again.

The server comes back with boxes for the leftover pizza and the check.

My phone vibrates with an incoming text.

Are you for real?????? I WOULD LOVE THAT!!!!!!!!!

I turn my phone around to show Del. He looks exactly as smug as I expect, but he has the good grace to not say anything.

I type back, **I'm just thinking about it.**

Del puts his hand over his mouth to cover a massive yawn. "I hate to rush off, but it's been a day. I'm ready for a hot shower and bed."

"Yeah, and apparently I have a trip to plan." I slide out of the booth. I'm trying to look stern, but the truth is, I'm excited. I'm so excited at the prospect of seeing Kat, but I'm also excited about taking a long drive, just me and the radio.

And all of a sudden, I'm excited about this stupid bucket list and the whole world of things I could add to it.

* * *

My Bucket List

1. ~~Buy a lottery ticket~~
2. Go through automatic car wash
3. Manicure
4. Get hair done in real salon
5. ~~Ask Del out on a date (!!!!!)~~
6. Get back into knitting
7. Visit Kat in Nashville

Chapter 16

Tuesday morning is much calmer at work. The computers are all back online and connected to the intranet. Del texts me that he got approval to start the process for doing the off-site backups. Kat has texted me nine hundred times that she really, really, really, really, REALLY wants me to come visit. So instead of doing actual work, I'm on my phone, looking up Airbnb rentals in Nashville. I find an available cottage three blocks from the university that's cheaper than I expect, so I hold my breath and book it.

I screenshot the confirmation email and send it to Del. **See? I can be impulsive.**

Wow that looks great! He texts back within a minute. A few seconds later, my phone buzzes again. **I'm impressed.**

Even though no one can see me in my cubicle, I cover my mouth to hide my smile. I feel my cheeks heat as I text back, **Me, too.** I can't believe I actually did it.

Then I text Kat that I'll be arriving Thursday evening.

She texts me back, **The new couch is super comfy.**

I won't need it. I end the message with a string of smiley faces and wait for her three-inch-long string of question marks. I send her a winky face and a screenshot of the Airbnb confirmation.

She sends back a shocked Pikachu gif followed by three dozen exclamation marks.

Is it close to your apartment? I ask.

Two blocks. It's perfect. I'm so excited, I can't wait!!!!!!!!!!!!!!!!!!!!!!!!!!!!!!!!!!!

A throat clears behind me.

Edmonds is standing with his arms crossed, glowering at my black computer screen. "Important business, I presume?"

I swallow hard and lean down to shove my phone in my purse. "Sorry." I touch my mouse and the screen comes back to life, showing the spreadsheet I'd been working on. Just my freaking luck to get caught the one time I'm actually screwing off.

"Do you have the Brighton reports done?"

"They're not due until Friday."

"I need them today."

I wait a beat to control my tone, because there's exactly zero chance he needs them today or any other day. "Sure."

"If that's a problem, Sandra, I can have someone else take care of it."

I hate this guy. Always have, always will. He's one of those smarmy corporate stereotypes who couldn't handle an honest day's work if it curled up on his desk and farted. I raise my eyebrows and innocently ask, "Who's Sandra?"

He sputters for a second and focuses on the brass nameplate affixed to my cube. He turns on his heel and leaves. If there's one thing he hates more than work, it's being called out for saying something wrong.

I go around and poke my head into Ellie's cubicle. "Edmonds is asking for the Brighton reports today."

She squeaks and looked panicked. "It's not due until Friday. I'm trying to finish the Wheeler files that are due tomorrow."

"Can you have Wheeler done by lunchtime?"

"Yeah."

"Just start on Brighton after lunch and get as far as you can. I'll handle Edmonds." I strongly suspect he won't remember what he asked for, and that he'd just picked an account out of thin air to punish me for slacking off. Whatever.

I go into our intranet system and check on the team. I note that Abby is a little behind on her monthly targets, which is unlike her. I submit my PTO request and then go across the room to Abby's cube.

"Is there anything I can help you with?" I ask her.

She runs a frustrated hand down her face. "This update is really screwing me up."

"What update?"

"The one we got from IT."

I lean down to look at a progress bar on her screen. "What is this?" I click and a window pops up showing something installing. "Oh, crap." I grab her mouse and try clicking to end the installation. The mouse clicks, but nothing changes. Hitting Ctrl/Alt/Del does nothing. Uh oh. I take her phone and dial Del's extension.

"IT, this is Del."

"Hey. It's Shasta. Abby's system has some sort of update going and it's locking up the system."

He lets out a string of colorful curses. "Okay, hang on." The background is a flurry of clicking. Then he says, "I got her station blocked from the intranet. I'll be over to look at her computer in a few."

I hang up and blow out a hard breath. This, on the heels of

yesterday's technical disaster does not bode well for Del's state of mind.

"Did I do something wrong?"

I feel like a stern schoolmarm with some of my employees, especially the younger ones. I have to be careful of her feelings while imparting the severity of the problem. "Did you click on a link in an email?"

"Yeah."

"Did you verify where the email came from?"

"It said IT."

"Did you *verify* that with IT?"

She blinks at me like I've asked the question in Klingon.

My exasperation builds. "You know that phishing training we just had?"

"Yeah?"

"This is exactly what the training covered. Not clicking links in emails."

"But the email said it was a critical update." She clicks on her email and opens the message to show me.

I pinch the bridge of my nose. "Abby. PAMECorp is spelled wrong. That's not even our logo." The amount of typos in the first sentence alone should have tipped her off. Shit. I'm going to have to write her up for this.

Del arrives at her cubicle and glances at the email. His nostrils flare as he pulls in a long breath. I know he's clinging to the last strand of patience he's got, because I'm doing the same. For a generation that is supposed to be so tech-savvy, it always seems to be the young ones who click the links, at least in my department.

"You might as well take lunch," he says sharply. "When you get back, you'll have to change all your passwords. For *everything*."

"That's such a pain," she whines.

"So is fixing this mess," he fires back.

Her eyes widen as if he's slapped her.

I share his annoyance, but there's no point beating a dead horse. "Abby, go take your lunch break."

She scurries away from her cubicle as fast as her legs will take her.

Del sits on her chair and begins unhooking cables. "Sorry to be touchy, but for crying out freaking loud, it's not that complicated. Don't. Click. Any. Links."

"Job security."

He snort-laughs. "Guess what. On top of all the shit yesterday, now they've decided that I have to be the one to deal with every single one of these internal security issues personally. Lucky me." He shakes his head. "Wanna grab lunch when I'm done here?"

"Absolutely. I'll be in my cage." I make my rounds, checking in with everyone, and make my way back to my cubicle. I'm knee deep in my own reports when Del taps on the edge of my cube.

"Need a few minutes?"

"Nope, I'm good." I click to save the spreadsheet and lock my computer.

"I'm going to have you lead a seminar on how to walk away from your station," he grumbles.

"Oh, shoot. I was supposed to leave it unlocked, wasn't I?

Perhaps with a notebook of all my passwords laying right here," I tap my desk.

"Yeah, with your unattended wallet right there." He points to the other side of my monitor.

Speaking of my wallet, I reach down to grab my purse and lunchbag, and only find my purse. "What the heck?" Immediately, a vision of my lunchbag, packed and ready, waiting on the kitchen counter, comes to mind. "Are you kidding me? I left my lunch on the counter this morning."

"My condolences."

"Condolences?"

"Well, everything in the cafeteria tastes like death, sooooo, yeah."

I laugh and lead the way to the elevator.

"I'm really impressed you actually booked your trip," he says when the doors slide shut.

"I honestly didn't think Kat would be so gung ho about it." I glance up and he's smirking. "What?"

He looks down at me. "Messed up your whole plan, didn't she?"

"I'm still not paying you twenty bucks. I never took the bet."

He shrugs, unbothered. "It was worth twenty bucks just to see you take the leap."

The elevator jerks to a stop and two people from the seventh floor get on, effectively pausing our conversation.

It jerks again at the fourth floor and two chattering salesmen get on, one of which is Trevor. He doesn't register the existence of the people around him, no surprise.

"Have you asked her out yet?"

Trevor shakes his head. "Not yet. Giving her a little bit at a time to make sure she's on the hook." He makes a casting motion and pulls back. "Then I'll start reeling her in, man, just reeling her in." He twirls his hand.

The other guy, I forget his name, guffaws like the follower he obviously is, since Trevor hasn't said anything remotely funny. "You think you'll keep this one a while? She's pretty hot."

Trevor snorts. "I'm strictly catch and release."

Eew. Seriously? Enough of the fishing metaphors. I'm pretty sure Trevor's never been fishing. It'd probably wreck his manicure.

His sycophantic buddy snickers. "One and done."

They fist bump and I'd like to bump my own fist into Trevor's face. With force. On behalf of all womankind. He's such a douchebag, and I'm pretty sure they're talking about Ellie. Apparently my face is doing that thing where it clearly broadcasts what's on my mind even though I'm not saying a word, because Del nudges my arm and his mouth is quirking like he's trying not to smile.

Thankfully, the elevator opens and we step off into the lobby. Del and I turn right toward the cafeteria while everyone else heads left.

"I cannot for the life of me understand why Ellie's so smitten with that smarmy weasel." I glare into the refrigerated shelves at the selection of pre-made sandwiches and salads.

Del shrugs and grabs a sandwich. "He's a good salesman, I guess."

"I wouldn't buy anything from him. So obnoxious." I pick

the least sad looking chef salad and a packet of ranch dressing. "Think we can return him to the Jerk Store?"

That earns a laugh. "Probably no returns."

We finish selecting our lunches and pay the cashier. I'm still annoyed when we sit down but I take a breath and let it go. "How bad was Abby's system?"

Del groans. "Extra paperwork bad."

"I was afraid of that." Which means that not only do I have to do paperwork to issue a formal reprimand, Del has to fill out paperwork about a security breach. And I'll have to listen to Abby whine about being assigned more training modules. Talk about punishment. Those modules are the most boring-ass torture to ever crawl up from the pits of corporate hell.

He waves his hand. "Let's talk about something better. What's your plan for Nashville?"

I tear open the dressing packet and drizzle it on my salad. "I don't have much of a plan yet, if you can believe it. I spent last evening mapping out the route and figuring how many rest stops I'll need and where. I know I want to see the Grand Ole Opry and I'd like to go to the zoo. And of course hit all the best food places. I might take one of those double-decker bus tours just to see what's there."

"How about Madame Tussauds?"

"Sounds like a brothel."

Del shakes his head and sighs. "It's the famous wax museum."

"Well. It sounds like it could be a brothel."

"No, it doesn't."

I poke at my salad. "Okay, then, what's a good name for a

brothel?"

"I don't know, probably something seedy like Miss Kitty's Playhouse or something."

"Not Miss Kitty's Cathouse?"

He considers this. "You might be onto something."

"Anyway. That's my agenda for tonight. Do some research and see what I want to do while I'm there." I spear some lettuce with the cheap plastic fork. "I'm sure Kat will have some things in mind, so I'll have to check with her and be flexible."

"Bravo." He finishes his sandwich and brushes the crumbs from his hands. "Does your car have a CD player?"

I envision my center console. "Yes. Why?"

"Just curious."

That was random. "I'm glad you encouraged me to check with Kat instead of just assuming she'd be too busy to entertain me." I'm simultaneously grateful and frustrated. I try not to think about all the trips I might have taken if I hadn't held myself back, afraid of being an inconvenience. "I need to see what grocery stores and restaurants are in the area near their apartment. I want to get her — them — some gift cards because I'm sure she'll be spending so much time studying that they'll probably be eating out a good bit, and she'll balk if I just give her cash."

"Sounds like Allie. As soon as she got out on her own, she'd get offended if I tried to give her money. Ben, on the other hand, is a big fan of cash. I swear I cash app that kid money every other day."

"I suppose I should be grateful she's so independent."

"I see where she gets it." He smiles at me over the top of his cup.

At least she's not independent to a fault, like her mom seems to be. I shift the topic. "Have you ever been to Nashville?"

"No, but I'd like to visit someday."

My heart leaps up and lodges in my throat. Should I invite him to come along? I feel like my brain is short-circuiting.

"Shas?"

I snap back to the present. "Sorry, what?"

"Where'd you go?"

I plaster a grin on my face and say, "Nashville. Just thinking about how much fun this trip is going to be." My mind has split into about ten different voices, some of them lobbying to invite Del — after all, I'm all about impulsive decisions these days, right? — and some of them saying I'm ridiculous and this trip is all about me. It's my birthday, after all. Well, me and Kat. But mostly me. I'm almost giddy at the thought of doing this myself, *for* myself.

"I want to hear all about the places you visit."

Okay, whew. He wasn't hinting about being invited, and that's stupid anyway. He probably can't take off with such short notice. And we're not official anyway, so definitely not on any kind of taking-a-trip-together level.

"I'll definitely keep you posted."

* * *

My Bucket List

1. ~~Buy a lottery ticket~~
2. Go through automatic car wash
3. Manicure
4. Get hair done in real salon
5. ~~Ask Del out on a date (!!!!!)~~
6. Get back into knitting
7. Visit Kat in Nashville

Chapter 17

The rest of the week passes in a haze of paperwork and tears. I gave Abby her written reprimand on Wednesday, and since then she's barely looked at me.

I'm so glad it's Friday. I clock out and look forward to spending my weekend not being here.

I'm on my way across the parking lot. It's approximately forty billion degrees outside and our dress code only allows for jeans on casual Fridays, not capris. By the time I reach my car, I've got swamp butt and I feel like I peed myself.

So of course this is the exact moment Del calls my name. He's wearing khaki pants and I mentally kick myself. I have khakis. Why didn't I wear them instead?

"Hey."

He jog-walks over to me. "Want to grab supper?"

"Yes, but." I peel my t-shirt out from where it's sticking to my stomach.

"But?"

"I need to go home and grab a shower first. I'm melting." I hope he doesn't require a deeper explanation, because I am so not in the mood to go over the effects of perimenopausal hot flashes in summertime.

"No problem. I'll stop by my place and give you like half an hour?"

"Perfect." I'm not sure if he has something more to say, but I open my car door to signal that I'm not interested in a lengthy conversation while standing here on the surface of the sun. Not even with Del. "I hate to rush, but I need to get some A/C going before I dissolve."

"See you in a bit."

I leave him standing in the parking lot and drive with my fingertips until the air conditioning cools off enough that my steering wheel doesn't feel like a branding iron. I flip the A/C on high and lift my elbows so the vents blow cool air toward my armpits.

I practically run into the house and dive into the shower, letting the cool water wash away all the yuck. I seriously don't understand how I survived as a kid, being outside from sunup to sundown no matter how hot it was. In fact, at that age, the hotter the better. I swear ninety degrees today is a whole lot different than ninety degrees back in the day. I squirt shampoo into my palm.

Back in the day? Seriously? I'm going on forty-seven, not seventy-four. Next thing you know I'll be shaking my fist at the neighbor kids and yelling at them to get off my lawn.

I dry off and slip into a sundress. Want to know how hot it is? I'm skipping the spanx. I towel my hair as much as I can. I twist it up and secure it with a clip to keep it off my neck. Now would probably be a good time to do number four on my list and go to an actual salon and get a haircut. Maybe a cute bob that would swing across my shoulders and be cooler than the mess I currently have.

I slip my sandals on and peek out the front door. Del's car is rolling to a stop, so I grab my purse and head outside, back into the wall of oppressive yuck. I wave my hand to stop him from jumping out to open my door. Chivalry is unacceptable in certain weather conditions. I'm totally sure Miss Manners would agree with me. And if not, maybe I'll write my own book on etiquette. So there.

The inside of his car is nice and cool. "Where to?"

"You look amazing."

I flush with pleasure. It's so weird and wonderful to hear his random compliments. "Thank you." I fluff the skirt of my sundress. "I got this at Goodwill for two bucks." I have no idea why I tell him this.

He raises an eyebrow and plucks at his shirt. "Target. Fifteen dollars."

"You just made that up."

"I did. I have no idea where I got this or how much it cost. But since that's where the bulk of my clothes come from, it's a good guess." He puts the car in reverse. "Where would you like to eat?"

"I could kind of eat at the BBQ place, but I'm not sure I want to eat anything heavy because it's so freaking hot."

"It's up to you. I was kind of hoping that's where you'd want to go."

"Yeah, let's go there. I can always get a salad or something."

He backs out of the driveway and just as he rolls to a stop at the light, huge drops of rain splat onto the windshield. "Oh, great," he grumbles.

"Maybe it'll take care of some of the humidity." I know that's wishful thinking, and I refuse to consider what the humidity will be like when I head to Tennessee. In the middle of August. That's the only thing I am not looking forward to.

Fat drops of rain dump out of the sky and pelt the windshield. Del flips the wipers on. It's still pouring when we park at the BBQ restaurant.

He turns the car off and sits, uncertain.

Since I've turned over a new leaf and make all kinds of snap decisions now, I grab the door handle. "I'm starving, and I don't care if I have to swim to the front door."

"Okay, let's go."

We jump out and run, our footsteps slapping the water skimming the asphalt. Steam rises up from the pavement as the cool water hits the scorching ground. We run up the steps and stop on the porch, laughing and breathing hard.

"I don't want to drip on their floor." I squeeze the water from my dress while Del takes care of wringing his soggy clothes.

The restaurant is packed, so they seat us on their deck, which ends up being the perfect spot. We're at a table along the railing. The rain has slowed from a downpour to a steady flow, and as I'd hoped, it took the humidity out of the air.

Del checks his weather app. "Looks like it's supposed to rain all night."

"I guess we could use it." We talk about the weather for a few minutes until I'm distracted by a bird down on the restaurant's lawn, tugging a worm from the ground.

Since the heat has calmed down, my stomach has decided that it no longer only wants a light salad. I end up ordering a grilled chicken dinner with a white sauce. I even splurge and order a cocktail.

Del orders a brisket dinner and a beer.

As we eat, we chat about everything and nothing. Our kids, my trip, our bucket lists. Until we're almost done with our main meal and overhear the people seated at the table next to ours.

The young man begins, "Sweetheart, you mean the world to me, and I— "

We both clam up when she interrupts him, trying not to be obvious that we're listening, but come on.

"Spencer, stop."

"I can't. Baby, I love you."

The young woman forces out an annoyed sigh and looks down, her long straight hair curtaining the sides of her face. "Don't."

Del whispers to me, "Don't do it, man."

Spencer pulls a box out of his pocket and sets it on the table. "We've both made some mistakes."

Her eyes flash up to glare at him.

"I know mine are bigger."

I feel myself lean closer, hanging on every word. I'm invested.

"I know we can work this out and be happy together."

"No. I can't do this." She tugs the napkin off her lap and tosses it on the table. "I never should have met you tonight."

"Sophie, my love." He slides off his chair and gets on one knee beside her. "Marry me."

A few people cheer and yell things like, "Say yes!"

Sophie jerks to her feet, the chair clattering away and falling. "No. I don't ever want to see you again."

Del and I gawk, wide eyed. It's impossible to pretend to

look away. Even a server is trapped in the middle of the room, holding a tray full of food.

Someone yells, "That's cold!"

Sophie bursts into tears and screeches, "He slept with my sister!" before sprinting from the deck.

Spencer calls after her, "It didn't mean anything! I said I was sorry!"

Del lets out a low whistle.

There's a beat of stunned silence, then the deck roars back to life. The server delivers the tray of food, and conversation starts back up, no doubt dissecting the scene we just witnessed.

"I don't understand," Spencer whines. He looks over at Del. "What can I do to get her back?"

Del's expression is the coldest I've ever seen. Dislike is written all over his face. "Maybe try not cheating. Grow up. As for Sophie? Stay the hell away from her."

You'd have thought Spencer cheated on Del's daughter, from his clenched jaw.

Spencer turns to the opposite table to find some understanding there.

"I'm going to the ladies' room. I'll be right back." I should have known better than to order a cocktail because alcohol goes straight through me.

I wind around the tables, into the main restaurant, and into the restroom, where someone is crying in the last stall. I do my business and after I wash my hands, I lightly tap on the stall door. "Sophie?"

She sniffles.

"Are you okay?"

The door opens a crack. Warily, she asks, "Who are you?"

I point over my shoulder. "I, uh, out there, I was sitting at the table next to you."

"Oh."

"Are you okay?" I ask again. I'm not sure why. Obviously she's not okay.

She wipes her nose on a wadded tissue.

"Do you have a ride home?"

She nods. "I called my friend to come get me." Every other word hitches.

"You know he's not worth your tears, right?" I can't help but think this is a preview of Ellie's future if she spends too much time with Trevor. "Spencer is a douchebag and you deserve so much better."

Her chin quivers.

"Is your friend coming?"

She nods.

"Do you want me to wait with you?"

She blinks a few times and nods again.

So we stand in the bathroom for a good twenty minutes until her outraged friend storms into the bathroom, vowing to cut Spencer's penis off and choke him with it.

I slip out the door.

"Sorry about that," I say as I sit back down. "Sophie was in the restroom and I stayed with her until her ride showed up."

Del smiles, but it's subdued. "I figured as much. I took the liberty of ordering dessert."

* * *

The ride home is quiet. I'm stuffed from the triple chocolate brownie cake with ice cream Del and I shared.

I glance over and notice that his jaw is tense.

"What's up?" I ask.

"Sorry, that whole scene just got me in my head. Dragging up ancient history."

I reach over and rest my hand on his forearm.

"My wife cheated on me," he blurts out. "A lot. I found out she'd been screwing around pretty much the entire time we were married."

"I'm so sorry." I know exactly how horrible that feels.

"Yeah. And then I was the bad guy for asking for paternity tests." He pulls into my driveway. "Maybe I was. I don't know."

We sit in the car, watching the rain in the headlights reflecting off my garage door.

I'm dying to know, but I'm never going to ask.

"They both came back positive. Not that it matters. They're my kids no matter what some stupid test says. Allie was old enough to understand, but I'm not sure Ben will ever forgive me for getting him tested."

I'm not sure what to say, so we just sit, holding hands.

Finally, he gives a little laugh and says, "She was totally not spongeworthy."

I laugh along with him, and don't even point out all the ways that makes no sense. I also don't say anything about the growing feelings I have, or the physical attraction, or the fact that Del is the most spongeworthy man I've been around in years.

* * *

My Bucket List

1. ~~Buy a lottery ticket~~
2. Go through automatic car wash
3. Manicure
4. Get hair done in real salon
5. ~~Ask Del out on a date (!!!!!)~~
6. Get back into knitting
7. Visit Kat in Nashville

Chapter 18

The days fly until Wednesday. At 11:30, I clock out and grab my purse. I can't remember the last time I left work early unless it was for an appointment. I'm giddy as I put my computer to sleep and push my chair under my desk.

Ellie must hear me shuffling, because she pokes her head around the cube and says, "Have a wonderful trip."

"Thanks. I hope so. I can't wait to see my daughter."

"Aww, I bet she's super excited to see you, too." She smiles and dips back into her own cube.

I glance back at my desk, then hightail it to the elevator. My heart beats fast, like I'm doing something wrong and about to get caught. Which is asinine. I work hard for this place, and I've earned every second of my accrued PTO.

The elevator slides toward the lobby and stops on the fourth floor. Edmonds strides on. I stare up at the digital number, cursing my luck.

"Hey, Sharon, when you get back from lunch I'm going to need some reports from you."

I bite down a smirk as my brain immediately goes to Bill Lumbergh asking for TPS reports in *Office Space*. "Ooh, sorry, Tom, I'm out of the office this afternoon. If you could get with Peters for those reports, that'd be great."

He sputters. I'm not sure if it's because his name is Tim or because Peters is his superior, but either way I'm pretty darn pleased with myself. The doors slide open to the lobby. I hurry out before he can reply.

I chuckle inside all the way to my car.

I stop at the gas station and fill the car up. After that's done, I swing by the grocery store and buy some snacks for the trip. I'm coasting home on autopilot, making mental lists about what I need to get done before I leave tomorrow morning.

Lists.

You know what? I'm going to cross something off. I drive past my house and loop around my street back to the main road. I go back toward the grocery store and turn into the car wash.

I follow the arrows around the back of the building. How the heck does this thing even work? Thankfully I'm alone in the parking lot, so I take my time reading all the signs and warnings. I inch toward the giant garage door and peer inside. I expected to see giant whirly sponges, but apparently this car wash is a little lower-tech. I pull up to a little box that instructs me to insert my money and select my wash. I had no idea there were different levels of washes.

The lowest wash is seven bucks, and the highest is twelve. What the heck. I'll spring for the undercarriage and extra foam rinse. Might as well have the full experience, right?

I slide twelve dollars into the machine and push the button. Inside the huge garage bay, a green light comes on and instructs me to pull forward. I inch ahead until I roll over a bump and the light turns red. The sign says to put my car in Park, so I do.

A second later, the machinery whirs to life and a wheel of large arms spin and spray water onto the car. A massive arch moves overtop my car, pulling the water arms along toward the back.

The machine cycles through the water and then squirts a colorful sudsy foam over the car. I'm tempted to turn the windshield wipers on, but I resist.

I sit through three foam cycles and rinses. It's actually really nice. The radio has no signal inside the building, so it's just me and the sound of the machines. After the second cycle, the scent of the soap fills the air inside my car, like the inside was soaped as well. I breathe it in.

The arch stops moving, and the light turns green. Massive blowers at the exit kick on, and I inch forward as they dry the bulk of the water droplets off the car.

I pull out and coast over to the bank of vacuums. Might as well clean the carpets while I'm here.

As the vacuum hose sucks a million tiny stones from my floor mats, I'm conflicted. It feels good to have done something new, but it feels silly that it's taken me this long to try it.

I'm in need of some real balance in my life. I've spent far too long letting fear win out and keep me from doing even the smallest things. I can't keep claiming to be a "realist" when the reality is that it doesn't benefit me to get a soda with no ice or spend twenty minutes hand-washing my car instead of zipping through the auto wash in two. It might save me a little money, but it's costing me time.

And it's high time I start valuing my time as much as I do my money.

* * *

My Bucket List

1. ~~Buy a lottery ticket~~
2. ~~Go through automatic car wash~~
3. Manicure
4. Get hair done in real salon
5. ~~Ask Del out on a date (!!!!!)~~
6. Get back into knitting
7. Visit Kat in Nashville

Chapter 19

I swear I've double checked my suitcase a hundred times. Clothes are packed, my spare phone charger is packed, my toiletries, everything. All I have to do tomorrow morning is get up, get dressed, and get on the road. I can just go to bed for the night. Except that it's only four o'clock.

I scroll through my phone and open the text thread with Kat. I do not message her again, because I know she's getting annoyed by how many times I've asked if she's sure she wants me to come. I quadruple check my Airbnb address even though I've got it memorized.

Now I just need to kill a few hours until bedtime.

At five after five, my phone pings with a text message. Del.

Can I come over?

Absolutely, I text back. It's disconcerting to me that the only thing downside to this trip is not seeing Del for four days. I'm used to seeing his face every day.

His car pulls in the driveway and he gets out with a plain white bag, a grocery bag, and a sparkly gift bag.

"What's all this?" I ask as I let him in.

"Dinner." He heads to the kitchen and sets the bags down. "I picked up subs and chips and dessert."

"I knew there was something about you I liked."

"My sparkling personality? My good looks? My irresistible charm?"

I dramatically roll my eyes. "Your modesty. But mostly I

was talking about how you show up with food."

"It's my stunning IT physique. I knew it." He leans over to kiss my cheek. "Do you have a DVD player?"

"I'm old. Of course I have a DVD player."

"Excellent." He pulls something out of the grocery bag and hands it to me.

It's gift wrapped, but it's obviously a DVD case. "Should I open it now?"

"Of course. We can watch it while we eat. Dinner and a movie."

We've spent so much time together over the past few weeks, but haven't gotten around to the whole dinner and a movie thing. I unwrap the present and do a little hop. "*Date Night*! I love this movie. Tina Fey and Steve Carell are hilarious. Thank you."

We take the food to the living room. Del opens the chip bags (one plain, one BBQ) while I start the movie.

"Have you seen it before?" I ask.

"Yeah. It's been a while, though. I saw it in a bin at the checkout and figured it was a good choice. Part action-adventure movie for me, part romcom with half-naked Marky Mark for you."

"You'll hear no complaints about that," I laugh.

We eat while the movie plays in the background. I have to hand it to him. This was the perfect choice. We've both seen it, so we aren't missing anything by talking over it from time to time.

I tell him about my run-in with Edmonds and he laughs long and hard at my story. "The timing was perfect. The elevator opened, and I just slid right out and went for the door before he could even say anything."

"That's brilliant." He smacks his leg. "'That'd be great.' I wish I could have seen his face when you told him to check with Peters."

"I know, right? I think he's afraid of him."

Del vigorously nods his head. "He should be. Peters is the only one who sees him for the jackass he is."

"Amen." I polish off my sub and half-watch the movie.

"Are you all packed up?"

"Of course. Packed, checked, double checked. Ready to roll."

"How's the oil in your car?"

"I assume it's fine. I just had it in for inspection and oil change last month."

"Okay, good."

It's sweet that he's concerned. To be honest, I wouldn't have thought about checking the oil. "Speaking of oil and car stuff, guess what."

"What?"

Now I'm second guessing myself because going through the car wash isn't a big deal for normal people, so this isn't exactly an exciting anecdote.

"Yeeessss?" He draws the word out, curious.

"Sorry, lost my train of thought. Anyway, after I got gas, I went to the car wash."

He lifts an eyebrow. "The *automatic* car wash?"

"That's the one."

"Awesome. What did you think?"

"I think it missed a few spots I would have gotten by hand,

but it was a lot faster and it smelled soooooo good. I'd give it a six point five out of ten. Will do again."

"Nice." He finishes off the chips.

"What are you going to do with your weekend off?"

"Off?" He looks confused.

"I mean since you won't have to see me this weekend."

He smiles, and that dimple on his cheek deepens. "I won't *get* to see you this weekend. Allie needs some shelves put up, so I'll be putting my handyman skills to good use."

"And taking her out for breakfast at lunchtime?" I think it's sweet. I'm guessing an aerospace engineer is more than capable of putting up some shelves and she just used it as an excuse to hang out with her dad.

"That's the plan."

We turn our attention back to the movie for a bit, laughing at the on-screen antics. Soon, the credits roll and I flip the television to an *I Love Lucy* marathon and turn the volume down low.

I lean back on the couch and Del holds up a finger in a "wait" gesture. "Don't move."

"Okay." I wonder what he's up to.

He rustles around in the kitchen for a few minutes, then comes back to the living room with two cupcakes. One of them has a candle burning on it. "Since I won't get to see you on your actual birthday, here you go." He sings, "Happy birthday to you, happy birthday to you. Happy birthday, dear Shasta. Happy birthday to you." He holds the cupcake out. "Make a wish."

All of a sudden I'm blinking back tears. I fight to compose

myself and hope he doesn't notice. I take the cupcake and blow out the candle.

He did notice. "Hey, what is it?" He sits beside me and puts an arm around my shoulders. "My singing's bad, but I didn't think it was *that* bad."

I laugh. "You just caught me off guard. I can't remember the last time someone sang for my birthday."

He doesn't laugh with me. "I'm sorry. That's really shitty. You deserve all the birthday songs and cakes and presents."

Now I'm uncomfortable. This feels too vulnerable and I don't like it, so I focus on eating my cupcake. "Well. Speaking of presents." I reach for the bright red glittery gift bag. I pull out the card and slide my finger under the flap. The card has cartoon bacon drawn all over it and huge letters proclaim, "You can't buy happiness." I flip it open and the inside reads, "But you can buy bacon, and that's basically the same thing. Happy birthday!"

This time my laugh is real. "Truth. Maybe I should spend the rest of my winnings on bacon."

He grins. "Totally worth it."

I shift the tissue paper and pull out an envelope. I open it and find a gift certificate to the Haus of Yarn. "I've never heard of this."

"I looked them up. It's like ten minutes away from your Airbnb."

My mouth drops open. "Seriously?" Oh, shit, I'm blinking rapidly again. When the heck did I turn so weepy? Then again, when had anyone ever done something so thoughtful for me? "Del. This. I. This." I hold the gift certificate to my chest. "Thank you," is all I can manage to whisper.

"I know it's like a thousand degrees outside, but I figured you might find something to work on for the fall."

Ever since I added knitting to my bucket list, I've filled an entire Pinterest board with hats and scarves and sweaters and afghans. I've been itching to get back to my hobby, and I know exactly what my first project is going to be.

There's something else in the bag. I pull out the thin rectangle. The pink unicorn wrapping paper is so cute I hate to tear it. I carefully peel the paper where it's taped and ease it open. "Is it a CD?"

He just shrugs and waits for me to finish opening it.

"It *is* a CD." The cover has a cartoon long-haired swamp thing holding a guitar on a stage.

"It's the best graphic I could come up with."

"Is it… is this monster rock?"

"You got it!" Del waves his hands in the air, celebrating. "I was afraid the reference was too out there."

"This is amazing." I open the case and realize it's a homemade CD. "You put it all together?" My jaw drops again and I turn to look at him. "Did you seriously make me a mixtape?"

"I did indeed." He points to the inside of the cover, which lists all the songs on the CD. "The best of '80s rock and roll, all carefully curated to be perfect highway sing-along songs. And, I must add, all legally procured."

"Del." I'm at a loss for words. And suddenly I'm glad for the trip so I can get some space from him. It's too much, too sweet, too thoughtful, too perfect.

He's unaware of my internal freak-out. "Nothing better than rolling down the highway, singing along with the music cranked all the way up."

I fiddle with the CD.

He points to the case. "I had a heck of a time getting a wig on the swamp monster."

"Heh. You'd think there would be plenty of stock images with swamp monsters wearing wigs." My voice feels too loud and I don't understand the pounding in my chest.

"Shockingly, there's not. I can't believe there isn't a big demand though."

"Right?" My heart rate is coming back down with the mundane conversation. I don't get it. I can't figure him out. Why he's here. Why he's here *with me*. Why he's so thoughtful and sweet and kind. Why he ever noticed me in the first place.

The walls are closing in again. I jump up and go to the kitchen to refill my half-full glass of water.

Del follows me and fills his own glass. I grab a dish towel to wipe the condensation off my glass, then set it down on the island. He's standing next to me and I can feel the heat from his body. Or maybe it's my imagination. Hell, I don't know. But he's close. Too close. Not close enough.

My brain buzzes with a hundred different voices and every last one of them goes silent when he puts his hand on my back. I slowly look up at him and his face is inches from mine. There's a little smudge mark on the corner of his glasses and he has a tiny scar above his eyebrow that I never noticed.

I can scarcely pull in enough air.

His lips gently brush mine and then not quite so gently and

everything short circuits.

* * *

My Bucket List

1. ~~Buy a lottery ticket~~
2. ~~Go through automatic car wash~~
3. Manicure
4. Get hair done in real salon
5. ~~Ask Del out on a date (!!!!!)~~
6. Get back into knitting
7. Visit Kat in Nashville

Chapter 20

I'm hovering in some bizarre time-space glitch where the world around me has ceased to exist except for me and Del and the ground under my feet.

His arms hold me tight against him and my fingers clutch his shoulders. The temperature has gone up about a thousand degrees and I'm feeling warm things I haven't felt in a long, long time.

We're kissing and breathing and the voices start again. This time they're freaking out about everything. My breath, the roll around my middle, the way his neck must be bent to lean down to kiss me and I wonder if it's uncomfortable... He's so tall and solid and holy shit is this amazing.

I can't quite remember why I've been keeping him at arm's length.

I also can't keep trying to convince myself he just wants to be friends, because friends don't kiss their friends like this.

He pulls back slightly, breaking the kiss and some small noise of objection squeaks from my throat.

My eyes are still closed, and I feel his hand leave my side and then his fingers are softly tucking an escaped lock of hair behind my ear. Then he presses a kiss to my forehead and I've never felt so safe and cared for in my entire life.

Hot tears sting the backs of my closed eyes. I try to focus on my breathing, but I'm just pulling in the faint scent of his cologne and soap or maybe it's detergent and holy shit it's just too much.

I pull back and tell myself to just keep inhaling and exhaling to counts of four. When I'm sure I've got the tears locked back inside where they belong, I open my eyes. My self-control floods back into my arms and legs and I take a little step back.

He's looking at me, one eyebrow cocked, waiting for my next move.

Why is he so patient? I don't get it.

I swallow hard, then grab my glass of water. The ice has frozen into one big lump and when I tilt the glass to take a sip, the ice shifts and sends a bloosh of water onto my face. I sputter and cough and start laughing.

Del takes the glass and sets it down. His shoulders shake with laughter he's trying to suppress. He wipes the water that splashed onto the island with the dish towel then tosses it onto the puddle on the floor.

Our eyes meet and we're both laughing. I can't stop. I'm laughing so hard I have to grab onto the island to keep my balance. Tears roll down my cheeks and I'm ninety percent sure there's a snot bubble forming, so I sniffle, which turns into a snort and now we're laughing harder.

Both of us hang onto the island until the gales subside and we compose ourselves. There's an unspoken mutual agreement not to look each other in the eye until we're in control.

A few minutes pass while we dab at our eyes with napkins and can finally behave.

Del clears his throat. "Well. That's not quite how I imagined this would end up."

Laughter bubbles up again but I keep it inside. Mostly. My

insides feel lighter. I'd been wound so tight and so wrapped up in my own head that I definitely needed a moment of hysterical laughter to break the tension before I snapped.

I reach over and put my hand on his. He shifts to squeeze my fingers.

"This is the best birthday-before-my-birthday I've ever had."

He leans over and kisses my cheek. "And you'll have the best birthday-day-of-your-birthday ever, too. I can't wait to hear what you and Kat get into."

"I'll text you updates at random intervals."

He grins and brushes that stubborn lock of hair back again. "Can't wait." He stands straight and inclines his head toward the living room. "I should head out so you can finish quadruple checking your suitcase."

"Yeah."

"Take lots of pictures and have lots of fun."

"I will, I promise." And I do promise. Not just him, but I promise myself that I'm not going to hold back. There's a whole world between reckless and immovable. It's time to take a step outside my comfort zone.

* * *

My Bucket List

1. ~~Buy a lottery ticket~~
2. ~~Go through automatic car wash~~
3. Manicure
4. Get hair done in real salon
5. ~~Ask Del out on a date (!!!!!)~~
6. Get back into knitting
7. Visit Kat in Nashville

Chapter 21

Stepping out of my comfort zone is easier said than done, especially at the crack of dawn after a nervous night's sleep. My palms are clammy as I climb into the car. I get back out and triple check the back seat for my suitcase, my tote bag with my toiletries and charger, and my insulated sack with cold water and snacks. I even walk around the car and poke at the tires with my foot, like I know anything about cars. Yup, gonna need to replace the johnson rod.

I can't even name all the emotions flooding through me. I'm nervous about this eleven hour — twelve or thirteen with stops — drive. Until now, my longest road trip was four hours to the beach. All the obnoxious "what ifs" run through my mind.

What if the car breaks down? *That's why I made sure my AAA is up to date.*

What if I get sick? *That's why I mapped out every urgent care facility along the way.*

What if I'm in an accident? *That's why I have my phone secured to the dash, with Kat's number on a sticky note stuck to the back of it.*

What if the GPS gets me lost? *That's why I printed out directions and have a paper atlas in the trunk.*

It's rather empowering to have all the answers. It makes that obnoxious voice a little quieter.

"What could go *right*?" I ask the rearview mirror. "The weather is beautiful, I'm prepared, and I'm going to hug my daughter before suppertime tonight."

That shuts the voice up. I haven't seen Kat in over a year and a half. Sure, we've done some video chats, but seeing her on the screen isn't the same as seeing her in person.

The little voice insists we forgot something important.

"You know what?" I shout into the car. "If I forgot something, I'll just buy one!"

Heck, yeah. Piss off, comfort zone.

The clock on the console reads 5:00. I slide Del's CD into the CD player and back out of the driveway. The GPS instructs me to turn left, not that I need help getting out of town.

About three hours in, I stop at a convenience store to put gas in the car and use the restroom and stretch my legs. I'm alone in the restroom, so I do a few jumping jacks to get the blood pumping.

I stop at the soda fountain and get a large cup. I pause and fill it halfway with ice before I get my soda. I snap a picture and text it to Del.

A few seconds later I get a shocked face emoji and a thumbs up.

I pay for my soda and get back on the road. At each rest stop, I send Del and Kat updates on my location. I take I81 from Pennsylvania to Maryland to West Virginia to Virginia, which I swear is never going to end. The bulk of my rest stops are in Virginia, because it is the Longest. State. Ever.

It's a million years before I cross the state line from Virginia to Tennessee. I still have more than four hours left, but getting into Tennessee finally feels like I'm getting close. I see signs for food and shopping, so I get off the highway in Bristol and decide to have my first major splurge.

It's just before one o'clock and I need a break from my car, so I follow signs to an Outback Steakhouse. Once I'm seated in a booth, I have a moment of insecurity about eating alone, but then I shove it aside. Baloney. I'm on vacation, and normal people eat by themselves in restaurants all the time. I order a bloomin' onion with extra sauce, and I ask for an extra loaf of the seriously-to-die-for dark honey wheat bread. I don't want anything too heavy, so I get some grilled chicken and go wild and add a skewer of grilled shrimp. I eat half of each and get the rest boxed up. The Airbnb listed an air fryer as an amenity, so these will be amazing as leftovers.

After lunch, I pop the leftovers in the cooler and stop to fill the gas tank at a nearby Valero convenience store, where I get another fountain soda with ice and text a picture to Del.

He sends another shocked face emoji and says, **Who are you??**

The afternoon is uneventful. I tense a little going through traffic in Knoxville, and I'm a little taken aback forty-five minutes later when there's a random sign informing me that I've gone from the eastern to central time zone. Luckily my phone does that magical thing it does and seamlessly jumps to the right time.

It's another three hours and one more quick stop before I reach my Airbnb in Nashville. It's flipping adorable. The little cottage looks exactly like the photos. I'm thrilled. I punch the code into the lockbox and it opens on the first try.

The inside is perfect. Cute and cozy.

I'm so relieved. I'd had nightmares about showing up and finding a dilapidated shack full of bugs and other unpleasant surprises.

I make two trips to bring everything inside and text Kat that I'm here. It's almost six — well, five with the time change. I put my leftovers in the fridge and walk through the cottage, peeking into every room to get familiar with the place. And to stretch my legs and get some blood flowing because my butt is numb and my back aches.

My phone dings and I squeal as I read the message.

Kat's on her way.

* * *

My Bucket List

1. ~~Buy a lottery ticket~~
2. ~~Go through automatic car wash~~
3. Manicure
4. Get hair done in real salon
5. ~~Ask Del out on a date (!!!!!)~~
6. Get back into knitting
7. ~~Visit Kat in Nashville~~

Chapter 22

I'm on the couch, zoned out and almost dozing when I hear a car door slam out front. I'm on my feet before my brain catches up to my legs. I fling the door open and dash along the sidewalk. Kat and I collide into each other's arms, hugging so tight it's a wonder either of us can breathe. We're both crying and rocking back and forth and I'm pretty sure my heart is going to explode inside my chest from pure happiness.

When we finally pull apart, I grip her shoulders just to get a good look at her. "I've missed your face," I say. "Your hair is so pretty!" I touch the silky blonde bob that is currently dyed with blue and pink highlights. "The pictures didn't do it justice at all."

"Aww." Her chin quivers and her eyes start watering again. "I miss you."

I haul her close and squeeze her again. To think I almost didn't make the trip because I was afraid she'd be too busy. Even if I headed back home right now, this hug was worth the drive.

I can't tell you how long we stand there before we finally make our way inside the cottage.

"This place is so cute." Kat slips her shoes off at the doorway and drops her purse beside them. "I can't believe you're actually staying in an Airbnb."

"As much as I love crashing on your couch, I thought this

would be less intrusive since it was a pretty spur of the moment trip."

She shakes her head, her sleek hair swinging just below her jawline. "I can't believe you came. I'm so glad you're here, but I think I'm still in shock."

"Me, too."

We laugh as we settle onto the couch.

"Tell me everything. How's your list coming? And more importantly, how's the Del sitch?" Her eyes are bright with excitement.

I can't keep the grin off my face. "He came over last night and brought subs and we watched a movie and he gave me a birthday present."

She swirls her hand impatiently. "And? What was it?"

"He gave me a funny card and a gift certificate for the Haus of Yarn here in Nashville and he made me a mixtape for the drive."

Her jaw drops. "Moooommmmm, that is so sweet. Since we've leveled up to birthday gifts, does that mean you're official?"

"No. No, of course not. We haven't even had a serious talk about it." My fingernail plucks at the seam of my shorts.

"But he's not seeing anyone else and you're not seeing anyone else and you obviously like each other."

"I mean, yeah, but it's still pretty casual."

She rolls her eyes, hard. "Casual? You can't even talk about him without getting all swoony."

"Bite me."

She laughs. "How about we bite some supper instead? I can

show you the apartment and we can get something to eat. It's up to you if you want it to be just us or if you want Daniel to come along."

"Of course he can come along."

I grab my purse and we get our shoes on and head out the door. We get in Kat's car and she drives a few blocks to her apartment.

"Wow, you were right about the Airbnb being close to the apartment. This is really nice." I look up at the building. It's sleek and modern and looks very well maintained.

She bounces a little, positively giddy. "Wait 'til you see inside." She swipes a keycard and the main doors open. She ushers me in and shows me the massive gym and then the first pool.

"First pool?"

"Yup." She grins. "One inside, one outside." She pushes open a door that leads to a big courtyard and I see that the building itself is a huge rectangle, so there's no access to the courtyard except through the building. The courtyard is manicured, with a massive pool with marked swimming lanes and lounge chairs. To one side are tables with umbrellas and to the other is a lawn with croquet and cornhole games set up.

"That's really nice. It seems pretty safe."

"The building has really good security." She takes me back inside to a bank of elevators.

I can tell she's both nervous and excited to show me around.

We ride all the way to the top floor.

"Are you in the penthouse suite?"

She laughs. "Not quite."

The door opens and we step out into a hallway. She leads me to a door and pushes it open.

I gasp. We're on a rooftop courtyard with a breathtaking view of the Nashville skyline. "You can see the Batman building!" I point. "Is that the river?" The floor is basically a manicured lawn with outdoor sofas and chairs set up at regular intervals.

Kat slips her arm across my shoulders. "I know, isn't it great? The other side of the building has another rooftop access that's mostly identical but it's dog-friendly."

"This is incredible."

"Let's head to the apartment." She ushers me back inside to the elevator, which takes us to the fifth floor. She unlocks the door and walks in ahead of me. "Here we are."

I take in the dark hardwood floors and gleaming white cabinets against black granite countertops to my right. A matching black granite island with stools serves as an eating area. It's an open concept, flowing directly into the living area.

"Kat, this is gorgeous." It's all very sleek and modern, including the furniture, which isn't really my personal taste, but it's perfect for her.

"Hey, Shasta. Good to see you." Daniel appears from a doorway and comes over to give me a hug.

"Good to see you, too. This place is beautiful."

"We were afraid it wouldn't live up to the photos online, but so far it's been beyond our expectations."

"That's great."

"One of the best things is that we can walk to restaurants or whatever."

I spy the sheer curtains at the far side of the living room. "Do you have a nice view?"

Daniel grins and Kat squeals. "Wait until you see it." She prances over and pulls the curtain back to reveal not a window, but sliding doors.

"You have your own balcony?" I rush over and let Kat give me the tour. It's a tiny balcony, with a tiny table and two chairs. The railing is chrome with plexiglass that is chest high, so no danger of falling off.

"We love having our coffee out here in the morning," Daniel says from the doorway.

"No wonder." The view is mostly industrial, but nothing to sneeze at. "This is incredible," I say again.

Back inside, Kat shows me the bedroom, which leads to a huge walk-in closet that houses a stacked washer and dryer. "We can even do our own laundry right here. It was such a pain in our last place to haul everything to the laundry room. And this door goes to the bathroom." She leads the way. "You can access the bathroom here, or through here." She opens a second door, and it takes us back out to the kitchen.

"No wasted space. This is wonderful." It really is. And even more important, Kat is positively beaming as she shows me around. "I'm really impressed."

"Are you hungry? I'm getting really hungry."

I nod my agreement. "I am." I look up at Daniel. "Where's a good place to go?"

He and Kat exchange a glance. "Anywhere you want. I don't know if you're up for walking, but Hunters Station is about ten minutes from here. Or we can drive, it's up to you."

"I don't mind walking. I've been in the car all day." Just in case my look was too subtle, I say, "Will you join us?"

He seems pleased. "Sure."

We go down to the lobby and out onto the sidewalk. It's humid and my energy tank is running out of gas, so we walk mostly in silence while they point out various establishments. The only one that stuck in my mind was the Donut Distillery, where Kat promised we would have breakfast because their donuts are beyond amazing.

We reach Hunters Station, which turns out to be a sort of freestanding food court. Kat and I head straight for the taco spot while Daniel goes for a gourmet grilled cheese. We collect our food and find a table.

I take one bite and groan. "This is so good."

After a few minutes of quiet, I ask Daniel, "How's your new job going?"

"It's great," he says with enthusiasm. "I'm already learning so much and the people I work with are great." He tells me a bit about his position and where he already sees opportunity for advancing.

"You're glad you made the move?"

He blushes and looks over at Kat. "I'm thrilled. I only stayed in Colorado for her anyway. I've been itching to move back east for a while."

Whoa. I did *not* know this. Daniel just jumped up several points in my esteem.

"How was your drive down?" he asks me.

"Nice. The weather was great. Just enough cloud cover that the sun wasn't blinding me."

"Del made her a mixtape for the drive," Kat chimes in.

"I didn't know you kids were so serious," he jokes.

"Ha, ha. It was part of my birthday present. He's very thoughtful like that."

"He sounds like a nice guy, from what Kat tells me."

"He is."

Kat's phone vibrates. She glances at it, but doesn't pick it up. It vibrates again. And again.

"You should check that," I say. "It might be important." I appreciate that she's being polite and not hanging on her phone while she's with me, but who knows. It might be something to do with school.

She looks at the messages, grins, and then just as suddenly, her face falls.

"What is it?"

"Nothing." She puts her phone face-down on the table. "It's no big deal."

Daniel and I both stare at her until she cracks.

"A handful of the people in my program are doing a sort of meet and greet brunch tomorrow so we can get to know each other before classes start. It's fine if I miss it. It's pretty last minute and I'm sure not everyone can make it anyway."

"Oh?" There's no way my kid is missing a great networking opportunity just because I popped into town.

They both look at me.

"What?" she asks.

"I don't want you to miss this."

She starts to object, and I put a hand up. "Kat. No offense, but I have purely selfish reasons. One, I had an extremely long day today, so this way I can sleep in late tomorrow, and then I can go to the yarn shop and take my time without feeling like I should rush because you're bored out of your mind. Then we can meet up in the afternoon and do anything you want to do."

"No, I don't feel right."

"Sweetheart. I am *not* just being polite, I promise. You go meet your classmates and I'll entertain myself."

"Are you sure?"

"One hundred percent."

"Okay, but Saturday is you and me all day long for your birthday."

"Deal." I hold out my hand for her to shake. "We'll start at the donut shop and keep going until bedtime."

She giggles and shakes my hand. "I feel like I should be with you while you're here. I don't get to see you."

"Trust me. By the time I leave on Sunday, you'll be glad to see me go."

She smiles but doesn't laugh. We both know she'd love to have me closer.

"And speaking of bed, I've had a really long day."

It's seven o'clock, which is eight for my body, and I'm ready to take a nice long shower and climb into bed.

Daniel gathers our trash and throws it away. We head back toward the apartment building. Kat asks me four million times if I'm sure it's okay if she goes to brunch.

"Would you rather hang out at the yarn shop for three hours?" I finally ask her. "Because that's my plan."

She makes a face. "Three hours?"

"I haven't done any knitting for a while. I want to fully

immerse myself back into the experience."

"Okay, I'll do the brunch."

All three of us laugh at that.

* * *

My Bucket List

1. ~~Buy a lottery ticket~~
2. ~~Go through automatic car wash~~
3. Manicure
4. Get hair done in real salon
5. ~~Ask Del out on a date (!!!!!)~~
6. Get back into knitting
7. ~~Visit Kat in Nashville~~

Chapter 23

Despite what I told Kat, I don't sleep in obnoxiously late. By the time I get dressed and make breakfast, it's just after eight. I text Del. **Have a good day.**

Are you meeting Kat for breakfast?

No, I'm on my own for a few hours. I text him about Kat meeting her classmates for brunch and tell him I'm going to the yarn shop.

That sounds fun.

Really?

Okay, it sounds like torture for me, but it sounds fun for you.

I send back a string of laughing emojis.

How was the drive down?

Great. I had some amazing tunes to keep me company.

Wow where'd you get those? He ends the text with a winking face.

Some guy I know.

He sounds great.

He's okay I guess. LOL

An eye-rolling emoji pops up followed by: **Gotta run, IT emergency only I can solve.** Several more eye-rolling emojis follow.

I text back: **It IS Friday the 13th. Good luck.**

Miss you. He follows it up with a red heart emoji.

A heart? What? Are we really solid enough to be sending each other heart emojis? I shove my phone in my pocket. Really? A heart?

I tell myself I'm reading way too much into it.

A little red cartoon heart on my phone shouldn't be making my own flesh and blood heart beat this much faster.

I push this new crisis aside and spend a little time relaxing and scrolling through my phone until the yarn shop opens. I follow the GPS and twenty minutes later I'm pushing open the door to the cutest yarn shop I've ever been in. I breathe in the unique scent of fibers and dye.

A friendly woman greets me, then leaves me to browse. I circle the store once, looking over all the skeins of yarn, touching them to feel their weight and softness.

I have a project in mind — a hat and scarf for Del. By the time I find my knitting groove again and finish them, it'll definitely be cold outside. I grab a basket and make my second pass around the store, selecting yarn for the hat and scarf, and then more yarn for hats and scarves for other people. I get a visual of Oprah in my head, pointing to an imaginary audience. "You get a hat and scarf! You get a hat and scarf! Everybody gets a hat and scarf!"

I find a gorgeous thick gray yarn with black speckles. Scratch the hat and scarf for Kat. This will make gorgeous throw pillows for her sofa.

By the time I'm done looking at yarn, I've filled two shopping baskets. I set them by the checkout counter and go to the wall of needles and accessories. A fancy set of carbon fiber needles is calling my name. I pull the package down to get a closer look. They're expensive, but so lightweight and sleek. And, after all, it's my birthday, right?

I select a few more accessories and I'm marveling both at the stuff in my hands and the fact that I'm not freaking out about treating myself. Partly because I have Del's gift certificate to soften the blow of the final total, and partly because I'm on vacation, and dammit, partly because I deserve to splurge every now and then.

Speaking of splurge, a project tote catches my eye. I check the price tag and sigh. Nope, not treating myself *that* much.

"Shasta?"

I startle and drop half the things I'm holding as I whirl around.

"Oh my gosh, it is you."

It takes a second to recognize my college roommate. "Tracey? Wow, Tracey!"

She pulls me in for a big hug and then helps me pick the fallen items off the floor. "How are you?"

I take in my old friend. "Good. You? Why are you in Nashville?"

"I was just about to ask you the same thing." She laughs, and it sounds exactly like it did a decade ago when we lost touch.

"I'm visiting my daughter. Kat. She just moved here to start the midwifery program at Vanderbilt."

"Wow, no kidding. We moved here about a year ago for my husband's job."

"Oh, nice. How is Mike?"

Her eyes widen, and she laughs again. "Holy cow it *has* been a long time, hasn't it? Mike and I got divorced nine years ago."

"What?"

She rolls her eyes. "Yeah, long and unpleasant story. How's Nick?"

"Wouldn't know. Divorced him eight years ago."

"We need to do lunch. Like, right now."

"Yes, we do." I'm giddy at the thought of having lunch with her, catching up and gossiping and reminiscing.

I take my items to the counter and when it's all rung up, I have a brief moment of panic at the three hundred and seven dollar total. Nothing like jumping back into a hobby with both feet, right? She deducts Del's gift card and says, "One hundred and seven dollars."

I can't possibly have heard that right. "Wait, the gift certificate was for two hundred dollars?"

A confused frown pinches her brows together in concern. "Yes, was that not correct?"

"Sorry, I had no idea how much it was for. It's just a lot more than I expected." I hand over my debit card for the balance. *Two hundred dollars??*

She smiles at me. "Always a pleasant surprise."

"Definitely." I return her warm smile.

She suggests I sign up for their newsletter, so I do. Kat will be living here for at least two years, so surely I'll be back, right?

Tracey comes to the register with six skeins of yarn and pays for them while I hover a few steps away. When she's done, we walk out together.

"I'm parked right there." I point to my car.

She laughs. "I'm right beside you." She gestures to the red SUV in the spot next to mine. "Where would you like to have lunch?"

"I have no idea what's around here."

She looks skyward for a second, then snaps her fingers.

"Blue Moon Grille. It's about ten minutes from here. They have an outdoor patio that overlooks the river. And the food is fabulous."

"Sounds perfect. I'll follow you?" I figure that's better than leaving one of our cars in the parking lot and risk being towed. And who knows if we'll end up heading in opposite direction afterwards.

"It's easy peasy. We'll turn left out of the parking lot and a couple more turns and we're there."

"Great. Just give me a sec to let Kat know where I'm going." I put my bags in the trunk and slide into the driver's seat. I start the car to get the air conditioner running and text Kat. And find the restaurant's address to plug into my GPS. A minute later I give Tracey a thumbs up and follow her SUV out onto the highway.

Her estimate was accurate. Ten minutes later, we pull into a parking lot and then walk across a little pier to get to the restaurant. We're seated outside at a wooden table against the railing. The river is literally flowing right next to us.

"Isn't it gorgeous?" Tracey asks.

"It really is."

"And the food is so good."

We order our lunches and she says, "I can't believe I ran into you. I've thought about getting in touch over the years but… well, I guess I don't really have a good excuse. Life just got in the way. Which is really lame."

I nod in agreement. "I know. Things sure don't end up the way you think they will, do they?"

"Not even close. So tell me everything."

"Well, let's see." I try to remember the last time Tracey and I spoke. Yikes, it's probably been ten years. "I'm a senior accounting manager now. Divorced Nick eight years ago. Kat lives here with her boyfriend and I told you she's starting the midwifery program at Vanderbilt. Yeah. That's about it." I'm even more boring than I thought. "Your turn."

"Gosh. I divorced Mike nine years ago. The boys and I got through that and moved to Kentucky for a while, then I transferred to Montana, where I met Alan. We got married four years ago. So with my three boys and his three girls, we had our own Brady Bunch going on. His kids are grown and on their own, and Tyler is the only one of mine still at home. We moved here last year for Alan's work and I honestly wish we'd have come here sooner because we all love it so much."

"Are all the kids in the area?"

"Two of the girls and Steven stayed in Montana. Alexia, Mark, and Tyler moved with us and soon after, the older two got their own places. Tyler's starting college, so we'll have a completely empty nest here in a few weeks."

"Wow."

"And as for me, I work at a small mom and pop accounting firm part time and I do volunteer work for the food bank as well. And I still knit, too."

"I'm just getting back into it. I used to knit all the time and then at some point I realized I hadn't done it in years. I miss it." I pause when the server sets my salad with grilled mahi-mahi in front of me. "It looks amazing."

Tracey eyes her crab cakes. "I'm telling you, their food is the best."

We eat our lunches, catching up and halfway through the meal we're back to laughing and talking like we've only been apart for a week instead of a decade.

"It's been hard to stay in touch with the friends I used to be so close to." Tracey pokes at a bit of crab cake with her fork. "When my marriage went south, I didn't know who to trust. Mike was going behind my back spreading lies. He even tried to get CPS involved to take my boys, and when I sued him over that, he backed off. But every now and then he'd say something that I *know* I'd only discussed with a close friend. It was really hard to trust anyone after that."

I nod, understanding completely. "I got sick at work one day and came home early. Nick was screwing my supposed best friend in our bed. So yeah, I get not knowing who to trust."

Tracey lifts her glass. "To being rid of the toxic dead weight."

I clink my glass to hers. "Hear, hear."

We exchange phone numbers and promise to stay in touch.

And you know what? I really think we will.

* * *

My Bucket List

1. ~~Buy a lottery ticket~~
2. ~~Go through automatic car wash~~
3. Manicure
4. Get hair done in real salon
5. ~~Ask Del out on a date (!!!!!)~~
6. ~~Get back into knitting~~
7. ~~Visit Kat in Nashville~~

Chapter 24

Kat and I meet up in the late afternoon. She's super excited that I met Tracey so now she doesn't have to feel guilty at all about going to her brunch. We pretty much hole up in my Airbnb and order pizza. We talk and laugh and spend the entire evening just enjoying each other's company. It's the best time I've had in a long time. (Sorry Del. You're a close second, though!)

"Have you talked to Del?"

"Not since I got here. We've texted."

"I can't wait to meet him."

I choke on my tea. "Whoa. What makes you think I'm going to introduce him to my family? We're not even dating."

"Bullshit."

"Okay, fine. We've been spending a lot of time together, but it's not official or anything."

"You're so full of it."

"What?"

"You're totally into him. And hello, he dropped two hundred bucks on a yarn shop gift certificate *and* made you a mixtape. He's totally into you, too."

"We're friends." It sounds pathetically lame, even to my own ears.

"Mom." Her voice is stern. "I'm really, really glad you're starting to come out of your comfort zone. I think this guy's good for you and I would hate for you to be too cautious and miss out on something that sounds like it could be amazing."

"You've never even met him."

"I just told you I'd like to."

I make a little "pfft" noise. "Well, that's kind of hard when he's in Pennsylvania and you're in Tennessee. Besides, it's probably not going anywhere anyway. You don't need to meet all my other friends."

She raises an eyebrow and levels her gaze at me. "What other friends?"

She's got me there. I've got tons of acquaintances and hundreds of Facebook "friends" but... yeah, this line of thought is too depressing, so I backpedal. "Look. Del's great. I like him. But at the end of the day, he's a man, and I think I've proven I don't need a man to live a fulfilling, wonderful life. Besides. I just had lunch with Tracey."

"Mom. Lunch with Tracey was purely serendipitous. And let's be honest. Dad was an ass. But that was a long time ago, and it's not fair to judge Del — or any other guy you might be interested in — by that pathetic example."

My instinct to shield her kicks in. "Your dad loves you very much."

"Stop it!"

I jerk back against the cushion.

"He's an asshole. He was a lousy husband and a lousy father. He never kept a single promise he ever made, including covering my books for this semester. He's a liar and a cheater and a shit person. I *appreciate* that you've done your best to not badmouth him or force me to deal with those issues. You've never said a bad word about him or tried to keep me away from him. I know that. I see that. But I'm an adult, and I'm entitled to my own experience and my own opinions. My father loves me as much as he is capable of loving me, and I love him, too, solely because he's my dad. But I don't trust him and I don't even like him very much and I'm certainly not going to make Daniel pay for his sins."

I'm too stunned to speak.

"I judge the people in my life by seeing if they measure up to *you*. Loyal and hardworking and devoted and kind and thoughtful. Maybe to a fault. I saw everything you did for me, and still do for me. But I don't think I understood how much you've denied yourself. I want to see you happy. Truly happy, not just okay. You should hear your voice when you talk about Del."

"Yeah? And what if it doesn't work out?"

She shrugs one shoulder. "What if it does? All I'm saying is that I think he might be worth the risk. If it doesn't work out with him, at least it won't be because he's a cheating narcissistic asshole."

"No…" When did she get so damn smart?

"Don't let what *might* happen ruin what *is* happening."

I run a hand down over my face. "You know what? You're grounded."

We start laughing, and she shimmies across the couch to give me a hug. "I love you, Mom."

"I love you, too."

Kat beams at me. "I have the whole day planned for your birthday tomorrow. I'm picking you up at eight, and we're starting off with donuts."

"Then what?"

She shakes her head. "Bad news, Ms. Gotta Be In Control. I'm not telling you anything else."

I grumble a little, but if there's one thing I love more than control, it's seeing Kat happy and excited. "Can't wait."

She squeezes me hard and kisses my cheek. "We're going to have a blast. I'm so glad you're here."

"Me, too."

She hops off the couch and goes over to the door to slip her shoes on. "You wouldn't be here if Del hadn't encouraged it, you know."

My eyes narrow. "Brat."

She shrugs and blows me a kiss. "See you in the morning. Love you!" And she's gone.

I flip the television on and text Del a picture of my haul from the yarn shop.

Can I call you? Blinks onto my screen.

Sure.

A second later, my screen lights up with the incoming call. "Hey, what's up?"

"I miss you." His voice is low and sounds so good.

"I might miss you too, just a little bit." I snuggle back against the couch and mute the TV.

"I see you found the yarn shop. Was it nice?"

"It was fantastic. They had a huge selection of yarn. I kept thinking of all the projects I could make but I had to put the brakes on at some point. And by the way, that gift card? Two hundred dollars? That's too much."

"Not really. If you were here, I probably would have spent a hundred bucks on a gift, and then if I took you out to a nice dinner, there's another hundred. So I just put the birthday budget together and used it for the gift card." I get the feeling he had this argument already thought out.

"I'm not complaining. It just surprised me that it was so much." I can't put into words that it's the biggest birthday gift I've gotten in my entire life. "Do all your friends get expensive gifts?"

He laughs. "My friends are lucky to get a beer and a hearty handshake."

"Wow, so I'm special." The word is out before I can stop it.

There's a beat of quiet before he says, "You're very special to me, Shasta."

Well, shit. Time to change the subject. "Kat says she wants to meet you. She seems to think you're a good influence."

"She's right, of course," he teases.

"I have to give you credit. I wouldn't be here if you hadn't encouraged me to get outside of my comfort zone."

"You get all the credit, babe. I just asked what you wanted to do, and you had all the answers."

Babe? Did he just call me babe?

"What's your plan for the big day tomorrow?" he asks.

"Uh..." I'm still stuck on the babe thing but I shake it off. "Kat says she has the whole day planned. She's picking me up at eight and we're starting with donuts. She wouldn't tell me anything else."

"Nice."

"I'm excited to spend a whole day with just her and me. I'm afraid to think how long it's been since that happened. I think only twice since she left for college. That's so sad, isn't it?" Not that I mind having Daniel around, but one-on-one time with her is so precious and rare.

"Nah, that's how it's supposed to go. They grow up and move on and we have a smaller role. Don't dwell on that, you've got all day tomorrow with her. Enjoy every minute of it."

"I will. Are you still planning to go to Allie's tomorrow?"

"Yup. Brunch, then manual labor." There's nothing but affection in his tone. "That's what dads are for, right?"

"Yup." That's what Kat's dad was supposed to be for, but he always had something else to do. "What are you doing this evening?"

Instead of answering me, my phone vibrates. A selfie of him holding a can of beer in his back yard fills my screen. An empty pizza box lays open on the picnic table beside him.

"Wild night, huh?"

"It's hot but there's a nice breeze going. I mowed the grass and figured the best way to cap off the evening was pizza and beer."

"Brilliant plan. I haven't even looked out back here." I stroll around the cottage and open the back door. "There's a nice little backyard. Ooh, there's a porch swing. It's even got pillows and a blanket right on it. These homeowners thought of everything."

"Sweet. You can sit and watch the fireflies."

I curl up on the porch swing. "More likely I'll watch the backs of my eyelids. I'm pretty sure when Kat says it's going to be a full day, that means I should get my rest."

"I can't wait to hear all about it."

"I can't wait to hear all about Allie's shelves. And now I know who to call when I need something done around the house."

"Just be aware that I do not guarantee results. No warranty, no money back."

"Talk about covering your ass. Do you have a waiver I'll have to sign?"

"Yes."

I laugh. "You would." I jerk to attention. "Oh! I didn't even tell you. I was so focused on giving you heck for spending so much on the gift certificate that I didn't tell you the whole story."

I hear the pop of another can being opened. "I'm all ears."

I tell him all about running into Tracey and having lunch. "I had the best time. It was a little awkward those first few minutes after we did all the catching up questions, but then we started talking like we'd just seen each other last week."

"That's fantastic, Shas. Maybe another item for your bucket list?"

"What, keeping up with friends?"

"Yeah."

I consider this. "Maybe. It's hard to think about getting close like that again."

He lets the thought hang for a moment, then says, "Tell me more about this salad at lunch. Was it a Big Salad?"

I laugh at the *Seinfeld* reference. "No. It was a big salad, but it wasn't a Big Salad. It did have grilled mahi-mahi on it though, which was spectacular."

He snorts.

I connect his reaction to another episode. "Yes, Del, it was real, and it was spectacular."

* * *

My Bucket List

1. ~~Buy a lottery ticket~~
2. ~~Go through automatic car wash~~
3. Manicure
4. Get hair done in real salon
5. ~~Ask Del out on a date (!!!!!)~~
6. ~~Get back into knitting~~
7. ~~Visit Kat in Nashville~~

Chapter 25

Seven o'clock comes way too soon. So does seven forty-five, which is what time it is after I closed my eyes for one more minute. Shit. I ended up talking to Del until almost midnight. So much for getting to bed at a decent time.

I rush to do my bathroom routine and get dressed. Kat arrives at eight on the dot, like I knew she would, even though I hoped she'd have some reason for running late. I let her in while I brush my hair.

"I figured you'd be up and ready."

"Yeah, I overslept."

"Wow, you really are cutting loose for your birthday, aren't you?" She snickers at me.

"Sorry."

"Don't apologize. I think it's funny. Like, have you ever been late for anything in your whole life?"

"Probably not."

"Well, happy birthday, Mom." She leans over to kiss my cheek.

"Thank you, baby girl." I hug her and say, "Let me grab my shoes."

A few minutes later we're headed down the road. Kat pulls in to the Donut Distillery parking lot. We take our treasures back to the car and sit for a few minutes inhaling them.

"You were right. These are the most amazing donuts I've ever had. I'm going to get some to take home." I lick the last bit of glaze from my finger.

We get back on the road and twenty minutes later, Kat pulls into the parking lot for a salon and spa. "Now you'll get to cross something off your bucket list."

"What did I do to deserve you?"

She shakes her head, "You must have been very, very good in your past life. Like Mother Teresa-level good to end up with all this." She points at herself.

"Never mind. You're kind of obnoxious," I tease as we get out of the car.

She laughs and slings an arm across my shoulders as we walk to the door.

Kat checks us in at the reception desk and informs me that we are doing manicures *and* pedicures. Before I can argue about my shoes, she whips a pair of flipflops out of her bag. "I got it all covered. You're not the only anal retentive control freak planner in this family, you know."

We're led to manicure chairs placed side by side. Kat informs the nail technician that we're both getting gel manicures, whatever that means. The tech points us to a wall of polish.

Kat tells me, "You can pick both colors now if you want your pedi to be different. The gel polish will stay on for up to like three weeks, so you'll end up with a little growth showing at your cuticle."

I make a face. That doesn't sound appealing.

"If you want my advice, I'd get a regular French mani, and then pick a bold color for the pedi."

"Is that what you're doing?"

"Yup."

"Okay." Once again I'm feeling silly because something that millions of people do every single day feels like a complicated challenge for me.

Kat picks a hot pink polish for her pedicure.

My eye keeps coming back to a certain bottle of polish. It's bold, but it's going on my toes, so it's not like anybody has to ever see it, right? Right. I hesitate, then I commit to my decision and grab the bottle of razzle dazzle red. It's a bright red with a super fine glittery shimmer to it.

Kat grins and high fives me. Obviously she approves.

We get our French manicures and after my fingers are done baking under the UV light, the nail tech puts a dollop of lotion on her hands, then grabs my right hand. She tugs and squeezes and massages my entire hand, then repeats the process for my left. It feels amazing.

When we're both done, she instructs us to wash our hands, then take our spots in the pedicure chairs. I'm convinced I'm going to fall into it or over it or somehow make an ass of myself climbing onto it. Thankfully, I get situated without calling attention to myself.

A different nail tech comes over and fills the soaking tubs with warm soapy water. We relax and chat until she comes back.

I keep holding my hands up to admire my nails. "I can't believe I've never done this. It's so pretty."

"Gotta treat yourself, Mom."

The nail tech looks up. "Mom? I thought you were sisters."

I'm pretty sure she says that all the time, but I flush with pleasure anyway.

Quite a while later, I'm admiring my razzle dazzle red toenails while Kat pulls out of the parking lot.

"Thank you. This was so great."

"See? Such a little thing and it feels so nice. I try to get my nails done regularly because it helps keep them from breaking. The gel is really durable. And when it's time to have it redone, do not pick at it or you can wreck your natural nails. You need to soak it off with acetone or have the salon do it."

"Okay." I'll take her word for it since I don't know diddly squat about caring for a manicure.

"Next up: lunch."

"Lead the way." I settle back in the seat and relax. Yes, relax. It's strange even to me how I've been able to let go and let Kat do her thing. I'm not worrying about what we're doing, what I'm wearing, or how it's going to go. I'm in the moment and I'm enjoying every bit of it. I also know this new state of being isn't permanent, so I better enjoy it while it lasts.

We grab a quick lunch. Kat keeps checking her watch, so I know there's something planned. "What are we doing next?"

"You'll see." She smirks and I'm not sure if that's a good thing or a bad thing. Either way, I'm here for it. As long as I'm spending the day with her, I'll even go ziplining if I have to. I hope I don't have to.

We go downtown and park. Kat rushes me for a block, then stops. In front of a camo school bus.

"Kat?"

She bounces on her heels. A tour guide directs a group of us onto the bus. The Redneck Comedy Bus.

I'm skeptical, but I climb on and take a seat with Kat.

It's not long before my sides hurt from laughing so hard. We tour the city, seeing all the famous landmarks like the Country Music Hall of Fame and the Grand Ole Opry. With a hilarious running commentary. By the time the 90-minute tour is over, my face hurts from laughing.

There's no time to recover, though, as Kat takes me to the Nashville Zoo.

"Aww, you remembered."

"Of course I did," she says. "When we talked about what you wanted to see, it's the only thing you mentioned three times."

"Three?" I don't remember saying it so often, but I'm sure she's right.

We walk slowly around the zoo, reading the little information signs on each animal and talking about everything under the sun.

There's something about walking side by side and not facing someone that makes it easier to talk.

She lets out a long sigh. "I'm glad you made me go to brunch yesterday. I think getting to know some of the other people in the program ahead of time will make it easier to settle in."

"What's bothering you?"

We stop at the tiger exhibit and stand at the plexiglass window.

She puts her hand against it. "I'm excited, but I'm also terrified. This program is intense and all-consuming and scary. Getting the scholarship was amazing, but it's so much pressure. What if I flunk out and have to pay back all that money?"

I let her keep talking, without interrupting. We both know she's going to excel, but hopefully putting the doubts into words will get them out of her head.

"I know it's just anxiety talking, and once I get started, I'll be fine. And I feel better after meeting everyone yesterday. It's just, you know, everything has been moving so fast. Six weeks ago this wasn't even on my radar, and now here we are, moved to a new city across the country, new job for Daniel... it's just a lot."

"It *is* a lot. I'd be scared shitless, too."

She huffs a laugh. "You? You're never scared of anything."

"Have you been drinking? I'm scared of *everything*. Why do you think I never leave my comfort zone?"

She frowns but playfully nudges my arm. "Because you're an anal retentive control freak."

I'm blown away that she doesn't think I'm afraid. "And why is that? Because everything scares me. Not being in control. Not having a solid plan and an equally solid backup plan. I'm afraid of changing, but I'm flat out terrified of staying the same. I'm afraid of getting attached and getting my heart broken because I'm not sure I'd know how to come back from that."

Kat puts her arm around me and leans her head on my shoulder. We watch two giant tiger kittens frolicking in the grass while the mama cat keeps a watchful eye.

"I don't think that's going to happen with Del. I really don't."

I rest my head against hers. "You've never even met him."

"I will." She squeezes me and taps the plexiglass. "You should get a kitten."

I watch them play-attack each other. "I really should. I've

always wanted one."

A few hours later, my calves ache from all the walking. We stop at the gift shop and I go a little nuts splurging. It's my party and I'll spend if I want to. I buy us both shirts and insulated cups and fridge magnets, and before we leave I grab shirts for Daniel and Del, too. Because why the heck not?

Kat laughs at me, swishing her fingers against her opposite palm like I'm making it rain dollars. In a gift shop. At the zoo.

For good measure, I buy a stuffed giraffe wearing a bow tie and name him Nash.

"Okay, we need to get moving," Kat warns.

"There's more?"

She grins and hustles me to the car.

We're quiet on the ride. Kat follows the GPS's directions and takes us to another parking lot.

"Whoa. Are we touring that?" I point out the window to a giant steamboat docked on the river.

"Yup."

We walk along a massively long sort of bridge to the gangplank that gets us onto the steamboat. "This is so cool." I run my fingers along the polished wood railing.

"Just wait." We go to a dining room that looks like a ballroom, complete with a stage at the front. Huge windows run along both sides of the dining room.

"Are we having dinner here?" It suddenly dawns on me and I gasp. "Is it a river cruise?"

She laughs. "Yes. I've been dying to do this. It's a three-hour riverboat cruise. We'll have dinner and a show and sightseeing from the upper deck."

I grab her in a huge hug. "This is the best birthday ever." I blink back those pesky tears that have been threatening me so often lately.

We spend the evening eating dinner (the rosemary chicken is to die for) and chatting with eight strangers (four of them on their first trip to the United States from Japan) around our large table. Kat tells our tablemates it's my birthday and they sing Happy Birthday to me over dessert, much to my embarrassment and joy. After dinner, we're treated to a show unlike anything I've ever heard. It's part country, part bluegrass, part oldies (think Elvis, of course), and a bit of comedy.

Between the comedy bus tour and this evening, I'm pretty sure I've given myself a laughter-induced hernia.

After the show, Kat and I find seats up on the upper deck, where we watch the beautiful lights of Nashville reflect off the river as we sail by.

Kat leans against me. "I'm so glad you came."

"Me, too."

* * *

My Bucket List

~~1. Buy a lottery ticket~~
~~2. Go through automatic car wash~~
~~3. Manicure~~
4. Get hair done in real salon
~~5. Ask Del out on a date (!!!!!)~~
~~6. Get back into knitting~~
~~7. Visit Kat in Nashville~~

Chapter 26

Once again, I get to bed way too late. Which especially sucks since I've got a full day of driving tomorrow. But I just couldn't bring myself to say goodnight to Kat. After we got home and divided up the zoo souvenirs, we stood at the trunk of her car for another forty minutes talking and hugging.

I hurry and pull out my clothes for Sunday's drive and smoosh everything else into my suitcase. The plan right now is that Kat and Daniel will be at the donut shop when they open at eight. They'll bring me a dozen donuts to take home and I'll hit the road.

I set three alarms for seven thirty to give myself the maximum amount of sleep possible. Instead, seven o'clock finds me wide awake. Responsible me kicks in and I repack my suitcase neatly and spend a little extra time double checking that I haven't left anything behind. I park my suitcase and bags next to the front door.

At eight fifteen, Kat and Daniel pull in. Daniel takes my bags to the car and puts the donuts on the back seat. "We got you three dozen. They told us they freeze really well."

"Three dozen?"

Daniel shrugs. "It's my birthday gift for you."

I give him a hug. "Thank you. And thank you for sharing Kat with me yesterday. It's the best birthday I've ever had."

He squeezes me hard. "I'm glad. And I hope you'll visit again soon."

Holy crap, I think he means it. I pretend to root for something in my bag before I start blubbering like a fool.

"I'll wait in the car. Safe travels, Shasta." He pats my arm and walks away.

"Thank you."

Then Kat hugs me, and I *am* blubbering like a fool.

I compose myself and wipe my face. "Do you need anything for school? Did you need money for books?" Before she can argue, I add, "There's still money in your college fund you can use."

"In that case, yes. I'll email you the receipts?"

"Perfect."

"Did you get gas?"

I shake my head. "It's my first stop on my way out of town."

"Got your GPS set?"

"Yup." I know she's stalling because I am, too. But I do have a twelve-plus hour drive, so I hug her tight once more. "I'll text you at every rest stop along the way."

"Drive safe."

"I will. Good luck tomorrow. I'm so proud of you. You're amazing and you're going to be such a wonderful support for so many mommies-to-be."

"Thanks, Mom." She's tearing up again, so it's time to go.

I kiss her cheek and pull back. "I love you."

"Love you, too."

I point her toward the car where Daniel's waiting. After she's in the car, I wave until they're long gone.

I take my last pre-trip potty break and final lap around the cottage before I leave the key per the homeowner's instructions.

In the car, I set my GPS for home. Thanks to Del, the speakers come to life with the electric guitar that starts Kix's "Blow My Fuse" and I crank it up and hum along until I pull into the gas station.

Like the trip down, the trip home is long but uneventful. It's just before nine o'clock when I pull into my driveway with a bag from Arby's. As hungry as I am, I couldn't handle the idea of sitting down somewhere to eat as I got closer to home.

I take my stuff inside, lock the door, text Kat and Del that I'm home, and crash on the couch with my food and soda. I'm so, so, so glad I also took Monday off. Originally I thought I'd use Monday to do laundry and put my stuff away. Now, I'm pretty sure I'll be using Monday to sleep.

* * *

On Monday, I jolt awake in a panic somewhere around ten o'clock before I realize I'm not supposed to be at work. I'd stay in bed longer, but I have to pee, so I guess I'm up for the day. I must have gone dead to the world as soon as my head hit the pillow, because I never heard my phone vibrating, but I have a dozen unread text messages and one missed call. The texts are from Kat and Del, and the missed call is from an unknown number.

I skim the messages. Nothing urgent, so I take care of getting dressed and brushing my teeth and settle in with a plate of donuts before I reply.

To Kat, whose first class starts in fifteen minutes: **Have an**

amazing first day!

To Del, who asked if he could come over after work: **Glad I took today off. Yes, subs would be amazing. You're the best!**

The donuts are so good I eat three of them. I put two dozen in the freezer just so I'm not tempted to polish them all off in one day.

I scroll through social media and stop. An ad for a local hair salon pops up on my feed. I click over to their page and scroll through before and after pictures of clients, and photos of their shop.

What the heck right? I'm still operating under birthday rules, so I call the salon to schedule an appointment. I pull out my paper calendar, but you could knock me over with a feather when they offer me an appointment for one o'clock. Today.

Serendipitous, right?

I spend the next couple of hours scrolling through Pinterest, looking at different hairstyles. What do I even want? Right now, my hair is down to the middle of my back. It's got a little natural wave and a few grays sneaking into my mousy-brown hair.

When I get to the salon, Holly, the stylist, immediately whisks me to a luxurious chair and flicks a black cape across my lap. She spins me to face the mirror, chatting as she fastens the cape around my neck and works her fingers through my hair.

"So what are we having done today?"

"I'm not really sure. I have some ideas on my phone."

"Great. Let's see."

I pull my phone from under the apron and pull up the pictures I saved. She squints and bobs her head back and forth. "These are nice, but to be honest, your hair won't end up looking like that." She fluffs the back of my hair as if weighing it with her hands. "Hang on."

Like I'm going anywhere. I watch her reflection cross the room. She bends over something I can't see and comes back with a hardback book. She flips a few pages. "What do you think about something like this? With the texture of your hair, this'll be a lot easier to maintain. We can totally do one of the ones you picked, but it'll take a lot longer to get ready in the morning."

"I definitely need something that's more wash it and go."

She flips another page. "Or something like this." It's a bob similar to Kat's, only longer and asymmetrical.

"Yes. That."

"Perfect. Let's grab a before picture." She snaps a couple photos with her phone, then pulls my hair back and starts snipping. "Have you thought about doing color today? You'd look amazing with some caramel highlights."

I know she's upselling me, and I'm here for it. "I've never colored my hair, but I think highlights would be great. I'm a little shocked I was able to get in today."

"Monday afternoons are our slowest time, and on top of that I had a full color appointment reschedule, which opened up my whole afternoon." She fluffs a bit of my hair. "Do you like thinner highlights or chunky ones?"

"Um, I honestly have no idea. Can you do whatever you think would look best?" Holy crap I'm having an out-of-body experience. I just turned over complete control of my hair — *my hair!* — to a perfect stranger and somehow I'm not freaking out.

She grins and turns me away from the mirror. "You're gonna love it, I promise."

Over the next three hours, she chats like I'm her bestie, talking about her salon, her clients, her kids, the amazing marinated pork she made last week, an expensive car repair she just had done, and her dad just starting to date again after her mom passed away six years ago.

It's completely unnecessary for me to do anything to keep the conversation flowing. I nod and make the appropriate noises at various intervals until she finally leads me to the sink. I lay back in the chair while she removes all the crap she put on my head and rinses my hair. She shampoos and conditions with something that smells absolutely divine.

"That smells so good."

"We've only had it for about a month, and I think it's my favorite now. I think we still have a few bottles if you wanted to buy some for at home."

Oh, yes, Holly knows how to upsell, but it smells so good it sold itself. The worst part? I know darn well that if I didn't have the lottery money, I wouldn't let myself get highlights or go along with the upsold shampoo and conditioner, no matter how much I wanted to.

She leads me back to the chair and keeps me facing away from the mirror. She walks this way and that, touching my hair and squinting at various pieces that she snips off. Satisfied, she clicks on the dryer and works my hair with a round brush as she dries it.

There's an awful lot of hair on the floor, but I can't yet tell how much shorter it is.

"Okay, gorgeous, are you ready?" She sticks the dryer into its cubby and takes hold of the chair.

"I think so." I close my eyes as she spins my chair to the mirror. The chair comes to a stop. I take a breath and finally open my eyes.

"Holy shit!" I slowly reach up to touch it. "Is that really me?"

Never in a million years would I have thought a trip to the hair salon could shave ten years off my appearance, but here we are.

My hair swings across my shoulders, the caramel highlights are perfectly blended with my natural brown, and it's all smooth and shiny and healthier than it's ever looked.

Holly grabs some after pictures and texts them to me, along with the befores. The mirror catches my manicure as I touch my hair, and I'm blown away at how put together I look.

I swear it's the first time in my life I want to keep staring at myself in the mirror.

* * *

My Bucket List

1. ~~Buy a lottery ticket~~
2. ~~Go through automatic car wash~~
3. ~~Manicure~~
4. ~~Get hair done in real salon~~
5. ~~Ask Del out on a date (!!!!!)~~
6. ~~Get back into knitting~~
7. ~~Visit Kat in Nashville~~

Chapter 27

"Holy shit!" Del almost drops the bag of subs on the doorstep.

I blush furiously as I step back to let him into the house. "I know. It's totally different." My hair now skims across my shoulders, with a combination of skinny and chunky highlights of caramel brown mixed in with my own natural light brown. After the big reveal, Holly got a tape measure, and we discovered that she'd relieved me of fourteen inches of hair. Even with that much taken off, it's still long enough to toss into a ponytail or messy bun. Because messy buns are the best thing ever.

I even went the extra mile and put on some mascara.

"It's gorgeous. Seriously. You look amazing."

"Thank you."

He leans over and gives me a quick kiss and heads for the kitchen. "You even got color."

"I can't believe you noticed that." I reach up and smooth my hair like I've done a million times since I left the salon.

"Of course I noticed." He puts the subs on the table and pulls me in for a hug. "I missed you."

I breathe in the scent of his cologne. "I missed you, too."

His chest rumbles as he chuckles. "Lies. You were too busy to miss me."

"Nope. When I was by myself, I missed you a lot."

His voice drops. "When you were by yourself, huh?"

Uh oh. Is it getting warm in here? It seems like it's getting really warm in here all of a sudden. I push back and slide the subs out of the bag. "What did you bring?"

"One ham, one roast beef. I like them both but I'm kind of hoping you'll want the ham."

"Ham it is." I take my sub and settle into my seat at the table.

Del opens the bag of chips and sits at the corner beside me. He unwraps his sub. "I want to hear about everything."

"Oh, my goodness. Where do I even start? The riverboat dinner cruise last night was phenomenal. The lights from Nashville reflecting off the river was just so beautiful."

"You had great weather the whole time, too."

"I did. There was one storm Thursday night, but it blew over by morning." I try to remember everything in chronological order. By the time we finish our subs and the chips, I'm up to the donuts on Saturday morning.

"They sound amazing."

"Well." I go over to the counter and get the box. "You can see for yourself."

He puts a shocked hand over his heart. "Whoa, you're going to let me have one of your super special donuts?"

"Only one. And only because I have two dozen more in the freezer."

"Two dozen? Sweet." He selects a donut and takes a bite.

I pick a donut, too.

"These are delicious," he mumbles around a mouthful.

"Kat totally did me a solid recommending this place."

"They haven't even been there long, right? And she already scoped out the best restaurants."

I lick icing from my finger. "Priorities."

"Smart. Once she starts classes, she won't have to worry about finding places to grab dinner." He holds up the last sliver of his donut. "Or breakfast."

We finish our donuts and Del says, "How was the boyfriend?"

"Great. He said something that really surprised me, though. When I asked if he was okay with leaving Colorado, he said he'd been wanting to leave all along and he only stayed there for Kat."

"No kidding."

"Yeah. All this time I thought she was staying there for him. Definitely gave him bonus points in my book."

"I'm sure it did."

We clean up the table and go to the living room. I cuddle up next to Del on the couch. "Does Allie have a boyfriend?"

"No one serious. She dates every once in a while, but she's really focused on her career."

"Aerospace has to be a tough job. I bet it's hard to meet someone as smart as she is."

"Oh, finding a smart guy is easy enough. It's finding a smart guy who isn't intimidated by her intelligence and tries to knock her down a few pegs that's the tricky part."

I believe that. My ex did not handle my successes well. "Ugh. How did Project Install Shelves go?"

He scrunches his eyes shut. "I'm pretty sure she's not getting her security deposit back."

"Oh no!" I laugh at his pained expression.

"Yeah. So guess who decided they didn't need to use a stud

finder. Guess who also put a screw in the wall that punched completely through the drywall."

"You didn't."

"Oh, I did. A twenty minute project ended up taking all afternoon because then I had to run to the hardware store to get stuff to patch the hole and watch a million YouTube videos on how to do a patch."

I press my hand to my mouth. I'm trying not to laugh, but I'm imagining the whole scenario clearly.

"Make a note. If you need anything electronic fixed, I'm your guy. If you need handiwork done around the house, I am not."

"Good to know." I yawn, and even though it's barely eight o'clock, I'm beat. All that driving has definitely caught up with me.

"You should have taken Tuesday off, too," Del says with a grin.

"Tell me about it. Hopefully I'll go in and no one will need me so I can just sit in my cube and get through the week."

* * *

Spoiler alert, I do not get to sit in my cube for the rest of the week. Tuesday was fine, but Wednesday brought an unscheduled audit, so we all had to hustle to pull reports and cater to our regulatory bigwigs. Super fun.

It wouldn't have been so bad, but they swoop in for a surprise audit, which makes sense, but then they act all pissy because we're not ready for them. It's ridiculous.

Now it's Friday and I flop my lunch bag down on the table and drop into the crappy molded chair. "These people are awful," I grumble to Del as I unwrap my sandwich.

"Agreed." He shakes his head. "They came in wanting a full twelve-month assessment report and when Pete ran it from last August first to July thirty-first, they complained because they only wanted year-to-date through last Friday's date. Then ask for year-to-date, morons."

I'm pretty sure every single PAMECorp employee feels the same way. Even Cecily's perkiness is only about an eight out of ten instead of her usual over the top twenty out of ten.

"Freaking Edmonds has been in my department barking every few hours. I'm ready to backhand him." I bite my sandwich with more force than it deserves.

"I understand why they do surprise visits, but holy crap they should come ready with a list of what they want, including dates, and then realize it's going to take a minute to get shit together for them."

"I know, right? Here, we need six hundred reports printed out in triplicate and collated. I'll come back in ten minutes to get those from you."

We spend the rest of our lunch grumbling. Which is pretty much how it goes for the next two weeks until the auditors finally leave on the Friday before Labor Day.

It's like déjà vu. We're back in the cafeteria, but in much better spirits. The past two and a half weeks have been brutal, running around like chickens with our heads cut off to pull everything the auditors needed.

"Thank goodness they're shipping out," Del says.

"Good riddance." I mock salute toward the door.

"Where do they even find these people? I swear their main office wants to be rid of them so bad they make up surprise audits just to get them out of the building."

I nod vigorously. "I think you're right. Every time they come in, it's a more obnoxious batch than the last time. And *dumb*."

Del rolls his eyes. "No kidding. Yesterday one of the newbies tried arguing with me that using a link to Google sheets would be more secure than an encrypted Excel file."

"Ugh."

He snorts. "He's probably one that clicks on links in his work emails and gets their IT department all in a tizzy."

"No doubt. We had to listen to the one guy bragging about his most recent hookups. Don't they have HR where they come from?"

"I think they hatch from pods."

I choke on my water and pound my sternum until I get my breath back.

"Seriously. They all have the same vacant look in their eyes."

"Del, I have some bad news for you."

"What?"

"You're old. Like, grumpy old man *old*."

He waves dismissively. "I'll be fine as soon as these damn kids are off my lawn."

"Only…" I check my watch. "Four and a half more hours to go. You can do it. Actually, I bet they're gone by two thirty. You know they don't stick around on Fridays."

He gathers our trash. "And it's Labor Day weekend. Speaking of which, I'm doing burgers and hot dogs on Sunday.

I'd love for you to meet Allie."

"Yeah, sounds great. What should I bring?"

"Just your gorgeous self."

"No, seriously. How about macaroni salad?"

He winks at me and gets up. "Macaroni salad will be perfect. Dinner tonight?"

"Sure."

"Pick you up at six?"

"See you then." He makes a face and heads back to work.

Hoooooely crap, I'm going to meet his daughter.

* * *

My Bucket List

1. ~~Buy a lottery ticket~~
2. ~~Go through automatic car wash~~
3. ~~Manicure~~
4. ~~Get hair done in real salon~~
5. ~~Ask Del out on a date (!!!!!)~~
6. ~~Get back into knitting~~
7. ~~Visit Kat in Nashville~~

Chapter 28

On Sunday, I anxiety-clean the kitchen, scrubbing the sink until it shines. The minutes crawl until it's time to leave for Del's place. I really want to meet Allie but I'm nervous about her meeting me. Yeah, I'm a hot mess.

I check the macaroni salad half a dozen times. For what, I'm not sure. Finally, it's time. I secure the bowl on the front seat and clench and unclench my hands a few times to get some blood flowing.

I get to Del's townhouse and find a parking spot on the street. My anxiety ramps up several notches. There are a lot of cars here. Maybe they're visiting the neighbors? I clutch my bowl of macaroni salad and head up the sidewalk.

The main door is open, but the screen door is closed. Someone hollers, "Come on in!"

I walk into the living room and somehow manage to smile at the crowd of faces. Why are there so many people here? He specifically said he wanted me to meet Allie. Sooooo… who are these people?

Del appears in the doorway linking the living room to the kitchen. "Shas!" He hurries over and puts an arm around me. He reaches for the bowl, but I hold it tight.

"You must be the girlfriend. It's nice to finally meet you." A man who must be Del's brother reaches to shake my hand. "George. We've heard a lot about you."

"Uh oh," I manage.

"All good, all good," he says.

Another man steps up beside George. He's the opposite of Del, short, fair, and blond. "Thomas. Nice to meet you." He waves behind him. "Those are my kids."

"And your *wife*," a woman says with a smile. "Hi. I'm Mila. For some reason, I'm married to this idiot. It's really nice to meet you. The kids are Ashton, Cooper, Alexis, and Kylie. There will be a quiz later."

Del squeezes my shoulders. "My folks are out back. Allie's not here yet."

Wait. I'm meeting his *parents*? It was bad enough to meet his daughter. I did not expect to be ambushed with the entire clan.

Del nudges me toward the kitchen. "You can leave the macaroni salad here. We'll eat inside since it's four thousand degrees out there." He's completely oblivious to the fact that I'm freaking out right now.

I let him steer me through the kitchen to the sliding glass patio door.

A woman, I assume his mother, immediately grabs me in a tight hug. "Shasta, it's wonderful to finally meet you. We've been so looking forward to this."

His dad is slightly more reserved, and settles for a meaty handshake where he pumps my entire arm. "Great to meet you."

I don't have to say anything, so I just smile and go along with it.

"Oh, heavens. Of course we're Marie and Fred, but I'm sure you figured that out already."

I chuckle but it sounds forced to my ears.

There's some sort of commotion from inside.

"Hey, great, Allie's here."

Great. My stomach churns. I was not prepared for this.

A gorgeous young woman comes out the sliding door, her focus lasered on me. Her big smile seems genuine. "Hi. I'm Allie. I assume you're Shasta."

"Good guess," I manage with a smile that feels stretched across my face like I must look like the Joker.

Fred announces that the burgers are done, so Del herds me inside. Everyone gathers around the island, where a massive quantity of food is unwrapped and ready to be served. Someone has taken the lid off my macaroni salad and added a spoon.

It's at this point I realize my bowl of macaroni salad is next to... another bowl of macaroni salad.

While Fred says grace over the food, I'm trying to focus on my breathing. I probably don't have any reason at all to be freaking out, but I can't seem to get that message through to my pounding heart and stomach that really, really wants to empty its contents back the way they came.

The other macaroni salad looks so much better than mine. The hard boiled eggs are in smaller pieces, and whoever made it added perfectly diced green and red peppers to give it some festive color. Is that... holy shit it even has little cheese cubes in it. I bet that's really good. And, of course, there's a Food-Network-worthy sprinkle of freshly chopped parsley on top.

Mine is... yellowish. The eggs, the dressing, the macaroni. It's all one uniform color. One bland, boring, awful, sad, unappetizing color.

Well. If this isn't a parallel to real life, I don't know what is.

"Shas?" Del nudges me.

"Huh?"

"Grab your plate."

"Oh." I get a paper plate from the stack and inch along at the back of the line of Del's family working their way around the island, piling their plates high with food.

There's no freaking way I'm going to be able to eat. There's also no freaking way I can get out of it without being obvious. I put a little food on my plate, and as we work around the island, I can't help but notice there's one sad, polite, small spoonful missing from my macaroni salad, while the pretty one is half-empty.

"Is that all you're getting?" Del asks at my shoulder.

"Oh. There's so much I'm sure I'll make more than one trip." Wow, does that sound lame and fake.

Apparently he buys it, because he laughs a little. "Same. I should take a page from your book and pace myself." He steers me to a seat at the long dining room table. The kids seem to have wandered off to find other seating. I'm trapped. I have Del on one side and his mom on the other. Allie is on Del's other side, while Fred is on the other side of Marie. Thomas's wife — Myra? — is directly across from me. A woman I haven't met is beside her. I assume it's George's wife since he's on her other side, across from Fred. There's an empty seat across from Allie.

"Did you meet Pennie?" Myra asks. No, it's not Myra. What the heck is it? Myra, Mina, I know it starts with an M. I feel hot and cold at the same time. Why can't I remember her name?

"No, I haven't. Nice to meet you. I'm Shasta." I have no idea how the words come out sounding coherent.

"Shasta. What an unusual name. It's pretty. Now we've got Mila, Aashi, and Shasta. And here I am, Pennie. It sounds so boring next to you all."

I must look confused. Marie helpfully clarifies, "Aashi is Dwight's girlfriend. They live in Taiwan."

"Oh. Nice." I poke at my food with the plastic fork. "Pennie's a pretty name. It beats being named after a soda can." Oops, I hadn't meant to say that out loud, but everyone laughs. It's a warm sound, nothing malicious, but I just can't get comfortable.

"At least you weren't named after a dead president," George offers. "Like all four of us were," he adds with a fake cough aimed at his dad.

I feel my brows crease.

Del sighs. "George Washington. Thomas Jefferson. Dwight Eisenhower. And Delano after FDR."

"I had no idea."

Thomas pipes in. "At least they didn't go with Grover. Or Herbert."

George adds, "Or Ulysses."

Del explains, "Dad used to be very into politics and history."

Fred mumbles something about the last halfway decent president being Eisenhower.

"I thought the last great president was FDR?" Thomas apparently enjoys poking the bear.

Fred snorts and stabs at his baked beans. "He was! Ike wasn't nearly as great as FDR, but he was better than all the posers that've come after him."

Pennie and Mila exchange a look. It's obvious they've heard this all before, but I feel left out of their shared history.

"Knock it off," Marie says. "We're trying to make a good impression here."

I startle a little as I realize she means for me.

"Might as well show her how things really are around here," Fred grumbles. He leans forward to speak to me around Marie. "These boys are always picking at me. I'm just an innocent, helpless, old man."

Allie snorts. "Don't believe a word of it."

"My own granddaughter. You hear this, Shasta? This is what you're getting mixed up with."

I laugh, but it sounds so unnatural to my ear. I can appreciate how hard they're working to include me, but I hate — *hate* — being the center of attention and this is super uncomfortable.

"Oh, hush. It's not like they're getting married anytime soon," Marie says, then casts a sly eye my way. "Are you?"

"Holy shit, Mom, slow down." Del puts his arm around the back of my chair.

"Language."

Wait, what? Did she just hint at marriage? What is going on here? We're not even technically a couple!

"I have to use the restroom," I say quietly as I push my chair back. I opt for the upstairs bathroom instead of the one right next to the kitchen. You know, the one that's only three feet away from the people I'm trying to escape from.

I close the toilet lid and sit down. This is too much. And

why hasn't he cleared any of this up? They're all assuming we're *together*-together, but we've never even had a conversation about it.

I wonder how long I can hang out in here before they realize I'm gone. Ugh. Probably not long. I flush the unused toilet and wash my hands, waiting for the sink drain to open up into a portal and suck me into another dimension. Please?

Nope, the only thing the drain devours is the soap bubbles. Thanks for nothing.

I suck it up and head back down the carpeted stairs. The living room is empty. From the kitchen, I hear voices I'm not supposed to overhear.

One of the wives says, "She seems nervous. I hope she warms up to us."

His mom says, "She'll have to since Del says she's the one."

Good-natured chuckling ripples around the table, but it hits me like a freaking shockwave. The one? What?!

His voice chimes in. "She'll be fine. You people are just a bit much."

I can't help but notice he didn't contradict his mom's words.

I need to get out of here.

* * *

My Bucket List

1. ~~Buy a lottery ticket~~
2. ~~Go through automatic car wash~~
3. ~~Manicure~~
4. ~~Get hair done in real salon~~
5. ~~Ask Del out on a date (!!!!!)~~
6. ~~Get back into knitting~~
7. ~~Visit Kat in Nashville~~

Chapter 29

I hover until I hear a chair scraping against the floor and rustling that I assume is everyone cleaning up the table before making an entrance.

Del smiles at me. "I wasn't sure if you were done?" He gestures to my mostly full plate. "We're heading out for the semi-annual Hudson Games."

Thomas says, "I hope you're not squeamish. It's a bloodbath."

"It was fine until the Lawn Dart Incident of 2017. Police cars, ambulances, fire trucks, the whole nine," George dramatically adds. I'm fairly sure he's exaggerating.

Mila rolls her eyes. "Thomas ran in front of a lawn dart and ended up with a tiny scratch on his leg."

Thomas throws his hands up. "Scratch! It was a gash. I thought I was going to lose my leg." He looks at me. "It was practically *severed*."

Pennie holds her thumb and forefinger about in inch apart. "I never heard a grown man cry so much."

"Now we do ladder ball because Marie put her foot down and banned the lawn darts."

Allie adds, "They were *real* darts from like the nineteen seventies. Sharp metal things. I can't believe they used to sell them to the general public."

"Ooooh, the nineteen seventies. Way back then, huh? Of course they were metal because plastic hadn't been invented yet." George grumbles at his niece good naturedly.

They continue going back and forth as everyone migrates through the door.

Marie hangs back, ripping plastic wrap off a roll to cover one of the bowls.

"Oh. Can I help you?" I ask, pulling away from Del's arm.

"No, no, you go outside. I'll just be a minute." She winks at me. "I'll let you help next time."

Oh, shit.

The afternoon drags and I'm in this bizarre sort of mental limbo where I want to just relax and fit in because everyone is so nice, but my anxiety is still at an eleven. My mind is whirling with so many questions. Like what is this, and why does Del's family seem to already have a label slapped on it? Does Del have a label on it? Because I sure don't. Do I?

I get wrangled into playing a few rounds, but I can't get my balls to wrap around the rungs of the ladder, so I bench myself.

Finally, blessedly, the torture, I mean *tournament*, is over — seriously, Marie had a notebook with playoff brackets — and Thomas and Mila are awarded the Hudson Cup — a plastic cup with foil shaped around it. It vaguely resembles a tiny trophy if you use your imagination. Thomas hoists it in the air and whoops, then points at his brothers. "IN YOUR FACE! AND YOUR FACE! Suck it, cuz I'm the CHAMPION!"

Mila rolls her eyes and says, "I don't know him."

"None of us do," Marie deadpans.

The guys clean up the game pieces and stow them in the plastic bin under the picnic table.

I let myself be swept inside with everyone else. Marie pulls the food out of the fridge. "Okay, everyone, make your plates up."

The kids descend like vultures and pile to-go plates with food. I notice Marie's subtle move of adding some of my macaroni salad to everyone's plates before she covers them with foil.

Awesome. She's giving out pity leftovers.

"Where's the other macaroni stuff?" the youngest boy asks. Connor? No, Cooper. It's definitely Cooper.

"It's all," Marie tells him with a keep-your-mouth-shut grandma look.

I stay off to the side, strangely feeling both invisible and exposed at the same time. Like I'm somewhere I shouldn't be. All I want is to be home. Alone. Now.

I suffer through the awkward goodbyes and finally it's just me and Del and Allie and my empty bowl.

"This was so great," I lie. "It was so great to meet everyone."

"Oh, are you leaving already?" Del asks.

"Yeah, I want to get home and call Kat."

"You okay?" His brow creases as he studies my face.

"I think I just got too much sun. It's fine." I turn to Allie. "I'm so glad I got to meet you. Your dad always has such good things to say about you."

"Likewise. We'll have to have dinner so we can actually talk. It was kind of chaotic today."

What an understatement.

"The whole family at once can be kind of overwhelming. It's hard to prepare for."

Before I can stop myself, I blurt out, "I wish I could have

prepared at all. I had no idea this was a whole big family thing." I grab my bowl.

Allie's eyebrows shoot up and she casts a meaningful look at her dad. "You didn't give her a heads up?"

"I'm sure I did."

I backpedal. "It's not a big deal. I have to go, though. Dinner would be wonderful." I inch toward the living room and give Allie the biggest smile I can muster. "I hope to see you soon."

She smiles back.

Del frowns and walks me out. "Are you sure everything's okay?"

"Sure."

"You don't have to leave."

I give him the first excuse that pops into my head. "I need to go to the bathroom."

He points over his shoulder to the house.

Seriously? Is he really being this thick? "Not something I want to do in someone else's house, if you know what I mean."

"Oh." Finally, recognition crosses his face.

"I really gotta go. I'll talk to you later."

"Okay." He leans down and gives me a kiss.

I pull back and hurry to my car. Hopefully the fact that I'm practically running reinforces the cover story about needing to use the bathroom, and doesn't make it clear I'm making my escape.

I get home and once I'm safely inside, I lean back on the door with a thump. I have no idea what's wrong with me. I shouldn't be this freaked out, right? The lid slips off my bowl and one single macaroni clings to the bottom. One sad, lonely, pathetic macaroni.

Because all its sad, lonely, pathetic macaroni friends were dished out to people who didn't want them.

Is that me? There's literally no one I can call to vent or cry to. I have so many vague acquaintances, but no one I'm close enough to that I can call right now.

Except Kat, and that's probably not healthy, is it? That my only friend in the world is my daughter?

I stare down at the lone macaroni.

Maybe I should just get back in my car and drive to the shelter and adopt seventy-five cats to complete my downward spiral.

Instead, I do something I haven't done in years and years. I curl up on the couch and I cry.

When I'm done, I wipe my face and I get the stupid notebook that started this whole damn journey of facing my pathetic life. I'm half-tempted to rip it in half and set the pages on fire, but I don't.

I click the Parker pen — even though I'm in some weird headspace right now I pause to appreciate how awesome this pen is — and I add a new item to my bucket list.

* * *

My Bucket List

1. ~~Buy a lottery ticket~~
2. ~~Go through automatic car wash~~
3. ~~Manicure~~
4. ~~Get hair done in real salon~~
5. ~~Ask Del out on a date (!!!!!)~~
6. ~~Get back into knitting~~
7. ~~Visit Kat in Nashville~~
8. Make time for friends

Chapter 30

I finish my one-woman pity party with a glass of wine. Or two. Or possibly three. I'm not sure, but the bottle's empty and my mood is greatly improved. I scroll through social media for a while, sipping on water, because even though I'm pretty tipsy right now, I remember how to avoid a hangover. So there. Suck it, hangover, you're not happening.

At some point, I wake up facedown on the couch. My phone is on the floor. The battery is dead.

Spoiler alert, drinking water didn't work. My head is pounding, my mouth feels like I ate sugar-crusted roadkill, my eyes are heavy and coated with sandpaper, and I'm half a second away from peeing myself.

I plug my phone in and shuffle to the bathroom. A few seconds later, I groan with relief. I swear I pee for half an hour. I'm so glad today's a holiday, because going to work would not be in the cards.

After I brush my teeth, I kick off my pants, drop the rest of my clothes onto the floor, and get into a nice warm shower. It's been three weeks since I got my hair cut, and it's just now starting to feel normal to shampoo this length.

The shower helps me feel better, right up until I turn the water off and realize I never got a towel. I drip all the way to the linen closet and carefully slosh back to the mat without slipping on the tile.

Once I dry myself, I toss the towel on the floor to sop up the mess I've made and get dressed. I flop back onto the couch. Speaking of messes... I have no idea how to handle the Del situation. I'm still mad at being ambushed with the entire family. It was so awkward and uncomfortable and...

As if summoned by my thoughts, my phone vibrates with an incoming call from Del.

"Hey, do you want to get breakfast?"

I squint at my watch. It's nine thirty. Yikes, definitely a good thing today's a holiday because I overslept by a lot. "Uh, maybe?"

"What's going on?"

"What are you talking about?"

"You were acting so weird yesterday and now it sounds like you don't even want to talk to me. I want to know what's going on."

"Wait, what? I just got out of the shower and grabbed the phone. I don't know what you think is going on." My brain catches up with what he said. "And I acted weird yesterday? Seriously?"

"Yes. Do you want to get breakfast or not?"

"Gee, it's super tempting, but I might be weird, so better not." I jump from mildly annoyed to pissed. He's the one who put me in an awkward situation, and now he has the nerve to be snippy with me?

"Oh, come on. You know what I mean."

Well, damn. Looks like we're about to have our first fight. "No, Del, I do *not* know what you mean. You keep saying I acted weird and your tone suggests you're mad about it."

"I'm not mad, I was embarrassed."

Record scratch. "Are you freaking kidding me? If you're embarrassed, it should be because you created the whole awkward mess."

"Me? I invited you to a cookout."

"No. You invited me to 'burgers and hot dogs' so I could meet Allie. Allie. That's one person. You didn't warn me I was meeting the entire family."

"I'm pretty sure I said I wanted you to meet my family, and even if I didn't, why would you assume I was having a whole cookout just for Allie? That doesn't even make sense."

"You didn't say cookout! I *assumed* that when you said you wanted me to meet Allie that I would only be meeting Allie. Why on earth would I *assume* you meant your entire family?"

"What is the big deal?" His volume has increased to match mine.

I shake my phone, wishing the motion would shake him on the other end. "Do you seriously not understand why I might need a little heads up that I'm meeting all of the most important people in your life? It's one thing to meet your daughter. It's a whole other ballgame to meet your daughter, your brothers, their families, and your *parents*."

"They're just regular people, Shasta. It's not like you were meeting the Queen."

"Meeting the Queen would have been less stressful!" I yell.

"I have no idea why you're so upset."

"Obviously!" My head thumps harder from the shouting and the frustration of him just not getting it. I don't even know how to explain it if he's not going to listen. "You don't think it was a big deal, so you don't think it should be a big deal for me, so there's no point in trying to explain it to you."

"It's *not* a big deal."

"To you! It *is* a big deal for me! Why can't you at least pretend to consider that for a second?"

"Okay, fine. It was a big deal."

Ooooh, his condescending tone is pissing me off on about twelve different levels right now. "Gosh, I'm sooooo sorry my issues are annoying for you. That must be very stressful."

"Wow."

"Wow indeed. I'm going to pass on breakfast. I have some things I need to get done."

There's a long pause. "Okay. I'll talk to you later."

"Bye." I hang up before he answers.

I stomp to the kitchen and anger-scrub the counters and the sink, even though they're already clean. When I'm calmed down, I make scrambled eggs to have with my breakfast of coffee and aspirin.

My social media app opens and I abruptly sit up straight. I've got dozens of messages and notifications. What the heck?? I'm invisible on social media. I rarely post. I wonder if my stupid account was hacked.

Nope.

It's all legit.

Messages from old friends I haven't talked to in six or seven years. Connie, Beth, Lucy, April, Kristy… what the heck inspired this? I vaguely remember wishing for friends during last night's pity party, but since I'm pretty sure there was no magic genie involved, this makes no sense. I tap on the messages, one by one.

Connie: Shasta!!!!!!!! It's been forever! I'm so super excited for you to join us this month!!

Beth: Glad you can make it. What are you working on?

Lucy: Long time, no see.

Connie: I added you to the group as well as the group chat.

April: Did Connie tell you we moved locations?

Connie (group): Big crowd this month, ladies! Sharon, be sure to order extra cupcakes!

Kristy (group): Jade's coming too for the first time in years! This month's going to be great!

April (group): Connie, update the location, it still has Meyer Street address!!!!

Connie (group): Oh shit, I thought I fixed that. Thx! CBWC's new meeting location is 14 Maple Drive!

This all sounds very interesting, but I have no idea what they're talking about. CBWC? Meeting location? What?

I click into my profile and search last night's activity. Wow.

Apparently I was serious about the friend thing, because I searched and searched until I found Connie. We'd been casual acquaintances after college, then friends, but when I had my troubles with Nick, I pretty much left everyone behind. She'd started a book club around the time I ghosted, so I never responded to the invitations she'd sent me. From the social media posts, the group has evolved into the Crafty Book & Wine Club, which meets on the second Saturday of each month. Which is set up as an event. Which I responded to. By saying I was going to attend.

My instinct is to block everyone and pretend this never happened. It's not like I run into any of these ladies on any kind of regular basis.

Instead, I close out of the app and text Kat. She responds by calling me.

I confess my drunken RSVP, which she finds much more hilarious than she should, then proceeds to grill me on why I was drunk in the first place.

Damn it.

She's sympathetic to my initial anxiety, but, as I expect, she gently suggests I might have let myself get too wrapped up in my discomfort and possibly could have engineered a better outcome if I hadn't gotten too into my own head.

At least she agrees that Del is being thick-headed and isn't doing a great job, either.

We end our call when Daniel yells for help because he set their tiny hibachi grill on fire out on their balcony.

I hang up feeling better, except for the lingering headache. I reopen the social media app and dive right into the group chat.

Hi, everyone! I'm so glad I found your CBWC page. I have to admit, I'm not quite sure what you do at these meetings, but it sounds fun. LMK what to expect?? and what to bring??

Forty-five minutes later, through a fast and furious storm of messages, I know that there's a book they read each month (which no one expects me to read by Saturday), and everyone brings whatever craft project they're working on (two other knitters and several crocheters in the group, as well as a few card maker/scrapbookers, and a clay artist, whatever that is), and they craft and discuss the book and eat snacks and drink wine.

By the time I put my phone down, I'm actually excited.

I really want to tell Del about it, but I remember I'm still mad at him.

* * *

My Bucket List

1. ~~Buy a lottery ticket~~
2. ~~Go through automatic car wash~~
3. ~~Manicure~~
4. ~~Get hair done in real salon~~
5. ~~Ask Del out on a date (!!!!!)~~
6. ~~Get back into knitting~~
7. ~~Visit Kat in Nashville~~
8. Make time for friends (IN PROGRESS)

Chapter 31

It's the middle of the afternoon and I'm sitting cross-legged on the couch, trying to read a hat pattern. Knitting instructions are like a foreign language and I'm sorely out of practice. *(WS) *K2, P2, rep from * to last 3 sts...* Ugh. I might have to watch some refreshers online.

A knock on the door startles me from my confusion. I set the soft gray yarn aside and answer the door.

Del stands on the porch, holding the screen door open. "It seemed like we need to have a face-to-face conversation."

I disagree. I don't want to have another big conversation. I've had too much emotional turmoil this weekend. I just want to relax and enjoy the rest of my day off. "Sure."

He comes in and sits on the chair.

I resume my position on the couch, pulling the yarn and needles back onto my lap. "What's up?"

His brow creases and he says, "You tell me. I thought everything was going good until yesterday. My entire family thinks you hate them. I thought you'd all get along great, but apparently not."

My jaw clenches a few times as I attempt to rein in my irritation. "This entire thing could have been avoided if you had just told me what to expect."

"I didn't want you to freak out about meeting my parents, like it was some big deal."

"So you *did* keep it from me on purpose. Why would you do

that? Why not just say, 'Hey, my family's coming over for a super casual barbeque, I'd like you to come and meet everyone?' and then I would have been able to prepare a little better?"

"What is there to prepare? It's just my family. It's not a big deal."

"Really? Because your mom seemed to think it was a big deal. And if it wasn't a big deal, why are you sitting here giving me a bunch of shit for not living up to your expectations? You just admitted you deliberately didn't tell me. So is it a big deal or not, because you can't have it both ways."

He shakes his head like *I'm* not getting it.

"I'm frustrated because you acted like it was just Allie and a few other people. I was prepared to meet her and so worried about making a good impression on her. Then all of a sudden — BAM! — I have to impress your parents, your brothers, their wives, *and* Allie. So I come in blind and start off on the wrong foot because now I'm blindsided and I freeze up. Everyone was finishing each other's stories and has all this history and you let me bring macaroni salad!"

He leans forward, his palms up, thoroughly confused. "Macaroni salad?"

"Look. I know it's not a big deal to guys, but it's a *thing* at a cookout to not bring duplicate foods, because look what happened! My sad, pathetic macaroni salad just sat there while the gorgeous Food-fricking-Network-level macaroni salad had everyone chowing down and going back for seconds." I can hear Kat's voice in my head, telling me I'm overreacting, but I can't stop myself from digging my heels in.

"I have no idea what you're talking about."

"I know you don't!" The ball of yarn is going to need rewound. It's unraveling around my clenched fingers. "I didn't impress anyone with my lame ass conversation, and I sure didn't impress anyone with my boring ass macaroni salad."

"Why are you fixating on the macaroni salad?"

"Why are you ignoring it?"

"Because it's irrelevant?"

"No, Del, it's not. It's very relevant. It didn't fit in with all the other food, just like I didn't fit in with all the people. Everyone was acting like we're together-together. Your mom brought up marriage like four times, Del. Marriage! We're not even officially dating."

He sits back and looks stunned. "Aren't we?"

At this point, I really want to scream. "Are we? I don't know. Because we've never had one single conversation about it. And you're not even batting an eyelash about your family talking about *marriage*."

"You're blowing this way out of proportion. They were trying to be welcoming and include you. That's all."

"Blowi— Del, you're ignoring what I said. Why does your family have this assumption about how serious we are when we've never even talked about being exclusive? We barely called it a date months ago the first time we went out, and there's been zero discussion since then. We're not even sleeping together!"

He has the audacity to shake his head like *he's* exasperated. "I know that."

I double down. "Oh, so you're mad because we're not

having sex? What, is that the endgame here?" I smack the yarn down on the cushion next to me and jump to my feet. "Sorry to disappoint by not jumping into the sack sooner. If that's the most important thing here..." I trail off because I don't even know how to finish the sentence. I can almost see Kat pinching the bridge of her nose, wishing I'd shut up with this nonsense.

"Give me a break. You know damn well I'm not worried about when we end up sleeping together. You seriously think I wasted the last two months of my life just trying to get laid?"

The air rushes from my lungs. "Wasted?" Tears sting the backs of my eyes before I can slam the hurt into a neat little box and shove it away.

"That's not what I meant."

My mouth moves, but I'm not sure any sound actually comes out. I clear my throat and try again. "Leave."

He stands up and takes a step toward me.

I take a step back and trip over the edge of the coffee table. I lose my balance and topple backward onto the floor. Del rushes forward to help me, but I scramble to my feet. The unexpected fall distracts me from being able to lock down my emotions. So I stand here, cradling my arm where it hit the coffee table, with tears streaming down my face.

"I did *not* say I was wasting my time with you."

There aren't a whole lot of ways to interpret what he said, and quite frankly my emotional bandwidth is stretched to its absolute limit.

"Shasta. I'm sorry. I know how that came out, but it's not... I didn't..." He runs a hand over his hair, then scrubs it down his face.

I bite my lips together and wipe at the tears, but they won't stop coming.

He tries again. "Shas…"

I shove past him and yank the front door open. I don't trust myself to speak without breaking down and sobbing, so I point.

"We're going to talk later." Reluctantly, he walks to the door.

I refuse to look at him, and eventually he sighs and walks out. He turns and opens his mouth to say something, but I close the door.

He sends me a few texts, but I ignore them all.

Tuesday comes, and I still feel like crap. I sneak out of the building and eat lunch in my car. I nearly choke on my sandwich when Del texts, asking where I am. I ignore that message, too.

Wednesday and Thursday are the same, except on Thursday he doesn't text me. It stings a little, but I can't expect him to keep chasing. A snarky, angry voice in my head adds that yeah, especially since he's not even getting laid in this relationship. Friendship. Whatever.

On Friday, I eat in the cafeteria. By myself. I pretend it doesn't bother me and scroll on my phone. The CBWC chat is rolling right along with excitement about tomorrow's meeting. I did borrow the book from the library, but could barely get through the first chapter.

The book is a romance novel, and I just can't stomach it right now. Not when I'm in this weird headspace. It's not even like I'm working through a breakup. You can't break up when you were never together, right?

I'm not even sure who I'm lying to with that line anymore. Even if I hold on to the most technical of technicalities, there's just no denying we were together.

And now we're not.

And it hurts.

* * *

My Bucket List

1. ~~Buy a lottery ticket~~
2. ~~Go through automatic car wash~~
3. ~~Manicure~~
4. ~~Get hair done in real salon~~
5. ~~Ask Del out on a date (!!!!!)~~
6. ~~Get back into knitting~~
7. ~~Visit Kat in Nashville~~
8. Make time for friends (IN PROGRESS)

Chapter 32

Saturday dawns and I'm nervous and excited all day. It's still my first thought to talk to Del, and I have to wonder how long it will be until he's not my first and last thoughts of the day.

I pack up my project bag with my needles and yarn. I was assured several times that first time guests aren't expected to bring snacks because there's a sign-up sheet at each meeting for the next meeting's refreshments.

The meeting starts at four. I plug the address into my GPS and am surprised when it leads me to a party supply store. I'm not sure if I'm at the right place when two more cars pull into the parking lot.

I haven't seen Connie in at least seven years, but she looks exactly the same. Her face lights up with a huge smile and she waves at me. Dragging my bag across the seat, I get out of the car. I rub my clammy hands on the front of my pants.

"Shasta!" She rounds her car and comes at me for a hug. When she's done squeezing the life out of me, she pulls back and grips my shoulders. "You look *amazing.* Where do you get your hair done?"

I give her the name of the salon.

"Nice. I think April goes there, too, but I'm not sure. Anyway, grab your bag, let's head in."

"I wasn't sure I was in the right place." I gesture to the building.

"Yeah, we had been meeting in my basement but it got to be too tight with the people needing tables to spread out their stamps and whatnot. Crocheting doesn't take up all that room," she adds with a laugh. "Then Kristy moved her party rental business into this building and it has a huge room in the back. We chipped in to get some secondhand sofas and some nice tables. You'll see." She pulls the front door open and we go inside.

Kristy is on the phone. I assume it's with a client, since she's talking about price lists and packages. She waves and gives me a big smile.

Connie leads me through an aisle of wedding table décor and through a door that opens into a big room. Just as she'd said, it's set up like a living room with sofas and a couple of recliners and three sturdy wooden dining tables whose tops have seen much better days and one long table against the wall that houses a coffee maker.

The room is set up in a sort of circle. I'm interested to see how this works.

And part of me is terrified it will be a disaster just like meeting Del's family.

* * *

By four thirty, there are nine of us in attendance. Jade, Sophie, and I are all new, so Connie helpfully gives a rundown of what happens. The first hour is a round robin discussion of the book and then whatever else people want to discuss. The second hour is quiet work time. The third hour is chitchat, and after that it's officially over, but sometimes there's a fourth or even fifth hour, depending on how it's going.

I'm reminded of Connie's years as the PTO president. She's definitely using those same skills to keep this group running smoothly.

"Since we have three newbies tonight, I thought we'd just go around and do a quick intro. Nothing fancy, just who you are and what you like to work on here."

Of the regulars, I know everyone except Gloria and Olive. I've also never met Sophie, but I do know Jade. It's nice. Kind of like a reunion only far less awkward.

The group is split pretty evenly between yarn crafters and paper crafters. And there's one quilter for some variety.

I slowly work on my hat, listening to the conversation about the book.

"I felt *awful* for Maude. I could totally see where she was coming from. She'd been so hurt and was trying to protect herself."

"Yeah, but what Robert did wasn't *that* bad. She used it as an excuse to go back into her comfort zone so she wouldn't get hurt."

Ouch. I don't know Maude and Robert's story, but it sure sounds familiar.

"And ended up hurting herself in the process."

"Maude knew what she was doing. That's what frustrated me the most. She knew she was going to end up breaking her own heart, but she did it anyway. Like, it was so not worth it."

I'm listening intently, wrapping my yarn around my needle,

but I'm not making any stitches.

"Aww, I could relate, though. Maude's first husband had cheated and left her with the twins. She'd been so betrayed by the people she trusted the most."

"I know, but Robert was so patient and the first time he screws up she wants to end it. Like, I wanted to shake her and be like, Maude, you're never going to find someone who's perfect and will never hurt your feelings at all. But there's a difference between hurting your feelings and *hurting* you. Robert was a good guy."

Shit. I feel like there's a spotlight shining on me, and Maude and Robert are code words for Shasta and Del.

"That's a really good point. Robert did hurt her feelings, but he never did anything to *hurt* her. He wasn't perfect, but he really was taking it slow because he loved her even with all the issues she had."

"And don't forget, he had issues, too, with his parents' betrayal."

"Oooh, yeah he did."

"It was so nice, though, seeing Maude make the grand gesture and apologizing instead of waiting for Robert to make the first move."

I watch the conversation ping-pong around the room and holy cow is it uncomfortable. It sounds like there are no bad guys in the story, just good guys who both screw up sometimes and both have things they should apologize for. Gee, why does that sound familiar?

Olive asks, "What did you think, Shasta?"

I jerk to attention. "Unfortunately I didn't have time to read it."

"Oh, that's right," Kristy says, "I forgot you only got the info a few days ago. I guess because most of us know you already it seems like you've been in the group all along."

I think that's the nicest thing anyone has ever said to me.

* * *

My Bucket List

1. ~~Buy a lottery ticket~~
2. ~~Go through automatic car wash~~
3. ~~Manicure~~
4. ~~Get hair done in real salon~~
5. ~~Ask Del out on a date (!!!!!)~~
6. ~~Get back into knitting~~
7. ~~Visit Kat in Nashville~~
8. ~~Make time for friends~~

Chapter 33

I sign up to bring brownies to the next meeting. I'm a big fan of sign-up sheets. No repeats of the macaroni salad disaster. As I drive home, I make a mental note to look up brownie recipes on Pinterest. There's probably some amazing fancy brownie I can make.

I'm just pulling in the driveway when the dash lights up with an incoming call. Kat.

"Hi, baby. I'm getting out of the car, so it might disconnect. Hang on."

"Okay." Her tone is light, so I can set aside any worry that she's calling me with some sort of bad news.

I get out of the car with my bag and keys in one hand, my phone in the other. I shut the door with my hip. "You still there?"

"Still here."

"Perfect. How was your day?"

"Meh. Daniel had to work, and I was studying all day, so not all that exciting."

"How's school going?"

"Great." She launches into describing her classes and classmates and professors.

As I listen, I can hear the excitement in her voice. It's a grueling schedule, but she thrives under pressure. And she's smart enough to know when it's too much pressure. She's so good at setting healthy boundaries around herself, and I don't know where she learned how. It certainly wasn't from me, and it damn sure wasn't from Nick.

"Have you talked to Del yet?"

"No."

"Mom."

When in doubt, deflect and divert, right? "I haven't had a chance. I just got back from my CBWC meeting."

"The what?"

"Crafty Book & Wine Club."

"You… Wait, this is the thing you drunk-RSVP'd to?"

"Yes."

"You actually went?" Her shock is loud and clear.

"I did."

"No shit. I really thought you'd bail."

"So did I. But I'm glad I didn't." It's my turn to give her every last detail about the meeting. "I signed up to take brownies next month."

"That's awesome, Mom."

"I'm excited. I haven't had any girlfriends to hang out with, so it was really nice. I'll definitely have to read the book for next month. They had a big discussion about this one and I didn't have a chance to read it." I might, though. Maybe Maude can give me some ideas on how to get back on track with Del.

"Good job distracting me, but you never told me what happened after the cookout." She should have been a detective, because she's impossible to sidetrack.

"There's not a lot to tell. He came over on Monday and we had a big fight and we haven't talked since. The end." I know she's not going to accept that as the whole story.

"What was the fight about?"

"Well, it boiled down to me telling him I felt ambushed and uncomfortable and annoyed he let me bring macaroni salad when someone else was bringing macaroni salad. Then he basically said I was ridiculous and overreacting. I asked him why his family thought we were headed for marriage — his mom literally brought it up like four times — when we're not even sleeping together and he said something about the past few months being a waste of his time and I cried and told him to leave and he left and we haven't talked since."

"Wait. He actually said the past few months have been a waste of time?"

I shift uncomfortably. "It was something to that effect. I was so upset I honestly didn't hear exactly what he was saying."

She stays quiet for a few beats. "That's a mess. What are you going to do?"

"I don't know. He did text me on Tuesday and Wednesday, but I never answered him."

"So it's possible he was going to apologize? Or clarify that bit he may or may not have said?"

"Anything's possible." I sigh. "I can sort of see where he's coming from. I probably could have handled the cookout a little better. And he could have been a lot more understanding."

"He definitely wasn't the hero of the story. I'm not saying he was a supervillain, but I agree that he has *some* accountability."

I hear her loud and clear. "And so do I." I pull in a long breath and let it out. "I should call him tomorrow. To… apologize."

"You should."

"Bossy."

"Learned from the best."

* * *

Sunday morning I get up and sit on the edge of my bed, staring at my phone. It takes me forever to gather the courage to text one simple word.

Breakfast?

I wait.

And wait.

And wait.

Ten minutes later, the description on my message changes from "Delivered" to "Read."

I wait some more, but he doesn't respond. Ouch.

All day long, I keep checking my phone, but Del never texts me. I suppose it's justifiable since I ignored his messages, but this tit for tat isn't going to get us anywhere good.

Sunday evening I make one more attempt to text him.

Can we talk?

It immediately flags as read, but he doesn't text me back.

I crawl in to bed, determined. I'll think of something. We're bound to run into each other at work eventually. Maybe I'll just make sure it happens sooner than later.

Monday morning rolls around. I wear my sky blue blouse because it's Del's favorite. I spend a few minutes putting on some eyeliner and lip gloss. Nothing crazy.

I get to the lobby and check my watch. He should be coming through the door any minute. Instead, Ellie comes in and begins chattering excitedly about her weekend. Apparently she went on a date with Trevor.

That snaps my attention to her. "Trevor? Ellie, he's..." How can I say 'dirtbag' in a nice way? "You deserve a great guy who'll treat you like a princess and be *faithful* and not leave as soon as he gets what he wants."

We get on the elevator and just as the doors close, I look out and... yep, of course. Del is walking across the lobby toward the bank of elevators. Damn it.

I want to give Ellie more advice, but I keep reminding myself that I'm her supervisor, not her mom. There's a professional distance I have to maintain, and let's be real — there are life lessons she has to learn on her own.

There are stars in her eyes. "He's such a great guy. Did you know he takes care of his sick grandmother?"

We all know I'm tight with money, but I would one hundred percent be comfortable betting every penny I have that there is no sick grandmother. "Huh."

We get settled into our cubes and I'm distracted with trying to think of ways to get Del to talk to me when the solution lands in my inbox.

"Update Your Chase Fargo Account Information"

I click on the email to open it. The poorly cobbled-together logo at the top of the email is definitely Del's handiwork. As is the deliberate grammatical nightmare of a message that follows.

I start to sweat. In my entire professional life, I've never been reprimanded or written up or even talked to about something that was legitimately my fault. (Obviously Edmonds and his nonsense doesn't count.) I've always followed the rules. Paid attention to the trainings (no matter how asinine). I've never, ever considered deliberately doing something to put myself on a naughty list.

I move my mouse. The cursor hovers over the "CLICK HEAR!" button. The misspelling is a nice touch.

This won't just go to Del.

I'll be on the "Id-10-t" list that everyone in IT snarks about.

This will be a blemish on my otherwise perfect employee record.

Worse, it might not even work.

Which would be doubly humiliating.

I close the email and drum my fingers on my desktop.

Actual work needs to be done, so I open a file and work for a while.

"Shasta? Do you have any aspirin or anything?" Ellie pokes her head into my cubicle.

"Sure." I grab my purse and pull out my handy little travel bottle of Advil. I hand it to Ellie and while she's getting what she needs, I look down at the bucket list journal I've been carrying around.

"Thanks so much." She hands the bottle back.

"No problem," I answer absently. The cover easily falls open and my eyes land on the bright orange sticky note with Del's handwriting.

I reopen the email. If this isn't a grand gesture, I don't know what is. The cursor once again hovers over "CLICK HEAR" and this time... I click it.

I'm not sure what I expected to happen. An alarm? Sirens? A nasty pop up on my screen confirming that I've just done something stupid? Whatever I expected didn't happen. In fact, nothing happens at all.

It's very anticlimactic.

* * *

My Bucket List

1. ~~Buy a lottery ticket~~
2. ~~Go through automatic car wash~~
3. ~~Manicure~~
4. ~~Get hair done in real salon~~
5. ~~Ask Del out on a date (!!!!!)~~
6. ~~Get back into knitting~~
7. ~~Visit Kat in Nashville~~
8. ~~Make time for friends~~
9. Make things right with Del

Chapter 34

I ride the elevator down to the cafeteria. It's been three hours since I clicked the fake phishing email, and still nothing has happened. I find a spot next to the bank of windows and scroll through the latest CBWC group messages while I eat my salad and leftover lasagna.

April has left a massive rant about her neighbors and I'm so riveted that the tray smacking down on the table scares the life out of me. I drop my phone onto the table.

"Shit!"

Del plops onto his chair. He pulls his glasses off and rubs his eyes. "Why?"

"Why what?"

"Why, why, why, did you click that link?" He squeezes his eyes shut and pops them open. "Shasta." His expression is exasperation, frustration, and I definitely see some amusement in there.

"I mean, it seemed totally legit."

Amusement is winning out. The corners of his mouth twitch. "Do you know the penalty for clicking those links is doing six hours of training modules?"

I suck in a breath. "Six?" Those things are stab-your-eyes-with-a-rusty-fork brutal.

He unwraps his sandwich and takes an aggressive bite. In a minute, he washes it down with his soda, which he points at me. "You're lucky you have a friend in IT."

"Oh?" Do I still?

"I took your name off the naughty list."

"You did?"

He shakes his head and laughs. "You know, if you keep doing shit like that, you're never gonna be my latex salesman."

Our eyes meet and we laugh at the *Seinfeld* reference. I lift my water bottle. "To Vandelay Industries."

"Long may they import/export." Del taps his cup to my bottle.

"I miss you."

He fiddles with his straw and finally looks up at me. "I miss you, too."

"I'm sorry I freaked out and overreacted with meeting your family."

He holds a hand up. "Nope."

I jerk back, not sure if he's rejecting my apology or dismissing it.

"This one's on me. Allie and I had a long talk last night, wherein she summarily handed me my ass about several things. First, I now understand how epically wrong I was to not tell you my entire family was going to be there and how much it must have felt like a setup. Second, apparently I was monumentally stupid about the macaroni salad. I truly did not know that two people bringing the same dish was a thing, but I have been thoroughly educated about the fact that it is a thing and I was wrong." He reaches across the table and stops just before his fingers touch mine. "I'm sorry. I never meant to ambush you with my family. I certainly never meant to hurt you or be dismissive or otherwise put you in any kind of awkward position. And I never, never, ever meant that I've been wasting my time with you. Think you can forgive me?"

I inch my hand forward and rest the tips of my fingers on his. "Yeah. My daughter also had some sage advice, which I personally think is bullshit that these kids have the audacity to be right sometimes."

He takes my hand and squeezes it. "It is absolutely bullshit."

"I'm sorry I didn't handle the situation better, and I'm sorry I sort of ghosted." I use his words because I am *so* not good at apologies. "Think you can forgive me?"

"Yes, but there is one more thing that was really bothering me."

Uh oh. I wait.

"It kind of got me that you kept saying we aren't together. Because we can be just friends, but that's not what I want."

I can't believe we're having this conversation in the cafeteria at work. I squeeze his hand. "I'm sorry. I think I was holding so tight to that little technicality because if we're official that means I'm really all in, and that's scary. Terrifying, actually, because I'm just handing you my heart and all I can do is hope you won't break it. But... scary or not... I don't want to be just your friend, Del."

His smile lights up his entire face and I really, really want to grab that face and kiss him. But... work.

"Can I tell Allie we're good?"

"Yeah. And I'll tell Kat."

We clean up our spots and on the way back up to the eighth floor, we're alone in the elevator so I do kiss him.

* * *

My Bucket List

1. ~~Buy a lottery ticket~~
2. ~~Go through automatic car wash~~
3. ~~Manicure~~
4. ~~Get hair done in real salon~~
5. ~~Ask Del out on a date (!!!!!)~~
6. ~~Get back into knitting~~
7. ~~Visit Kat in Nashville~~
8. ~~Make time for friends~~
9. ~~Make things right with Del~~

Chapter 35

Two months later
Thanksgiving

I'm not sure who's more excited, me or Del. I'm frazzled because we're hosting Thanksgiving at my house, but mostly I'm okay. We were supposed to have dinner at noon, but Kat and Daniel had to stop overnight at a hotel in Winchester, Virginia because of a freak snowstorm, instead of arriving last evening. So we've pushed the meal back to six o'clock instead.

Much to my gratitude and surprise, even though I agonized about changing the mealtime, no one complained. In fact, Marie texted me three times to make sure Kat and Daniel were safely on their way.

It's been a crazy couple of months. After the air was cleared between me and Del, Marie invited me to join a few of their Sunday evening family video chats, which has helped me feel like I'm starting to fit in. Then they invited Kat, which is obviously the fastest way to my heart.

After the first time Kat joined in, she called me immediately afterwards and said, "I *told* you I liked him."

Yeah, yeah, kid, you were right. Again.

Del's entire family is coming, including Dwight and Aashi, who are visiting from Taiwan for two entire months, much to Marie's delight. (She's already making plans for a Christmas even the Rockefellers could only dream of.)

I baste the turkey for the billionth time because I'm so worried about it drying out. The entire counter is lined with crockpots filled to the brim with a whole holiday spread.

Just before five, Kat's voice rings from the living room. "We're here!"

I drop my oven mitts and run in to grab her in a massive hug.

Del and Daniel shake hands. When Kat pulls away from me, she hugs Del warmly. "It's so great to finally meet you in person."

He's ever so slightly choked up. "You, too."

His family starts pouring in and soon the house is packed with chatter and laughter and food and bodies *everywhere*. Kat and Allie are fast friends and look like they've known each other forever. I have a sneaking suspicion they've been talking outside of the family chats.

We get everything loaded into serving dishes and onto the dining room table. Del shouts to get everyone's attention and the river of people flows into the dining room. He and I are the last to sit, so we sit at the end closest to the kitchen. It suits me fine, so I can jump up and grab anything that anyone needs.

The conversation comes to an abrupt halt as Fred says grace over the meal. Everyone murmurs, "Amen." Then the bowls make their way around the table as everyone piles their plates.

The scene in front of me is exactly the sort of family gathering I've dreamed of ever since I was a little girl. I can't remember ever feeling so happy.

Del's arm slides around my back. He speaks close to my ear. "Everything okay?"

I wipe a tear and smile up at him. "Everything's perfect."

And it is. I'm almost overwhelmed by the easy love surrounding the table.

"Is there pie?" Cooper asks loudly.

Marie swats his hand. "Not until everyone's finished with their meal."

"Awwww," he groans and leans back in his chair.

I finish eating and lean over to Del. "I'm going to cut the pies."

"I'll help," he says. "Do you want to help, too?" he asks Allie. It's weird how he enunciates the question.

Her eyes widen. "Yes."

"Kat?" he asks.

She jumps up.

Whatever. I'll take all the help I can get. I open the drawer to get the pie server out.

I turn and drop it on the floor.

Del is down on one knee, holding a velvet box. The girls are on either side of him. "I was going to do this as a big spectacle in front of everyone, but I think this is better."

I squeak something, but it's definitely not a word.

"Shasta Moonflower DeAngelo. Will you marry me?" He pops the box open but I can't take my eyes off his.

"Yes."

He grins and gets to his feet, sweeping me up in a hug. I wrap my arms around him and kiss him.

When I pull back, Del hands me the box. "The girls helped me design the ring. So if you hate it, blame them."

We all laugh. It's an emerald-cut peridot — my birthstone,

which looks like a clear, bright green diamond. It has smaller diamonds on either side, set in a band with channel-set diamonds on the sides. It goes without saying that I love it. And it's all the more special knowing Allie approves of me enough to have helped.

Kat adds, "All the stones are lab created ethical stones. It turned out even more perfect than I imagined."

"It's beautiful," Allie says quietly.

"I love it." I look up at Del. "And I love you."

"I love you," he whispers back and pulls me close and kisses me.

"Eww, get a room."

"Yuck."

The girls head back to the dining room, giggling together.

We have a moment of peace until the demands for pie get out of hand.

Del slips the ring on my finger. It fits perfectly.

Once the pies are gone and everyone slips into a subdued turkey coma, Del announces our engagement to the crowd.

After all the hugs and tears (his mom, mostly), we all work together and clear the table.

"Hey, schmoopy." Del pulls me aside.

"Yes, schmoopy?" I laugh, more content than I think I've ever been.

"I have one more thing for you."

What more could this man possibly give me today?

He hands me a wrapped gift that feels suspiciously like a book. "Open it."

I peel the paper to find a soft leather journal just like the ones PAMECorp gave us back in July. The only difference is that the front of this one is etched with "OUR Bucket List."

I hold it close to my heart. "I can't wait to fill this with you."

Epilogue

Two Years Later

OUR BUCKET LIST

~~Get married in Vegas (by Elvis!!)~~
~~Meet Mike Tyson (AT OUR WEDDING!!!!!!)~~
~~Visit Kat and Daniel in Nashville (and visit with~~
~~Tracey!)~~
~~Visit Ben in Ohio (saw 3 of his home games!)~~
~~Buy a house together~~
~~Create a budget and retirement plan together~~
~~Buy a junk '69 Chevelle to restore~~
~~Volunteer (I teach a financial independence class at~~
~~a women's shelter while Del does pro bono tech~~
~~support for several local non-profits.)~~
~~Go salsa dancing~~
~~Plant a garden~~
~~Donate blood~~
~~Take all 3 kids (and Daniel) on Alaskan cruise~~
~~Get a kitten (okay, two kittens)~~
~~Fifty random acts of kindness (half must cost~~
~~nothing!)~~
~~Take a date-night cooking class~~

~~Catch fireflies~~
~~Learn to install drywall~~
~~Go skiing (this was not fun for either of us!)~~
~~Go kayaking (this was!)~~
~~Enter afghan in the county fair (I got an honorable~~
~~mention! Jade got the blue ribbon!)~~
~~Build patio furniture from reclaimed pallets~~
~~Throw a massive neighborhood barbeque (only one~~
~~macaroni salad!)~~
~~Watch every episode of *Seinfeld*~~
~~Live happily ever after~~
Start a new bucket list

Author's Note

Dear Reader,

It was fun to take a detour from my Hickory Hollow series to write The Bucket List. I loved writing Shasta's story, and I hope you enjoyed her and Del as much as I do.

I don't have an official bucket list, but I do have lots of things I'd like to do "someday." (Like learn to drive a stick shift and see the Pyramids in Egypt.) It was a lot of fun to bring Shasta out of her shell and see what things inspired her to inch out of that comfort zone. I also felt really bad about the macaroni salad situation. It's the WORST to roll up to a potluck with a dish only to find out someone else brought a better version!

It was fun to write in a corporate setting for a change. Special thanks to my son Austin, who works in IT and answered a bunch of questions about internal phishing alerts. (FYI, YES, people who click on those phishing emails create a lot of work for their IT department!) And yes, those brutal training modules were a throwback to my old day job, and yes, they truly were so boring you would rather stab yourself with a rusty fork.

As always, thanks to my husband Scott for his amazing support. He's not great with tech, but he's my real life Del, sweet and supportive.

Lastly, thank you to YOU for reading this book! If you enjoyed it and have a moment to spare, leaving a review online would be very helpful to me. (Even if you didn't buy it online, you can still leave a review.) If you'd like to hear more from me, sign up for my newsletter! You'll get exclusive sneak peeks, behind-the-scenes info, notice of upcoming releases, and all that jazz. (Sign up at carriejacobsauthor.com)

Be sure to follow me on Facebook (facebook.com/writercarriejacobs) for notice of upcoming events and more importantly, pictures of my furry editorial assistants.

Best,

Carrie

About the Author

Carrie's love of storytelling began in early childhood and never wavered as time marched onward. She reads in pretty much every genre imaginable, but found her writing happy place in contemporary romance and romantic comedy.

From that love came Hickory Hollow, a mashup of her hometown and places she's either visited or would like to. Her favorite part of Hickory Hollow? The residents don't have to drive an hour to get to Target, like she does in real life.

Carrie lives in beautiful central Pennsylvania with her family and very spoiled furry editorial assistants.

Connect with Carrie through her newsletter or social media!

Website: carriejacobsauthor.com
Facebook: facebook.com/writercarriejacobs
Instagram: instagram.com/carriejacobsauthor

Made in United States
Troutdale, OR
09/10/2024

22717972R00166